TIME RI[

And a dotted [
Round and round ana round a tree,
Yellowing its greenery
Keeps a watch on all the world,
All the world and this old bull
In the forest beautiful.

Ralph Hodgson, *The Bull*

prologue

The thunderous sound of the shells exploding seemed endless, shaking the ground mercilessly. The old, Italian monk stood next to a side door of the noisy, crowded building. Except for a young woman across the doorway, he was separate from the terrified villagers. Most of the civilians were not being detained against their will.

The monk touched his sleeve. The room smelt of blood, sweat and fear. He stole a glance at the front of the building; he did not want to go through another interrogation.

At that moment one of the German soldiers turned and looked straight at him. The monk's seventy year old heart pounded and he felt faint: He needed to get out; he needed to breathe. He couldn't take any more questions. Unconsciously, he again touched his sleeve and noticed the girl watching him.

Then, with a mighty roar, one end of the building exploded, followed by a cacophony of blood-curdling screams. Many were killed instantly, their cries of pain and terror never heard. Steel, dust, debris and body parts formed a swirling picture only hell could paint.

This was no place for a monk. In one motion he grabbed the girl's wrist and was through the door. 'Come!' He had to shout to her above the screams. She followed him. They ran toward the woods and two more explosions sounded their exit, the building burning and crumbling.

The monk did not know the girl but felt she would be trustworthy. She was very pretty and had an intelligent face but most of all she seemed to have a wisdom that exceeded her years. He touched his sleeve and they stopped running for a moment. He breathed hard, trying to catch his breath. The girl offered him a concerned look.

There was another explosion not far away and the monk dropped to his knees at the base of a hollowed tree. She watched him closely as he pulled out a scroll that was hidden in his sleeve. He placed the scroll deep within the hollow.

The monk spoke to the girl. She nodded. Then, the monk stood up and they both started to run off down the hill. They crossed a road and ran down a dirt path that ran parallel to the road. They ran hard.

But moments later the monk stopped abruptly, clutching his chest. He told the girl to go on and then he collapsed. She went to him and touched his face. He was dead.

The girl sobbed briefly, turned and ran through the woods toward her village around the hill. Amongst the trees she found her lover, who was talking with a friend.

Sometime later she returned to the tree hollow with her lover and they retrieved the monk's scroll. They married and had a son. They named him after the friend.

Their boy developed a keen interest for both adventure and archaeology. He liked to find things.

And one day he found something.

chapter 1

It was hot; very, very hot. The sun's size and brightness seemed to border surreal. Heat waves shimmered over the blistering sand of the Algerian desert, the quietness broken only by the sounds of the camels' hooves swishing gracefully across the barren landscape and the shuffling boots of the soldiers. Occasionally, one of the wounded moaned.

The trek was tedious and long, dune after dune. The direction of the platoon's march was aimed at El Khajira, an oasis several miles away. And then after a rest, straight back to Fort Ghardelle- where the legionnaires called home.

The year was 1939 and the French Foreign Legion was constantly

TIME RING

N. C. SLY

BOOKSLY

ISBN: 978-0-9565973-0-4

This is a work of fiction. All characters, names, places and incidents portrayed are either figments of the author's imagination and bear no resemblance to any event, locale, person, living or dead, or are used fictitiously. Any resemblance is entirely coincidental.

Author's Note: Chapters and paragraph sections shown in italics are random time periods whereas chapters in regular type are of a continuing time frame, starting in the spring of 1939.

This volume consists of over 100,000 words.

Published by Booksly BN16JS, United Kingdom
Printed and bound in Great Britain

battling the Tuareg Arabs for vast and various patches of the Sahara Desert. The warfare usually ranged from hit-and-run to find and expel.

Guerilla warfare versus search and destroy. This time the Arabs had won.

Having suffered their worst battle ever, the men were retreating from Has al Kabir- a large settlement held by the Tuaregs. Even worse, the soldiers had seen it coming in the lieutenant's eyes. Lieutenant Salvatore Bationi had argued with his captain for days that the attack- the *offensive*- would be disastrous. The plan was sheer folly Bationi had pleaded.

Higher up the chain of command it had been decided that Has al Kabir would be earmarked as a future fort site. The problem being that it was crawling with the enemy.

And so, Lieutenant Bationi had taken and followed his orders. He had a fairly experienced platoon of sixty-four men, fifty-five camels and two beautiful new British-made howitzer cannons (though he had not wanted to drag them halfway across the desert first time out!) which he had sequestered for months and had finally only recently arrived.

And now they were gone, lost in the most horrifying ambush Bationi had ever seen. In addition to the lost cannons, forty-five camels were missing. Thirty-six legionnaires were killed, and many wounded. It had been a hasty retreat; a narrow escape.

The platoon was still a couple of hours away from the oasis. They were low on ammunition, spirit and water. Salvatore turned his head around, still walking, and regarded his remaining troop.

Among the healthy there were French-Jewish brothers Ibriam and Julien, Chief Corporal Phillippe Patek, the Swede, Tommy the English kid, Klauss- the sullen Swiss, the American, Treselme and Hassef. Hassef, a nomadic Arab with French lineage who was a most important addition to the unit, was the lieutenant's best scout.

Two of the Belgians were still alive, as were LaMonde and the Greek. Also, there were Pierre from Paris and his close friend Louis from Lyon, the Dutchboy and a few others.

The lieutenant looked at Phillippe and caught his eye, nodded subtly once, and the corporal understood. He moved quickly to the lieutenant's side, ready to take orders.

Salvatore pointed to a rocky, dusty rise that was accompanied by a large array of boulders. He said, 'Phillippe, allez avec Hassef et Pierre et Louis et regardez a qu'est-ce que c'est derriere les rochers.' Bationi did not speak French very well but the corporal understood nonetheless. Phillippe gave a quick salute then went off to get the others.

The lieutenant let out a small sigh as he marched alongside his soldiers, his eyes locked on the boulders.

The legionnaire who was from the United States wore a lugubrious expression on his face owing to the fact (*not to mention the battle!*) that he had parted with an old keepsake, his lucky wrist-watch.

He hadn't lost it during the ambush at Has al Kabir, nor did a Tuareg pry it from him. He had traded it for water. The watch he had bought in New York, all those years ago.

Oh, well: he thought to himself. It was cracked and had to be wound every day. *Who needs a watch out here?* The legionnaire mixed a grimace with a smirk and managed to find a trace of humour, though somewhat sardonic, in his melancholy. He looked back over his shoulder through the marching soldiers until his eyes met the Algerian's, whose name was Hassef. Hassef was grinning.

The legionnaire smiled back and said, 'Hey, Hassef. What time is it?' He pointed a finger onto his left wrist.

Hassef did not speak English but he understood the gesture and raised his left wrist, wriggled it about, and put the watch to his ear. Hamming it up perhaps but it was in good nature. The legionnaire let out a soft chuckle.

The men walked in pairs and after a long period of silence they began to engage in quiet, muffled conversations. The American legionnaire let his mind drift back to the day he had moved to Manhattan and bought the watch from a street vendor who called himself Fast Lenny.

Jeez, Fast Lenny! When was that? Oh, yeah. 1932: All those years ago.

The soldier marching alongside the American broke the legionnaire from his daydream. 'You regret tradin' yer watch, eh, mate?' said Tommy, an English lad from London.

The legionnaire looked at Tommy solemnly and said, 'Yeah.'

'Water's more important out here...'

'I guess so. Anyway, it could be worse.' Both men thought of the dead and wounded as they continued their trek across the burning sand.

A few rows back Hassef watched the English boy talk to the

American, who was named Jack. He wondered if they were talking about the wrist-watch. He smiled to himself; it was a good trade. The watch seemed to have an emotional effect on the American. That was good. At some time later Hassef would sell it back for cash, coins or script.

Hassef stored up water for times like this, for these were profitable times. The new European recruits- usually French, German, Spanish or Italian- suffered greatly in the Saharan sun and would gladly give whatever they had for a drink of water.

Hassef was from the south-western regions of Algeria and could walk through the desert on very little water. Some of his fellow legionnaires believed he was really a camel; but nicer.

He was also shrewder than a camel. During the afternoon he had collected the American's watch, the Belgian's compass and a favorite of his- a pair of (almost) new woolen socks. Growing up he had gone barefoot during the day but had worn woolen socks at night. They were apparently his father's, who had died on Hassef's sixth birthday. He wore the socks at night for years until they were merely a few threads.

Thick, wooly, grey socks; it did not take much to make some men happy...

Hassef noticed the corporal was running down from the front of the line. He was followed by Pierre and Louis and seemed to be looking at Hassef. The corporal called out, 'Hassef!' and beckoned with his hand, a flick of wrist and fingers, and the Algerian moved out of the marching line over to the corporal.

The corporal told Hassef to come with them. He spoke French. 'We are to see what is behind the boulders,' Phillippe said, breaking into a jog. Pierre, Louis and Hassef followed him. Lieutenant Bationi watched the four soldiers jaunt hesitantly towards the rise. He raised his palm and yelled, 'Halt!'

The platoon came to a standstill. A couple of the camels kept walking and their reins were quickly grabbed. All eyes were on the four scouts as they approached the boulders. The men were silent; a camel snorted.

Every step that the scouts took weighed heavily on the lieutenant's mind. He felt anxious, his stomach muscles tightened. The sun beamed forcefully onto the left side of his body and face.

Hassef reached the scattered boulders first. Moving in from his right were Pierre and Louis. Phillippe, walking now, brought up the rear. The scouts made a quick search of the boulders, some very large, and then headed toward the crest.

Hassef disappeared over the top, and the other three followed him. All four were out of sight.

The lieutenant drew his pistol and took a few steps toward the rise. One by one, more like two by two, the legionnaires took the lieutenant's silent cue and began sorting their weapons. The sound of metal filled the desert air as the soldiers attached their bayonets.

Kneeling now, Bationi motioned for the Swede and the Dutchboy. They quickly moved to him and crouched alongside their lieutenant, who was watching the rise intently.

Suddenly...Hassef appeared: He was alright. He was shouting, 'Ca va!' *It's okay!*

Bationi could hear him. He felt relieved. He saw Phillippe, Pierre and Louis casually walking into sight. He sighed.

Looking back to face the platoon the lieutenant swung his arm back, then forward- indicating for the men to move ahead. The soldiers continued their march across the hot, lonely desert.

Hassef was running down the slope, a beeline for the lieutenant. Bationi wondered where Hassef got the energy.

Hassef came to a running halt. 'Rien, Lieutenant,' he said. *Nothing.*

Bationi nodded once and said, 'Bon.' He rubbed his eyebrows, turned and headed to join the line, with Hassef in tow.

A slight gust of wind caught his perspiration, and Salvatore was thankful. He tugged his beard; it was getting bushier these days. He put the pistol back in its holster.

The corporal and the other two scouts were angling their way down the rise to join the platoon. When they did, Bationi decided, he would give the soldiers ten minutes rest and then let the four scouts ride on camels for awhile. All but four of the few camels left carried severely wounded men.

It was still very hot and the afternoon sun tilted only slightly to the west. But they were heading west and it would only be a matter of time before the sun shone directly in their eyes. By Bationi's reckoning, he figured the platoon would reach the oasis well before dusk.

Rolling dunes filled the landscape as the rise of scattered boulders disappeared into the men's past.

Ahead, one of the camels snorted but otherwise the platoon was silent. Has al Kabir had been a quick and savage battle; and the men were greatly fatigued. From the oasis they would be heading straight to Fort Ghardelle.

And then possibly be assigned new units. The skeletal crew would be temporarily disbanded and then pieced into various other units.

The soldiers walked in pairs but no one was speaking. Talking would only use up energy unnecessarily. There was still a lot of walking to do and there was the chance that Arabs were in the vicinity.

The platoon's offensive had pushed them deep into an area controlled by the Tuaregs. The strength of the attack was to have been the element of surprise but it was the legionnaires who had been surprised. The reconnaissance report issued by the Legion to Lieutenant Bationi and his superior, Captain Versailler, underestimated the number of Arabs at Has al Kabir. The report had said that there would be fifty (maybe seventy-five but no more) feebly armed Tuaregs in the area surrounding the small, rocky settlement and the strategic desert peak that watched over it. There must've had to have been two-hundred and fifty, at least; maybe three-hundred, maybe more.

They'd had rifles and they'd had swords.

It had been a bloody affair. The lieutenant replayed the battle in his mind. He thought: how could it have been avoided? *Maybe I could have sent an advanced scout party to each flank on the approach to Has al Kabir.* Or not follow the orders of his commanding officer who had insisted on a straight forward attack. *I could have circled around and used the small slope to minimize any surprises...I could have...*

There was nothing he could have done to change the outcome. They'd been surrounded and they had been surprised. And they'd been vastly outnumbered in terms of men, camels and weapons. Oh, the cannons? They had not been used. Lieutenant Bationi had made such a fuss to his superiors about getting the cannons (he'd wanted six, plus more infantry) and had waited so long for them. And now they were gone, captured by the Tuaregs; as well as their shells and the camels that'd been carrying the shells.

The platoon sergeant had been killed. He'd been friends with the lieutenant for years. His name was Rene Leliat and he'd had a wife and four children. Upon returning to the fort the lieutenant would have to write to Rene's wife informing her of her husband's death. The lieu-

9

tenant decided that if he were to ever be killed in battle that he would not want his family to find out about it in a letter. He would want one of his soldiers to personally notify his family.

Lieutenant Bationi's wife was French. Her name was Yvonne, and she and their daughter lived in France in a town called Chateaurenault. He had not seen them in quite some time and he wondered if he would ever see them again.

Salvatore barely remembered their home, a maison at the edge of his wife's hometown. He had seldom been there. The last eighteen years of his life Salvatore had been with the Legion. He had always wanted to be a soldier and had joined the Italian Army at the outset of the Great War. But after a few years he had become disenchanted, feeling that Italy did not take its military seriously. He had not been able to rise above private and felt as though he was looked on as a peasant. Disillusioned, he left the army and joined the French Foreign Legion. He handed over his passport and signed a mandatory five-year contract. He'd been there ever since.

The Legion had given Salvatore a fresh start. He'd climbed his way up on his own merit and when there were opportunities he'd taken them. He felt lucky as there were only a small percentage of commanding officers that were not French. His record as a commanding officer had been quite impressive until now, but his reputation would surely be affected by this latest fiasco. It'd been by far the worst defeat of his career.

Then he thought of his parents and his brothers and sisters; he hadn't seen *them* in well over a decade. They were all still back in the small villages nestled among the mountains south-east of Rome. I must write Mama and Papa more often, he thought as he shuffled through the dunes.

The lieutenant sighed. He stopped for a moment and raised the field-glasses. He looked to the south-east; then panned around slowly. They were on an elevated stretch of sand and the lieutenant had a good, panoramic view. Satisfied, he put them down to about waist level and gently cleaned the sand out of the lens with his uniform. He continued walking and then noticed Phillippe looking at him so he signaled to his little corporal that everything was okay.

He wanted a cigarette. Scanning the line quickly Salvatore spotted LaMonde, a Frenchman who smoked. He thought: LaMonde should have a cigarette. After a few seconds, quickening his pace, the lieu-tenant caught up with LaMonde. Salvatore asked him, 'Henri, avez vous une cigarette?'

'Oui,' answered LaMonde, handing his lieutenant a cigarette.

'Merci.' Salvatore pulled a matchbox from his left shirt pocket and took out a match and, stopping momentarily, struck it- lighting his cigarette. He inhaled deeply; as he exhaled smoke came out of his mouth, nose, and possibly ears. He thought: French cigarettes, not too bad, but not as good as the English or American brands.

Salvatore's favourite brand was Players Number 6. The English le-gionnaire, Tommy, had brought several packets of Players with him when he had joined the Legion. But Tommy did not smoke- they'd been a gift from an uncle- and so he had given them to Salvatore. Since then, the lieutenant hadn't been able to find any Players, but he counted them as his *favori*.

Several steps behind Lieutenant Bationi walked Julien and the hairy Frenchman named Dupree. They were helping a wounded soldier who was slipping off of a camel. Salvatore couldn't see the soldier's face but he guessed that it was the Czech named Pilzer.

This was the best unit he had ever had and they had been wasted-decimated- on this futile attack, thought the lieutenant. This was not their fault. *It was mine.*

Still, what was left could be considered a crack unit. If all the wounded return, although by the look of some of them that seemed unlikely, there may just be enough men. Salvatore wondered if he could convince his superiors to assign him more men to bring it back to numbers. No: heads will roll. And he knew that his was first in line.

He watched his men marching through the sand, a little bit uphill then a little bit downhill...and then all over again. Quickening his pace a little he moved up along the line. The sun beamed down hard on his well-tanned face.

Salvatore was due for a leave so he would go to France and see his wife and daughter. It was something to look forward to.

But before that he would have to get back to Fort Ghardelle and face the humiliation and pray for his wounded and dead soldiers. Right now his top priority was to get the platoon safely to the oasis where the men would get water and shade and rest. The territory around the oasis was not hostile; its occupants were usually nomads passing through. It was a relatively small oasis but there was ample shade there and at the far end by the hillside there were a few date trees. The wounded needed to get cleaned up and rested properly. The medic was dead.

The minutes passed; the quicker, the better. Sometimes a few miles seemed like a hundred out here in the desert when it was this hot. But the men were starting to talk a little and that was good. The time passed quicker when they conversed. They still had to remain vigilant even though they were leaving enemy territory. The sun was tilting to the west and it was in their eyes. The lieutenant raised his field-glasses and looked back to the east, and then north. There was no sign of life, although Salvatore knew there were all kinds of life moving about through the sands. He put the glasses down and looked at the ground just as a skink skimmed across the dune.

He kept close watch on his flank guards. On the left riding camels were Pierre and Louis, and on the right also on camels were Hassef and Phillippe. Taking up the rear guard walked Treselme and one of the Belgians, Limoges, nearly thirty metres behind. They should be entering safe woods, thought Lieutenant Bationi. But things were a little out of the ordinary. The oasis was now less than two hours march and he forced himself to be thankful.

The heat was still blazing, though it had cooled a fraction and the men were exhausted. But they- the healthy ones- were feeling a little better. They were not speaking in hushed tones anymore. Someone even laughed. It was the Greek, who was talking with Tommy. The lieutenant wondered what could be funny about all this but if there was a joke to be found the Greek would find it. There was still over an hour before they would reach the oasis but the thought of water and shade *and rest* seemed to have brought new life, if not new awareness, into the men.

Lieutenant Bationi did not blame the men for being happy; it was a good oasis. They had been there many times and there had always been plenty of water and plenty of trees. And it was away from enemy territory.

Bationi decided that it was time to change turns on the flanks. He whistled sharply to his right and Hassef and the chief corporal looked over. He waved them in and then pointed at the Greek, who had stopped talking when he'd heard the whistle, and sent him out. With him went a regular corporal, a German named Hensch. On the left Pierre and Louis had angled their camels toward the marching line and were getting ready to dismount. The lieutenant replaced them on the left flank with the Dutchboy and a Spaniard whose name was Martinez. Dupree and one of the Belgians fell back and took up the rear. The line seemed to be so much quieter with the Greek out there, thought the lieutenant.

Salvatore relaxed. He borrowed another cigarette, this time from an unsavoury character named Divitto. 'Grazi,' he said to his fellow countryman. Divitto grunted.

The lieutenant scratched his beard and thought of the soft, welcoming breeze that awaited them at the oasis. He decided that they would rest at El Khajira a few hours and then continue their trek after nightfall.

Jack watched as Hassef took a spot in the marching line in front of him. 'Psst. Hassef...' he said. Hassef turned around, grinning. 'Listen, I got an idea,' Jack told him through parched lips. Hassef looked puzzled and dropped back to walk alongside the American.

Hassef said, 'No parle *English*.' He was still grinning. The sun shone on his white teeth.

'Hassef, when we get back to the fort I'll give you the fifty francs for the watch; plus fifty more for some water now. That's a hundred francs; that's what? Nearly two bucks? You can't pass that up, fella.' His dry mouth cracked. It was still very hot and the sand was like fiery coal.

There was no breeze, just dune after dune.

Hassef dropped his grin and shrugged.

Jack said: 'What? What does *that* mean? Look...' Jack held up ten fingers five times. 'Cinque-...cinquense francs. Okay?'

Hassef still did not understand. Jack pointed at his empty canteen.

The Algerian's face was blank. He knew the American wanted more water but he also knew that he didn't have any money out here.

Jack turned to Tommy, who was walking nearby, and said, 'C'mon, Tommy buddy. I forgot how to say "fifty" in French. You gotta help me out with this. You talk better French than me. Tell him I'm good for it.'

Tommy smiled. 'Yeah, okay, Yank.' He turned to Hassef and spoke in fairly rapid French.

Hassef understood completely. They were nearly home free so there

13

was very little chance that the American would be killed before they reached Ghardelle and Hassef was sure the American would be true to his word. He felt it was worth the risk. But still, Hassef had to barter. It was part of the business. He mumbled to himself; 'soixante...sept? Non; soixante-quinze: Oui, soixante-quinze.'

Now it was Jack's turn to look perplexed. He said to Tommy, 'What? I couldn't hear. What's he sayin'?'

Tommy chuckled. 'Sounds to me like 'e's upped ya, mate.' Then added, 'He wants seventy-five francs for the water, plus the fifty for the watch later.'

Smiling, Jack shook his head. 'Oh, no, no. Hassef...' He looked at the Algerian right in the eye. With a straight face Jack said, 'How about trente francs?' He flashed up ten fingers three times. 'Trente...for the water.'

Hassef replied, 'Okay. Cinquante francs. Five. I joke with you. It good. Fifty francs. Okay? Here water...' He stopped to pour water into Jack's canteen. He finished pouring and looked up at Jack. He grinned, 'Oui, okay, Jack. Cinquante francs?'

Jack said, 'Yeah, cinquante. Fifty francs.'

'Et cinquante aussi pour...le *watch*,' said Hassef.

'Yeah, pal, I know. Plus the fifty for the watch...Cent francs.'

I knew you'd come around.' He smiled and began drinking from his canteen in earnest. The water tasted wonderful.

Hassef watched the American guzzle his drink. He knew that Jack was from a far-away place called America and a large village called a New York. Hassef guessed that Jack must have learned his bartering skills there.

Jack put the cap back on his canteen and sidled up closer to Hassef. 'I thought you didn't talk- I mean- speak English...'

'I...little...no much. No...'

The American laughed.

The American's actual name was Charles Hamlyn and he'd been born in Hoboken, New Jersey when the Great European War was in full swing. He'd taken the name Jack from his initial encounter with Hassef, who'd joined the Legion shortly after he had, nearly a year and a half earlier.

Jack and Hassef had been speaking in French, trying to communicate. To pass training the Legionnaires had had to learn at least a basic, rudimentary knowledge of the language. Hassef had asked Jack what his name was: 'Quel est votre nom?'

Jack had understood and said, 'Uh...je m'appelle Charlie,' and had pointed himself in the chest with his index finger.

Hassef had repeated what he'd heard, rising in a questioning tone at the end. 'Jar-...lee?'

'Yeah, you know, I mean, uh..,' Jack had remembered to try to speak French. 'Uh...je suis Charles; Charlie, Chuck...'

'Ah, oui! Jacques!' Hassef had grinned; he'd heard that name before. His father had had a brother named Jacques. 'Oui, je sais. Jacques!' He had stood there grinning and nodding.

Jack had said, 'No, not Jacques..,' and then had paused for a moment, remembering back to the time when he'd handed over his passport to the Legion and how he'd been offered a new identity if he'd so desired. He had declined the offer but he'd considered it. Suddenly, an impulsive thought had come to him. '...Well, yeah, okay. *Jacques*. I mean...oui, Jacques. Sure. Yeah, oui...or just plain Jack...'

Hassef had said, '...Jack?'

'Oui, je m'appelle Jack,' Jack had said.

The French-Algerian had grinned again and he'd pointed both hands toward his chest: 'Bon jour, Jack. Je suis Hassef.'

Jack remembered that it had been wet that day and wished it were raining now. It was hotter than hell.

Thank God for the water, thought Jack. The summer had not yet begun and it was already this hot. *How will I make it through another summer?* He looked over at Hassef; *or I'll be penniless.*

The oasis waited, beyond the dunes. The legionnaires walked into the sun; as though they were following it. Jack drank from his canteen. The water tasted good.

There was still a ways to go.

After thirty minutes the lieutenant looked around to see who was next to sit on the right flank camels. Dupree and Descartes both needed a rest. He told his *chef caporal,* Phillippe, to inform them. He whistled sharply to his right and Corporal Hensch and the Greek cocked their heads. There was a small commotion a few rows behind the lieutenant. He turned and looked over his shoulder.

One of the wounded soldiers had lost consciousness and had fallen off his camel. Regaining consciousness he immediately screamed in

15

pain. A few of the men rushed over to help him up. Bationi saw that it was Gorentz, who was one of the worst off. At Has al Kabir he'd had a sword go through his left side. And now he'd possibly broken a rib. It was painful just looking at him, thought the lieutenant.

Bationi noticed Dupree and Descartes walking up to Hensch and the Greek, and taking over the camels. The new flank guards climbed on the camels and gave their legs a much needed rest, though their eyes would have to remain vigilant. As the other two neared the line the lieutenant could hear that the Greek was still talking and laughing.

An agama lizard scuttled away from Jack's feet. A pair of Desert Sparrows flew over high above and the sun shined directly in the American's eyes. He was walking alongside Tommy.

Tommy was saying, 'Well, me old cock. Shouldn't be long, now.'

'I'm still waiting for a turn on the camels.'

'Me too, mate.'

'My legs are cramping up and I'm hungry. I hope there'll be some more of them dates. Like last time.'

'I thought you didn't like dates, Jack...'

'I'm starved...'

'There won't be any dates at the oasis; the Greek told me.'

'Whaddya mean?'

'They've all been picked clean by now.'

'Ah, hell...'

'As I said before, old cock. It could be worse...' Tommy's words trailed the direction of his eyes, setting them on a legionnaire named Mendes who had lost some fingers when- having been caught off guard- had tried to shield off a wielding sword with his hand; a gruesome sight. The nearest proper medical facilities were at home- Fort Ghardelle. The medical supplies that the platoon had brought with them had been lost in the scuffle at Has al Kabir. With no morphine on hand the wounded were in great pain. The drugs had gone along with the medic.

Mendes was shuffling along a few rows ahead of Tommy and Jack, trying to open his canteen with two hands and five fingers. He managed to open it but immediately he dropped it. The water spilled, sinking wastefully in the sand. He made a whimpering sound as he bent down to pick up the empty canteen. He looked at Tommy and Jack as they walked up.

Tommy had joined the Legion at the very same time as Mendes. They had been in the Legion's recruitment center in Paris on the same day, less than seven months ago. Tommy felt sorry for him; he wasn't a bad sort. He handed the Barcelonan his own canteen and Mendes grabbed it thankfully, taking a quick drink and then nodding to Tommy in gratitude.

As Tommy watched his comrade struggle to drink some more he scratched the back of his neck and was glad that he still had fingers. Tommy hadn't been in Africa long but all he had seen was a lot of blood and death. Not quite the adventure filled escape he had envisioned. Mendes handed him back his canteen. It was empty. Tommy didn't mind.

Jack had stopped with them. He still had a drop of water left. He offered to Mendes who took it and drank.

The dunes were rising and dipping in greater contrast. There was no wind. One of the wounded was moaning.

Tommy thought about the life he'd left and was missing his family in central London. The endless buildings of the city were in complete contrast to the empty landscape of the desert. But at the same time, he greatly enjoyed the feeling of being away from home, the feeling of independence and of being a man. He was only eighteen. But he'd signed up for the mandatory five years and now that seemed like a very long time. With the sun glaring forcefully on his face his mind wandered to a more comfortable place.

A nice, hot cuppa by the fireplace: Blackcurrant scones with sugar and butter.

The only tea here is bloody awful.

All this walking: *All this bloody walking.*

Tommy was the only Brit left in the platoon. The other, a Scot, had been killed at Has al Kabir. He had learned some French in school so he could communicate fairly well out here in his new life. Lieutenant Bationi had already asked him if had ever been interested in being a corporal. He'd never given it a thought, but had been honoured that the lieutenant had singled him out. *Maybe one day when I am more experienced.*

He was used to the overcast English sky. The Saharan sun shined down hard on Tommy's pale skin. Any exposed skin quickly reddened and there would be no tan until several peelings. The heat had reduced

17

his already skinny frame into what best resembled a lamppost. He didn't mind the sun usually. But it was quite hot today and with everything that had happened, nightfall and sleep were too far away.

Tommy tugged his trousers up and reminded himself to cut another hole in his belt, to tighten it, when they got to the oasis. As he walked through the endless sand he watched the American, whom he had become friendly with, wearing a look of frustration on his face as he tried to follow a conversation between Phillippe and Treselme. The American could follow basic orders and one-word sentences, but he was at a lost when the conversations turned fluid. He and Jack were now the only two English speaking legionnaires remaining in the platoon, as far as he knew.

Tommy listened to the conversation for a moment, then he said, 'Don't worry, Yank. You're not missing anything new.'

'Yeah, but it drives me nuts. Why can't they talk slower. Then I'd know what they're talkin' about.'

'Listen, mate. You just 'av to 'ear the key words. The rest is all, you know, bollocks.'

'Yeah. Thanks, pal. But it still drives me nuts.'

chapter 2

Trees loomed from both sides of the road, obscuring the late afternoon's sun from the two horses and the driver. Speckles of light sparkled through the lovely green foliage as they moved along.

The carriage trundled along the thoroughfare at a quick but somewhat casual pace, the sounds a pleasant mixture of horse hooves, reins tinkling and the strong oak wheels that creaked quietly but steadily. There was no breeze. It had been a warm day and was only cooling slightly, very nice for autumn, but the driver of the carriage could see dark clouds forming on the horizon ahead.

Several metres ahead, a squirrel scurried across the road at breakneck speed, darting invisibly into the bushes on the other side. The carriage thundered by, leaving dust in its wake.

The driver and his wife- she was in the coach- had been travelling most of the day. They had stopped hours earlier for a midday meal of bread, cheese and ale but would soon have to stop for supper. The

18

driver's name was Benjamin Bathurst, who was middle-aged with a heavy beard. He and his wife, Helga, were on their way home to Staffordshire after a week's business in London.

A man and a woman, both carrying two large sacks apiece, were walking along the road when they'd seen the approaching carriage coming toward them and moved to the side. They watched it go by, and walked on. Moments later, they heard a horse galloping and turned around. It was a lone rider- a neighbour of the two people. They recognized him from the long dark coat that he always wore.

The rider turned left off of the main road down a lane and was swallowed by the trees.

The couple went on their way. They had things to do.

Helga looked out of the carriage at the passing foliage. She'd seen the couple and guessed that they'd had a hard life. The sacks seemed terribly heavy, she thought. Wouldn't it be better to have the servants do that sort of thing?

She knew that they would be stopping before too long. I'm famished. And Benjamin must be, too. *A fine meal and expensive wine awaited them at the popular inn that they had patronized on many occasions through the years.*

Helga had bought many fashionable garments that past week in London, some of them were quite risqué. She was very buxom. Her husband liked her to dress in the busty, revealing manner of the day and she loved wearing the current trends.

Benjamin and Helga would normally have a driver but their coachman had suddenly taken ill recently. Benjamin had insisted he'd be fine handling the carriage.

'But Benjamin,' she had told him. 'You are an old man. You should not have to do this.'

'I am not an old man,' he said, winking. 'Remember last night?'

She remembered. 'I would rather you be in the coach with me.'

'Don't worry.' Until his string of antique businesses became successful Benjamin had driven the carriage to London all of the time. But that had been ages ago. 'This is an important trip and we have no one to handle the carriage. So, I will do it. We must leave soon.'

Helga had said nothing more; there would've been no reason to.

A rider passed by the carriage at a quick gallop. He hadn't seemed to have slowed down, as Benjamin had.

Helga licked her lips, wondering what delightful food would be available. They'd be there soon. She sat there in the coach, alone, thinking about juicy meat and succulent vegetables; and luscious wine.

Benjamin was tired and weary, much more than he'd anticipated, but the horses were running well and they were making good time. He was glad for it and though exhausted, felt somewhat exhilarated. He knew they were close to the inn; it was just up around the next bend.

He slowed the horses as they approached the clearing. There was low brush and bushes on either side, so the area was brightened by the lowering sun. But not far off the darkening clouds gathered and were moving towards them. Benjamin felt a distinct change in the air and suddenly felt a chill. But then just as quickly he caught the sun's rays again, feeling some warmth.

Benjamin looked at the beautiful sign that hung on a post next to the wood and stone building. The sign read: The White Swan Inn.

chapter 3

The legionnaires were feeling a little bit lighter for they knew it wouldn't be too long before the oasis came into view. They could see the top of the hillside that ran along El Khajira. Though thoroughly fatigued and many in pain, the men's heart's jumped with thoughts of water and shade and, most of all, rest. The platoon laboured up a dune and off in the distance appeared the outline of the oasis. The Greek laughed and made celebratory gestures.

The men were greatly relieved. Lieutenant Bationi sighed; it was a safe area. Nonetheless he called out, 'Hassef!' As Hassef came up to him he glanced around at his left and right flanks; everything seemed to be fine. Behind Hassef, Salvatore could see the rear flank walking. He looked at his top scout and pointed to the oasis. Hassef understood and ran off to make sure the oasis was safe.

Salvatore made eye contact with Limoges and Grizzo and they followed after Hassef. *Better safe than sorry.*

A camel snorted and sneezed into Jack's face as he walked by the beast. He was a little disgusted. 'Oh, that's great,' he mumbled sarcastically. Tommy was about to say something but Jack stopped him and said, 'Yeah, yeah. I know, I know...*could be worse.*'

The platoon had turned northward so that the lowering sun was now on their left. Bationi had to squint to see the left flank; the Swede and Martinez made a silhouette against the sunshine. It was still very warm, but a strong wind suddenly blew sand on the legionnaires and they had to cover their eyes. 'Crikey...' said Tommy. 'Damn it,' said Jack.

Hassef was up at the final dune rise before El Khajira. Limoges and Grizzo were several steps behind him. Hassef looked back and waved his arm twice. He turned, faced the oasis and stood surveying the area; the oasis looked deserted. Hassef briefly looked over his shoulder back at the platoon and then back to the oasis, standing still for a few moments for Limoges and Grizzo to reach the crest before he would run down for a closer look. As he stood on the soft white sandy hillcrest with the date trees jutting from the oasis beyond him and the sun shining down he created a striking image, embellished by the beautiful blue and white Legion uniform.

The Lieutenant wiped the sand from his face and studied the scouts. Hassef did not look concerned.

Water: beautiful water. The men could smell it: *Water, water, water.*

Then the wind kicked up again, even more fierce than before. The solid breeze lowered the temperature and that was good but the sand flying everywhere was quite bothersome. Lieutenant Bationi saw Hassef give the okay signal: one hand, two waves. Then he saw Hassef go over the last dune just as Limoges and Grizzo reached the crest. He closed his eyes again when the wind whipped up some sand in his face.

Seemingly full of energy, Hassef sprinted down the dune to the oasis. Limoges followed him. Grizzo stood at the crest. More wind.

Suddenly a shot rang out. To the left, into the sun, Bationi saw Martinez fall off the camel. A second later the other left flank guard, the Swede, fell too.

Charging from the direction of the sun was a pack of Tuaregs on camels, an ambush. They shot while riding and they were screaming a war cry: They shouted, 'Allah Allah!' There were many of them.

The lieutenant screamed out, 'Disperser!' The men spread out but quickly had to set and fire. There was no cover. Bationi heard shots from behind him and turned around to see the rear guard drop to their sitting firing position, firing behind them. Then one of them fell; and then the other. The wind was not stopping. It picked up bucketfuls of sand and rained it back down on the battlefield, swirling in all directions.

Out of a dune nearby from the east appeared several Arabs on foot; they must have laid low when the platoon had marched by moments before and the right flank had somehow missed them. The platoon was nearly surrounded. Bullets and the war cry filled the air: 'Allah!'

Tommy and Jack both knelt and shot side by side. Jack cursed beneath his breath as he fired. The flying sand made it difficult to get off a good shot. A bullet pierced the sand just to his right. 'Jesus..,' he muttered.

The Arabs were nearly on them. Once again, Bationi and his men had found themselves outnumbered. The ambushers seemed to have risen out of the sand. They were yelling; 'Allah ul Alluh: Allah!'

The attackers were now among and around the legionnaires. As if the gale was not bad enough, a gust of wind on loan from Hades suddenly burst out- blowing hot sand into the eyes of the surrounded platoon. The Tuaregs were everywhere. The south-west end of the company was in hand-to-hand combat. Despite the conditions, the aim of the legionnaires was good and the charging camel riders fell in numbers. But many were getting through.

Hassef and Limoges were running back from the oasis. Limoges stopped to fix his bayonet. As Grizzo stood and fired at the attackers he heard Hassef run past him. A Tuareg's bullet whizzed into Grizzo's skull and Limoges watched him fall.

Tommy glanced back to the rear and to his horror he saw a sword rip into LaMonde's chest. He fired at the Arab and missed. Sand blew in his eyes. He attached his bayonet while he frantically rubbed the sand from his eyes; then he fired into the melee and missed.

Jack was still near Tommy, also firing into the melee that was getting closer by the second. But they were also being attacked on almost all sides. They were nearly surrounded. Jack took two deliberate shots and killed two attackers. He felt lucky; the sand was making it very difficult to shoot.

The Tuaregs were everywhere. They were still shouting praise to Allah as they dismounted their camels amongst the fatigued legionnaires. Some had rifles, most had swords. A few had both.

The platoon was in trouble with hand-to-hand in this case. Normally a bayonet would hold its own against a sword but on this chaotic stage in hell a sword beats a bayonet like a flush beats a straight.

A legionnaire's elbow was jarred by a camel as he was set to plunge a bayonet into an Arab: He missed his target and the Tuareg took full advantage of this reversal of fortune and embedded his scimitar, a curved sword, into the legionnaire's arm. The soldier screamed in pain. It was Phillippe, Bationi's chief corporal.

The little corporal held his rifle up with one arm, it would be too difficult to pull the trigger and aim, and pointed the bayonet as menacingly as possible at his foe who was circling him as a vulture would circle a wounded animal.

Tommy yelled to Jack. 'The rear's fallin' apart, Jack!' He ran several steps through the sand and dived. Lying prone, he took careful aim. This time his shot was accurate and an Arab fell to the sand. He looked around and saw Phillippe trying to fend off two swordsmen while holding his rifle with just one hand. Tommy quickly raised his rifle to shoot but, horribly, a sword sliced deep into Phillippe's neck and the brave little corporal fell dead.

Tommy fired at the Arab and missed, but before he could fire again the Arab fell dead. He could tell where the bullet had originated. 'Thanks, Yank,' he said, though not loud enough for his friend to hear. Tommy fired at Phillippe's other assassin. His first shot missed, but his second found its mark.

Tommy turned to look at Jack who was now firing towards the right flank, to the east. Sword wielding Arabs were approaching on foot. Tommy glanced quickly around hoping to see where the lieutenant was at but something caught his eye.

He saw Klauss, the Swiss legionnaire, fire into a melee but it was one of the legionnaires that fell. It was Ibriam, one of the Frankmeier brothers. Tommy wondered for a moment whether he had seen correctly. But his doubts quickly disappeared as, astonishingly, Klauss fired once again into the melee and another legionnaire fell. This time it was Ibriam's brother, Julien.

Tommy then turned his attention to the east, knelt and started firing alongside Jack. The desert landscape was littered with dead and wounded men. On both sides the numbers were dwindling rapidly. The wind continued to create miniature dust-devils.

The eastern charge had reached Tommy and Jack. In front of Tommy, Pierre was jabbing his bayonet left and right at two Arabs-keeping them at bay. Another was running straight at Tommy. Tommy turned, straightened and positioned himself but there was no time to shoot. He stood and thrust his bayonet at the Tuareg and it pegged straight into the heart. He yanked it back out and the Arab fell dead. For just an instant Tommy felt sickened. He noticed that the Arab was just a boy, barely an adolescent. He looked around hastily. He saw Jack shoot two more at close range and then heard him mutter, 'Jesus...' Jack had to reload.

Tommy fired off four shots at an Arab that was running at him with a raised sword. The fourth hit and the attacker fell but was still moving and trying to get up. Tommy fired thrice more into him before he laid still.

A few feet behind the slain Arab, Pierre was lying dead.

When Jack had been reloading an Arab ran at him, swinging a sword. Jack had been caught off guard and dropped his bullets. He hadn't fixed his bayonet and had barely raised his rifle in time to stop the blade from cutting him in two. When the Arab had quickly turned and swung again Jack could only throw up his rifle in defense, but it had slipped from his hands and skidded across the sand. The Tuareg had stood in front of Jack with his sword at his side, waving it deliberately. Then Jack had backed up slowly, never letting his eyes off of the attacker's.

Now, barely six feet separated them. Jack put his left hand into a pocket and pulled out a round, apple-sized object. He was still moving back and the Arab was advancing on him. Suddenly, Jack ran away from the Arab at full speed. Then, just as sudden, he came to an abrupt halt, turned around and heaved a rock at great speed- a hundred miles per hour- at his sword-wielding attacker, who was chasing him.

The rock smashed into the swordsman's head, smashing his skull into fragments of bone and tissue and he was killed instantly. Jack ran and retrieved his rifle. He knew he had been able to load a few bullets before he'd been attacked. He saw Tommy and the Greek fighting an Arab. The giant Greek pinned the attacker to the sand with his bayonet.

Jack looked around and could see that only a handful still stood. They were all legionnaires. For a moment there was silence. Even the wind had ceased.

Then, an Arab feigning death made a run for the lieutenant, coming up behind him.

Jack saw what was happening, raised his rifle and fired once. The Arab fell. Lieutenant Bationi turned around.

The surviving legionnaires continued to swivel their heads back and forth. Limoges ran around the Arabs looking for their wounded. He found one lying still with a bullet wound in his shoulder. The attacker's scimitar was nearby in the sand, almost within reach. Limoges met his foe's eyes and fired twice into them. This had been a suicide attack and there would be no mercy.

Divitto took the Belgian's cue and found five more wounded Tuaregs feigning death. He killed them all.

Bationi, whose eyes had been scanning the dune horizons in a panoramic view for any further attack, saw what was happening and shouted. 'Assez!' *'Enough!'* He ordered the men to gather the camels, collect weapons and spare any other wounded. He wanted prisoners because he wanted answers. *Je veux des reponses!* The attacks today had seemed so full of vengeance, more so than the usual, the lieutenant felt.

'Corporal Hensch, take care of it.' Hensch was now second in command. 'Oui, Lieutenant,' said the German.

The bodies of Arab and Legionnaire alike were strewn across the desert dune. It was quiet as some men checked the Arabs and others checked their wounded and dead comrades. The lieutenant counted the dead legionnaires. *Quinze:* Fifteen.

Fifteen more: Of the surviving thirteen, five were wounded. Every Arab was dead. It had been a suicide attack; there was no doubt about it.

There were now more camels than men. The badly wounded legionnaires that had been hanging on a string since Has al Kabir and that had made it this far, only hours away from home, had been cut up in the attack and finished off. Mendes had been beheaded.

Lieutenant Bationi conversed quietly with the Greek and Louis. Louis was nursing a severe bullet wound in his leg.

Tommy grabbed a camel by the reins and walked over toward Jack, who was gathering swords. Almost every sword was bloodstained. Tommy asked himself: *Had I seen right?* He knew he had. *Should I say something?* He hoped he would. He looked at Jack and for a moment he started to speak, but nothing came out.

Not now. Not yet. He glimpsed at Klauss.

Bationi gave the order to gather what they could and move down to the oasis.

A few of the soldiers walked into the desert pool and sat down. Others kept their guard up in case of any further attack. One or two did not care. A camel bull dropped its head into the water and drank. The lieutenant stood under the shade of a tall, thin tree and leaned against it. He shook his head in disbelief. Would they ever make it back to fort? The soldiers still had another three to four hours march through the lonesome desert before they would reach Fort Ghardelle.

The Greek was not talking very much now. He held his rifle with his right hand and his left hand covered the side of his hip where a scimitar had grazed him. He was okay, though. He walked over to where Jack and Tommy sat at the edge of the water. Tommy was looking at the ground. Jack was staring forward, mumbling, 'Jesus fucking Christ...'

Hassef had survived. He was throwing water on his face. He was next to Treselme, who was sitting in the water facing out toward the dunes and scanning the horizon with eyes full of anxiety.

Louis came limping over, his leg wound bleeding badly. He was crying; Pierre was dead: *Mon bon ami...*

Louis walked in and lowered himself into the oasis pool. The water turned red.

After a few hours of much needed rest, the men prepared to depart. The temperature was finally dropping and the platoon had regained some of their energy. Lieutenant Bationi had decided that the best route back may not be the obvious one so he'd felt it would be best to march west a ways and then north back to the fort, instead of moving in a straight north-west direction. It would cost them a little time, but the lieutenant could not count out the possibility of another ambush.

It would be dark before too long. The lieutenant gave the command and the legionnaires, what was left of them, moved into single file and started on their way.

Tommy was still silent. He had not told anyone of the killings he had witnessed earlier. From time to time he'd glanced over at Klauss, making sure not to make any eye contact. He did not, of course, want Klauss to suspect that he had seen anything.

Jack was walking behind Tommy. He looked at his skinny British friend, who had said not one word during the whole time at the oasis.

Jack figured that his fellow comrade's silence must stem from one too many altercations. Poor guy, thought Jack. *He's only been on patrols a few months and there's been one battle after another.*

Of course, there hadn't been much talking from anybody since the ambush. Most of the time the soldier's eyes were fixed on the horizon. The horizon to the west, the east, the north, the south...

Jack spoke. 'Hey, Tommy, buddy ol' pal. Long time, no hear. You havin' second thoughts about life in the Legion?' It was a redundant question: Every legionnaire had second thoughts about it: And thirds.

Tommy turned around and looked at Jack for a moment. He wanted to speak, or even give a half-smile, but could not. He turned and continued his march, staring straight ahead.

Jack said, 'Well, I dunno about you but I'm thinkin' about gettin' out.' Desertion was not exactly smiled upon by the Legion, though it was very common. But the soldiers all understood when one deserted; they all secretly wanted to at one time or another- and some thought of it all the time. But the punishment was severe if a deserter was caught. However, Lieutenant Bationi had always had a low percentage of deserters.

'I don't think we'll be ambushed again,' said Jack. 'Damn Arabs...' He paused to give Tommy a chance to speak. Tommy remained silent, looking straight ahead.

Jack continued: 'That last ambush must've been a fluke. El Khajira has always been a safe spot. When I first joined up it was victory after victory. They'd be dropping like flies. Until lately, we hadn't been doing too bad...' His voice trailed. Still, Tommy said nothing.

'But I gotta tell ya, buddy ol' pal, there was somethin' fishy about Has al Kabir. Bationi's a good man; a good commander. Now we're headin' back to the fort with our tails between our legs.'

The camels' hooves swished through the sand. A bull several feet ahead of Jack and Tommy let off some gas. A moment later the stench entered Jack's nostrils and he gagged. 'Ugh...pee-yew. I was just thinking about how hungry I was and then I smell that...' Then the odour was gone and his hunger returned. 'When I get back to the fort I'm gonna stuff my gut. I could eat a horse. I could eat a *camel*. Well; not a camel. But I'm gonna eat all the slop they throw at me.' Jack reached forward and tapped Tommy on his back. 'What about you, buddy? You gonna try and put some weight on that toothpick body of yours?'

Tommy remembered his belt; he'd forgotten to cut another hole in it so that he could pull it tighter. He tugged his pants up. He finally spoke. 'Bloody hell. I forgot to make another 'ole in me belt.'

Jack's eyebrows raised in semi-mock surprise. He said, 'Hey! He speaks! I thought you'd gone deaf and dumb, fella.'

There was a pause for a few seconds and then Tommy said, 'No...no. I'm just tired, that's all...'

'Yeah, well it seems to me to be a little more than fatigue,' said the American. 'Like somethin's botherin' you. If there is, y'know, you can always tell me.' He waited; then added, 'Of course, if you don't wanna tell me then that's okay, too.'

Tommy took a quick and extremely subtle glance at Klauss from the corner of his eyes. Klauss was less than ten metres away. *Too close.* Tommy wondered whether Klauss could understand English. He'd heard him speaking French quite fluently. But, he *was* Swiss, after all. It suddenly occurred to Tommy that he had never spoken to Klauss.

Tommy turned to Jack for a moment and said, 'No, mate. Nothing's botherin' me. If there was, you'd be the first to know. Like you said-just 'aving doubts about this line of work, that's all.'

'Yeah, well, me too, buddy. I know exactly what you mean. We've all felt that way.' Again, they walked in silence.

A while later the few men that were not riding camels took their turn, among them Jack and Tommy. Most of the camels that were not carrying wounded were laden with weapons and ammunition.

Lieutenant Bationi and Corporal Hensch rode up front. Behind them Hassef dismounted and Klauss, who had been stringing along several packed camels, handed over the reins to Hassef and mounted the camel. At the rear rode Treselme and Limoges. They dismounted when they reached Jack and Tommy, who had stopped walking.

Tommy took hold of the camel, taking quite a few moments struggling to climb up on to the beast. He dropped his rifle. He bent over slowly to pick it up.

'You okay, little buddy?' Jack asked.

Tommy gave a sort of grunt, looked up the line and he watched Treselme and Limoges get farther from them. Klauss was a good twenty or thirty yards away. Klauss was still too close. Tommy was still too nervous. He wiped the sweat from his brow, which lead to an impromptu performance wherein he knocked his kepi off- *whoops!* pretended to be blinded by the sun and finally found the flat-peaked cap behind him. He picked it up, placed it back upon his head, and mounted.

Jack was sitting on his camel waiting patiently. He was watching the English boy closely. He was a little *a*mused; and he was a little *be*mused. Tommy rode up next to him and they started off casually to join the end of the line.

'What was that?' questioned Jack.

'What?' Tommy said innocently.

'Cut the crap. What's goin' on?'

Tommy looked at Jack, revealing an earnest gaze. Quietly, without moving his lips, he said, 'Shush.'

Jack listened.

Tommy spoke in a hushed tone. 'Listen carefully, Jack. You asked me earlier if somethin' was bothering me. I said "No"...'

Jack nodded subtly. 'Yeah, I remember.'

Tommy glanced up the line, then back to Jack. 'Well, there is something botherin' me. During that last ambush at the oasis, I saw...something.' He paused.

Jack looked up. 'Something?'

Tommy continued. When I was shooting, well, I mean...I could be wrong. In the heat of the battle, I mean, what I saw...' Tommy nervously looked up the line.

Jack interjected the trailing words. 'What you "saw"? What did you see?'

Tommy stared at Jack for a moment, straight in the eyes. He opened his mouth to speak but did not. Instead, he let out a deep breath.

Jack: 'Well, partner; spit it out.'

'Keep your voice down a bit, mate. I'm a bit nervous.'

'You're tellin' me...' said Jack quietly.

'This is between you and me,' Tommy was almost shaking. 'Now, when I tell you this, I don't want you to look up ahead. Just keep looking at me. I think...I think I saw Klauss- *don't look forward!* I saw Klauss shoot, and kill, the Frankmeier brothers. I mean, I couldn't bloody believe it. 'He shot 'em right before me bloody eyes...'

'Are you sure? I mean you might've just thought that's what you saw.'

'I know. I know what I said. But I know that's what I saw. I just

29

couldn't believe it. I mean: why? Why would 'e? It doesn't make any sense.'

'Maybe he owed them money.'

'Don't be funny, mate. You don't kill someone over a bit of dosh.'

'You'd be surprised...'

Tommy glanced quickly ahead. He saw that Klauss was still far up the line, riding his camel and staring straight forward. Tommy looked over at Jack. 'I think we ought to tell the lieutenant, don't you?'

'"*We*"? Whaddya mean, "*We*"? This is your baby. You saw it- not me. I find it best not to get involved in these kind of things.' Jack waited a moment then broke into a grin. He said, 'Just kiddin', buddy. If you need help, I'll help. Just be real careful. If this is true, then this guy could real dangerous. Are you sure he hasn't seen you watchin' him?'

'No. I'm sure 'e 'asn't. I'll tell the lieutenant when we get back.'

'Yeah, well, come to think of it the guy does kinda give me the creeps. He joined up soon after me. When I first went up to introduce myself I put my hand out to him to shake but he just walked away.'

Tommy was shaking his head slowly. 'I just don't understand why 'e would kill 'em like that. Maybe he's an escaped murderer. You know the Legion; they'll take just about anybody. All they'd asked from me was me passport.'

As Tommy began to feel a little more at ease having unburdened his dilemma, Jack was starting to feel a little more on edge. 'Well, buddy, the best thing for now is for us to keep quiet about it 'til we get back. Try to think of whether or not you saw somethin' else. And try not to keep glancing over at him. If he catches you lookin' at him he might get suspicious.'

'Well, 'e makes me nervous.'

'Yeah, well, you and me both. He isn't gonna try anythin' here, so don't worry. Let's can it for now, okay buddy?'

'Right-o, mate. And thanks for listening.'

'Forget it. Now, save your energy. We got a lotta sand to travel over. Think of some of them poems that you read from that book of yours.' Tommy had a book of poems back at the fort.

The time passed and the evening turned into night. The remnant platoon headed into the desert sunset and the moon grew brighter by the minute. The men would soon turn to march north. In a flash the sun was gone. To the left of the moon sat Venus twinkling in imitation of the stars that would soon fill the desert sky.

Most of the men looking at the bright planet assumed that it was indeed a star. Venus caught Jack's eye and he said to his friend, 'Here's a poem for ya.' He pointed at Venus. '*"First star I see tonight; I wish I may I wish I might; I get the wish I wish tonight".*'

Tommy chuckled. 'I don't think so, Jack. There won't be any women at the fort.'

'Well,' said Jack. 'A man can dream; can't he?'

chapter 4

The sign was expertly crafted, hanging from the wooden post that stood outside the entrance to the inn. A heavy wind could sometimes blow it off its chain, but there was little breeze today. The horses slowed, and the carriage pulled up along the path that led to the front entrance. Benjamin basked for a moment in the sunlight. The sun's early evening rays felt wonderful on his face. He looked at the inn; he knew that the food would be good. He and his wife had eaten there several times on their business trips between London and their home in Staffordshire. He glanced at the well that was off to the left; the horses would be thirsty and need a drink.

Helga waited in the carriage. She would not get out until the horses were completely still and Benjamin had opened the door. From the opening she watched Benjamin climb down and pat one of the horses on the head. Then he walked by smiling at her and went to the rear of the carriage; maybe to check the wheels, she thought.

She leaned over and looked back but she could not see him now. He was out of view.

The horses were glad for the rest. They would soon have water to drink and straw to eat. The horse on the left, they were both brown with white speckles, cocked its left ear. A fly landed on the horse's nostril and crawled up its nose, causing the beast to huff.

The house servant had looked through the window and recognized the carriage upon their arrival. He informed the proprietor, who in turn instructed him, 'Prepare a table for Mr Bathurst and his wife.' The house servant went off to perform his duties. The proprietor walked off

31

to the kitchen to speak with the cook- his daughter.

Outside, Benjamin bent down to pick up the object that had caught his eye just as the carriage had pulled up. It shined in the sun's reflection. He picked it up. It had a couple of chains attached to a band and a ring, with a round object halfway up one of the chains. Very curious, he thought; very curious indeed. What was it? Benjamin immediately felt that it was something valuable: But what? What could he sell it as? It looked quite modern; it was not rusty. So: not an antique. Jewellery? He dealt with jewellers; they would know.

He placed the ring on his finger. It fit, although slightly loose. He saw that maybe the metal- silver? band went on the wrist and put the band around his left wrist and closed it together. It snapped together smoothly. He unsnapped it and it came apart easy. He smiled. He closed the band again, and again it snapped neatly together. Benjamin felt very clever.

He heard a yelp; or something. Or some thing: an animal crying out? Moments earlier he had thought that he'd heard some small creature scurrying about; but it was probably just a grouse. Maybe our dinner! He looked back at the object; the ball part rested neatly in his palm. He twiddled with it.

He heard Helga calling out from the carriage. 'Did you say something? Benjamin, what are you doing?' she asked.

He was about to answer her but his thumb rested on a knobby bit on the ball as it rotated slightly in his palm. He twisted and released.

Helga opened the carriage door cautiously. 'Benjamin? Benjamin, I'm coming out.' She climbed out of the carriage and moved to the rear, but there was no sign of Benjamin. She called out again, 'Benjamin? Where are you? Benjamin?' She looked around; nothing. There! What was that? The bushes by the well: an animal? Was it Benjamin? She cried out once again, 'Benjamin?!' When she looked in all directions this time she could tell that she was becoming frantic.

The proprietor came out of the front door smiling. He said, 'Good evening, Mrs Bathurst. How are you?' He glanced around. 'Where is Mr Bathurst?'

She looked away from him and into the direction of the bushes she yelled, 'Benjamin? Benjamin?!' She turned and looked at the proprietor, who was no longer smiling. She told him, 'I don't know.'

chapter 5

The fort gates opened and Lieutenant Bationi's platoon marched through with much awaited relief. The wounded were immediately taken to Ghardelle's medical quarters and seen to.

Salvatore went immediately to report to his commanding officer, Captain Versailler. The healthy troops were sent to rest. It was one order that they did not mind.

Versailler was sitting at his desk as Bationi stood and described the battle: *The battles*. Not battles: *Two ambushes*. The commanding officer frowned as he listened to Salvatore's retake of the day's events. He was greatly displeased, especially the part about the cannons disappearing into the Arabs hands: And the men? Only thirteen out of sixty-four survived! Versailler threw Bationi a look that was steeped in disapproval.

The lieutenant mentioned that they had been greatly outnumbered and that that had been the fault of the reconnaissance, not his. The men had fought bravely and the thirteen that were left had been lucky to make it back alive.

Versailler spoke. 'Je ne veux pas entrendre des excuses.' The captain did not want to hear excuses; only results. He told the lieutenant that he should melt his platoon into one of the other sections and be relieved of his duty. He said he would have to think about what to do with Salvatore and his men. He also said that he would now have to turn around and go to his superiors and inform them that Has al Kabir had still not been secured.

Bationi seethed. Captain Versailler was more concerned with saving face; and he would not be taking the blame for Has al Kabir. Bationi had been a sergeant under Versailler when the captain had been a lieutenant. He never liked him. They never liked each other, but Versailler needed Salvatore because he was a good leader. But this was bad, and the lieutenant knew he was expendable.

The captain stood up. He glared coldly at Salvatore. He said, 'Votre chef caporal est mort. Vous aurez a ecrirer les notifications de mort.' *Your chief corporal is dead. You will have to write the death notifications.* The lieutenant already knew this; at one time it had been one of his duties. He noticed that his commanding officer was speaking more quick than usual, purposefully making it difficult for the native Italian to follow. But Bationi knew what was being said. Versailler continued, 'Cela vous prenda un temps long, donc vous avez eu mieux commence.' *That will take you a long time, so you had better get started.'* The lieutenant's expression was stony. He was not going to display any emotion.

'Cela est tout, Lieutenant Bationi.' *That is all, Lieutenant.* Salvatore saluted and left the captain's office.

Jack walked into the soldier's quarters and sat on his cot. Food had been put out for the famished survivors and Jack had dived in mouth first. Tommy was the only person in the room and was already lying on his cot, reading from his poetry book. He looked up when Jack had entered.

Jack said, 'You didn't eat much...'

'Not that hungry.' Tommy put the book down.

Jack whispered. 'Y'know, I was thinkin' about what should be said to the lieutenant about...what you saw. These things can be pretty tricky...how it's worded.'

Divitto walked into the room. The American looked at his English comrade; they would have to go outside to talk. It'd be too risky speaking indoors. The walls have ears.

Lieutenant Bationi was angry. He sat at a desk in the NCO's cramped office space. He found a pen and pulled out some paper from a drawer and prepared to write the death notices. Of course, this was normally the duty of the *chef caporal,* but Corporal Patek's family would be receiving a letter themselves. Little Phillippe had served the lieutenant well.

This particular duty had used to make Salvatore very sad. But all he felt now was anger.

He put the pen to paper and thought about how to word the first letter, which would be sent to Sergeant Leliat's wife and family. Salvatore looked at the typewriter for a moment, then pushed it aside to give him more room to hand write the notification. He would not be sending this letter typewritten.

Salvatore thought of his long-time friend. He and Rene had been through a lot together. A lot of battles, a lot of wine, a lot of laughs...

He stared at the wall. He wondered: *What do I write? How does one write such a letter without coldness?*

He began to write: *Violette, je regrette que votre mari, mon ami Rene, etais detruire durant se battre. Il etait un bon homme. Il etait un bon ami. Je regrette*

The lieutenant stopped writing. His eyes glinted and then he threw the pen, hard as he could, at the wall. He cursed in Italian. He rose from the desk and went to open one of the two bottles of wine that he had brought into the office with him. Just then, he noticed Tommy was standing in the doorway.

Tommy said, 'Excusez moi, Lieutenant...'

Salvatore regarded the lanky English soldier, who he felt was much too thin. He said to Tommy, 'En Italian, il est "mi scusi".' Tommy replied, 'Mi scusi, Lieutenant.' The lieutenant managed a weak smile. 'Oui. Qu'est-ce qu'il y a, Legionnaire Smith?' *What is it, Smith?*

Tommy entered the room and started to pull the door closed as he did so. The lieutenant was pouring a large glass of wine. He motioned Tommy not to bother closing the door, but Tommy nodded solemnly and closed it anyway. He faced Salvatore and said, 'Oui. Je besoin...'

Lieutenant Bationi took a long gulp of wine. The young English soldier looked scared, but how bad could it be? The day could not get any worse. Bationi gestured for Tommy to continue speaking.

'I don't know how to tell you this,' said Tommy as he quickly tried to translate his words into French.

The lieutenant told him, 'En Francais...'

Tommy stumbled over his words in his nervous haste. 'Oui, d'accord. Je ne sais pas...'

Salvatore took another big gulp of wine. It tasted good. He told Tommy to relax; they were home now; just get some rest and come back in the morning.

Tommy shook his head. He was finally able to string together some words so that the lieutenant could understand what it was that he was saying.

Salvatore drank as he listened to Legionnaire Smith tell him that he had witnessed Klauss purposely shoot and kill the Frankmeier brothers during the ambush at El Khajira. The lieutenant had the feeling that this day would never end. He lit a cigarette and offered one to Tommy. Tommy politely refused.

Jack was out in the hallway standing guard and straining his ear to the door. He wouldn't be able to understand anyway. He basically knew already what Tommy would be saying as he had briefed his skinny friend beforehand. But what would Lieutenant Bationi say? He looked up and down the halls but no one was around. He edged closer to the doorway and was startled as Tommy opened the door and walked out. Jack jumped. 'Jesus,' he said to his English buddy. 'You scared the hell outta me...'

They walked down the hall and out into the courtyard. Jack led Tommy to a far corner that had an edge jutting out. Perfect. He looked around, pulling out a pouch of Moroccan tobacco. The only men in sight were the sentries on duty, quite a distance away. He rolled a cigarette quickly. Before he lit it he asked Tommy, 'Well, what he say?' He struck a match and puffed.

'Said that he would, you know, record that the information was anonymous: no names. That's what we wanted...'

Jack smiled. *Name*s. *We.* He said, 'Good. That's good. Anything else? Are you sure he understood what you were saying?'

'Yeah, mate. I 'ad to go over the story about three times because he couldn't believe it.'

'Did he say what he was gonna do?'

'No.'

'But he's gonna file the report?'

'Yes.'

Jack scratched his cheek. He looked around the fort. It was quiet. He couldn't see it nor hear it. But he could feel it. It was gloom. He turned to Tommy. 'Anything else?'

'No. Well, somethin' about his family in France.'

'Family in France? But the lieutenant is Italian...' Jack's words trailed off as he noticed a couple of figures walking over in the distance. He saw that it was Treselme and Limoges smoking cigarettes. They weren't close enough to worry about. He continued; 'Wouldn't the lieutenant have family in Italy?'

'No. His wife is French.'

'I never knew that.' Jack pondered for a moment; then said, 'Hm.' He looked at Tommy and asked, 'Is that it?'

'Uh, well. The information will be reported as anonymous...'

'You already said that.' Jack looked a tiny bit exacerbated. 'What I meant was, *is that it* about the family in France? Why would he talk about that?'

'He was 'avin a booze-up by the look of it. Gettin' nostalgic, I guess. So he told me that if 'e was ever killed that he wouldn't want his family to read about it on some typed piece of paper. 'He would want one of his men to go to France and notify his family in person.'

'That's it? That's nuts...' Jack took a puff from his cigarette and then let it curl up into his nostrils from his mouth. He then exhaled back out his mouth. He said, almost to himself: 'French-style.' He looked at Tommy.

Tommy seemed embarrassed about something. Jack noticed and said, 'What? What is it, kid?'

'I sort of promised 'im that I'd personally see to it that, well, his family was notified. After all, he's doin' us a favour by leaving our names out of the report. The lieutenant is doin' us a favour; so we should do one for 'im.'

Jack chuckled softly. He said, 'There's that *we* again...' He was tired, but he was alive. And he was glad. He blew out smoke and dropped his cigarette butt to the ground, and rubbed it out. He smiled at his friend. 'Tommy, buddy, how on earth could you keep that kind of promise? You plan on runnin' the Legion someday?'

'I would never need to. The lieutenant can survive anything. But if I had to, I'd find a way.'

Jack caught a glimpse of Tommy's face in the moonlight. The kid looked sheepish. Jack said, 'Okay...out with it.'

'Well, I actually told Lieutenant Bationi that we-...I sort of promised on your behalf as well.'

'Buddy, I don't like making promises I can't keep...'

'Sorry.'

Jack shrugged. He said, 'I take it then that you told the lieutenant you'd told me.'

'Well...yes.'

'Okay. I just needed to know. I'm gonna hit the sack. It's been a long day.'

They walked across the dirt ground wondering what nightmares would be awaiting them in their sleep. Tommy spoke almost inaudibly: 'Sorry about gettin' you involved, mate.'

Jack said, 'No problem, little buddy.' He grinned. 'You think I give a crap? Involvement is my middle name.'

In a matter of minutes they were both sound asleep. Well, one of them was.

Lieutenant Bationi finished another letter and leaned back in the wooden chair so as to reach the second bottle of wine. *Vino.* It was nearly empty. He and Rene would normally be sharing the bottles. He was alone in the room. Pouring the wine and raising his mug, the lieutenant looked upward and found the imaginary face of his friend. He managed to smile though he was still very angry about the massacre, the death, the waste. Bationi spoke Italian. 'Here's to you, my good friend: In bocca al lupo...' *Into the mouth of the wolf!* Salvatore toasted his dead friend and drank. If he were alive, Rene would reply: Crepi il lupo! *May the wolf burst!*

Putting the mug on the desk he looked down at the ashtray and picked up one of the bigger butts. He lit it. Most of the fort would be asleep as it was past eleven and *reveille* would be at 0500 hours- five o'clock in the morning. He gathered his thoughts.

Salvatore could have had Corporal Hensch do some of the paperwork but Hensch was a bit oafish. Hensch was older than him, and had fought in the Great War for the Germans. The huge German *caporal* was very strong and very loyal, but he was also very stupid at times and tactless. The lieutenant did not feel that Hensch would be able to handle such a delicate task.

He thought of his platoon: What would happen to it? What *happened* to it? Maybe, it had become too large; realistically, it could have made up at least two sections. But there was a shortage of lieutenants at the moment and the battalion was awaiting replacements. Bationi turned his mind to other thoughts.

The mug was empty. He turned and grabbed the bottle, taking a long swig from it. When he had gone to the toilet earlier he had brought back with him the file on Klauss. Klauss Lenz. He had already glanced at it but he hadn't noticed anything that was out of the ordinary. Now, it was on the table to the side and as it caught his eye he suddenly heard a faint bell ring. It was not a real ringing; it was in his mind: Something. He scratched his beard. He decided to file the report now while Smith's account was still fresh in his mind. The other letters would have to wait.

He emptied the remainder of the red wine into his mug. He lit up a fresh cigarette and started typing.

Several minutes later Lieutenant Bationi pulled the sheet of paper out of the typewriter. The report on Klauss was finished. He turned, still sitting, and placed the report on top of Klauss's file. He reclined on the seat, stretching. The wine was almost gone. He put the mug to his lips and sipped. He wanted to relax but couldn't. He felt a presence.

There was a small tap at the door. The lieutenant looked up and said, 'Entrez.' The door opened slowly, and into the room walked Legionnaire Smith.

Tommy entered. He pulled the door closed after him and this time the lieutenant did not stop him. Tommy said, 'I couldn't sleep, sir.' Bationi nodded, and sipped his vino. Tommy continued. 'I wondered if you had done the report yet...' He was speaking French.

The lieutenant nodded. 'Oui, j'ai.' *I have.*

'Did you leave my, uh-...our names out?'

'Oui, d'accord.' *Yes, of course.*

'I'm sorry for disturbing you. I will go, now,' said Tommy. The lieutenant could see worry-lines etched into the young legionnaire's forehead. Too much worry for someone that young.

Salvatore raised his mug towards the young soldier. He said, 'In bocca al lupo!' He smiled and drained the last of his wine.

Tommy did not understand Italian but smiled back. 'Merci, Lieutenant,' he said as left the room. He closed the door and was gone.

Salvatore slipped a sheet of paper in the typewriter and began typing more death notices. Then he bolted upright. The faint bell in his mind had come to light. Quello e esso! *That's it!*

He stopped typing. He remembered now. Over a year ago there had been a fighting incident, though it was commonplace in the legion, involving Klauss and a Belgian named Hollstein. Hollstein had died last year. Come to think of it, thought Salvatore, Hollstein had died in a melee situation. And then he recalled that the legionnaire who had reported the incident, Sancho, had also perished in a melee.

The lieutenant pushed the typewriter aside and tossed the Klauss Lenz file onto the desk. He searched for his packet of cigarettes. *Ah, there they are.* Still sitting, he leaned over and grabbed it- taking one out. He looked at the clock on the wall. He wished he could just go to sleep. Smoke filled the room.

There had been no *appel*- evening roll-call- tonight for Bationi's

39

unit; *what was left of it.* The weary lieutenant sighed. He looked down at the file.

He studied some details: Swiss national, thirty years old...

Salvatore cursed as he accidentally dropped the cigarette onto his trousers. He brushed it to the floor and bent down to pick it up. He felt the air change. He sensed that the door may have opened. He looked up, and Klauss stood in the doorway. A shiver ran down his spine as Klauss closed the door.

The lieutenant told him, 'La porte ouvrir.' *Leave it open.* Klauss ignored him, pretending not to hear.

Klauss spoke. 'I have something to report...'

Bationi demanded, 'Que voulez-vous?' *What do you want?* He was not in the mood. He straightened up in his chair.

Klauss moved slowly forward. He again said, 'I have something to report.'

'Oui. You have said that.' The lieutenant's eyes narrowed as he watched the tall legionnaire lean inches closer. He saw Klauss scanning the desk. *The file! The report!* He tried to nonchalantly cover the papers on the desk, but only made it obvious. Klauss had already seen his name.

Klauss grew angry. He asked the lieutenant, 'What are those papers?'

Salvatore grew impatient. He told the Swiss legionnaire, 'Ce n'est pas de votre inquietude.' *It is not of your concern.*

Klauss smiled. 'Is that my file?'

'No.'

Klauss paused; his eyes locked with Salvatore's. He glared intensely across the desk as the lieutenant stood up. Klauss changed from French to Italian, the lieutenant's native tongue, and acidly said, 'Bugiardo...' *Liar.*

Game on. Salvatore reached for his pistol but Klauss pounced on him, diving over the desk and immediately rapping the lieutenant on the face as they both stumbled into the chair and onto the ground. Salvatore had the weight of Klauss on him and was quickly struggling to his feet when, from the corner of his eye, he saw the motion of his opponent's arm thrusting toward him.

An instant later Salvatore felt cold steel ripping into his throat, savaging his vocal chords. With blood pouring from his neck he instinctively tried to grab Klauss, but the murderous legionnaire was stabbing him repeatedly in the chest in a frenzied manner. The lieutenant's hands were sliced mercilessly as he held them up to shield his heart and lungs.

Salvatore weakened; he was losing massive amounts of blood. He thought of his pistol again but just as quickly he realized that it was too late. He was off balance, and he could not stop the onslaught.

As the blade sunk into his temple he thought of his wife back home, her image one full of worry. It was his last thought. Klauss pulled the dagger out of the lieutenant's skull and Salvatore fell lifelessly to the floor.

Klauss grabbed his file and put it in a drawer. He turned off the light and closed the door as he left. He took the report with him.

Klauss read the report under the moonlight: *Anonymous letter?* It could be anyone, he thought. He could not kill everyone in the platoon; besides the soldier may have told anybody by now. He decided that he must vacate the premises: *Immediately.* It was not easy getting out of the fort, but Klauss managed to.

The desert sky was expansive. Klauss had been walking, sometimes running, for hours through the night. He would have to rest soon, or risk collapsing, so he stopped to drink water from his canteen; it was half empty. He looked up at the stars and amongst them he saw the morning star, sparkling beautifully above the desert horizon, knowing that it was not a star; that it was a planet. He had been to see many a Wagnerian opera.

Klauss walked on through the sand, which had become less soft. He was entering an area of the desert that was called *reg*; the gravelly ground made up of broken stones and stunted vegetation. He would make good time through it.

He thought of how the American had pointed to Venus and had recited some childish verse, mistaking the planet for a star. Idiot: *There should be laws against such ignorance.*

Klauss Lenz was really Klauss Gelfroher. He was not just a member of the French Foreign Legion. He was also a member of the German military branch called the Schutzstaffel. It was more commonly known as the SS. He had sworn solemn oath and allegiance to the Nazi party, and its leader Adolf Hitler.

He was on assignment. He had joined the Legion for the purpose of

41

gathering intelligence. He was to observe troop numbers and quality, and to study tactics used by the field commanders. If Germany and France went to war, and his superiors were planning it, they would want to know what kind of reserve France could pull out of Africa. This information could be very useful.

Three years ago the Germans had marched into the Rhineland, previously a demilitarized zone. Soon, they would want France.

Last year, the Nazi's entered Prague and Hitler chillingly announced to the world: 'Czechoslovakia has ceased to exist.' A fellow officer who'd been in Prague had told Klauss in Germany that key information had been found in the Czech military archives. Incredibly important data such as sketches that had been made of the insides of the Maginot Line, France's concrete defense structure that stood along the new German-Franco border.

Every little bit helped.

Klauss had been picked for this role because of his expert knowledge of the Mediterranean countries. He spoke fluent French, Italian and Spanish; as well as some Greek and Latin. He knew a smattering of Arabic. Although not fluent, he could converse in English and naturally spoke German. His contact was in Switzerland. It was simple enough. He would write a letter to his 'aunt' in pre-determined code. The Legion scrutinized everyone's mail, but Klauss was careful. However, the mail would sometimes take months to be delivered. He had sent his last letter only days ago.

His legs were turning into rubber, and he urged himself to go on. He had seen what the Legion did to deserters. What would they do to murderers who desert? The thought of it stopped him from resting. The ground was becoming firmer. He was glad for that; his trail would be hard to follow here. When he had distanced himself a kilometre from the fort earlier, after killing Bationi, he had begun a series of false trails. He would double back a ways, jump as far he could and roll, walk on and then do it all again. Then he would trek for awhile; then repeat the whole process again. He was confident that this would deter a small posse following footprints but it would not fool a large search party on horseback. He felt sick. He halted abruptly, feeling faint.

He sat down; then lay on his side. He was asleep in seconds.

Klauss had wanted to join the German Army during the Great War-his three older brothers were soldiers- but he was not old enough. They were much older than him, but they had been close to him. All three brothers perished during the third battle of Ypres. He had yearned to enter the battlefield and avenge his brothers.

He hated the French. He had learned French for the sole purpose of using it against them one day. He wanted to kill every Frenchman; one at a time if need be. He had once been an instructor for the Nazi youth and had used any opportunity he could to instill anti-French feelings. He had told the boys and girls that the French were an evil race that needed to be eliminated.

That was the way Klauss had felt when he'd killed the Frankmeier brothers. In espionage, it had been a terrible move by Klauss. The killings were most definitely *not* part of his assignment. For Klauss, the murders were strictly added pleasure. But his superiors would not be pleased by this turn of events.

Klauss slept heavily. He welcomed the darkness. He hated the glaring sun. After several peelings his skin had tanned. His darkened skin disgusted him.

He wished his leader would hurry up and declare war on France: the sooner, the better. He even dreamt of it.

Hate; kill. Hate; kill.

His mind was a dark furnace.

chapter 6

The boy looked down at his finely tailored suit and rounded the corner into the crowded town centre. He turned his head purposely to his left. His timing was perfect. Umpf!

'Ow!' he cried out.

'Oh, my apologies,' said the well-dressed gentleman who managed to stop the boy from falling by holding on to his coat. The boy regained his balance and dusted off his trousers.

The man regarded the lad. He thought to himself that the boy looked like he came from a family of high standing. And such fine shoes: best be careful not to offend. He asked the boy, 'Bist du gut?' Are you alright?

They were speaking German. The boy answered, 'Ja.' Then he smiled

43

and added, 'Danke.' He bowed and left.

The gentleman watched the boy walk off across the road to an alley and disappear. He thought it was strange that the boy would bow, like one would on a stage. Making sure that he did not collide into anyone else he cautiously continued on his way to the bank, as he always did first thing on Friday mornings.

It was overcast but not so cold. Too warm for this coat, he thought as he approached the bank. It was turning out to be quite a pleasant day. He was glad the boy had not been hurt. He vowed to be more careful.

He opened the door and entered the bank.

The boy had bowed because it was a stage. What an act! He could have stolen more but this was good, several coins. He hoped the man was so well off as to not notice a few coins missing.

He waited outside the baker's back entrance, glancing around left and right. He saw a customer open the front door to the bakery and go in. Now!

The boy moved quickly. Zip. Zip in; zip out. Nobody noticed.

Zip: Two loaves of bread and a piece of strudel pastry.

He walked briskly off and headed down a lane that led to the woods.

The gentleman had left the bank and had gone straight to a local alehouse called the Bergenhaus. He'd been there a few times before, and though it was early in the day he'd felt celebratory. Spring had arrived!

He stood before the barman with a perplexed look on his face.

The barman was tall and had to look down at the gentleman. He was drying beer steins with a cloth. He noticed the look of confusion and so repeated the price of the ale.

The gentleman shook his head in realization as he placed the coins onto the bar.

The barman scooped up the coins and said, 'Thank you.' Then added, 'Is there something wrong?'

'No. Well, I may've been pickpocketed. This morning; in the town centre.'

'That is too bad,' said the barman, who then tended to the elderly man who was waving a walking stick.

The gentleman sat down alone on a wooden chair and sipped his ale. Oh, I see now, he thought. That was why the boy had bowed. And that was why he had said 'Danke' the way that he did; as though he was saying 'Thank You'.

The bustling sound of the townsfolk decreased as the boy ventured into the foliage. There were several paths through the trees, some leading somewhere and some leading nowhere. This dirt lane would lead the boy- his name was Kaspar- to a clearing in the dark heavy forest where he had pitched a small camp. After a short while he came to a particular trail that led off the lane and slunk on to it. The trail was old and not used and only circled back to the lane. But there was a fairly new trail, unseen, that ran off it. Kaspar ducked into a bush and onto the new trail. In a few minutes he came to his campsite in the clearing that bathed soft, warm rays on his face. He basked in the sun for a moment and then sat down to eat his bread and pastry.

He looked at his campfire; he would need it later. The wind was beginning to pick up and the clouds were moving across the sky, obscuring the sun. It went cold as the sunlight disappeared off of his face. He would have to go back into town later and find his supper. He was thinking that he would have to leave the area soon but he'd had a good run of it. He'd found plenty of food and had saved several dozen coins, which always made it easier when he went to the next town. He stayed away from the villages and stuck to the towns. He wore fine garments and splendid shoes. It was his cover. His modus operandi *was deception.*

The clouds moved away and the sunshine returned to the clearing. Kaspar enjoyed the rays; he knew they would soon be gone for the day.

Much later the boy had gone back into town for the evening's pickings, an especially fruitful time when alcohol began to flow throughout the many bierhaus' and inns that dotted the town. He had stolen food, a book, a photograph of a horse, matches and, of course, a lot of coins. He had spent a few of the coins on a nice meal at an inn. One of the fellow diners had recognized him and politely said hello. That was good, thought Kaspar, because it meant that the diner had not noticed from their first meeting that he had lost an ink pen to the pickpocket's deft fingers.

It was dark now and much colder; but not as cold as winter. He walked slowly through the forest trail, his eyes and ears straining to maximum. The woods could be extremely dangerous. The boy was not

45

stupid; he was very scared. And he was carrying quite a lot of booty. He moved stealthily through the greenery, hoping that it would not start raining. He walked off the lane to the old trail and soon came to the hidden trail. He stopped for a moment to listen intently. No one or no thing was following him. He sighed, ducked and disappeared into the thick wood.

It was almost pitch-black as Kaspar moved quietly and deliberately through the final trail to his campsite. He could hear his own heartbeat and muted breaths. He dropped the book and his eyes looked down into the darkness. He had to feel for it; he found it and picked it up. When he continued on his way his eyes adjusted and he could see firelight through the trees, glowing faintly in the direction of his camp.

chapter 7

Tommy was in the middle of a forest. The trees dripped thick gooey blood. He was trying to plant a date tree but its towering trunk kept bumping into the wooded oaks, and a branch of sharp pine speared a camel. The camel had the face of a young desert boy. The camel hated Tommy but he did not know why. But then the spear was in his hands now and he hated *it*. It started raining and the rain washed away the blood. The forest had turned into the park that was next to his cousin's brick house in Greenwich. His cousin was laughing and kicking a football. Why wasn't his cousin sad, too? The ball was kicked to Tommy and he kicked it back. He started laughing and running and kicking the ball around. Then he saw Jack in the park, in full Legion uniform, smoking a cigarette. Jack was yelling but Tommy could not understand what he was saying...

'Wake up! Hey!' Jack was shaking Tommy's shoulder. Tommy awoke startled. He looked at Jack, puzzled.

There was a lot of commotion and Tommy felt as though he had just fallen asleep. He was groggy, the images of his bizarre dream still lingering in his mind. He sat up. 'Wha...What's goin' on? It's five o'clock already?'

'No. Just after four. They're gettin' everybody up. Treselme says the lieutenant is dead.'

'No...'

'Immediate roll-call. In two minutes. Get dressed.'

'Crikey...' Tommy dozily climbed off his cot and grabbed some trousers.

'One of the sergeants from second section found him in the NCO's office. Cut to pieces.'

Tommy shuddered. He thought for a moment; then started to speak. 'Do ya think-'

Jack cut him off. 'Shush.' He pointed to Tommy's boots. 'Hurry up...' Jack's expression was sombre.

Tommy quietly and quickly finished dressing. They went out to attend roll-call. It was nearly sunrise. They both noticed that Klauss was nowhere in sight. There were other units going through roll-call across the fort. Only four other soldiers stood shivering with Jack and Tommy: Corporal Hensch, Treselme, Limoges and Hassef. Captain Versailler walked over to the group with another officer. He looked at the half a dozen bedraggled legionnaires that now represented Bationi's unit. He spoke angrily, looking at Hensch. 'Where are the others?'

Hensch answered, 'In the hospital, sir...'

Versailler seemed to be genuinely shocked. 'My god...' He had not quite grasped the severity of the battle.

Jack moved forward. 'There's, uh, one missing, I think...'

Hensch cocked his head quizzically.

Versailler snapped his head towards the American. 'What? Who?'

'Uh, I think Klauss was not hospitalized.'

Hensch spoke up. 'Yes; Klauss Lenz. He should be here, sir.'

The captain spoke to the officer who silently stood next to him. The officer ran off. Versailler faced the platoon and said, 'I'm sure you have all heard the news by now; Lieutenant Bationi has been slain. He was murdered late last night or very early this morning. If anyone has any information they need to tell me, I will be in my office.' He turned to Hensch. 'Corporal, come with me.'

Jack and Tommy exchanged looks. The platoon remnant stood near each other for a few moments and then slowly dispersed. When they had distanced themselves from their comrades, Jack spoke quietly. 'Do you think the captain has read the report?'

'No,' said Tommy. 'He would've noticed Klauss's absence right away.'

'Yeah,' said Jack, pondering. 'Maybe the lieutenant didn't have time

47

to type the report.'

'No. 'E wrote up the report, alright. I couldn't sleep for awhile so I went to to see 'im. He'd already finished it.'

'Why didn't you tell me?'

'You were snoring...'

'Oh, yeah.'

'I think, me old cock,' Tommy said, rubbing his eyes. 'We have to go see the captain.'

'Yeah. Klauss could still be here. It wouldn't be that easy sneaking out of here.'

'But at least they'll be looking for 'im, now.'

'He won't get far, pal. They'll hang him for this.'

'I hope so. I bloody 'ope so...'

They stood outside Captain Versailler's office. They were hungry, their bowels rumbled and Jack wanted a cigarette and some coffee. Jack said, 'I could do with a cup of joe, right now.'

'Yeah. And I would like a cuppa an' all, mate.'

Jack rapped on the captain's door. A moment later the door opened. The sergeant who had found Bationi's body entered the doorway, held the door open for Jack and Tommy, and- seeing the captain nod- left the room. The two English-speaking legionnaires walked into the office. Versailler sat at his desk. Hensch was stood next to him.

'Hamlyn,' said the captain in rapid French. 'You noticed that Klauss was missing...' It wasn't exactly accusatory, but it wasn't friendly either. Jack knew what Versailler was saying. He'd listened for the key words.

Jack retorted in English. 'It doesn't take a mathematician to count to seven.'

Versailler did not understand English, and took the reply to be hostile. He told Jack, 'En Francais, sil vous plait.' It was an order, not a request.

Jack needed help. He looked at his friend. 'I think you'd better take over from here, buddy.'

'Yeah,' said Tommy hesitantly. He turned to Versailler, who looked quite angry. Tommy paused, looking at Hensch then back to the captain. The captain understood. He sent Hensch off so the three of them could speak in private. When the door closed, Tommy continued.

48

'Avez-vous vu le rapport?' *Have you seen the report?*

Versailler was puzzled. 'Quel rapport?' *What report?*

Tommy glanced at Jack. Jack had a thought. He spoke to Tommy. 'If the report read anonymous informant, he would wonder how we knew.'

Versailler interjected. 'En francais!' *In French!* The captain was becoming impatient.

Jack was looking straight at the captain but out of the side of his mouth he said to Tommy, 'I think we better tell him the whole story...'

Legionnaire Smith explained the entire story, as best he could, to Captain Versailler as Legionnaire Hamlyn tried his hardest to follow the conversation. The captain listened intently. Just as Tommy was finishing the account, Hensch was back at the door. Versailler called him in. 'Corporal?'

Hensch walked in, saluted. 'There is no sign of Klauss anywhere in the fort.'

'I see. Bring me the Arab- al Hemed Rouge- and prepare him a camel: On the double, Corporal!' Hensch ran off to tell Hassef to report to the commanding officer; immediately. Versailler turned to Hamlyn and Smith. 'Why did you not come sooner?'

'We only just realized at roll-call,' said Tommy. 'Captain, may Jack and I join Hassef in the search for Klauss?'

Jack heard his name but did not understand what Tommy had just said.

Versailler thought briefly. 'Yes. Your platoon will not be needed in the field for awhile, and three men should suffice. You will have until sunset tomorrow to find him. Then the Legion will have set up a proper search party involving other outposts. If you do find him I want him brought back here alive but if you have to kill him that is fine. If you do kill him, just be sure to bring back his head.'

They all waited in the office for Hassef. They did not have to wait long.

Two more camels were added for the search, prepared with food, blankets and water. Each man would carry a rifle and ammunition. The gates opened and Jack, Tommy and Hassef rode their camels out of Fort Ghardelle. The early morning sun would soon rapidly turn warmer.

Some legionnaires had located footprints that were likely to be from

49

Klauss. The camels retraced the steps and followed that direction. The trio departed and the wooden walls of the fort slowly disappeared from their view. Their quarry had had a good head start on them. Klauss could have had as much as a seven hour leeway. But he was on foot and the posse was on camels.

All three legionnaires had admired and respected Lieutenant Bationi. All three wanted Klauss dead.

The hours passed and the afternoon sun was becoming unbearable. They'd followed the footprints but the prints had ended. They'd circled the area when they lost the trail and had picked up another, following it until it, too, had disappeared. Hassef seemed to be impressed. He thought that they would have caught up with Klauss by now or at least be hot on his trail. But the trail had gone cold. Still, Hassef felt that he knew in which direction the lieutenant's killer would go.

They decided to stop and rest at the rocky outcrop that they had come to which offered them some much wanted shade.

Hassef dismounted, pulling out dates from a pocket and sitting down in the shade. Jack and Tommy followed suit. They all sat there in silence, eating dates and drinking from their canteens. A solitary skink perched itself on a rock, watching them. It had never seen a human before.

After several minutes the lizard became bored with the humans and moved on to other, more interesting things. Tommy was eating flat bread as they talked of the search. Hassef felt they should head toward the mountains that were to the west. Tommy wondered out loud whether they should consider north, but Hassef grinned and pointed west and said, 'Morocco.'

Jack agreed, nodding. He was trying to force down a date. He swallowed it. 'Where I come from this is old people's food.'

Tommy told him, 'If you don't want them, mate, just give 'em to me. I'll have 'em.'

'Oh, I'll eat them...'

Hassef listened to them, but did not understand. Then, Hassef stood up and grinned at Tommy and Jack. They looked at him.

Hassef started talking to Tommy in French. He became animated, running a few steps and then stopping abruptly. He made a quick turning motion and then mimicked throwing an object, all the while accompanying it with verbal, expressive commentary that was stocked with hoots and hollers. Jack, who at first was just trying to follow the conversation by picking up words, realized he did not need to hear the words to know what Hassef was talking about.

Jack felt a pang in his stomach, but it was not from hunger: He watched Hassef's pantomime with reluctance.

Hassef put his palms over his own face and made a gesture of an explosion, then with full sound effects. Jack felt sick.

Hassef seemed very excited about it all. That was the end of his story and he was grinning at Tommy but glancing over at Jack. Tommy, smiling as one does when they are impressed, was saying, 'That's amazing! Bloody hell, Jack, is that true?'

Jack said nothing. His expression was void.

'Hassef says you threw a rock at an Arab and killed 'im stone dead. Right into his face.'

Jack stared at the ground, nodding his head very slowly.

Hassef's grin dropped as he watched Jack. Tommy noticed Jack's sudden melancholy. He said, 'You okay, mate?'

Jack shrugged.

'Is there something wrong?' Tommy asked.

'Long story...'

'Oh. Well, we 'av a lot of time...'

Jack looked up at his fellow comrades. After quite a long pause he said, 'We'd better get on with the search. I'll tell ya later.'

The posse started off once again on their search for Klauss. Jack's mind drifted to his younger days. He had dreamed of becoming a major league baseball player as a pitcher for his favourite team: the Boston Red Sox. During the Great Depression he'd left school and then had played semi-professional ball in New Jersey, making very little money. During the fall and winter he had worked in the docks of Manhattan. It'd been hard work and most of the workers were older and burlier than Jack but there'd been plenty of things for him to do.

He had done very well as a player and before he was eighteen, after two years of playing semi-pro, he'd caught the eye of a Red Sox scout. He had signed the contract, one of his happiest moments ever, and the ballclub sent him to play for their minor league team in Syracuse- only miles from his hometown. And boy could he play.

He was a southpaw; the nickname attached to all left-handed pitchers. He hadn't made it to the major league yet but he'd gotten so close

51

he could taste it. In his first season he'd been one of the best pitchers in the minor leagues.

Hassef was talking to Tommy, who then turned and translated to Jack. Tommy said, 'Hassef says we should soon come across footprints if 'e was headed north; so, look for them. But 'e still thinks Lenz is heading for Morocco. Whatcha think?'

'Uh well...Hassef knows what he's doin'.' Jack's mind shifted now to Yankee Stadium: *The bases were loaded and Hank Greenberg was batting...and somebody wanted peanuts.* And the throw from Charlie the peanut vendor had been right on the money.

His mind kept wandering as he watched the rippling desert heat waves snake across the horizon. It ended up on the ocean liner that he had worked on as a kitchen worker when he'd left New York; in particular a conversation between him and a fellow employee about exotic women. And the desert. And Beau Geste. And...the French Foreign Legion.

Many times Jack had asked himself *how did I get here?* And the answer always was: That conversation.

Tommy wondered what Hassef was up to. The Algerian had said their quarry was headed west so they went west but then they'd turned north, then west again, north again and now were skirting the reg westwards. It seemed impossible to him that they would find a trail. Mountain peaks loomed far in the distance. Tommy and Hassef had had a few discussions about each other's lives and he knew that Hassef had been a nomad until joining the Legion. His father had been a Frenchman named Henri Rouge who'd gone to Algeria to teach and ended up marrying a desert girl. His mother had died giving birth to him and his father was quite old, dying when Hassef was a small boy. He and his five brothers were left to roam the Sahara and fend for themselves by tending sheep, camel herding or, most often, thieving. But when two brothers were killed attempting to steal a goat, Hassef had decided to journey north to see the ocean, something neither he nor his brothers had ever seen; something their father had told them was a very beautiful thing.

The day turned into evening and the posse grew tired. It would be dark soon and they would try to sleep for a couple of hours. Hassef was looking disappointed and yet still seemed optimistic, thought Tommy. They had all been very silent and subdued the last several hours as they searched diligently through the desert for any traces of their prey.

Finally, Tommy broke the silence. 'Y'know, Jack, I was thinking...that oath I made for us with the lieutenant...'

'Oath? I thought it was a promise...'

'No, well, see, it was an oath because I kind of swore on our mothers graves.'

'An oath to our dead lieutenant...that's just great. Great, pal. You know I take those kinda things serious. Jeez. It's a matter of honour. And since there's no way of us keeping that promise, that means- I dunno- it's just bad.'

Hassef spoke. 'Ici.' *Here.*

Tommy was silent. Jack said, 'Yeah. Here's as good a place as any.' They all dismounted. They gave the camels water. They ate, they drank. They went to sleep.

The figure scurried away from the nomadic herdsmen unseen. He had stolen their water and taken it to where his camel was tied. He had killed a lone shepherd earlier this morning in order to obtain the camel. He was very hungry. The large town where he was heading to was almost one hundred and fifty kilometres away: Days away. Before getting on the camel and scurrying away, Klauss drank greedily.

To the east of the posse the night was giving way to the creeping light. They rode the camel bulls in silence, straining their eyes for clues in the semi-darkness. They each had a two day's supply of food and water left. Hassef rode in front. He was determined to find Klauss. He wanted to bring back the lieutenant's killer's head. Many treated Hassef like a peasant, a thief or, at best, just hated him. But not Lieutenant Bationi: or his officers. The lieutenant had been like a father-figure to him. Hassef thought of his remaining three brothers; they would no doubt still be roaming the Sahara. He hoped that one day he would see them again.

Tommy knew they had to find the fugitive before sunset tonight or stop the search. But, by his reckoning, they would run out of food and water about ten or twelve hours too soon; they would have to find it elsewhere if they were to make it back to Fort Ghardelle. We're on a wild goose chase, he thought. A sonnet from a book he had picked up on one of his excursions came to mind for some reason. He began to recite a small bit that he had memorized, speaking softly. *'From fairest creatures we desire increase, That thereby beauty's rose might never die, But as the riper should by time decrease, His tender heir might bear his memory.'*

'What the hell was that?' asked Jack, looking back at Tommy.

'Shakespeare.'

'Oh.'

'Y'know, Yank, we need to find Klauss before noon or we might run out of water...' Tommy's voice trailed.

'Yeah, I know, buddy. But there are settlements that're okay for us to go to. We're in safe territory, at least. It's strange that we haven't seen anyone at all.'

'It's getting lighter,' said Tommy. He looked beyond Jack and nodded once. 'He looks confident.'

'Good. I'm not. But I wouldn't like anything better than to walk through the fort gates carrying the bastard's head.'

'Aye.'

It was nearing midday and the heat was fierce. They had skirted the reg all morning and had found nothing. They would soon rest and then decide whether to continue the search. Hassef spoke to Tommy in French. Hassef said, 'I think I would like to desert, too. I miss the freedom.'

Tommy was shocked. But pleased. He said to Hassef, 'Vraiment?' *Really?*

Hassef grinned. Jack wondered what they were talking about.

Tommy went on. 'Because I'm fed up with the Legion already and I was thinking earlier about, well, desertion. I'll go with you, Hassef.'

Hassef grinned, but said nothing.

The conversation seemed interesting, thought Jack. He was curious. 'What the hell are you two talking about?'

'We're both going to desert the Legion, Yank.'

'What? Why?'

'Well, 'e wants his freedom and I, me, well...I've seen enough death already to last me a bloody lifetime. And besides, I can go and honour the lieutenant's death wish.'

'Is that really why you're deserting? Because of a crazy promise? That's nuts, buddy.'

54

'What about honour, mate? You said-'

'Forget what I said...' Jack looked back and made eye contact with his friend. 'Look, they'll torture you if they catch you and then throw you in prison. I can't let you go.'

'I'll stay close to Hassef.'

'Tell you what. *I'm* through with the desert. It ain't Beau Geste. I'll go with Hassef. I don't even care if they catch me. But if they don't, then I'll go to France and honour the lieutenant's last request.'

'Yank, I don't think I could let-'

'Can it, pal. You're going back to the fort. I don't wanna hear another word.' They stopped to rest. As they climbed off of the camels Jack said to Tommy, 'How the hell do we know where the lieutenant's family lives?'

Tommy pulled a piece of paper from one of his pockets. He held it out for the American to take and said, 'His address; he wrote it down...'

Jack took the paper and glanced at it. He said to no one in particular, 'Chateaurenault...sounds like a kind of wine.'

Klauss had changed into the shepherd's clothing when he had acquired the camel and buried his legionnaires clothing sometime later, except for the boots. He had hardly rested in days and was beginning to wear. At one point he had fallen asleep on the camel and then slipped off. The mountains were getting closer, though, and if he could make it that far, he believed, he would be home-free.

He watched the vultures flying high above him, circling nearby. But they were not interested in Klauss. He was still moving.

The trio did not rest long. They'd decided between them to keep searching just a little bit longer. They mounted the beasts and as they started off Tommy spoke to Jack. 'Y'know, mate, you never told us the long story. You know- from yesterday. We'll probably never see each other again...'

'Sure we will.'

Tommy shrugged. 'I don't see how.'

Jack eyed his young friend. After a moment he said, 'Okay, I'll tell ya the story. I've talked to you about baseball before...'

'Yeah, mate. You're favourite team is the Red Sox.'

'Right. Well, I was pretty good. A pitcher; I threw with my left hand...'

'The pitcher's the one who throws it to the batter.'

'Yeah. When I was seventeen my favourite team-'

'The Red Sox...'

'...They signed me to a contract to play for one of their minor league teams-'

'Minor league?'

'It's like your second division in football...'

'Gotcha, mate.'

'Anyway, I threw hard and I had pinpoint control- that is to say, I had good aim. I won eighteen games and lost only two in my very first season. One sportswriter said I was the next Lefty Grove.'

'What's a lefty grove?'

'Not a what. It's a who. He's the greatest pitcher in baseball...my idol. Anyway, to make a long story short I started off fantastic the following season but in a game against our rivals I, uh...something happened.' Jack looked down.

Tommy could tell the tone had just changed drastically. He was not sure whether to pry.

Jack continued. 'This guy- Doug Gilly- well he was crowding the plate. But I wasn't gonna let him push me out of the strike zone. Like I said, I had great aim, and I was confident that I could place the ball at high velocity on the inside part of the plate. And I can throw hard, some say as hard as Walter Johnson threw. The score was tied one-all. I threw the ball...hard...' Jack seemed to choke a little, thought Tommy. Like there was a lump in the throat.

'I threw the ball hard and I smashed his face in. That was it- the end of his career. He never played another game. And he was a good little player. He might've made the majors.'

'And you..?' said Tommy. 'Did you make the majors?'

Jack looked down, then away; and let his eyes fall on a spot on the horizon that was far, far away. 'No.'

Tommy didn't know what to say. *Should I ask?*

Jack still stared at the endless landscape. He could feel his friend wanting to ask, so he made it easy for him. 'You wanna know what happened?' Jack didn't see Tommy nodding, but he knew that he was. 'I lost it. That's what happened- I just plain lost it. After that I was afraid to throw it anywhere near the plate. My game was gone. I never recovered my form and before the end of the year I had quit. So, now you know; I'm a quitter.'

Tommy understood now why Jack had been so upset the day before when Hassef had brought up the story.

'Anyway, then I got a job at Yankee Stadium selling peanuts to the spectators for a couple of years.'

They were both silent for a moment. Then, full of unbridled glee, Hassef pointed excitedly. He was saying, 'Regard! La-bas! La-bas!'

He was pointing at footprints.

Hassef had found the trail and was quite confident that he knew exactly which way Klauss was headed. They had stopped to analyze the prints. Hassef told Tommy, 'Je le trouverai et le retour au fort avec sa tete.' *I will find him and return to the fort with his head.*

Tommy was confused. 'Hold on a minute, Hassef.' Then, in French: 'Je'ai pense vous desertaient...' *I thought you were deserting...*

Hassef decided to show off his English skills. 'No..,' he said, grinning. 'I joking you.'

'What?!'

'I joking you.' Hassef was still grinning.

Jack asked Tommy, 'What's goin' on?'

'He's going after Klauss, but he's not deserting,' replied Tommy.

'Now that I've got it in my head to desert,' said Jack, '...I really want to get outta here.'

Tommy suggested: 'Just come back to the fort, old cock. You were right- it was a stupid idea. Hassef is going to go after Klauss.'

'No,' said Jack. 'I will go with Hassef and we will find Klauss. You go back to Ghardelle and tell Versailler we are on his trail. Remember, Tommy, follow the stars- not the moon.' He was on his camel, next to Hassef.

Tommy started to protest but Jack stopped him with a hard look, so he resignedly waved goodbye to Hassef. 'Au revoir, mon ami.' Hassef waved back, grinning, and turned his camel around. Hassef's camel then began to trace their prey's tracks. Tommy looked at Jack and said, 'Good luck, mate. See you soon.' But Tommy had a feeling that he wouldn't be seeing his friend ever again.

Jack turned and followed Hassef. He looked back at his skinny young friend and called out, 'See ya, buddy.'

Jack and Hassef rode in deathly silence as they stalked their quarry.

Jack's mind began to wander again. The idea of deserting the Legion was becoming more feasible. *Hell, I could go back to the States and start playing ball again. I'll regain my form, get noticed and then...voila. I'd make the best of my opportunity this time and before I knew it I'd be in the majors- maybe even with the Red Sox. Maybe facing Hank Greenberg with the season on the line: And this time throwing curveballs instead of peanuts.*

Well, a man can dream; can't he?

chapter 8

Kaspar edged up to the clearing's outskirts and watched the trespasser enjoy his campfire. His stash of money and wares was many paces away from the campsite down another secret trail, and he knew that it was hidden safely underground. He watched the lone figure, a man, drinking wine from one of the wine jugs that were on the ground. It was not Kaspar's wine; he did not drink alcohol yet. The man did not seem dangerous, thought Kaspar. But you could never be sure.

He had seen the man's face upon arrival to the clearing, but now had moved around to behind the intruder. He watched him as he silently ate chocolate amongst the trees and bushes. He could see that the man was getting quite drunk. That could be very good, thought Kaspar, or very bad.

The boy noticed the man pull something from his coat. He caught a glimpse of it and it looked valuable. The man seemed to be looking at it. Was that gold?

As he quietly slinked to a better point of view he could see the man attaching the object to his wrist and finger. Kaspar watched closely, noting how it was worn. He was still moving to get a better angle when he stepped on a thin, fallen branch. It snapped. Kaspar froze. He heard a voice call out.

'Wer gibt es?' Who's there?

Kaspar could feel his heart trying to pound its way out of his chest. He stood perfectly still. He saw the man put the object back into a coat pocket. Inside, top left side, Kaspar noted professionally. The man stood and started walking cautiously, as well as drunkenly, towards him. Kaspar's eyes were as big as saucers. He wondered if the man could see him. The trespasser was not far from him and moving closer. The boy thought of running but he still was not sure that he'd been seen.

Then the man squint his eyes and stopped. He was looking directly at the boy. The man held up his left hand and said, 'Seien Sie erschrocken nicht.' Do not be frightened.

Kaspar knew he had been spotted. He slyly placed most of his coins at his feet- just in case- bending to the ground. He would take a chance and if he had to run then he would run, he reasoned. No sense in igniting a chase, though, and so he walked into the clearing slowly. The scared, young lad watched the man guardedly.

The man smiled when he saw the adolescent emerge from the darkened forest and said something that the boy did not understand. But Kaspar understood what the man said next.

'Was ist Ihr Name?'

Kaspar had no choice but to use charm. He smiled at the man and answered, 'Mein Name ist Kaspar.'

The man seemed relieved. He told the boy, 'Ich bin Hansel.'

Kaspar sat by the fire and let the flame's flicker dance on his face. The man, Hansel, had offered some wine to him and he'd had a small amount, but it had tasted bitter. The man had travelled from far-away lands, he'd just told Kaspar, and was travelling through.

Kaspar in turn told the man a little about himself- that he had been from a wealthy family and had been orphaned as a young boy, living in the woods ever since. He told the man that he, too, was just passing through. The man took a liking to the boy and Kaspar did not feel in any danger. But you never knew.

As the fermented grapes saturated the man's bloodstream he quickly became sleepy. They were both glad that it had not rained. The man lay down to sleep on a cloth as they watched the fire get smaller and smaller. It was better to fall asleep in the dark, felt Kaspar. He'd heard tales of the 'ham farir'- ordinary men who became wolves under a full moon. But the moon was not full tonight; and his new friend, Hansel, was most likely not a werewolf.

But you never knew. So, Kaspar pretended to fall asleep while keeping half an eye on the man. It wasn't long before the man was snoring; he was fast asleep.

Kaspar crept over to him. His fingers skillfully probed the inside of

Hansel's coat until he found the pocket that he was feeling for. He found it and slipped the object gracefully out of the pocket.

A few moments later Kaspar disappeared into the lonely, dark and deep forest.

Kaspar had looked briefly for the rest of his coins in the darkness but was unsuccessful. There was no time to waste, he had thought; it would be better to go back along the hidden trail, to the circular trail and down the narrow dirt lane and away for a day or two. Then, he would return to find his coins and gather his secret horde, and move on the next town- any town as long as it was not one he had visited before.

He walked down the nearly pitch-black lane full of fear. The boy was apprehensive and walked briskly. The man could wake at any time and discover the missing trinket and come searching for him. There were still a few coins in the boy's pocket. Nearby, an owl hooted and it startled the little thief. He quickened his pace.

After several minutes Kaspar was growing quite tired. The town was not far and there were some cottages coming up on the left hand side of the lane. He was going to sleep somewhere around here tonight. Stopping to think for a moment, he took out his recent acquisition. Kaspar stared at the beautiful piece of jewellery, holding it closely in the darkness. He thought of when the man had put on the bracelet and was now doing the same thing.

The next thing he was aware of was that it had suddenly become daytime and that the cottages looked very clean. He heard a woman cry out, 'Ach!' and when he turned around he saw that she looked very frightened. When he went to speak, the woman ran away screaming and shouting, 'Geist! Geist!' Ghost! Ghost! *Kaspar was becoming increasingly confused and disoriented. Why was there daylight? He looked at the ornament and it was still in his hands. The woman had run to her cottage screaming. There was no sense in standing around so the boy had to make a quick decision. It was not an easy choice. He chose to go to his secret horde and gather his things now, and then leave town as quickly as possible. He hoped he would not run into the man named Hansel.*

Kaspar was soon digging his fingers into the soft earth searching for the chest that stored the pickpocket's belongings. He was bewildered completely because he knew that this was the spot where the chest should be. He checked again, looking around; yes, this was the spot.

He was certain. Why was it daylight? The chest couldn't have been found, he reasoned to himself. The dirt had not been disturbed. Maybe it was deeper in the ground. He continued to dig, becoming somewhat frantic. Finally, after quite a long while, Kaspar ceased digging.

The campsite trail was gone but the boy found the clearing anyway, following off the old circle trail. But there was no campfire and no sign of the man named Hansel. No wine jugs or anything. He searched around for the remaining coins but did not find them either. Life was becoming very strange for the charismatic, friendly young thief, and it was time to run away from this scary place where women shrieked at you and night became day in the blink of an eye.

Kaspar left with the few possessions he still had: a few coins and some matches, his clothes and a photograph of a small brown horse.

chapter 9

Klauss sat by a window in a small cafe somewhere in the middle of Lisbon, drinking lukewarm coffee and, from time to time, peering out from the corner of his eyes. The waitress, a Portuguese woman in her thirties, brought over some more coffee which she poured into his mug and without saying anything she went on to another table. He sipped the brew; it was also lukewarm, but he did not care. It was not yet eleven o'clock in the morning and already the temperature had risen to about twenty-five degrees Celsius; but much cooler than in North Africa.

He had been down at the docks at dawn on general espionage duty, having been reduced to what Klauss believed were very menial tasks, and the area had been teeming with spies. To him, they were easy to identify and he hoped that he was not as noticeable. His body hardly moved, just his head to glance occasionally and his forearm to raise the mug and sip. In his mind he began to construct the next message, which was to be sent to a contact in Madrid.

The official bureau of German military Intelligence was the Abwehr, and they were greatly bothered by the incident that had happened at Fort Ghardelle. Klauss Gelfroher had risen quickly but now had faltered and was awaiting further instruction. He'd had almost no contact and was beginning to feel isolated. As much as he craved being alone, he did not want to *feel* alone.

Naturally it was possible that his superiors were timid of keeping close contact with him because they believed he might be being followed by French agents, as even Klauss believed at times. He thought back to his escape through the desert; the thirsty days, the hungry nights. The lizard that had tasted good...the trek through the Moroccan mountains...

The pavement outside the cafe window was busily crowded with the inner city populace and horns honked behind impatient drivers. The cafe was filling up. Klauss called the waitress over and she waved back to let him know that she would be there in a second. When she came over to the small table he told her that he wanted soup. She smiled briefly and hurried off to tend to about a million things.

Even though he despised the darkening of his skin, which it had done after several peelings in the Sahara, he knew the tan helped him blend in fairly well here on the Iberian Peninsula. The cafe was becoming very noisy with lunch-time chatter, and the native language bounced off the walls. Klauss could follow it- he could speak fluent Spanish- but Portuguese was not his forte.

The soup arrived and the bill was paid. Klauss eyed it suspiciously but picked up the spoon and tasted the brown, broth-like, vegetable liquid meal hesitantly. It was delicious; he was pleasantly surprised for once and set to eat it quickly, for he was late getting back to his rented room on the outskirts of the town centre. He liked to get back before the mail arrived so as to be there to receive it immediately. The landlady of the rented room could be quite nosy at times. Klauss had got himself into big trouble because of what'd happened in Algeria; he did not feel like having to kill anyone else for awhile: Too much headache; *Mucho caca.*

He slurped a second spoonful of the soul-warming broth and just as he was about to dip for a third he heard a fly buzzing close by, and then saw it fall into his soup bowl. It was two flies; they were mating. Klauss was disgusted and grunted loudly as he banged his fist on the table. He flipped the bowl over and it bounced on the table, then off to the floor. The soup spilled and the drenched flies shook themselves dry. The people had all stopped talking for a short moment, looking at the angry man. He looked back at them, showing infuriation, and they resumed their conversations. Klauss strode from the cafe swiftly, cursing himself for losing his temper.

The angry man no doubt meant nothing to the customers, but it was terrible form by the spy.

After trying so hard to be incognito it was just plain stupid to attract attention like that. To be noticed.

Making sure no one had taken any further interest in him, Klauss hailed a taxi and gave the driver directions that would have the beat-up old automobile zigzag its way to the rented room. The taxi ride was bumpy, stuffy and the horn seemed to be permanently held down as the driver wildly careened through the narrow streets. The angry man fought his instinct to yell at the driver to stop honking and concentrated instead on keeping an eye out for anyone following the taxi.

The noisy car rumbled past cafes, shops, people, vendors, mules, horses, houses and churches and then approached another crossroad. There were no stop signs at the corners and the driver was going to plough straight through it. Klauss leaned forward and told the driver to turn right. The driver skidded as he sped into the turn, wheels screeching. The spy watched through the back window for several moments and, feeling satisfied, turned to the driver and said, 'Vire a esquerda.' The taxi made a left turn.

'Pare aqui,' said Klauss as he kept an eye on the last intersection. The taxi pulled to a stop and Klauss paid the driver. He had not been followed.

Klauss walked two streets until he came to a footpath that led to a string of partially crumbled buildings, one of which was the house that he was staying in. Dozy chickens squawked and scattered as he moved down the sunny path. The landlady was standing outside holding letters in her hand, and a small dog was barking at her feet. The mail had arrived. She caught sight of her tenant and waved somewhat excitedly. *Mein Gott*...I have a letter, he thought, quickening his pace.

Klauss was excited, also, but he tried to mask it. However, as he neared the dwelling he said, 'Dia bom, senhora.' *Good day, madam.* Stepping forward and handing him the letter, she noticed him smiling; it was the first time she'd ever seen him smile. The landlady was a kind, tough old woman and was glad that the letter had brought a smile to his face. It was the second letter he had received since moving into the room a month ago. The old woman thought, being charitable, that though it was a smile, it was not a very nice smile.

After scrutinizing the envelope for signs of tampering Klauss thanked the landlady and took the letter into his room to read. He closed the door, turned to the sunlight that was coming through the window and opened the letter. He did not feel so alone now. He took out the piece of paper and read it, but it would not mean anything to him until he had deciphered it. This would take a few minutes.

While he was decoding the message the landlady knocked on his door, asking her tenant if he would like some bread- *pao*- that she had made earlier. She could bring it to him with jam if he liked, she told him. Irritated by the interruption, Klauss tried his polite best to tell her to just leave it in the kitchen and he would have it soon. *Damned old woman! Why can't she just leave me be?*

After deciphering the letter and reading the message the smile from Klauss had long disappeared. And it was not coming back any time soon, for he realized that though being reassigned to Marseille- he was glad about that- he would be facing a sort of disciplinary hearing on account of his actions in North Africa. That was not something to look forward to, but it was something that had to be done. It would not be that bad, he finally convinced himself; because even though he was Abwehr, he was also SS. And the SS was a much bigger, more frightening fish.

Klauss was to leave immediately. The rail line ran from here to Madrid, and from Madrid to Barcelona. From Barcelona he would have to get as close to the border as possible and then cross into France by foot. From a shirt pocket he pulled out a box of matches and lit one, igniting the letter and watching it burn completely.

He opened the door and left the room, heading for the kitchen to eat the bread and jam that the kind, old woman had left him on a table. The landlady had gone out and Klauss was alone in the house. He silently sat eating the home-made *pao* and chewing slowly while he gathered his thoughts. In a matter of minutes he would be leaving the dwelling with his few possessions and stride towards the rail station, hoping to find a taxi on route. He had done enough walking these last couple of months. Just ask the desert.

Jack and Hassef had followed the trail of Klauss through the reg though it had not been as easy as following footprints in the sand. The gravelly, rocky ground had left few clues for the two-man posse, but

Hassef was able to find enough evidence to warrant continuing their search. After several hours they had come across a dead, naked shepherd. He had been cut up.

They'd known that Klauss would've had a knife on him, presumably the one that he had used on the lieutenant, but they had not been sure whether he had a firearm. Any gun would have had to have been stolen because the posse knew that Klauss had left his rifle and bayonet behind. Captain Versailler had ordered a weapons check and all were accounted for before the posse had set out. So, they'd doubted that Klauss had had a gun; it was bad enough to desert from the Legion but to desert with a weapon was sheer stupidity; hence the reason for the small posse instead of a manhunt.

The lieutenant's murderer had left his bayonet bloodied so it was at first assumed to be the murder weapon but from what Versailler had told Tommy about the killing before they'd left, the posse had assumed that Klauss had had a secret knife. The rotting sliced up body that they had come across in the reg confirmed their suspicions.

Hassef had guessed correctly that Klauss had been headed for Morocco but at one point when the trail had been wearing thin the two legionnaires had had to come to a decision on whether to concentrate on a search in the direction of Fez or in the direction of Marrakech. They'd decided that Hassef would head toward Fez and Jack would go to Marrakech in the hope that one of them would find their quarry.

They'd started to communicate a little better on their search through the reg. Men on the hunt always did. Hassef had conveyed that if he did not find any trace of Klauss in Fez that he would return to the Legion and possibly face desertion charges. He had told Jack that the Legion was his home.

But Jack had had a taste of freedom and he'd wanted more, so he'd told his Algerian comrade that he would probably not be back, and this was goodbye. He'd told his friend: 'Au revoir.'

Hassef had said, 'Attente...j'ai quelque chose pour vous.' *Wait...I have something for you.*

Jack had been surprised to see Hassef hand over the watch that he had bought from Fast Lenny all those years ago but he'd then said, in English, to his now-new but soon-to-be-old friend, 'No, no, buddy...you keep it; you earned it. And you're gonna be doin' *time*; so you might as well *keep* it. Get it? *Keep it?*' Jack had chuckled to himself but

Hassef just grinned, not understanding much of it except that Jack had been trying to hand back the watch.

'Oh, c'mon, Hassef...' Jack had pleaded. 'Really, I want you to have it.' But Hassef had just sat on his camel grinning.

Finally, in well-spoken French, Hassef had said, 'Il a ete signifie pour etre avec vous.' *It was meant to be with you.* Jack had taken the watch and they'd both gone on their separate ways.

That had been about two months ago.

The sleek express train travelled swiftly through the beautiful, green French countryside en route to Paris. It was a splendidly warm, sunny midsummer's day all across the south-western area of Europe.

Jack was wearing the watch on his wrist at this very moment. It had stopped ticking a few minutes earlier but Jack hadn't noticed because he had other things on his mind, like making sure he did not come across anyone that was official and asking questions- because he did not have identification or a passport. And also on his mind was that the Legion would be keeping an eye out for him with some assistance from Interpol and the French military. And, of course, there was the honour of the lieutenant's request- a pledge to be delivered beyond the grave. And most importantly...an extremely sexy, high class woman adorned in the latest fashion was sat directly across from him.

A small, laughing child somewhat dangerously ran down the aisle of the fast moving train with its mother in hot pursuit, calling the child's name; 'Yvette!'

To Jack's left were two French sailors presumably on leave to Paris. Earlier, he had wondered what kind of shenanigans that they would get up to in the City of Light; and he sort of wished that he could be going along, too. Maybe, thought Jack devilishly, that after the business was taken care of in Chateaurenault that he would take a chance and spend a few nights in Paris. The Legion was a presence there and he did not want to be arrested even though he had thought vaguely about turning himself in.

The beautiful, kittenish woman of fashion had only got on the train at the last stop, Tours, and when she'd sat down in front of him he had thought, *Ooh la la.* But she had been busy with the contents of her purse since sitting down and Jack hadn't yet had a chance to flirt, though he'd enjoyed observing her style of dress: short red skirt, revealing grey top and knee-length black boots. She had black hair, blue eye-shadow and thick red lipstick. At last, the woman closed her purse and looked up- their eyes meeting. Jack smiled.

She smiled back; and *wow* what a smile, thought the ex-legionnaire. Their smiles held on for a few moments so Jack said with a fairly decent French accent, 'Bon jour...' Still smiling, she nodded back. He went on. 'Mon nom est Jacques et je suis artiste.' His idea of a false identity was to be an artist named Jacques. Not a very good one considering it was based on the fact that he just liked saying, *'je suis artiste'*. He couldn't draw worth a lick.

She was nodding her head and politely said, 'Ahh...'

At least she was still smiling, thought the deserter: The quitter.

The sexy woman could see that Jack was a good-looking man with a cheeky, though subtly hampered and possibly skeptical- as well as tired- twinkle in his eye. He had a bright smile, she thought, and the blue shirt was very nice but his ensemble was questionable and he didn't look very cosmopolitan; or rich, for that matter. She was still smiling, pleased by the attention. She told him her name. 'Babette,' she said. Even her voice was sexy. 'Vous etes artiste...'

'Oui,' said *Jacques*. His accent had gotten better since coming to France. 'Je vais a Paris...bientot. Mais, pas maintenant...pas aujourd'hui.'

'Pas aujourd'hui?'

'Non.' He stopped to think for a moment; his vocabulary was still very limited.

Babette broke the silence and said, 'Je suis dans les affaires de fasion.' She spoke at normal speed, which was too fast for Jack, though he thought that he might have understood that part. 'Me dire,' she continued. 'Cette chemise est-il de Paris?' *Did you get that shirt in Paris?* He didn't know what Babette'd just said but she was looking at his shirt.

He was nodding as he followed her conversation but now she'd asked him a question and was smiling, waiting for an answer. He didn't know what to say so he said, 'Uh...oui.'

Babette went on. 'Oh, vous devez dire le nom de l'endroit...' *Oh, you must tell me the name of the place...*

Smiling, Jack just nodded and said, 'Oui.' She tilted her head, slightly puzzled.

Babette said, 'Eh? Ou c'est?' *Huh? Where is it?*

Where's what? Jack thought. He had stopped nodding but held up the smile: Might as well smile as you hold on to the mast while the ship sinks. He unconfidently said, 'Oui...' But she replied with a vacant stare, realizing that he could not really speak French. He knew that he now looked like an idiot so he tried cute, raising his eyebrows and holding his palms out pleadingly. In a questioning tone, he repeated the answer: 'Oui?'

Babette smiled back and politely said, 'Vous ne parlez pas le Francais, n'est-ce pas?' Jack shook his head and his smile faded slowly. No, *I do not speak French*, he thought. Not *really*.

He offered an explanation. 'Je parle en peu de Francais,' he said in an accent that was getting better by the minute. She nodded. He gave her a resigned smile and mumbled, '...Un peu.' Jack was at a loss for words- literally. The beautiful cosmopolitan woman gave him a final smile and then returned her attention to her small, black purse.

Jack looked slowly down at the piece of paper that he held in his hand and remembered why he was there. He had to focus.

His thoughts were interrupted; the French sailors were laughing and gesturing toward him in what looked like good-natured ribbing. They were speaking too fast for him to understand but he smiled back, nodding and mumbling, 'Yeah, yeah...' He guessed that they were saying the French for: *She's outta your league, pal.*

A moment later it became obvious that the train had begun to slow down gradually. Jack looked out his window and noticed the rectangular wooden platform signs that came into view proclaiming the station. The train stopped and only a few doors opened.

Jack alighted. He watched a porter help an elderly woman who had much too much luggage with her. Jack travelled light, carrying only a small duffle bag which contained a few clothes and a shaving kit. And a baseball-sized round rock; he did not carry a knife and dared not carry a firearm. The guard blew his whistle and the locomotive steamed off to Paris as he walked along to the end of the platform, descending the stone steps to the road whilst absorbing the lush beauty. The village looked like it belonged on a postcard.

Klauss had left the landlady a note saying that he would not be returning. When he reached one of the more busy streets he found a taxi and hailed it. The car came to a screeching halt when the driver had seen the hand go up and the German spy ran up to it and jumped into the back seat. It was the same cab as before and it lurched forward violently before speeding off in the direction of the station. The driver pressed down hard on the horn, blaring out at anybody that was near, because he thought that his fare had an urgent train to catch. Either that or the driver just liked honking.

They did not converse at all and when the taxi arrived at the station Klauss paid the manic driver, went into the depot and headed for the ticket booth where he bought a single- *one-way-* ticket to Madrid. When he reached the capital he would then buy a single fare to Barcelona. There had been no need for the taxi driver to have rushed; the next train to Madrid was an hour away.

Klauss made his way over to plataforma dois and climbed the stairs that would take him over the bridge to the platform. At the bottom of the stairs on the other side there was a newsagent and he bought a Spanish newspaper to pass the time. He moved to a quiet bench where there was nobody around and sat, unfolding the newspaper and commencing to read it under July's bright afternoon sun. There did not seem to be much in the paper that was newsworthy on this day in 1939. Nevertheless, the daily journal provided ample reading for him to while away the minutes.

Sometime later more passengers arrived on the platform and the few provided benches were all taken now except for a spot next to Klauss. A mother carrying an infant was walking with her two small children over to the available bench seat and the German agent glanced at them from behind his newspaper. They sat down on the bench beside him and immediately the baby began to cry.

Klauss huffed in discontent and then after taking a deep breath sighed heavily. He tried to continue reading but the infant's cries became a sharp, high-pitched wail. The mother struggled as she discreetly lifted her top while holding the baby, but managed to place the child's mouth to her ample milk-filled breasts. The baby stopped crying and a train pulled up to the platform across from them. The two young children, a boy and a girl, were drifting away from their mother. She told them to stay by the bench.

The train opposite them departed and the children moved back to the bench. Then, the boy said something to his sister and she shrieked in play fright. He made spider motions with his fingers and the pretend spider crawled toward her through the air. She emitted a shrilling, piercing scream that stunned Klauss, and the brother began chasing her around the bench. She shrieked again and laughed, calling out for help: 'Mamae!' But her mother was busy breast-feeding.

The boy caught his sister directly behind where Klauss was sitting and she squealed scathingly into the German's ears. The little girl giggled as she slipped away from her older brother. She ran to her mother for temporary cover but mamae was occupied. The children stopped for a moment to catch their breath, giggling at each other.

The train to Madrid did not depart for another thirty minutes and Klauss was growing impatient. When he attempted reading again, the children took it as a kind of cue to start up again. The boy lunged for the girl; she screamed and started running and giggling again as he pursued her while laughing and yelling. The mother told them to stop running but they ignored her, and continued to run round and around the bench shrieking with delight.

Klauss did not hear the announcement over the loudspeaker that said the Madrid train would be fifteen minutes late. He had strained his ears to hear it but the shrill sounds of the children had made it impossible for him. But he saw the expressions on the other passengers waiting who were bound for Madrid and he could see from them that it was not good news and guessed that the train had been delayed. But nobody had left the platform, so he deduced that the delay was minimal.

The *criancas* were getting louder and louder and their *mamae* could not quiet them as they ran faster and faster around the bench until the boy decided to end the chase and grab hold of his sister. She let out a piercing scream that matched all of the others put together. She was just inches from Klauss's ear.

Klauss's eyes were still widened from the sting of the piercing cry of the tiny girl when he turned and looked at the children and slammed his newspaper down hard on the bench and yelled, 'Parada!' *Stop!* And then: 'Acabamento!' *Finish!* The two small *criancas* stared at the angry man, and with saucer-sized eyes they moved quickly to huddle at their *mamae's* side. The mother avoided eye contact with the tall, furious stranger and tried to comfort her *criancas*. The little girl sobbed in quiet, stuttered gasps.

Just as Klauss was about to enjoy the silence the infant pulled from its mother's nipple and started crying. The mother tried in vain to

70

continue the feeding but the baby was wailing now. The older brother joined his siblings and began to weep also.

Klauss had had enough and got up from the bench and walked to the newsagent where he bought some mints. He then went to the other end of platform two where he would no longer have to hear the crying *criancas*.

About thirty or so minutes later the train bound for Madrid rolled into the station and Klauss gave his ticket to the porter and then boarded the train. Klauss moved down the aisle and opened a compartment door and went inside and sat down by a window, across from an elderly gentleman. Klauss looked at the old man briefly and then opened up the newspaper. Doors slammed shut as passengers hurried aboard. The whistle blew and the train lumbered out of the station, slowly picking up speed.

Nobody else had come into the carriage compartment- though the train was almost full with passengers- and Klauss was glad for that. It was about time I had a little luck, he thought as he sat reading- swaying to the train's gentle movements.

Klauss peered out from his paper and he noticed the elderly gentleman was watching him. The German made eye contact with the old man, who then quickly averted his eyes toward the window and pretended to watch the passing landscape.

When the old man glanced back he saw that the stranger was still staring at him. Embarrassed, the old man smiled politely but Klauss sat motionless, staring at the man, and did not acknowledge his politesse. The elderly traveller's smile disappeared and he looked away from Klauss with a resigned expression that was mixed with a dollop of fear.

They travelled in silence for a couple of stops and then the old man left the compartment. He did not bid adieu. Klauss noticed that the man had not alighted at the last station; he had simply moved on to another compartment.

Was it possible that the old man was really a French agent and had gone to get help? No, thought Klauss; that is ridiculous. The old man had been afraid of his own shadow; unless it was an act. No, no. Must settle down, he told himself. It was a long way until the train reached Salamanca, where he would change trains for Madrid, and he might as well get some rest. He had the cubicle all to his self and it was the perfect time for a siesta, though he would never actually allow himself to fall asleep in such a public, unsecure place.

The day turned into night.

Klauss watched the full moon as the train slowed, pulling into the station at Salamanca. He waited for the train to stop and then he climbed out of the carriage, looking left and right until he had an idea which way to go. He went left where there was a sign that read: Trains to Madrid. The night air was warm as it bathed over him on the platform and the full moon was bright in the rural sky. He found out that the next Madrid-bound train was due in five minutes and it would be the last train to the capital today.

Klauss moved quickly to the correct platform and when the train rolled up he boarded it. He searched for an isolated seat and planted himself down. There was still a long way to go and he wondered what the new assignment would be. Marseille was a very busy port city and Klauss had been there many times and he knew there were many things to do in a place like that.

His mind wandered to the hearing. Perhaps his superiors have lost confidence in him because of the Legion mishap, he thought. Mishap as in unlucky accident; and unlucky accident as in he was caught out.

Those damned French Jews! They're dead and I killed them and still they curse me from the grave! As he thought this Klauss's eyes widened and squinted at the same time, giving him the appearance of a homicidal maniac. Moving through the aisle in front of him a pretty young girl had caught the frightful gaze and walked warily by him to the end of the carriage. He had not noticed her watching him. He was thinking of Marseille: there will be plenty of opportunities to kill Frenchmen.

This brought a smile to Klauss's face, the second of the day.

Madrid was a very lively city but by midnight things were gearing down and there weren't many taxis waiting at the rail station. But the German spy only needed one and after he'd found a taxi he had the driver take him to a moderately priced hotel. He would be staying the night in the capital and leave for Barcelona first thing in the morning. The full moon gave the city the appearance of a black and white photograph. Madrid had seen a lot over the past decade, including a bloody civil war, and graffiti was splashed everywhere pledging past and present allegiances.

The taxi stopped outside a hotel. Klauss paid and tipped the driver, then watched the cab fade away into the distance- seemingly swallowed by the buildings. He turned and walked back to a different hotel, one that the driver had *not* mentioned, that they had passed earlier on, not wanting the taxi driver to know where he was staying.

The sun shined warmly the next morning and Klauss set off for Barcelona; he would have to change trains at a place called Alagon around midday and hopefully be in Barcelona by early evening. The carriages had no compartments and he had to sit next to people amongst the rows; the smell of sweat permeated the air in the crowded train and he felt sick. He thought of the flies that had gone for a swim in his soup. 'Ticket, please,' said the porter. The German handed over his ticket and the porter punched it; then handed it back. The man in the seat behind him was coughing phlegm and two young lovers in berets were cloying each other in front of him. Across the aisle from him a small boy sat picking his nose and eating the contents, all the while smiling up at Klauss. The father of the boy looked drunk already and had fresh scratches on his face. And sat next to him was an ancient looking codger who, Klauss suddenly realized, had just soiled himself.

Klauss was in hell. And he would be for the next four, five hours.

But Klauss survived; he always did. He was in Barcelona by supper time and ate at a restaurant near the station. The fish was fresh and the one beer that he allowed himself was refreshing. Nobody was following him. No one was interested in him. *Good.* He still had one more train to catch- to Figueras, a town near the French border, and would not get there until midnight.

From Figueras he planned to steal a car and drive to a point near the border and then walk into France along the beach in the moonlight.

His train to Figueras was scheduled to depart in twenty minutes. Klauss paid the bill and went on his way.

chapter 10

Kaspar did not like this strange new world that was identical to his old one but different. He'd left the town where he'd had the campsite in the clearing where he'd come across the stranger with the mysterious

73

ring-bracelet. He still carried the object, either under his coat in a hidden pocket or in a hiding place buried under the ground in a chest with his other precious belongings.

Kaspar had travelled throughout the Schwarzwald- Black Forest- and surrounding woods and villages, and had stopped at towns where the populace had been ripe for the picking, thieving-wise. The small pickpocket had encountered many mind-boggling questions since that day when he'd strolled along the dirt lane, when night had turned into day.

He'd been on his way toward Stuttgart when he'd noticed his well-made shoes began to show wear and decided he would find a cobbler at the next town who could mend them. He had dug up the chest and carried it now- which he does not like to do- with just a few possessions, among them the few coins that he'd kept in his pocket at the clearing in case the campsite intruder had turned out to be a robber requiring some sort of monetary appeasement. He'd had opportunity to use the coins but he was fond of them as they were from another place; a place from before that night in the clearing. He'd stolen coins regularly and used them for the fundamental needs that were not filled by his thieving.

But then he'd come to a town with the shoes falling apart and had had no coins on him- bar the special ones. Kaspar had found a cobbler in the town centre and was in the shop watching the cobbler examine the coins that he'd handed over for payment in advance. Kaspar asked the cobbler, 'Gibt es etwas falsch? Is there something wrong?

The cobbler's eyebrows burrowed and he held up one of the coins close to his eyes for better inspection. Finally, he looked at Kaspar and said, 'Es gibt etwas fremd hier...' There is something strange here. *The cobbler had looked closely at Kaspar then, noticing how young the small boy suddenly looked. He had continued, 'Wissen Sie was es ist?'* Do you know what it is?

Kaspar did not know and said so. 'Weiss nicht.'

The cobbler went on, speaking German. 'The coins are all dated years from now. Look..,' he'd said as he looked at the coin held by his fingers. 'The shiniest one is dated 1879. Why does it have 1879 on it?' He gazed at Kaspar in hope of an explanation.

But Kaspar only said, 'Weiss nicht.' I don't know.

The cobbler shook his head in puzzlement and could not think of any

74

other questions for the boy except one: 'Why do you have a coin that is dated 1879?'

Kaspar shrugged. He could not think of any other answer except one: 'Weiss nicht.'

The cobbler told Kaspar that he could not have his shoes mended there using those coins. He told the boy, 'Diese sind von keinem Gerbrauch...' These coins are of no use to me...

Kaspar was dumbfounded and looked at the cobbler blankly.

The cobbler then said, '1879...it must be a mistake. That is what..?' He had to think for a moment. *'That is fifty-one years from now. These are no good to me but I will buy them from you for one coin...'*

Kaspar told him, 'Nein.'

'Suit yourself,' the cobbler said as he'd handed the coins back to Kaspar, whose shoes still needed mending.

When Kaspar had reached Stuttgart, a city that he'd visited once before, he realized that it had changed a lot. It had seemed so much different than what his memory was insisting.

He had started to grow taller and he'd begun to see hair grow under his arms and around his testicles. The world was changing in so many ways for the nearly feral orphan who lived in the woods but worked in the towns. He had thought that there weren't any trains running anymore and that had made him sad; however, when he'd arrived in Stuttgart he'd finally seen a train- though it had been a very old fashioned one that had moved very slow. At least it'd been very clean and had looked brand new.

He also had wondered what an '1879' was. He knew about days and weeks and years and months and seasons but he hadn't quite grasped the magnitude of how odd his life had become.

In Stuttgart he had found that the stylish clothes that he'd loved so much- his cover- had attracted too much interest at a public house amongst the noisy, nosy patrons because of the advanced craftsmanship of the garments. He'd always wanted to look dandy but to stand out would be counter-productive to his business.

He had left Stuttgart in a carriage that had been filled with the wares of a clothes merchant. He'd snuck into it and had not known where it was going. He had not cared.

When the carriage had come to Nurnberg it stopped and Kaspar had crept out, blending quickly into the dark, early morning street.

75

Five years had passed since that early morning and Kaspar had become somewhat of a local celebrity, stemming from the time that he'd brandished his strange coins to a room full of fellow drinkers at a popular watering hole that was in the centre of town; and so he was thought of, in some circles, anyway, as something of an enigma. He had never left Nurnberg since arriving on the clothes carriage.

He still concealed his precious belongings underground in a chest at a secret hiding place in the woods outside of the city. But he would only pickpocket tourists and visitors; he'd sometimes found odd jobs and had been trying to make a better effort to join society. But he still lived in the wild and had built a small wooden shack to live in, though he hoped to move into a cottage one day; maybe even start a family.

Kaspar sat on a wooden bench that was next to a wooden table and drank ale from an old wooden mug. He was a young man now and he'd come to very much like the taste of fermented hops- though he still loathed even the smell of wine, much less the taste. It stirred up bad memories by reminding him of the good old days.

He was very sad. He'd become interested in the opposite sex but he had no social skills in that department. He was street smart, physically adept and could speak well, but when it came to girls he was inept and would fumble his words. He always ended up looking foolish and the only sex he'd ever had was when he would have the occasional wet dream.

But Greta was different. He believed that. She had laughed at his witticisms and animations, and had smiled at him nicely when he had come to her father's tailor shop to look for work. He arose from his seat to go buy another mug of ale and was already starting to lose his coordination, stumbling into a bench and disturbing a large, bearded man who looked at Kaspar angrily. The pickpocket had been becoming angry as well as being sad, but his anger did not match that of the large, bearded woodcutter's, so, with eyes widened, Kaspar apologized quickly and moved on to get more ale.

After Kaspar had sat back down and taken a large swallow from his mug he looked across the room at the object of his affection. He had come to this alehouse purposely for he knew that Greta came here with her father often on the days at the end of the week. Kaspar had seen her there several times before; she was the reason why he'd gone to the tailors looking for work; he'd wanted to be close to her. He was drinking to forget, or to find courage; he'd already forgotten which. He gulped down the ale and the mug was nearly empty. The large, cavernous alehouse had filled up and was now quite noisy.

To impress the girl- Fraulein Greta- Kaspar had brought his most prized possessions with him: his odd coins, the bracelet-ring and the photograph of the small, brown horse- all dug out from his secretly stashed chest earlier in the day. He hoped that one day he would present these to her as a gift. He'd also brought plenty of normal coins to buy her whatever she would want in the hope that she would think of him as a possible suitor.

She'd walked through the doorway earlier but she'd not been with her father; she'd come in with a tall, handsome young man and they'd been holding hands. Understandably, Kaspar had not liked that.

He was still, an hour later, trying to think up an alternative plan.

They were one of the more organized street gangs and even though they probably would call Berlin their home, they travelled about and frequented other cities such as Liepzig and Munich. There were six in the gang as they left Munich to return to Berlin. They had done well and were carrying the booty that they had not sold, yet. They'd decided to try and sell some fancy hats, among other things, in Nurnberg as they passed through. They'd arrived in the day and had sold many of the expensive hats already, at low-cost; and now they were relaxing in three-man shifts. Three in the gang were brothers and they had gone to a public drinking house to relax while the other three kept watch on the remainder of the booty and their horses. All six gang members were extremely furtive looking characters.

The brothers were quaffing their beer as their eyes searched around the busy alehouse looking for potential victims. They did not need to tell one another the obvious: look for the ones that were alone, drunk, looking for company and most of all, carrying many coins or valuables.

'Look,' said the eldest brother surreptitiously. 'There's one...'

The heads of the other two brothers didn't move but their eyes did- to the corners where they could get a furtive glance and watch the lone young man, using the peripheral vision of their sly, furtive eyes.

chapter 11

Jack had left the station and had gone in search of lunch. He'd been famished and had found a small cafe where he'd had coffee and a pastry. From there, after having been told where to find the bakery, he'd bought two warm loaves of elongated bread, a Viennese finger and three meat-filled pastries, without having had a clue what kind of meat it was.

After leaving the tiny, yet well-stocked bakery, Jack had walked down the cobblestone street to a bigger road and had found the sign that pointed to the town of his destination: CHATEAURENAULT.

As he had strolled along the road Jack had had nagging doubts and second thoughts about his *mission* to *inform* Lieutenant Bationi's wife of her husband's death; surely, she would have found out about it by now. *Will it open fresh wounds? What if she tells the Legion? Will I turn myself in, anyway? Do I even tell her that I am officially a deserter?* The gnawing thoughts had been stopping him from drowning in the beauty of the Loire Valley that surrounded him.

He had come to the town and found the street name that was on the small piece of paper but had not walked down it; instead, Jack had wandered into the wooded countryside to sleep in the bushes that night: to sleep on it.

He'd risen from his sleep the next morning- *yesterday*- and had been none the wiser on what to do about his dilemma. So, Jack had meandered through the greenery all day wondering if this would be one his last days of freedom. He'd bumped into a pair of pretty French girls- *les filles*- who were on a day trip and had flirted with them but hadn't been able to allow his self the luxury of gaiety that afternoon.

That was yesterday.

The American deserter had once again slept rough amongst the bushes and trees and had actually slept very well. The birds were chirping. Jack opened his eyes and immediately thought: what a wonderful sound to wake up to. He rubbed the sleepy dust from his eyes and when he arose he'd disturbed something in the bushes. He listened for a moment and heard nothing as the creature slithered away quietly. He walked over to a stream and threw water on his face: *Water, water, water.*

Jack finally made a decision on what to do about his quandary, though he had known all along- *really*- what he would do.

The deserter lathered his face and commenced shaving. He had to look respectful for when he delivered the message that day to the lieutenant's wife: That *morning*.

Lieutenant Bationi's request: The *expressed wish*.

Walking through the woods Jack had startled a couple of deer that had seemed to have sprouted wings as they'd recoiled into the bushes with such celerity that he hadn't been sure whether he'd even seen them. His heart pounded quickly from the start.

Now he was on the road and would soon be coming to Rue de Paradis- the name of the street written on the paper. A blonde girl walking past Jack stopped and turned to face him. She wore a yellow summer dress and was quite pretty, and was smiling at him. The girl was saying something but Jack could not follow and besides, he had important things to do.

Jack wanted to talk and flirt with the friendly girl, but instead he just smiled politely and said, 'Je ne parle pas...'

He had promises to keep.

A few minutes later Jack came to a white sign post with black lettering that read: Rue de Paradis.

'Well, he thought; this is it. *Here goes nothin'.*

He regarded the lovely cottage: the front garden splendidly adorned with a variety of flowers, the quaint face of the small, simple house that projected a halcyon state of mind, the metal number five that hung from a nail by the entrance door, the A-framed roof that may or may not harbour a grieving widow...

He knocked on the door. He waited.

A young girl opened the door and looked at him. She said, 'Oui...?'

Jack had not been expecting that; he had assumed that the lieutenant's wife would answer the door. He looked at the girl: her eyes, her nose, her mouth, her face, her hair; her lips. She was the most beautiful girl that he had ever seen.

It took him a moment to remember the speech and he went to speak, opening his mouth, but no words came out. He was lost in her eyes.

The ex-legionnaire pulled his self together. 'Je suis un soldat de votre..,' he'd begun to say; then stopped. The word that he had rehearsed to say next was *mari*- the French word for husband- because he had thought the lieutenant's wife would answer the door.

79

He had to think for a moment to remember the French word for *father*. He knew what it was but his mind had gone blank; his eyes were lost in hers again and he'd lost his train of thought. *What am I doing?* Finally, after too long a pause, he said, '...Votre pere.'

The girl stood silent.

Jack suddenly realized that the girl may not be Bationi's daughter at all; she might be a niece or a neighbour. Maybe it was the wrong house, he thought, or a new family had moved in. He felt fatuous. Jack raised both eyebrows and repeated: '...Votre pere?'

The girl scrutinized him carefully. The man standing in the doorway had been one of her father's soldiers. *But what was he doing here?*

Jack allowed a small smile and she smiled back; a small smile. He scanned down her shapely, curvaceous, lusty body- his eyes calmly resting in hers. His mind was filled with devilish intent and he looked away quickly, suddenly feeling embarrassed. Looking back at her, trying to think of what to say next, he noticed that she was still smiling-though her eyes were saddish as though weighed with unanswered questions.

He said, 'Etes-vouz...' *What was the word for daughter?* He could not think of it. '...Salvatore Bationi's..?'

She nodded, understanding.

Jack was at a loss for words and he tried to smile politely, but the sadness in her eyes just made him want to protect her.

A voice called out from behind the lieutenant's daughter; a woman was walking up. 'Maria? Qui est-ce?'

The girl turned around and spoke to the woman. 'Mama, il etait soldat du pere.' *He was a soldier of father's.*

'Que?' the mother said. 'Que veut-il?' *What does he want?*

'Je ne sais pas, mama.' *I do not know.*

The woman was next to her daughter now. The girl turned back to look at Jack and smiled. He looked back at her and then, turning to the mother, bowed in respect.

The mother was pleasant but had not smiled. She asked Jack, 'Que voulez-vous?' *What do you want?*

Jack forced a formal smile. 'Madame Bationi?'

'Oui...'

'Est-ce Salvatore Bationi votre mari?' *Is Salvatore Bationi your husband?*

'Oui,' said the lieutenant's wife.

'Je m'appelle Jack. Je suis un soldat du votre mari...' His words hung in the air.

Then the lieutenant's wife began to speak very quickly to both Jack and the girl. He could not understand what it was that she was saying, and he started to feel uneasy.

Then Mrs Bationi looked at Jack and said, 'Je suis Madame Bationi.' She took her daughter's hand. 'Et ceci est Maria.' The American understood that part, be he still displayed puzzlement. She noticed, continuing: 'Parlez-vous Francais, non?'

Jack just stood there for a moment. 'Non. Well, en peu...' Then: 'Je parle Anglais.'

Mrs Bationi turned to Maria and said, 'Vous parlez Anglais, Maria.'

Maria replied, 'Oui, mama.' She looked over at Jack and said to him, 'I speak a little English...I learn; two years in school.'

The girl spoke English. Thank fuck for that, thought Jack.

Jack glanced at Mrs Bationi, then back to Maria. He spoke slowly and deliberately. 'I have come with bad news. Your father wanted one of his soldiers to deliver this message in person.' He looked at the ground and his fingers scratched the side of his mouth. He continued, 'Well, anyway, he didn't want you or your mother to read about his death in a letter.'

Jack stopped talking and brought his gaze back up to Maria, awaiting a response. His eyes asked Maria if they had already heard, though he was sure of it.

Maria glanced at her mother; then back at Jack and said to him, 'Oui...yes. We have letter...two months ago.'

'Two months ago?'

'Oui.'

Jack stood in the doorway turning to the side and rubbing his neck. He felt embarrassed about the foolish, whimsical plan.

Maria asked him, 'Is that why you...come here?'

He nodded his head slowly. Maria turned to her mother and interpreted what had just been said. The girl looked back to her father's soldier and said, 'My mother would like to thank you for coming all this way.'

'Well; it was his dying wish,' he said, exaggerating only a small amount. He watched Maria speak to her mother and her mother speak back. They were translating.

Maria said to Jack, 'It means a lot to her that...father's men would go so far to honour his wish...'

Shrugging, Jack said, 'Well, uh...you know...'

Maria gave him a heartfelt smile and said, 'Thank you.'

Mrs Bationi said to Jack, 'Merci.' She leaned close to Maria and said something that the American could not hear.

Maria said to Jack, 'Would you like to stay for coffee..?' She paused, then added, '...Jack?'

He smiled. 'You bet I would.'

Maria and Mrs Bationi moved to the side as Jack entered the doorway. The opening to the side led to a warmly decorated lounge, and the lieutenant's wife smiled politely at him and pointed at the sofa. He took the cue and went over and sat down on the comfortable seat.

Mrs Bationi looked at him for a moment, thinking that he reminded her of someone. Then she disappeared through a door and into the kitchen.

Maria sat down on a cushioned chair across from Jack. She was wearing a blue skirt, about knee length, with a white top that had short sleeves. She sat with her body forward, her legs pressed together and her hands folded in her lap.

Jack was looking around the room. He made eye contact with her and she smiled. He smiled back and couldn't help but feel good. He thought to himself: wow, what a smile she has...

Maria said, 'What else are you doing in France, Jack?'

'Huh? Oh...that is it. Just to deliver the message.'

'*Vraiment?* Really? Did you need...special..,' she used the French word; '*permission...* from the Legion to come here?'

Uh oh. '...Uh, well...' He had to think about this for a moment. '...Well, not exactly.'

Maria went on. 'My father always...have much trouble with the Legion...about...coming home.'

'Well, to tell the truth, I kinda left the Legion.'

Maria wasn't quite sure what he had meant but could see that he was uncomfortable about it. She asked him, 'Where do you..,' she paused to think. '...go to from here, Jack?'

He was relieved that the conversation had changed from his desertion. Or had it? The deserter was not sure whether or not that it was wise to divulge such information. But he trusted her and blurted out, 'From here I'm goin' to Paris...and then maybe Marseille.'

Maria's eyes lit up. 'Oh Paris! How wonderful! I can not...wait to see it again!'

'You have been there?'

'Oh, oui,' gushed Maria. 'Yes. I have be there many...cinque- five-...'

'...Times.'

'Yes; *times*.' Her eyes widened as they talked about Paris. 'It is a wonderful city...you must see it, Jack.' She moved around in the chair, wiggling from the excitement of the conversation about Paris. She relaxed a little and her legs parted slightly, allowing Jack a dirty glimpse. His heart raced and his head went numb. His body tingled. Looking back up at her he noticed that she was smiling and he smiled back, trying to look nonchalant. He wondered whether she knew that he'd been trying to peek up her skirt and did not hear her last question.

'Jack? Did you hear me, Jack?'

He composed himself. 'Oh; uh. No. I was daydreaming...' It may've been the truth. The ex-legionnaire continued, 'I'm sorry, Maria. What did you say?'

'Are you going to Paris to...live?'

'No. Just visiting.'

'Oh...'

Jack watched her head bow and she stared downward. He thought: hmm, that's interesting- she sounded as though she was kind of...

Then he thought: *Nah*, couldn't be. He observed her; she still gazed at the ground. Jack decided to take a shot in the dark and said, 'Uh, Maria...'

She raised her head.

'Y'know, when I get to Paris I, uh, well...I will need a guide.'

Her *eyes* smiled. *Yes, oui. Vous aurez besoin du guide.*

Jack's heart grinned: I think that was a yes.

Mrs Bationi walked into the room at that moment with a tray on which three cups of coffee sat. She said to Jack, 'Sucre?' and pointed at the sugar bowl.

He said, 'Yes, please.' Then he corrected himself. 'Uh...Oui, s'il vous plait.' Jack looked over at Maria, who was stirring her coffee. They smiled at each other and Jack thought: *I have waited all of my life for that smile.*

Mrs Bationi said something but Jack sure as hell didn't hear it. She watched her daughter's eyes shimmer and sparkle in the company of the strange American who had been one of her husband's soldiers. She figured out who he reminded her of: Tyrone Power, the American actor.

Maria told her mother that Jack had asked her to go to Paris with him and from the look of it her mother did not seem to disfavour the idea, concluded Jack. Mother and daughter chatted for a moment, sipping their coffee. Jack was watching them; they were speaking too rapidly for Jack to follow. He drank from his cup.

At one point of their conversation Jack had heard the name Tyrone Power, and so he knew- then at least- what they were talking about as he had been compared looks-wise to the actor; and that was good.

But then the topic moved on and Jack once again was clueless as to what they were saying. Mrs Bationi said something to Maria and they both laughed. The daughter smiled at her mother, then looked over at Jack; and then back again to her mother. The mother's tone changed to one of motherly advice. She patted Maria on the knee and smiled.

Jack was puzzled; they'd been talking too quickly. Now they were looking at him and could see that he felt left out.

Maria said to him, 'I will translate. Okay, Jack?'

Jack nodded. The lieutenant's wife pointed to a large painting on the wall of a pretty, but gloomy quayside during a rainstorm. She said, '"Il pleut, encore"...'

He could understand that bit of simple French; but let Maria tell him, anyway.

Maria translated; 'The title of the painting is: "It rains, again".'

Not to Jack it wasn't. In fact, in Jack's mind it was sunny.

Sunnier than hell.

Later that evening, having spent the day together wandering around Chateaurenault, Jack and Maria had gone back to the cottage where Mrs Bationi decided that Jack would be welcome to stay the night and he didn't have the slightest problem with that.

It was dark outside and the lieutenant's wife had gone off to bed after making them all supper. Maria had gone to the kitchen and when she'd returned to the lounge she held two glasses in one hand and a bottle of red wine in the other.

She handed one of the glasses to Jack and poured him some wine. 'Merci, Maria,' he said. She smiled. The lights were off, the only light being the two candles that flickered and made their faces dance. He whispered, 'Are you sure it's alright...I mean the wine and everything...'

'Yes. Why not?' She gulped down some wine. 'What do you mean by "everything"?'

Jack had been putting his glass down and hence did not notice the kitten grin on Maria's face. So, he thought for a moment that she may be angry. As he went to apologize he glanced up and saw Maria smiling. Embarrassed, he broke out in a grin and chuckled. She went over to the sofa and sat down beside him.

Maria said, 'Shall we...?' She raised her glass.

Jack filled in the word. '...Toast.'

'Yes. Toast.'

'Sure. You know any?'

She thought briefly; then said, 'Oh, okay. Here is one: "A votre sante"...' Their glasses clinked.

Jack asked her, 'What's it mean? "A votre sante"? To your *what*?'

Maria gestured with her hands, rolling them in question- then putting them on her chest. Jack raised an eyebrow. Then it clicked. He said, '*Health*. Of course: "To your *health*". Their glasses clinked again.

Jack announced, 'I got one!'

'Shh.' Maria was giggling. She whispered to him, 'We have to be more quiet...'

'Okay..,' he said, conspiratorially.

'What is your toast?'

'Oh, yeah,' said Jack. '..."To France and all its beauty"...' *Clink.*

The candlelight sparkled in their eyes.

An hour or so had passed and the first bottle of red wine was empty and the second one half gone.

They had discarded their glasses and now drank straight from the bottle. Jack was tired and horny. So was Maria. She took a hefty swig from the bottle and then handed it to Jack. It had become silent the last couple of minutes. The two candles flickered.

Their faces slowly gravitated toward each other and stopped only inches apart. Jack looked deep into Maria's dark, soft brown eyes. Then her eyes fell down to his lips and he moved his face closer

...closer. Maria closed her eyes and opened her mouth; he kissed her.

Maria got up, went over and blew out one of the candles. She returned to the sofa and sat back down beside Jack. She leaned over to the other candle and looked Jack straight in the eye. Then she coyly smiled at him before blowing out the last candle.

Jack's heart skipped a beat.

A few minutes later their kissing had become more than passionate; more like frenzied lust. Jack's hand reached down and slightly lifted her skirt. He gently squeezed her warm, soft thigh and ever so slowly moved his hand upward where he found a pair of very moist lace panties.

She didn't mind; but he did. This was too real to cheapen. He stopped kissing and his eyes dived into hers. 'I think I'm in love...' The voice was his but he couldn't believe that he'd just said that. But he was glad that he had. He waited.

He did not have to wait long; she breathlessly whispered, 'Aussi...' *Me, too.*

In a short while Jack and Maria fell asleep on the sofa. They slept in each other's arms.

chapter 12

Mid-summer in Poland can be quite warm and today had been no exception; therefore all of the windows were open at a house made of brick that evening in the capital. Inside sat a family at the dining table eating their evening meal of fish stew filled with potato, carrot and onion. All six seats were occupied by family members: the mother and father, two children- boy and girl- and the mother's parents. The meal had just started and they were eating in silence. The spoons and the bowls were creating a rhythm all of their own.

The father of the children spoke after several mouthfuls. 'Janna is going to see your parents,' he said to his mother-in-law.

The oldest woman at the table said, 'Oh? Janna, ktory jest cudowny.' *Janna, that is wonderful.* 'They will be delighted to see you. When are you leaving?'

'In three weeks, Matka.'

'Pod katem jak dlugi?' asked the eldest man at the table, Janna's father. *For how long?*

'JA maja byc tam tygodniowo, Ojciec.' *I will be there for a week, Father.*

Janna's father nodded; then shook his head and shrugged his shoulder one time. 'Are you going alone?'

'Tak.' *Yes.*

'They will be so glad to see you. You have always been their favourite.'

'Oh, Father...' Janna was embarrassed. 'It is not true.'

'It is true. Is it not true, Anya?' Janna's father looked at her mother, who just smiled at him noncommittally. He turned back to Janna and said, 'It is true...'

The children were well-behaved and ate silently. They were occupied with mouthfuls of bread. Their father turned his head to speak while still chewing and it caused him to choke. He coughed and cleared his throat.

Janna asked him, 'Are you alright, Dimi?' Her husband nodded and drank from his water glass.

'Tak. Dzieke, moj kwiat.' *Yes. Thank you, my flower.*

'Please pass me the bread,' said the older woman. The little girl handed the bread to Janna, who then passed it over to her own mother. 'Dzieke.' *Thank you.*

They had finished dinner and Janna was clearing the dishes from the table. Her mother was helping her and the men had gone to the sitting room to smoke their pipes and talk about the world. The children were outside the house and playing in the dirt and gravel that made up the front garden. The bustling city around them soaked in the sun's warm rays but there was a sense of doom over the old city that had seen its share of war.

They had few toys but it did not matter; the children were very happy and laughed often.

Janna and her mother had moved to the kitchen where Janna washed the dishes whilst her mother dried them.

Janna's mother spoke. 'The boy and the girl are such nice children, Janna. You have done well with them.'

'Dzieke, Matka.' *Thank you, Mother.*

The old woman held a dish towel in one hand and a tea cup in the other. She'd stopped for a moment and was looking at her daughter, who had begun to acquire a few wrinkles around the eyes. Janna stopped also, noticing her mother regarding her. Her mother was not smiling but she looked very happy. Janna smiled back.

Her mother told her, 'Wy jestescie dobrymi matka.' *You are a good mother.*

'Dzieke, Matka,' said Janna as she hugged her mother. 'Wy jestescie takze.' *And so are you.*

Part I, epilogue

Kaspar was getting drunk and as he bought another ale he dropped several coins to the floor, swaying when he picked them up. He sounded rich. Kaspar was starting to stagger now and as he walked back to his table this time he spilled some of his ale. He shared the table with about six or seven other people but had not been able to start up a conversation with anyone. He thought about going to one of the public houses where he would be recognized as the boy with the mysterious coins; and may find a friend there.

But he did not want to leave here because Greta was here and it was still not too late. He could still woo her, he thought drunkenly. He was thinking about going over to Greta and her date when just then the tall, handsome suitor stood up and went through to the outside lavatory. My chance!

Kaspar started to get up but had to steady himself. He took a long guzzle from his mug and staggered over toward Greta. He had a lop-sided grin as he approached her and bumped into a woman sitting, slurring his half-apology. Greta looked slightly shocked. A furtive voice several tables away from Greta's and Kaspar's ears whispered, 'Look at that...'

The drunken pickpocket stared at the beautiful Fraulein and then sat down at the table where her suitor had been sitting and would soon be returning to. My chance! Quick! *He drunkenly fumbled through his pockets.* 'Here...I have something to show you. These are old coins; See? This one's an "1879". And this one..,' *he could not see the numbers properly as he was experiencing double-vision for the first-time in his young life. He put the coins on the table for her to see and she sat there not knowing what to say.*

Six furtive eyes watched closely.

Fraulein Greta was feeling increasingly uncomfortable as Kaspar rushed through his words, stuttering and slurring. She saw the people sitting around her take notice of the spectacle and a few even laughed. The Fraulein was very embarrassed but too polite to send him away. A couple of people leaned closer to glimpse at the strange coins and others in the room noticed it, edging ever closer to Kaspar.

Kaspar was searching through his coat as Greta started to get up. He put his hand on hers; she looked at him. He said, 'Warten Sie nein! Schauen Sie dies an...' No, wait! Look at this... *Kaspar pulled out something. It made Greta's eyes grow wide with interest but there was a hint of danger. It was a piece of fancy jewellery with a silver band and a gold ring attached to it. It was beautiful, she thought, though she hadn't a clue what it was. She had never seen anything like it and stared at the trinket for quite a long moment. Then she looked at Kaspar, slightly open-mouthed. She did not know what to say.*

Kaspar told her, 'Es ist schon, ja?' It is beautiful, yes? *'Es ist hubsch, wie Sie...'* It is lovely, like you. *He tried to look at her sweetly but it was hard to focus and he was swaying. His eyes were large and pleading but Greta stood up all the way this time and looked toward the door that her handsome suitor had gone through. Kaspar's heart began to sink. He quickly put the trinket back into his coat and started to gather his coins from off the table.*

Greta moved away from the table as he put the last coin in his pocket. He turned to follow her. Two opportunistic patrons saw the vacated seats and immediately occupied them. Three professionally opportunistic drinkers huddled together only feet away.

'Did you see that, Rolf?' The youngest brother asked.

'Ja,' said the eldest brother.

'What was it?'

'Weiss nicht.' I don't know.

'But whatever it is,' said the middle brother, 'it is valuable.'

'I have a plan.' said Rolf, the eldest.

Kaspar was following Greta through the crowded alehouse, stumbling, bumping and tripping as he strode to catch her. He was calling to her but she was pretending not to hear. He shouted, 'Greta! Wartezeit! Halt! Zuruckkommt!' Greta! Wait! Stop! Come back! *He caught* up with her at the bar counter and looked at her. *She looked back and he saw that her sadness and embarrassment had turned to anger. She was glaring at Kaspar, and for a moment it sobered him.*

My chance! My chance! *Kaspar was standing in front of her, and Greta was trapped in the crowded area of the bar unable to move. She looked anxiously for her suitor and wondered: What's taking him so long? The beautiful, blonde Fraulein had no choice but to hear Kaspar out.*

My chance! *He looked as deep as he could into her startling blue eyes and told her, 'Ich liebe Sie.'* I love you.

It was pathetic and sad. Greta finally spoke to him. Firmly, she said, 'Kaspar, gehen Sie nach Hause...' Kaspar, go home... *Kaspar looked at her sadly; he had no home save for a few sticks in the forest.*

Standing at the crowded bar a pair of furtive eyes watched Kaspar and Greta patiently. The eldest brother was only two feet away from the potential mark. The gang member saw the drunken lad fumble around in his coat pockets for something. As the inebriated pickpocket made a last ditch effort to impress the girl of his dreams, the furtive eyes landed on the item that Kaspar had pulled out of his coat. It was a strange looking 'painting' of a small, brown horse. Yet, at the same time it did not look like a painting.

'Greta, please. Look at this. It is called a photograph..,' said Kaspar as he held it out for the Fraulein to look at. She was intrigued for a second but she did not want to get involved, so she said nothing. She looked away.

A photograph: What's that? *The mind that sat behind furtive eyes wondered.*

Greta was relieved; her tall, handsome suitor had come through the door and was walking up to her. Kaspar was shrinking. He watched Greta say something to her suitor and the couple hurriedly exited the alehouse leaving Kaspar at the bar amongst the crowd still holding the photograph of the small, brown horse in his hand. As the sad boy turned to order another beer he was sure that he could actually feel his heart break in two.

He put the photograph back into his pocket and tried to get the attention of the busy bartender. He jostled for position but when he did he would get dizzy and wobble. Finally, after a few minutes, he had got his ale and was looking for a seat but there were none available so he

90

stood- swayed- by a wall. He felt like crying and the alcohol was starting to make him feel queasy.

Someone asked Kaspar, 'Bad night?' The bleary-eyed unsuccessful suitor glanced up with sad eyes. He did not answer.

'The Fraulein was not interested..,' said the voice. It was Rolf, the eldest brother. Kaspar remained silent. 'She is a fool; you are much more handsome than her tall, suitor,' Rolf lied.

Kaspar immediately felt better. A friend! He said, 'Really? I am?' Then added, 'Maybe she will change her mind, then...'

'Ja, maybe. But you would be better off finding a new Fraulein to turn your intentions to.'

'Weiss nicht...' I don't know.

'I am going to a bierhall where there are many Fraulein. Why don't you come with me? Finish your ale, quickly, and we shall go there.'

'Weiss nicht...'

'You must. There will be many girls for you to choose from. Now, drink up. You do not want to stand around here looking like the fool, do you?'

Kaspar shook his head. 'Nein..,' he said softly.

'Good! Then it is done. I will even buy your first ale when we get there. My name is...Wolfgang,' said Rolf.

'I am Kaspar.'

Outside the entrance of the alehouse the youngest brother sat pretending to be a beggar by, well, begging. The middle brother, who had gone to fetch the rest of the gang but was back now; stood inside by the entrance waiting for Rolf to leave and then would follow. The alehouse was still crowded and noisy as Kaspar and his new friend exited the building with five followers- unnoticed by Kaspar.

They were near the town centre and there were several people still on the streets. But there were plenty of dark lanes and deserted paths, as well as a myriad of inner city alleyways. There weren't many street lamps to speak of in the first third of Nineteenth century Nurnberg.

'What part of town did you say it-'

Rolf interrupted. 'Just up here a ways, beyond the river road.'

'Oh...' Kaspar was drunk and sad but he was also street smart. Alarum bells began to ring throughout his brain. Wait a minute...

'What is the matter, Kaspar?'

Kaspar was wising up: Too late. 'Uh, I think I am too tired to drink more,' he said as he slowed his pace. They had reached the river road and suddenly it was very, very dark. 'I am going to go...home.' Kaspar felt sad when he'd said the word 'home'. He added, 'I live back the other way. Thank you for your invite but I must be off now.'

The lonesome pickpocket stopped and went to turn around to go the opposite direction, though when he did an arm grabbed hold of him.

Kaspar was about to try pulling away but he was suddenly surrounded by five more dodgy-looking characters. A dozen furtive eyes stared at Kaspar, who was looking around the road in the hope that there would be passers-by. But the street was deserted. Kaspar was sobering up by the second but he was still swaying.

'Give us a look,' said the youngest brother. 'Show us the trinket!'

'Shh,' said the eldest.

'But Rolf...'

Kaspar thought: So, his name is not Wolfgang. I should run...

'Give us the trinket, the coins and the painting..,' Rolf ordered Kaspar. 'The painting; what did you call it?'

Kaspar was confused. He said, 'Painting?'

'Of the horse. You showed the Fraulein at the bar...' The other five gang-members wondered what their leader was talking about.

'Oh,' said Kaspar, who was shaking uncontrollably as the gang moved closely around him. 'The photograph.'

'Yes! That's it..."photograph".'

The middle brother asked, 'What's a "photograph"?'

'Shh,' said Rolf, who then turned to Kaspar. He told the scared, drunk and lonely boy, 'Give us those things now or we will kill you.'

Kaspar was aghast. These were his most prized possessions, his only link to a world that was his own; not this world of people who did not know what a photograph was and only had a few old-fashioned looking trains. No. These were the only things that he had...the things that made him who he was. He could not give them up. He would not give them up. Kaspar glanced around at the evil faces and had to make a quick decision on which way to run.

Rolf told him, 'Give those things to us NOW!'

There! Kaspar decided to make a run for an alley he thought he could slip through. He broke through the gang members and ran for the alley. His legs did not move like he had wanted them to.

For a brief moment Kaspar thought he had made it; he'd gained a *few steps on the robbers at first, but his drunken gait allowed the fiends to catch him and they pulled him to the ground. Kaspar struggled with all his might but there were six of them and only one of him. He threw fists at them and kicked out but they had swarmed on him.*

Then, Kaspar was shuddering as several knives began to tear at his flesh. It was over in seconds and the murderers found the items in his handsome coat. They took the trinket, the coins and the photograph of the small, brown horse as well as his coat and shoes. They left him there in the dark on his back, eyes staring vacantly at another world. Blood poured from Kaspar to the dirty alley and seeped into the ground.

TIME RING, Part II

Come away o human child
To the waters and the wild
Take a faery hand in hand
For the world's more full of weeping
Than you can understand

William B. Yeats   *The Stolen Child*

prologue

Tall buildings towered over the street, lending some shade to the pe-
destrians that littered the sidewalks of Manhattan. The few trees that
could be seen were in the process of changing from green to yellow,
orange or brown. Amongst the throng walked a man with his young
son at his side, holding the boy's right hand tightly as they whisked
through the crowd, strolling past restaurants, coffee shops, shoeshine
boys, liquor stores, corner bars; the boy was excited. Though they
lived nearby, their neighbourhood was quite plain.

A drunken man was openly begging at a busy street corner, lurching
at people as they criss-crossed the road around him. The boy asked his
father, 'What's that man doing?'

'Nothin'. Come on.' He steered them away.

Cars filled the roads: honking, stopping, starting. Yellow taxis
pulled over to the curbs: picking up or dropping off passengers, or sat
at stop lights with the cabdriver hanging out the window shouting
obscenities. Cyclists moved along in between the automobiles and the
masses. It was a virtual sea of humanity. Sometimes, at these moments,
the man longed for wide open spaces. The nearest place to that from
here was Nebraska, he thought, or New Mexico. Nevada? Would Ne-
vada be deserted enough? Maybe not for him; but the main thing was
that his son really enjoyed these walks down the avenues and through
the streets.

The autumn sun shined on their faces as they weaved along. The
father pointed ahead and told his son, 'Just up here, Mass. We make a

94

left.'

'Okay, Dad.' There was a liquor store at the corner called Barney's Liquor. Its sign was yellow with red letters. The boy saw the sign and said, *'Oh yeah, I remember now. Can I go in and get a Clark bar, Dad?'*

'Sure, kiddo. You've been a good boy, eh? And maybe they're still selling cigarette cards; the Series ain't over yet.'

'Dad...'

'What?'

'The kids call 'em bubblegum cards these days...'

'Since when?'

'Since about a hundred years ago. Since the Giants won the World Series...'

'What, 1954? That was only two years ago.'

'Dad, that's engine...injun...um,'

'"Ancient"...'

'Yeah, um...that's ancient history, Dad.'

'Listen, wise guy; when I was a kid we had to buy a packet of cigarettes just to get a card.' He smiled at the boy and they laughed as they went through the open door.

'Ancient history, Dad...'

'Yeah. I know. Go grab a Clark, son.'

Several long city blocks away and moving along briskly was a dark-featured fellow who carried a small sack, passing by the tall, run-down apartment buildings that lined the littered street. Up ahead on his right, perched on some steps that lead to one of the buildings, sat a woman who was dressed in a revealing manner. She was dark-haired and nice looking but on close inspection looked tired and worn. The fellow knew her from the neighbourhood. As he passed by the steps he noticed her.

She waved at him and said, *'Hiya, Johnny! Hey, you lookin' for a gal? I can give you a good time, Johnny. Whaddya say?'* She smiled weakly but friendly.

'No, I'm busy, Flo.' He had business to attend to.

Johnny Needles was a bettor's runner for the mob's bookies. He picked up the bets from the local population and, unless it was an unusually large amount of cash, he made the pay offs. In the 1930's when he had been barely a teenager he'd run numbers for the Penny

Lottery where customers picked a number from zero-zero-zero to nine hundred ninety-nine; the pay-off about six bucks for every penny wagered. Johnny remembered back on those days fondly; he was young and ambitious and on the way up. But that had been nearly twenty years ago.

He was on his way to meet one of his regulars, who he had met every morning during the World Series. He remembered this customer made a bundle last year betting against the beloved hometown Yankees in the Series. Nobody but nobody had bet on Brooklyn, he thought, but this guy had. But still, the customer had given it back to the bookies as they all did eventually.

A few pigeons were swarming around some rotting delicacy that they had found lying in the gutter. Johnny went on by, disgusted. Rats with wings, he thought, crossing the road. The summer was gone, it was the ninth of October, but the sun was bright and it wasn't cold. Johnny felt good; things were getting better all the time, albeit slowly but surely.

He stepped onto the other curb and as he passed by a crevice between the buildings a shadowed figure that was lurking emerged and moved quickly to Johnny's side, matching strides. In the light of day the figure uncovered itself to be a greasy-haired dodgy-looking bug-eyed slimeball; someone to be wary of.

The creature spoke with a West Side accent: 'Hey, Johnny. How ya doin', Johnny?'

Johnny was walking faster now and ignoring the good-for-nothing creep whom he knew only too well. But the creature kept up with him.

'Probly got a pile a money from collectin' bets, eh Johnny? In the sack?'

'Go away...'

'C'mon, you wanna fix? I got one just for you, Johnny. I know you wanna. How 'bout it, Johnny; you wanna? Tell you what; I'll sell you a dime bag for a nickel. Okay?'

'Yeah? Maybe I should tell my bosses what you want to do with their money...'

The dope dealer recoiled slightly. 'Yeah? It ain't like you're connected, Johnny. And you never will be. You're half-Irish...'

'Scram, creep...' Johnny quickened his pace.

'Just askin', Johnny. Just askin'.' The creep gave up and stopped, but

before slinking back into the shadows he added a parting shot at his former cohort. 'You got somethin' against a guy tryin' a make a livin', Johnny?'

There, but for the grace...

Johnny turned at the next corner.

The man and his son had left Barney's Liquor store and they were walking down the side-street, having to pass around a couple who were carrying several bags of groceries. The couple were both short and stout, and resembled - to the man, anyhow- two solid squares moving along the concrete. 'That Clark bar is for after lunch...'

'I know, Dad.'

They crossed an intersection and kept going straight; they were on the sunny side of the street. A yellow cab making a hasty left turn screeched at the corner, leaving a skid mark on the road. Ahead of them a man walked in their direction.

The boy pointed. 'There he is, Dad!'

'Yeah. Good eye, son.'

'Are you gonna bet on the Dodgers again?'

'Yeah.'

'But you lost yesterday...'

'Who woulda thought that Larsen would pitch a perfect game with the Series on the line?'

'You didn't, Dad.'

'Yeah, I know I didn't, wise guy. Here he comes, so hush up a minute.'

They stopped on the sidewalk when the man approached. The father said, 'Hi, Johnny. Put this on Brooklyn...' He handed the runner a couple of five-dollar bills.

Johnny told him, 'You should be a Yankees fan. You'd win more.'

'I do just fine, fella.'

'That's what they all say,' said Johnny Needles as he left to collect more bets.

The man turned to his son and said, 'Bettin's a mug's game, Massy. The only thing you can predict for sure is that in the end the bookies are gonna take your money.'

'I know, Dad.'

'Okay. Now, let's get you off to school.'

At that exact moment three thousand miles across the Atlantic Ocean, in South-West England, a woman was stirring sugar into a cup of tea that she was about to take out to her husband. Her very young daughter tugged her skirt and asked, 'Mummy, where did Daddy go?'

The woman smiled and looked at the open door. She said, 'He's in the garden by the flowers, poppet.' The child ran outside and across the lawn. The sun was fighting to peek through the overcast sky. Her father had his hand in the dirt, planting some beautiful blue and yellow pansies.

The little girl stood next to her father. 'Daddy! Mummy said you were here!'

'She did, did she?'

'Yes. And, um, that you were, um, in the flowers.'

'Yes, I am.'

'Can I help, Daddy?'

'Yeah; go on.' The woman came over with the hot tea and handed it to her husband. He turned to her and took it. 'Thank you, luv.'

They smiled at each other. Then, from inside the house they heard crying. The woman said, 'The baby's awake.' She went back to the house.

The little girl said, 'Is Baby Julie hungry, Daddy?'

'Yes, poppet. Do you like our new home?'

'Yes, Daddy.'

'Me, too. I love you, poppet.'

'I love you too, Daddy.'

chapter 1

Jack and Maria had been in Paris three days now and they'd captured all the landmark sights: The Eiffel Tower, the Arc de Triomphe, the Louvre, the Champs d'Elysees and a few others. They had enjoyed a moonlight stroll along Quai d'Orsay where Jack had almost asked *the* question. They were both very tired after a few excitement-filled days of walking, talking and, well; other stuff.

When they had checked into the inn that they were staying at, Le Taureau Ancien, they'd checked in as a married couple. That night Jack and Maria had made love for the first time: and second; and third.

At dawn on the fourth day Jack was awake first, as he had been every morning and parted the curtains to check on the weather. Dark clouds had gathered and rain threatened Paris. He let the curtains fall back into place and went to the sink and brushed his teeth. His memory was waiting for the bugle call for reveille and he glanced over at his wrist-watch, placed neatly on a table. The time it showed was two-thirty, which was not correct. The watch had stopped again and Jack would rewind it after finishing with his teeth. Jack guessed the time was about six o'clock.

Maria slept peacefully and her snoring was almost inaudible. Jack listened to her sleep as he wound the watch that Fast Lenny had sold to him all those years ago. When he looked at her while she slumbered there seemed to be a content smile on her face.

Jack had a lot on his mind: the Legion and its tentacles which included the French police forces and Central Bureau; what was he going to tell Maria about his desertion; would he turn himself in; he had no legal identification; he had no job...

He had no prospects either, as far as he could see. For the past couple days he had been entertaining the thought of marriage; but he had nothing to offer Maria, at the moment, except for a life on the run.

And besides, he thought, people get married and then all they do is fight.

Jack peeked out the window again and there was no change; it would probably start raining soon. Maria was lying on her back now and Jack could see her lovely breasts outlined on the bed sheet, under the cover. He was thinking: I am not in love...that's nuts; I only just met her.

Maria stirred, stretched and then one glazed-from-sleep eye opened slowly. She saw Jack and smiled; turning and yawning. 'Mmm,' she said cozily with her eyes closed. Then both eyes opened and she sleepily mumbled, 'Quelle heure y a til?'

'Around six o'clock, I think,' answered Jack.

'What, um...your watch...time?'

'It stopped ticking during the night.'

Maria rubbed her eyes. 'You need new watch...'

Jack did not have to think about it; he said, 'Not a chance.'

She stretched her arms up and yawned deeply, emitting a small, comfortable 'Mmm...' Watching her, Jack realized he was getting aroused- wearing only boxer shorts. Maria noticed. 'Mmm,' she said.

'Est-cela pour moi?' She smiled seductively.

Jack walked to the bed and leaned over her, moving his face close to hers. His eyes washed over the sexy girl before resting in hers. He said softly, 'Vous etes tres joli...tres beau.' The besotted pretty French girl smiled. Jack told her, 'I looked this up at a bookshop yesterday..."Vous yeux sont comme les diamants". Did I say it right?'

She stared up at him with a contented, peaceful smile on her face. Her eyes danced from Jack's left eye over to his right, back and forth. Maria was smitten with him. He told her, 'Je t'aime.' *I love you.*

They started kissing and as they did she pulled the covers back on the empty side of the bed. She playfully grabbed at his crotch; he was hard. Jack slid his hand over the sheet which covered her breasts and she pulled him onto the bed. When he was on top of Maria and gazing into her eyes, she remembered what he'd said a few moments earlier: Vous yeux sont comme les diamants. *Your eyes are like diamonds.*

chapter 2

The hilly, green plains of Western Poland sat softly beneath the late summer's warm sky and the birds sang the song of nature as brown cows stood about lazily chewing the turf. All seemed normal and off in the distance a raven cawed, causing the cow to raise her head- owing to instinct. The cow could hear the raven but what she couldn't hear was heavy engines, only miles away, which ploughed through the open countryside at almost breakneck speed.

It was the first day of September in the year 1939 and German armoured divisions, supported by motorized infantry divisions, rumbled their way toward Warsaw, the Polish capital.

Far away, south from the striking force, Janna was outside in the garden picking flowers with her grandmother, enjoying the warmness of the sun's gentle rays. 'Such a beautiful purple,' Janna remarked as she clipped one at the stem. They were collecting flowers to put in a vase for the dining table. Her grandfather was inside the house listening to the wireless; he liked to hear the classical music that they played at this time of day.

'Yes. They are very lovely,' said the old woman with a raspy voice. 'They are my favourites.' She smiled at her granddaughter, who had been a full-grown woman for quite some years now, and she still thought of her as the young girl who had ran yelling and giggling through the mud of the countryside when the world around them had been enveloped in a savage war. But her granddaughter did not seem so carefree anymore, she thought. However, the old woman, who'd had a hard life herself and wished that she had laughed and smiled more in her long lifetime, immensely enjoyed seeing her granddaughter.

The grandmother pointed to her left. 'And these...these are nice, Janna. They are called...' She paused, looking at the ground. '...I don't remember.' She wore a look of slight embarrassment.

'You will remember in a moment, Grandmother,' Janna reassured. 'It is good to see you and Grandfather. It has been a long time.'

'Yes. Too long.'

'The children have not seen you since they were very small. I promise to bring them over soon.'

'That would be very nice.'

'They would love to see you both.'

The old woman smiled weakly; she was getting tired. They both stood admiring the garden when a cloud moved in front of the sun. A cool breeze sliced a chill through the warm air. 'I think I must go in and sit down.'

'Yes, Grandmother. I will make us something warm to drink.'

They were just starting to move down the garden path when the front door flung open. Janna's grandfather was yelling at them and they were startled, both wide-eyed and eager for understanding. It quickly became clear as the grandfather shouted more coherently, 'The Germans have invaded!'

Janna hugged and kissed her grandparents goodbye and mounted the old, rusty bicycle that represented the best means of transport available. Her grandmother was sobbing now and a bit unsteady. The grandfather put his arms around his wife and told Janna to be careful; it was an old bike.

With a shaking arm the grandmother held out a chunk of wrapped cheese. 'Take this...'

Janna reached out and took the food and put it in the small bag she was holding that contained her money. She told them, 'Dzieke.' *Thank you.*

She wanted a train; she needed to get to her family in Warsaw.

101

When Janna had reached the main road the panic had become more evident. Janna was finding it more and more difficult to steer the bicycle as masses of people filed onto the concrete strip that headed southward; she was riding north. Every now and then a car or two came hurtling through the people, sending pedestrians to the side of the road. The eerie thing to Janna was the quiet; it should be noisier, *shouldn't it?*

There was no way for Janna to contact her family; she would have to make it to Warsaw by bicycle, train, car, bus or however. Warsaw was over two hundred kilometres away.

With every passing hour the narrow road had become more congested, not only with people and cars but also horse-drawn carriages, carts full of possessions, lorries, bicycles and the occasional military vehicle heading north. Janna struggled with the squeaky, old bike as she steered into the oncoming, southbound traffic. She would constantly have to slow down or move to the side of the road. Dropped items began to litter the road. It was warm; sweat dripped into her blue eyes.

The road dipped and rose through the hilly terrain and Janna noted that her environment was becoming noisier. Tempers were beginning to flare as the fleeing civilians bumped into each other in their haste to reach the southernmost regions of Poland, away from Warsaw- the Germans main objective. Nobody noticed the beautiful countryside that surrounded them.

She pulled to the side of the road when she heard an engine roaring up behind her and watched the crowd disperse in the lorry's wake. When this happened Janna quickly rode the bike through the brief opening before it closed up again. It wasn't long before she was back to weaving through the exodus. Still, she was making good time; it was mid-afternoon and she'd travelled over fifty kilometres.

It had been very arduous and now hunger was becoming the dominant thought in her mind. She was also very dehydrated and would soon be stopping for a proper rest. Once again Janna had to move to the side, this time for an oncoming convoy of civilian automobiles headed south. Behind car windows wide-eyed faces stared at Janna as they went by her. When the last auto passed she jumped back on the old, rusty bike and continued her journey. She had a long way to go.

A chicken ran about aimlessly amongst the people's legs while being called after by its owner and Janna steered the bicycle carefully past them, listening to the fowl's squawks fade as she moved away from the scene. There should be a village before too long, she thought. A brief spot of open road gave her inspiration to overcome the fatigue and she cycled as hard and fast as she could. She must eat and drink. She must keep going.

She must find her family.

The soft hills allowed her to coast downhill at times and the sensation was soothing, wind caressing the face. She rounded a bend at good speed and suddenly found herself hurtling toward an old lady who was trying to steer and push a cart overladen with stuff that quite possibly carried a life's worth of possessions. The old lady saw Janna coming toward her and panicked; falling, she let go of the cart and it crashed to the road- spilling items everywhere. Janna steered the bicycle away sharply to the left, just avoiding hitting the old woman, but she rode off the side of the road and down a short embankment that lead to a dirt pathway. The bicycle landed solidly and Janna was thrown off and landed harshly but not severely. Her hands and knees were scraped and bleeding from where she had landed and she was a bit shocked; but she was okay.

The bicycle was not. The tyre was punctured, the wheel was bent and the handlebar had nearly broken off. It was unfixable.

A dark cloud moved in front of the sun as Janna climbed back up the embankment to the road. There were a group of people walking by and they regarded her standing there bloodied, her summer skirt torn. She looked back down at the bicycle forlornly.

Behind her the old lady was shouting. Janna turned around to see her picking up her possessions off of the road and placing them back on the cart. People were passing by; most trying not to take notice, some offering expressions of sympathy. After a few well-aimed glances from the old woman Janna realized *she* was the target of the rants. *Was it my fault?*

Janna moved toward the old lady. She asked, 'Do you need any help?'

'You want to help me more?'

'I am sorry.'

'Look at my things!'

Janna bent down to pick up some clothes. 'Let me help...'

103

'You should look where you are going.'

'I rode off the side,' said Janna. 'I did not collide with you.'

'And I should be grateful?'

Janna placed the clothes on the cart and bent back down to pick up a broom. 'I *am* sorry. The bicycle is broken...'

'Should I feel sorry for you?'

This was getting to be hard work; Janna was exasperated. '...No, but-'

The old woman interrupted. 'Look what you have done! You foolish woman! The broom goes in last!'

Janna had had enough. 'If you had not panicked and fell then I would have ridden around you...'

Scornfully, the old lady hissed: 'So, it is my fault, then?'

Janna watched the crazy lady remove the broom from the cart and drop it to the ground. If an automobile came by it could be dangerous but that was not Janna's problem. 'Goodbye,' she said as she walked away from the angry, old woman.

She set off at a brisk pace but soon slowed to a more conservative, steady pace. There was still no sign of any village. The road started to fill up with refugees once again and vehicles were pouring through.

Her stomach grumbled and growled. She stopped and asked a man if he had any spare food that he could sell.

'I have only some for myself and my wife. But there is a village that we have just passed through, not more than a kilometre beyond that bend in the road.'

Janna said, 'Dzieke.' *Thank you.*

There was a village bakery but it was empty and the shelves were, too. But further down there was a shop and people were in it. Janna ran to it, went inside and quickly gathered a loaf of bread, some cheese, apples, three tins of kippers and a few other things. The queue was long but she did not mind. It was busy and fairly noisy, though not many people were talking. She opened her purse and counted her money; she did not have much, maybe enough for a couple of days or so.

Outside the shop several military vehicles roared north along the road. Some children waved at them. Afternoon had turned into evening and Janna felt chilly as she left the shop with her food, looking for a suitable place to eat. She wished that she had taken one of the crazy old lady's sweaters; there must have been about twenty of them.

She found a spot off the road and sat down, wolfing down bread and cheese. She nearly choked in her haste to swallow and told herself to calm down. Taking off her shoes, Janna massaged her feet.

Her family was a long way away. She finished eating and acknowledged the greying sky; it was time to move on. She stood up and began walking again; left foot, right foot, left foot, right foot...

Over the next few hours, having made several rest stops, Janna had walked a further dozen or so kilometres closer to Warsaw. The sun was gone now as she approached the train station in Kivosk. Polish soldiers stood guard at the entrance; it would be the same at this station as it was at the one near her grandparents. The railway was closed for military use and wasn't open to the public.

She made her way out of town and followed the main road to the capital. The surge of refugees had died down some and that made it easier for Janna to walk but she was getting extremely tired; she would not be able to continue much longer without proper rest. She would soon have to find a place to sleep.

The Berlin sky was cloudy and rain threatened. The pawnbroker moved away from the shop window and went to his chair by the counter. He ran a good business with plenty of nice items and clothes but also a lot of junk. He was sort of a middleman for the jewellers, a broker, because he knew a fair amount about jewellery and could make a nice profit for himself. His reputation of trade in quality goods was what brought the next the customer in.

The shop door opened and the pawnbroker watched a man enter. It was Rolf, the eldest brother and leader of the gang. He was alone. The door closed.

The rest of the gang safely guarded their current booty nearby. Rolf was here to sell two specific items that he'd felt would demand the highest price: a strange ornamental bracelet with a gold ring attached and a picture of a small brown horse. He walked up to the counter.

'Guten Tag,' the pawnbroker said. Good day, sir.

Rolf grunted. He had already been to many pawnshops in a number of cities and had been disappointed at the amounts being offered for these particular items. The gang usually sold off the stolen goods quite quickly but these two items were different. Rolf was sure that they were worth far more than what he had been offered. He was already disappointed that the rare coins had been sold too cheaply. He wasn't going to make that mistake again, he told himself.

Rolf looked at the pawnbroker carefully. He pulled out something from his pocket and said, 'Ich habe dies.' I have this. *He placed the picture of the horse on the counter.*

'Was ist es?' What is it?

'Ein Pferd...' A horse...

'I can see that with my eyes. I mean, the texture; and.., the image. It is quite astonishing: Very peculiar.'

Rolf watched the man's eyes acutely as they studied the image of the horse.

The pawnbroker lifted his gaze from the picture and asked, 'Do you know how it was made?'

'It is called a "photograph", Rolf answered.

'A "photograph"? I have never heard of such a thing. Hmm...'

Several moments of silence passed as the two men calculated their own positions for the coming barter. Rolf spoke first. 'You will give how much?'

'What do you want for it?'

'I have had many offers...'

'But you have not sold it?'

Rolf cursed silently; one point advantage to the pawnbroker. Must rebound; these pieces are valuable and not to be parted with cheaply. His face was like stone. He said, 'No one has offered me what I want. If your offer is an insult then I will walk away at once and you will not have another chance.'

'I have done business with you before. You think I don't know how you came to this?'

'You make an offer...or I leave.' Rolf waited. He would give the pawnbroker a few extra seconds to allow him time to regain any potential loss of face. He had the man off balance now. The fish was on the hook.

After a long pause, the pawnbroker finally spoke. 'Ja...let me see. It is quite lovely; I should be able to pass it along. How about, say, ten; maybe fifteen-'

'Fifteen?' Rolf asked full of indignation. He turned to leave.

'I meant twenty!'

Rolf stopped to look back at the man and shook his head slowly before continuing toward the door.

'Twenty-five is the most that I could pay!' The man held his palms upward when Rolf halted and turned around.

'Make it twenty-seven and it is yours.' It was five times what Rolf had been hoping to get.

'Ja. Ja, twenty-seven.'

Rolf took the money from the pawnbroker and handed over the photograph of the small brown horse.

The man said, 'Danke.' Thank you.

Rolf grunted and then said, 'I also have this.' He carefully and dramatically pulled out the bracelet with the gold ring, his eyes fixed intensely on the pawnbroker's face and mouth and eyes. The pupils in particular; Rolf noticed that the man's had dilated hugely. This was good.

The man spoke. 'Fascinating. A beautiful piece of jewellery...' His words trailed.

'Make me an offer.'

'I have a feeling that you want quite a substantial amount of money for it...'

'I already have an acceptable offer. If you can match it then I will sell it to you for paying me a fair price for the photograph.'

'What was your offer?'

'What is your offer?'

The man thought carefully. 'Twenty? Ja, twenty...'

'That is not good enough. Auf Wiedersehen.'

'No! Wait! Just tell me what you want for it.'

'Seventy-five.'

'You have been offered seventy-five? By which pawnbroker?'

Rolf did not answer him. He just stared blankly.

'I can give you forty...'

'My previous offer was fifty. You may have it at that price.'

The pawnbroker thought long and hard. He thought: What am I doing? Will I be able to make a profit from these two items? He had never paid such a high price for stolen or used things but the truth was he wasn't sure if he would even want to sell the 'photograph' or the 'bracelet'. They were both exquisite.

He looked at Rolf and said, 'Ja. I will give you fifty.'

The years passed and 1833 turned into 1863. The pawnbroker was old *now and still ran his shop in the same old building which was now run-down somewhat. He had no children and his wife had passed away many years earlier. He went to visit a long-time friend who was a jeweller and ended up staying over for the night. In the morning he returned to his place of business in the heart of the city.*

As he walked through the shop door he realized immediately that he'd been burgled. The place was a shambles. He scanned around, taking mental inventory and evaluating what had been stolen. He quickly realized that the best and most expensive items were missing. The ring boxes were missing from the shelf where they were hidden in hollowed out books. The secret jewellery drawer had been found and so was his money stash. Old coins, paintings, tools, nice clothes...

All of the good stuff was gone. He sighed and moved to the back room fearing the worst; for that was where he had hidden his two most prized possessions: the photograph and the bracelet.

It was a miracle; they were both there, safely tucked below a floorboard.

The old pawnbroker did not know what to do. There was nothing left in his shop but junk, most of that broken, and he had no money. He sat in his chair at the counter and looked at the broken window. He would have to clean up the glass soon. The photograph and the bracelet were on the shelf under the counter. The old man rose up and went to lock the door; he would be closed today.

He was startled when a man suddenly appeared at the door. 'Are you open?'

The pawnbroker felt that he recognized the man. He asked, 'Have I seen you before?'

'Ja. I came here two years ago. I bought several rings. Do you remember? I am English. I live near Coventry in the Midlands.'

'Ja. I remember now. Come in; but you see, I've been burgled and all my rings have been taken.'

'That is terrible.' The Englishman entered through the doorway. 'Have you nothing of interest?'

The pawnbroker paused; he did have two things that were very interesting. He needed money. He said, 'I may have something that you might be interested in.'

The Englishman followed him to the counter and the old man handed over the photograph. After a moment, the wealthy Englishman said, 'It is just a photograph of a small horse.'

The old pawnbroker explained. 'Ja. But it is a photograph from before the photograph was invented. I bought this in 1833; or was it 1834? I forget. I am old. But it is very valuable.'

The Englishman thought it over. 'Nein. Danke.' No. Thank you. *'It is just a photograph...'*

The pawnbroker felt sick; was it worthless? Was it just a photograph? There was still the bracelet, his favourite between the two, and that was certainly valuable. The ring was gold and the chain was silver; its value must have risen. If he received a fair offer he would take it. The old man lifted the bracelet-ring and placed it on the counter.

The Englishman marvelled at the sight. 'My God,' he said. 'What is it?'

'Weiss nicht.' I don't know.

'I must have it. It will go splendidly in the display room at my mansion. How much for it?'

The pawnbroker wrote a figure- many times higher than what he had paid for it- on a piece of paper and slid it forward on the counter toward the Englishman, who looked at the amount.

'I think we have reached an agreement, sir,' announced the man from the Midlands as he pulled a wad of cash from inside his coat.

The pawnbroker took the money and watched the Englishman pick up the bracelet-ring that he had cherished so many years. He smiled ruefully and watched the man leave.

Janna was exhausted. The next large town was Rodem but that was still about forty-five kilometres away. Refugees still dotted the road; it was for the most part quiet but the atmosphere was sombre. She came to an elevated bend in the road and scanned the area for a place to sleep.

There were a farmhouse and a barn just down a ways on the right; that was one possibility, she thought while walking down the road toward it, her head swiveling left and right as she surveyed the countryside for any other options.

The quiet was broken when a lorry carrying soldiers sped through from behind her. She moved to the side, as did the other people. A bearded goat had to be yanked by his owner at the last moment, avoiding a messy collision. The lights of the truck disappeared around the next bend. The goat bleated.

Janna decided on the farmhouse and headed for the dirt road that led to it. The barn would provide shelter if there was a way in, she thought, and it would be cool tonight. But at least it wasn't cold. She still only wore a short-sleeved shirt with a light skirt that was torn.

There was light in the farmhouse so someone must be there. She walked cautiously as she turned onto the dirt road. The barn was just beyond the farmhouse so Janna would have to go past it, unless she circled all the way around. She had to make a decision in the next few moments, before getting to the gate and fence. The fence posts were liberally spaced with a single piece of wood connecting each, so it would be easy for Janna to get through. But that wasn't the problem. She was concerned about whether or not the people in the farmhouse would mind her borrowing their barn for a night. It was just a small favour to ask, she thought, given the circumstances.

She came to the gate and paused. Her heart was pounding now but her legs were glad for the rest. A gentle breeze washed over her face softly and it momentarily calmed her. She took a deep breath. *I will rely on instinct.*

The gate pushed open easily. With skirt torn and bloodied, her arms and knees scraped, scratched and forming scabs, Janna moved along the pathway to the front door of the farmhouse slowly but confidently. *I will be civilized and ask permission to sleep in the barn.*

Suddenly the door flung open and an old farmer stood in the entrance holding a shotgun. Janna froze; eyes wide. The old man asked her, 'Co czy potrzeba?' *What do you want?* 'Jak duzo rezygnowac ty?' *How many people with you?*

She didn't know what to do; she was afraid to speak. Her eyes wandered from the farmer's glare and landed on the barn. This seemed to anger him. 'Oh, I see,' he said. 'You are with them...'

Janna was confused. *Them*? Who are *they*? Then she realized and found her voice. 'Nie. Nie JA jestem sam.' *No, I am alone.*

The farmer was still pointing the shotgun at Janna but he was looking at the barn. It became obvious that there were people staying in the barn: Unwanted guests. She reassured him, 'I am not with them. I only seek shelter for the night. I have my own food.'

An old woman peered out from the doorway. It must be the farmer's wife, thought Janna. The farmer turned his attention away from the barn and said, 'And you want to stay here...'

'No...I mean; I came to ask permission to sleep in the barn.'

'You can take your chances with those people. But at daylight I am going to chase them out with this...' He held his gun up.

Janna looked over at the barn and suddenly it did not seem very inviting. It looked foreboding. 'Dzieke,' she said as she turned to move toward the barn. A possibly treacherous barn and an old man with a shotgun; she felt caught between a rock and a hard place. She stopped. Maybe I should just go back to the main road, she thought.

The old woman stepped out of the doorway. She said to her husband, 'Look at her. She is all cut and torn and weak. She is not with the others and she is not a threat. We could let this one in. Yes?'

'It is a risk,' he said.

'No. It is not a risk. I can tell,' said the farmer's wife.

The old farmer studied Janna closely for a moment then nodded solemnly. He glanced at the barn and then quickly at the gate area, then at Janna. He moved aside at the door and told her, 'Przyjsc wnertze.' *Come inside.*

Janna couldn't believe her luck and quietly entered through the door. The farmer took one last quick glance outside and then ducked back in through the door. The door shut.

The eastern sky was pink and the farmer, who had been up all night sitting on a chair in the kitchen, sat up and went into the next room to wake up his house guest and his wife. The old man had barely slept five minutes but he had things to do. Dawn was approaching.

Janna had slept all through the night but she still felt exhausted when the farmer woke her. 'You must go now. It is nearly daylight and I have business to attend to with my barn.'

She was quite groggy. 'Yes,' she said. 'May I wash my face before I leave?'

'Of course.'

Janna picked up her bag of food and went into the kitchen. While she was washing her face the farmer's wife walked through the entrance holding a coat. She told Janna, 'You may need this for warmth at night. Warsaw is a long way.'

'That is very kind, but a coat may be too hot and heavy to walk with during the day...'

111

'Do you want a sweater, instead?'

'Yes. That would be very helpful.' Janna towelled her face and watched the old woman dash off and then return in moments with a cream coloured sweater. Janna said, 'That is lovely. You are very kind.' The farmer was nearby gazing out the window. She put the sweater on and opened the door. The old farmer followed her out. When she was outside, Janna turned and smiled. She told them, 'Dzieke.' *Thank you.*

Left foot, right foot, left foot, right foot...

After a few hours of straight walking the exercise becomes almost hypnotic. She had tried to wave down an automobile a couple of times but to no avail. So she walked...and walked...and walked.

On the plus side she was making fairly good time and must have traveled more than fifteen kilometres or maybe even twenty. But now Janna was worn out and she had finished off her food at breakfast. She'd had only two rest stops and it was past mid-morning. The flow of refugees increased as the morning progressed. The sweater was wrapped around her waist.

It was time to rest, she thought. She would have to find food soon. Last night at the farmhouse she had been able to wash and clean her wounds, and the cuts were looking much better. She still wore the bloodied skirt.

Her mind was wandering. She knew that the town of Wodzke was not far off. Hopefully, she thought, there would be shops open for business. A family of six pulled their carts along the road ahead of Janna so she moved to the centre of the roadway. Other refugees used the other side as they moved to pass the family; they were all south-bound and Janna walked sandwiched between them northbound.

Then, without any warning, an automobile came screeching up from behind Janna. She instinctively started to her left but the family was there, now panicking. She twisted to her right; the others were scattering. The auto's wheels slid sideways as the brakes clamped hard. People yelled. Janna dove to the right.

The driver managed to bring the vehicle to a halt without hitting anyone. Refugees were lying left and right, scraped and bruised. A few men were yelling at the driver, who best decided to straighten up his auto and drive off quickly. The curses didn't stop until the vehicle was out of sight.

Janna sat nursing her ankle; something did not seem right. It felt funny. She also had a few new scrapes to add to her collection and was bleeding superficially in several places. The warm sunbeams were her only consolation.

She tried standing but nearly fell over. She balanced herself with one foot down and the other gingerly tiptoed. Trying to walk she fell and landed on her rump; the ankle could not take much weight. Janna sat with her head bowed and began to cry quietly.

She didn't sit long and tried once again to walk. This time she was more successful and began limping her way to Wodzke, all the while keeping an eye out for a stick to use as a crutch. She stopped several times to rest and finally came upon a suitable stick to use.

Over the next two hours Janna had barely traversed two kilometres. The town of Wodzke was busy and her stomach grumbled. It was busy and she found a food shop down a side street. She hobbled over to it.

She bought bread, pastries and cheese; and apples and chocolate. There was a radio on and Janna listened to the news bulletins of the German assault. Poland was being invaded from the north in East Prussia, the west from Germany and now, out of the south through Slovakia. The stream of refugees was heading straight into the German's southern attacking force. They would all have to turn around later, she guessed. *This is madness.* Janna left the shop hobbling and clutching on to her bag of sustenance.

It was difficult to carry the bag and walk so she decided to eat now and lighten her load. She sat down against the wall of the shop.

A man came out through the shop's door carrying an armful of food and drink. He went to his black automobile and put everything in the back seat. Janna watched him. He turned and looked at her; then asked, 'Dokad idziesz?' *Where are you going?*

'JA jestem zamierzac Warszawa.' *I am going to Warsaw.*

He told her, 'JA jestem chodzenie trzydziesci kilometry za Rodem.' *I am going thirty kilometres beyond Rodem.* 'Czypotrzeba pewien jezdzic?' *Do you want a ride?*

Janna smiled. 'Tak.' *Yes.*

As they rode, Janna still kept her eyes on the passing refugees for she had a small feeling that maybe her husband had got the family out of Warsaw and were heading to her grandparents in the south. She ate and rested her ankle. The man was quiet; they had spoken briefly on the developments of the invasion and she had told him her story, but that was all. He had to keep his eye and concentration on the road as they drove through the hordes of people and animals. Other vehicles were a menace, too, but when the road cleared they could cover several kilometres in just a few minutes.

It was still early afternoon when they came to the town of Rodem. The man asked Janna if she would like to be dropped at the train station. She told him, 'No. It will be closed like the others.' It would be better to stay in the automobile; it would take her thirty kilometres closer to her home and family. Warsaw was now only approximately eighty-five kilometres away.

Well over an hour later they came to the turning in the road that would take the man to his destination. The auto slowed and then stopped. They had long left the hills of the south and were now surrounded by flatland. Janna hopped carefully out and grabbed her bag and walking stick. She thanked the man for the ride. 'Dzieke,' she said as she watched him pull the door shut from the inside. He waved and then drove off. Janna started hobbling in the direction of Warsaw, about fifty kilometres as the crow flies.

It was hard going for the determined Polish woman. Her ankle was very sore and each time it made contact with the ground it was painful, but Janna did not think it was broken. She hadn't washed her wounds properly for some time but had cleaned up as best she could during the ride. The bruises weren't even noticed, but the cuts and scratches were bothersome. Her shirt was bloodstained from using it as a wipe cloth.

But she wasn't hungry and the weather was quite warm, though clouds were starting to fill the sky. She kept to the side of the road but the refugees were growing in numbers and it was becoming extremely difficult to walk through the surge. Soon, afternoon would be giving way to evening and she planned to keep going until nightfall. Janna walked on.

Left stick, right foot, left stick, right foot...

It was dark. Janna had hobbled the better part of five hours and covered perhaps a half dozen or so kilometres. She found a grassy area behind some trees just off the side of the road and settled down to eat some of her bread and cheese. As she ate she listened to the sounds of the people filing by on the road. The repetitious shuffling sound was somewhat surreal to Janna, though she wouldn't attempt to put a word to the feeling. She just felt empty. She thought of her children, Anja and Stanis. *They must be so scared.* She tried not to think of the worst and hoped with all her spirit that they were alright.

She took the last bite off an apple and lay down for a moment. She had the sweater on now, the one from the farmer's wife, and she needed it. The night had brought the cold with it.

Janna closed her eyes and calmed herself with thoughts of being reunited with her family soon. In moments she was fast asleep.

By the early hours of the morning the temperature had dropped quite considerably and Janna woke up shivering. She went to get up but jarred her bad ankle and she let out a small shout. She sat up. It was still very dark. She took out some bread and began to chew, wrapping her arms to cradle herself. It would be too cold to try sleeping and she felt as if she'd had sufficient rest, so she decided to walk until the morning brought some warmth; then take a comfortable nap. There were less people on the road at this hour and so it would much easier to travel in this condition, she reasoned.

After several hours she had walked several kilometres. The sun had been up for quite some time and now the air was warm. A refugee warned Janna that the Germans were two days from Warsaw but that would not deter her. She pressed on until she could go no further, finding a place to take a nap. Again, she was asleep within seconds.

Janna slept for three hours and then continued her trek. The ankle was swollen badly and she had to be very careful with it. The throng fleeing from Warsaw was reaching epic proportions. She wondered if her family was amongst them. Ignoring her pain, she got on with it.

By the late afternoon Janna had crossed off another half dozen or so kilometres. Her ankle was throbbing and she stopped for a moment. She asked a couple of men if they knew how far Warsaw was. 'Thirty kilometres,' said one. '...At least,' said the other. 'Maybe forty...'

'No,' said the first one. 'More like thirty.'

'No,' said the other. 'More like forty.'

'No. Thirty! More like thirty!'

Janna nodded her thank you but they did not notice. She walked on, leaving them to their debate. She guessed Warsaw must be about thirty-five kilometres away. In a little while she found a suitable place to put her head down for a few hours. She was exhausted. Clouds moved across the sky but it was still warm. She closed her eyes.

The cool night air caused Janna to wake. The road traffic was only half of what it was earlier and Janna was thankful for that. She marched on through the late evening past midnight and had hobbled her way maybe five or more kilometres closer to her home before collapsing in a heap just off the side of the road. It would be hours before the cold air would awaken her this time.

At dawn Janna rose. People were walking nearby on the road. She rubbed her ankle and it seemed to be getting better. A convoy of military vehicles filed along the roadway heading to the capital.

Janna looked toward Warsaw and saw that there was smoke floating from the distance. She noticed that the people were looking more desperate, more dishevelled, more scared and more burdened with sadness. She set out once again, determined to reach her family by the end of the day.

By midday Janna discovered that she was a little closer than she had realized. She was told that the capital was less than fifteen kilometres away and she could see the continuous smoke billow from it. She could hear explosions.

Janna rested and ate. Then, back to hobbling. But the road was thick with humanity and machines and animals. The tide of the fleeing masses flowed into her like lava.

In the late afternoon she was helped aboard a lorry that had stopped for a moment because of the crowd. She rode on it for about five kilometres but then had to get out. Janna managed to walk for nearly three more hours but had to stop to rest and finish the rest of her food. There wasn't much daylight left. She listened to the explosions and looked up at the sky and saw the German aircraft.

Janna tried to swallow her food as quickly as possible, almost choking: *Must get there.* She stood up and, still chewing, tried to walk on. But her legs felt funny and rubbery, especially the right one. It had taken the brunt of the gruelling walk so as to lighten the load off of her sprained left ankle. She grimaced and tried again but the leg went wobbly and she fell.

Janna was at the outskirts and crawled to the side of a building and sat with her back against it, watching the *unreal* real world around her. She felt dizzy and passed out.

Shells blasting startled Janna and she woke to see brilliant flashes of light from the explosions fill the darkening smoke-filled sky. The body was weak but the mind was willing. She rose to her feet and forced herself to move in the direction that would get her to her family. The streets were filled with all kinds of activities: refugees starting out of the city, civilians trying to go on with their lives, soldiers, firemen and other city helpers, looters, the newly homeless, the previously homeless and many others.

Janna was nearly home.

chapter 3

The two French policemen were on extra high alert this evening. They were told to keep a normal atmosphere while among the public so as not to instill any panic but at the same time be extremely vigilant and watchful of anything that was out of the ordinary. They were at war now and things would be different.

The policemen strolled through the lovely park and watched the people that still were enjoying the dwindling daylight of the warm end-of-summer day. Both of them were tall, thin and dark with small black moustaches and looked like they were twins, even though they weren't.

They turned onto a path and everything seemed normal. Up ahead there were two benches, one on each side of the path. On the left a woman tended to her purse as a young boy about fourteen years old played with a football on the grass nearby. On the bench opposite the woman sat a man who was engrossed in the daily newspaper. They could not see his face and assumed he was probably the woman's husband and child's father.

As the policemen walked past the benches they noticed the headline blaring from the man's newspaper- the same headline that they had seen all day obscuring a population of heads: FRANCE AND BRIT-AIN DECLARE WAR ON GERMANY.

Jack was in Marseille.

He'd told Maria that he would have to turn himself in and face desertion charges. She had not wanted him to go. 'But Maria, we would be running our whole lives. Where would we live? They will find me and take me. If I go in voluntarily I may get a lighter sentence,' he had said.

'We would be together.'

'We *will* be together. Eventually.'

'Non! It is no good. *Non* Good...Do not leave me, Jack.'

'...Maybe you should just forget about me; it will be a few years...'

'Maybe I *should*...' The words had hung in the air like a foreboding dark cloud.

He'd gone to Marseille to turn himself in for a reason. The Legion had offices at both places and Paris would have been the obvious choice being closer. Klauss was Swiss, Jack had thought, and would be heading for Switzerland. Marseille was an obvious point of entry. It was part of his cover story; that he'd tracked Klauss this far but had lost him. After all, Hassef and Jack *had* continued on in the full hope of finding Klauss. But Hassef had said he would return to the Legion and face possible charges for extending their search. And there was the possibility that Hassef had found Klauss, which wouldn't help Jack's somewhat fabricated story because after Marrakech Jack had ran for freedom- albeit first he'd had to honour Lieutenant Bationi's death wish.

But falling in love with Maria had changed his mind. He'd already been in a dilemma about turning himself in simply because he did not like life on the run. Jack loved the freedom but not the price of it.

Freedom at any price? Even conscience?

'It would be like a lifetime,' she had said in reference to the wait.

'Maybe less than we think, because of circumstances. The story is a good-'

'It is bad story. They will see it is a lie.'

'Some of it is true...'

'Listen to yourself...'

'I'm sorry, but I couldn't make you live this life with me. I want to give you more.'

'If you care for me, then stay with me. I do not care about all that...that...'

'Will you wait for me?'

'If I have not found a husband by the time you return, then maybe...'

'Fine,' Jack had said sharply. Then calmly he'd added, 'I will come back to you, and if you are married I will just go away.'

'Bon,' Maria had said. 'Goodbye, Jack.'

But things were different now. Jack walked into a park and he felt happy. The sun was setting and there was a slight breeze. He was on his way to the station at Marseille to catch a train. A train that would take him to Maria; he'd changed his mind.

Fuck honour. Honour doesn't keep you warm at night.

He'd already written her three days prior and told her he'd be coming back; he hoped she'd received the letter by now and was expecting him. He *really* hoped that she was no longer angry with him.

Jack had a spring in his step and the park seemed so green and pretty and the rays of the sunset sliced reddish colours out from the trees. The lush grass carpeted vast areas of the park. He walked along the path and came to a fork of which both ways lead to the station on the other end of the park. He chose the right turning.

Up ahead he noticed a couple of benches; it would have been a nice place to stop and have a cigarette but both benches were occupied and besides, Jack had things to do and places to go...and someone to see.

The setting sun shined into his eyes as he walked toward the benches and he closed them a moment as he walked along. He felt a little blissful. He passed by the benches and moved along the curving path up a slight incline.

Jack was thinking about Maria; he wanted to do something special for her but could not come up with anything. She would be glad to see him; but then again- *what if she wasn't?* Suddenly, the thought made him anxious and that made him quicken his already lively pace. He was up the rise and moving along the path at the crest of the hill when another thought hit him; *what if she did not want to see him anymore?* He started to worry, doubling his walking speed. Then-

Jack stopped abruptly; he hadn't been paying attention. His stop lasted less than a tenth of a second- he quickly continued as though he had never halted- but it was noticeable. He tried to avert his eyes casually and move normally but the policemen had been watching Jack walk up the path. They'd seen him slow and both had seen his eyes full of fear- if only just for an instant. Jack tried his best to stroll nonchalantly past the policemen but they both moved in front of him and stopped. It was too late to run.

'Your papers, Monsieur?'

Jack was done for. He looked at the ground: *How could I be so god-damned stupid?*

The hearing had gone well for Klauss. He'd received a slap on the hand for his 'mishaps' in Algeria thanks largely to support from his SS superiors. *Nice to have friends in high places*. The downside was that he'd been relegated to routine espionage duties such as straight reconnaissance and the like, observing port activity and watching the main station here in Marseille.

But his standing was still surprisingly high within the organization, mainly due to having a few very influential officers on his side who shared his passion and zeal. Klauss's hatred for the French was well-known and in some circles well-respected and now was a good time to have that quality, for the two countries were at war.

The demotion of duties was to appease the Abwehr's more mainstream superiors but there were some within the Schutzstaffel who had bigger plans for Klauss Gelfroher.

Today Klauss had been a well-dressed businessman watching the station and the area around it, and it'd been a long day. The daylight had been disappearing fast when he'd suddenly felt very hungry. Tonight he would treat himself to a nice restaurant as he was already dressed for the occasion. He had plenty of cash.

Klauss had scratched the nicely trimmed beard he'd grown and had decided to go to the Le Coq d'Or restaurant; there was a short cut to it through the park. As he'd been walking along a park path he'd seen two policemen in the distance walking in his direction. Klauss quickly sat down at a bench across from a woman and her son and buried himself in a newspaper.

In less than two minutes they'd already passed him and then he'd watched them walk up the tiny hill and stop at the crest.

A man had walked past Klauss but Klauss had been squinting through the sun's glare at the crest where the policemen had stopped and did not take notice of the walker.

Klauss had gone back to his newspaper. He'd thought about the following day- tomorrow- when he would be observing the docks and be disguised as a painter. He would be wearing a long overcoat and a beret. He would have the paint and the canvas and the easel. Klauss was not a good painter but he could do well enough to pass for a well-intended enthusiast. But it would be the last time that he would use that cover; France and Germany were at war now and painting docks would no doubt draw suspicion.

He'd looked at the woman across from him and had seen that she'd communicated with her son using a kind of sign language, concluding that the boy must be deaf. Pretending to straighten his tie, Klauss had glanced up at the crest to give one last look before he'd leave for the restaurant when he'd noticed the man who had passed by a minute earlier reach the crest of the hill where the two policemen had still stood.

Moments later, Klauss had realized that the police were stopping the man.

And now Klauss was watching them arrest the man and take him away. The German spy rose from the bench and briskly walked off in the opposite direction. There was food to eat.

chapter 4

It was after sunset when Janna entered through the front door of her house; she'd finally made it. She called out, 'Dimi?' There was nobody home. She looked around briefly and then went to the neighbour's house, dropping her walking stick. She did not bother picking it up; she felt she could move faster now by limping on her left foot.

There was no one home at the neighbour's either. She wondered whether there had been a note left at the house. If Dimi had left one then surely it would have been in plain sight. She decided not to waste time looking and headed for her parents' house, only a few streets away.

Explosions thundered and Janna glanced up at the grey sky and saw that it was filled with aircraft: German aircraft; the Luftwaffe.

Bombers.

The bomb doors opened and Warsaw screamed.

The bombs were getting louder and that meant closer. Janna limped as fast as she could go without losing her balance. She rounded the corner and heard a building nearby get hit by a bomb. The sound was deafening. People were running out of buildings and houses screaming at the terror. The German planes were also dropping incendiary bombs which spread fire throughout the ravished city. Janna hopped, limped and skipped down the street through all this in her ripped, torn and bloody clothes. A row of houses on her left were burning and more people were crying out.

She came to the next corner and turned right, screaming when yet another bomb exploded nearby. She fell. A man holding a rifle helped her up and then ran off. He did not look like a soldier, she thought as she tested her ankle. The streets were dusty and smoke filled the air. The roar of the explosions was tremendous. Janna kept going.

She made it to the next street and went left. Her parents' house was now visible. She quickened her pace, her eyes wide with fright and anticipation. *They must be there!* The bombs crashed all around her and she stumbled, falling to her hands and knees. This caused fresh new cuts and opened old ones but at least she wasn't hit by any of the falling debris that tumbled around her. On all fours, she gave a quick glance over at her mother and father's home as she moved to stand up. Incredibly, at that moment a bomb roared into the house and exploded.

No. It cannot be. She froze, refusing to believe what she had just seen.

Then, running out from the burning house was her husband. He was on fire. Janna overcame her shock and ran to him, not noticing the pain in her ankle. She watched him roll to the ground and could hear him screaming horribly. She called out to him, 'Dimi!'

He was no longer on fire. Janna made it to his side and sat on the ground with him and held him; she could see he was suffering. 'Oh, Dimi,' she said. 'No.'

His eyes met his wife's. He raised an arm feebly and pointed to the house. Janna told him, 'I will be right back.' She ran to the door but the flames chased her out. As she moved to the side of the building she looked through a smashed window. *There must be a way in.* The front of the house was engulfed in flames.

Janna hopped around to a side window and smashed it. It was the toilet window and there seemed to be no flames coming through. She went to climb through but a ceiling beam gave way and swung down, part of it catching her on the arm. It burned her and she let out a piercing scream. Janna screamed out for her children. 'Anja! Stanis!'

She quickly went to the next window and looked into the bedroom. The room was in flames and there would be no way in through that window. But just as Janna was about to look for another way into the house the wind changed direction inside and she could see to her utmost horror the burning corpses of her parents and her children huddled on the bedroom floor. She stared at the scene and let the reality soak in: entering hell was never easy. *Dimi!*

Janna ran back to her husband. He was barely alive and in great pain. She sat holding him, cradling him. She told him he would be alright but moments later he was dead...

She looked up to the sky and screamed.

The bombing subsided and after more tears than any mother should ever have to endure Janna had no option but to leave her family, heading back to her home to gather some things. She did not want to stay here any longer, though she had no idea of where she would go. The Germans would soon overrun the whole country. Her grandparents' area had already been attacked from what she'd heard but where else could she go? And her two sisters had both married German men, one of whom was a soldier, and lived near the Rhine.

Grabbing a few clothes and items, such as a knife and a pen, she set them down by the door ready. Janna washed up in the bath and tended to her wounds. In the kitchen she ate whatever food she found.

Several houses nearby were burning. It would not be safe to stay too long but she decided to spend the night here in her home.

At daybreak Janna set out from the house. There would be no reason to stay; there was nothing left. She'd decided to head back to her grandparents in the south; they were her only real family left. She hoped they were alright.

Janna walked down the streets of the city where she had lived her entire life and watched it turn into floating ash.

Warsaw burned; a deep scar left by the Nazi branding iron.

The house was very large; in fact, it was a mansion. It was not far from the main road that led to Coventry but it was secluded. It perched atop a small hill that overlooked a farming community nestled along the river. It was dark. Rain fell down from the grey-black clouds, dousing the roof incessantly. Silver on display in the dining area watched silently as raindrops pelted the windows. Paintings on the wall came alive with each flash of lightning. The thunder shook the china.

The owners were away.

A key slotted into the front door. It turned. The door opened. It was the caretaker and his wife. They had a separate dwelling nearby. The caretaker was to keep an eye on the house as well as the property while their employer was away on family emergency.

It was late and he had gone outside his home to empty his bladder when he'd heard some suspicious noises. He had told his wife, who'd insisted on following him to the house.

The caretaker slowly entered the hallway. He lit a candle with a match and the hallway brightened, the darkness ebbing away down the hall and retreating into the doorways of the adjoining rooms.

Oriental rugs covered pine floors. It was beautiful. There was only the sound of the rain and occasional thunder. The doorway to the right lead to the study; to the left was the dining area that opened up to the lounge. Down the hall there were other doorways which lead to guest-rooms, a staircase and further on the left another entrance to the lounge. There was no electric light; the light bulb hadn't been invented.

The caretaker turned to his wife. 'Stay here,' he whispered. But she shook her head. He didn't like the looks of this. He whispered again. 'I may need a weapon. Let's go back.'

She nodded; then whispered, 'We must get help from the village.'

'There is not enough time, lass. Also, we do not know if anyone is, indeed, here.'

Suddenly, there was the unmistakable sound of broken glass.

Now they knew there was someone there. And there was no time. The caretaker ran toward the end of the hall. His wife gasped, 'No!'

The caretaker shouted into the darkness, 'Stop!' He heard shuffling, then a wooden bang. The French doors! He knew where the intruders were; a display room off one end of the lounge. It was completely dark. His wife was running down the hall after him, pleading with him to stop. He passed the stairway and entered the lounge.

The darkness stopped him. For an instant he was blind; it was pitch black in front of him. His wife came up behind him, stopping in the doorway; her silhouette faint against the hall candles.

Their ears strained. They listened. They heard nothing. Their eyes began to adjust.

And then, lightning. Light bathed the room and the caretaker and his wife saw the French doors wide open; but there was nobody in sight. The thunder roared.

The caretaker sighed. His wife sobbed silently, from relief.

Another flash of lightning illuminated the room. This time the caretaker noticed many items missing in the display room. The thunder rumbled. He lit some candles and then they ran over to a field shed where there was a rifle.

He would have to take inventory but first he had to take his wife down to the village where she'd be safe; then seek assistance. He knew he could not pursue the burglars without help in these conditions.

Tomorrow, the caretaker would somehow have to arrange for a telegraph to be sent to his employer. There was a telegraph office in nearby Coventry.

The road from Warsaw was even more crowded as Janna hobbled along with her new walking crutch, holding a sack with her few possessions. The ankle was still swollen and damaged, but to what extent she did not know. However; she felt it seemed to be getting a little better. It had been several days since she had left her home in the capital.

She had a cloth wrapped around the upper part of her right arm that covered the burn she received at her parents' house when the beam fell. She had cleaned it well, and kept it clean, and was thankful that there were no signs of infection and that it was healing slowly but surely. Janna had only made it to the town of Wodzke and had left the flat land behind at Rodem. She was back in the hills. The refugees were heading in both directions and military vehicles also sped both north and south. Many people were stopping and reversing directions. Here at Wodzke the majority of people were turning around and heading back north but Janna kept on moving southward to her grandparents' home near Miekow.

The word was that Krakow was in German hands and their southern army was moving toward L'vov in the east and to Warsaw in the north.

Straight into Janna.

Stubbornly, she trod on and it wasn't long before she heard explosions. But she kept walking; toward the shells.

The explosions became louder. The fleeing civilians before her were moving quickly; they were panic stricken and running for their lives. Behind Janna a transport truck came barrelling along. She hobbled forward, ignoring the rumblings in her stomach.

She was nearly knocked over by a running man and with all the chaos around her at this moment she wondered if now would be a good time to rest. She was down to crusts and crumbs and had no water. Janna was dehydrating and as she moved along slowly and watched the madness she closed her mind and shut out the world, walking as though in a trance.

Her eyes watched the transport truck roll down the road but Janna was not thinking about that. Her mind had floated to a cloud-like place where she was gently urged to sleep: Peaceful.

But her trance was broken into tiny pieces when a shell smashed into the transport truck and exploded, sending metal and limbs flying.

Another shell exploded nearby and Janna was finally beginning to think that trying to reach her grandmother and grandfather would be an impossible task. The Germans were closer than she had thought. However, she pressed onward south with the idea that she would walk east at the first opportunity and then at some point go south with the hope that she could still make it to her grandparents'.

Janna found she was going against the flow of the crowd once again and though jarred many times, did not fall. She hobbled up to the next curve, just beyond the smoking and wrecked transport truck, and halted. Her heart stopped. Up ahead German troops and vehicles were moving up the road. Now the heart pounded. She hopped carefully but quickly off the roadway and into some bushes. Janna lied down in a foetal position and tried to calm herself down.

It was impossible to relax for even a millisecond; people ran by her yelling and screaming and shouting. Janna felt that at any moment other people would join her in the bushes. Would she be glad? She did not know. There were refugees scattering into the hills.

Janna just wanted it to all go away. It was all just a bad dream and now it was time to wake up. Her mind attempted to wander: birds, flowers, trees in the wind, butterflies...burning houses, burnt flesh, her husband, her...*Oh God in heaven make it stop!*

The sounds of the hysterical fleeing masses had quieted some on the road; the German soldiers were getting close. Janna strained her neck to get a glimpse through the bush. She reached an arm through the branches and pushed one aside slowly. She nearly fainted.

The gray-uniformed troops of the Wermacht were upon her and she could see their faces and even their eyes. The source of the rumbling sound and vibration she had become aware of exposed itself: Two German tanks fifty metres down the road.

Her heart sank. She let go of the branch and curled into a ball and closed her eyes. Janna listened to the troops footsteps as they marched by and it wasn't long before the tanks passed by her. Then the tank stopped. Her heart pounded so fiercely that she thought it might explode: *Surely they weren't stopping for me!*

Far in the distance there were explosions. A turret swiveled its head and then a metal hatch clanked. Janna opened an eye but couldn't see anything. A moment later there were voices by the tanks. The temptation to get up and run and scream was great but there was no use in that, she reasoned to herself. Besides, she couldn't run anyhow. *What I am going to do?*

Lie still. What else could she do?

After several minutes the tanks moved on. Janna was only slightly relieved; the troops were still filing by.

Just as she was starting to get somewhat used to the abysmal scenario, feeling a small reprieve as it were, a German voice suddenly grew in volume. Janna could hear footsteps moving in her direction. *I've been seen!* She fought back the urge to scream, her eyes bulged and she wanted to tilt her head back to get a look.

The German soldier was almost on her and still moving. *Is he going to shoot me?* She began to slowly roll her head back. She peered through the branches just as the soldier came to a halt. She could see him; he was looking straight at her.

Or was he?

He pulled out his penis and after a moment began to urinate. His gaze moved to the north and then to the sky. He hadn't seen her. She watched him finish and then shake the dribble off. The soldier went back to the road.

Janna sighed relief, curled back into a ball and closed her eyes.

The whole evening German troops, motorcycles, military vehicles and the occasional tank passed by Janna. There were times when the road possibly was clear enough for Janna to head for the hills to the east but she had not mustered up the courage to attempt it. *They wouldn't shoot me, would they? A fleeing, unarmed and wounded civilian...*

The evening turned into night and though her heart pounded mercilessly most of the time she, at one point, amazingly fell asleep for a few hours.

The sun's distant glow announced the day's arrival. Janna opened her eyes groggily and took a moment to wake up. She looked around and listened; there were birds chirping. Had it all been a dream? She pushed branches aside and peered out at the road. It was empty.

Her limbs were sore, her muscles stiff. But maybe now was the time to try getting away from the bush. She moved her arms so as to position herself to rise up. But...

Her ears picked up a sound. *Was it?* Yes, more troops.

Janna cursed beneath her breath; she would have to wait. It would be hard to spend another day here in the bush, she thought. But for now there was nothing she could do.

Janna wondered where she could go if not to her grandparents. Though Dimi's parents were both dead, his mother had been Greek and he had family in Greece. She did not know any of the names or where they lived, however, so it would be impossible to find them. Still, Janna knew that Poland and Greece were close allies and maybe it would be a safe place to go. All that she knew about Greece, really, was that they grew olives and that it was very warm.

Janna would still try and make it to Miekow from the east but she wasn't very optimistic about her chances. She rubbed her thighs and calves and continued to wait in the bush.

At around mid-morning there was a noticeable pause in the noise so Janna stretched out and looked up to the road. A few troops were walking along silently. She sighed. Something light and tickly flew up her nose and it caused her to sneeze; a muffled sneeze. She froze.

Footsteps... Voices...

'Was machen Sie?' *What are you doing?*

'Ich habe etwas gehort.' *I heard something.*

The footsteps shuffled next to the bush that Janna was under. The soldier was squatting down and peered in through the branches and leaves. His eyes locked with Janna's; her's as large as the moon. She peed herself a little and felt as though her head would explode. They stared at each other. A voice from behind him asked, 'Was ist es?' *What is it?*

'Es ist ein Verwundeter Hund...' *It's a wounded dog...*

'Stellen Sie es aus Schmerz.' *Put it out of pain.*

Janna and the soldier still watched each other. Then the German, pale and blonde with blue eyes, told his fellow soldier, 'Nein. Es Ist nicht Verwundeter.' *No, it is not wounded.* He smiled at Janna, only briefly, and took out a small tin. 'Es ist nur eschrocken.' *It is just scared.* He poured water into the tin and held it forward and placed it in the bush a ways, toward Janna. 'Ich werde ihm Wasser geben.' *I will give it water.*

Janna could not believe it. She made eye contact one more time and mouthed the word *Dzieke*, though she remembered right afterward that the German word for thank you was *Danke.* A moment later he was gone.

Janna pulled the tin carefully toward her and savoured every single sip.

It was noon before the road had cleared significantly enough for Janna to gather up the courage to move on. She rose stiffly from the bush and looked all around. She propped up on her crutch and clutched her bag and then hobbled across the road, making her way into the hills. Janna ducked and hid when she needed to and after several minutes she found herself walking alone down a dirt path heading east. She finally gave up the thought of making it to her grandparents.

Her destination was Greece, though Janna did not know how she would get there. At the moment, food and water were her top priorities. Far down this path she could see a house and headed for it.

Her stomach rumbled and her legs stumbled but soon Janna was at the door, knocking. There was no answer. It was abandoned or at least appeared to be. She moved around to the back of the house, a rustic old cottage, and there didn't seem to be anyone around. The back door was locked. Janna found a rock and, after pausing and looking around, smashed it through a window. After knocking out all the glass with a small broom, she carefully climbed through. It was quite difficult but Janna made it in, enduring a few small cuts.

She called out but there was nobody there.

In the kitchen Janna found very little food left in the cupboards; in fact, almost nothing. To be precise, there was a half empty- *half full?* jar of blackberry jam. She used a spoon to scoop it out and eat.

Janna moved to the next room and settled into the most comfortable chair and sat spooning her jar. Her eyes began to feel heavy. Exhaustion overcame her and brought sleep.

It wasn't long before her rest was interrupted; she was shaken from it when someone shouted from outside. Janna bolted upright and, still holding her jam jar, hopped quickly to the window. There was a young boy running toward the house and at least two adult men calling after him. She grabbed her crutch and her bag, putting the jam jar in it, and headed for the back door. Janna pulled the latch, went out through the door discreetly and hobbled over to some trees. She wasn't seen.

The men did not seem dangerous, thought Janna, though they did not seem particularly trustworthy either. She waited in the trees, eating out of the jar with her fingers. She had left the spoon indoors.

The strangers stayed in the house until nightfall and then they left; it was not their home.

Janna watched them leave and then went back to the house. This time, she simply walked in through the door.

The night was warm. Janna lay down on the bed and went to sleep.

chapter 5

Lunch was over.

The student walked through the doorway and moved to his right toward the back of the classroom. He picked a desk and sat down. He still had three minutes to go before class would start. He glanced to and fro at the incoming surge of his new classmates as they filed in through the door. The teacher faced the chalkboard, writing her name: Mrs. Evans.

The student reflected: first day of a new school; first day of college. It was nearly over. The clock on the wall showed two minutes before one o'clock.

The previous evening he'd had dinner with his mother and father at the Delgado Hotel, where his parents had booked a room for the night. The three of them had had a wonderful time eating an amazing meal at an expensive restaurant and they'd had drinks- Bloody Mary's- in the bar afterward. They'd given him money. They had told him that they loved him. They'd announced that they would be going to Europe and the Middle East for a visit that would last about two months. And that they were leaving for the airport back in New York mid-morning to-morrow in the rental car.

And his parents had told him that they were proud of him.

He was thinking of that now. It made him feel good.

He remembered waving goodbye to them as they stood smiling, waving back from the hotel entrance steps as he drifted away in the back seat of a yellow taxi-cab.

He started to realize that he'd never been away from his mom and dad for that long. He would not be seeing them again until about Thanksgiving. Suddenly he felt alone.

Oh, well, he thought. They're proud of me.

He snapped out of it- his momentary daydream. Then, he noticed that the classroom had hushed to whispers, then silence. Some students stared at the teacher, awaiting instruction. Some looked nervously down at their desk or the floor or at the wall. Some looked at each other. One, who seemed angry to be there, looked uninterested out the window. A student, embarrassed, rushed into the room; thirty seconds late for class. The teacher motioned him to close the door and he did.

The teacher had gray hair, cropped short. Her wrinkling face looked hard, but kind.

'Hello, class. I am Mrs Evans. Ancient History 01.'

There were a murmur of hellos from the students; the class clown made a stake for his claim early, muttering something about ancient history. Nobody laughed, though.

It wasn't high school anymore. This was college- University! *This was serious. This was life.*

The clown- his desk dead center of the room- felt foolish and, somehow, somewhat betrayed. That would've worked last year! It would've been funny!

The silence was only moments long but the entire classroom felt awkward. Almost happily, the teacher said, 'Oh, that old one.' Then she smiled. The students chuckled. Most had even caught the ironic humour of her reply.

The proud one did. He thought: Yes, I am here with like-minded individuals. Quick, witty, intelligent, even-balanced; wisecracks and pranks had been left to distant echoes in the corridors of high school. Irony and witticisms and intellectuality were now the order of the day.

Mrs Evans spoke. 'OK, first let me read out the names to see who's

131

here.' She glanced up and scanned the unfamiliar faces. The only one she recognized was the smart aleck from moments before. He sat quietly, looking slightly glum. Overall, they seemed to be a nice array of kids, she thought.

The teacher looked down at her class sheet and started roll-call. She called out, *'Gregory Adams...Greg?'* She glanced right, then left. On the left she saw a hand raised. After a pause she said, *'Like this: "Adams?" then, "Here." OK?'* Her eyes went back down to the sheet and she read the next name. *'Lori Browne?'*

A girl in the front row smiled cheerily and chirped, *'Here!'*

'Thank you, Miss Browne,' said Mrs Evans. She continued. *'Alice Bunning...'*

'Here.'

'Mike Cardenas...'

A hand rose from the back. *'Here.'*

'John Carroll...' She waited a moment, looking around. *'Jonathan Carroll?'*

'Yeah. Here.'

'Marilyn Daley?'

'Here.' Catching sight of the blonde bombshell, the proud one could almost hear imaginary wolf-whistles. *Wow! What a dish!*

He watched the roll-call, attaching the names to the faces and placing them to his memory.

'Samantha Grant...'

'Here.'

A sound: Feet running.

The proud one was sat near the door so he had seen the quick motion to his left, someone flashing by the windows and then stopping to open the door. At first he assumed it was somebody else late for class.

The runner, a young woman, paused for a moment as she looked at the classroom- but quickly averted her eyes away. She walked somberly toward the teacher.

Mrs Evans had stopped roll-call and was looking at the woman with a hint of puzzlement. *'Gertrude?'* she asked. Gertrude was one of the receptionists.

The class watched as Gertrude approached the teacher. She moved closer and leaned her head to Mrs Evans' ear, whispering something. The class shifted and shuffled nervously as the mood had now *changed. Gertrude had brought with her a kind of darkness; a kind of gloom.*

Mrs Evans looked sad. She stole a look at the class, then back to Gertrude. She nodded and Gertrude left the classroom, taking one last quick look at the students. She looked sad, also.

The comedian wanted to lighten up the mood by saying, 'Geez, who was that? The grim reaper?' but he'd already learnt his first college lesson. Instead, he folded his arms and said nothing. He turned to Mrs Evans; she had started to speak.

'Um, I'm very sorry...' She paused. She looked around at the faces but only the male ones. She continued, speaking slowly. 'Would Massy-'

The proud one's heart sank. Me?

This was not good. No, not good. She sounded underwater: something-something. Then he made out, '...please come forward.'

His legs felt weak as he rose from his desk chair. The teacher's face wore a grave expression. Not good. Not good! He felt himself trembling.

He forced his legs to transport him to the front of the class: To Mrs Evans; to something he did not want to hear. Not good!

He stood in front of the teacher. He looked at her. She looked as though...as though she wanted to cry? Not good! She leaned toward him, gently placing her right hand on his shoulder.

Quietly, Mrs Evans told him, 'You must go to the principal's office immediately.' Then she added, ' It's your parents...'

Not good! 'What? What is it?' he cried out, loud enough for everyone to hear. She shook her head.

'You must go,' she said, dropping her hand from his shoulder.

He ran. He grabbed the handle and flew out the doorway and into the hall. Mrs Evans listened until she could no longer hear his footsteps echoing down the hallway.

The teacher turned and faced the somber room. She continued roll-call. She softly called out, 'Brian Harrison?'

'Here.'

As the Rhode Island police officer spoke you could have thrown a brick at the proud one and he would not have noticed: 'parents', 'car crash', 'killed'. These were words that when put together were NOT GOOD!

133

He thought maybe it was a dream; no, not a dream- a nightmare.

Finally, the numbness began to subside. It was all real: It was Not Good. Tears started to well in his eyes. His face began to distort into a morph of wrack and grief and he could hear the policeman saying, 'I am sorry, son. You'll have to come with me to make a formal identification.'

Massy dropped to the floor in a heap, sobbing uncontrollably.

The officer moved forward and placed a hand on top of the young man's head. He said sympathetically, 'I'm sorry, son.' He didn't know what else to say.

Massy struggled to speak through his gasping sobs: 'But they...were...proud of me...'

chapter 6

It was just over a week later when Janna arrived at the Dneister River, which she'd been told was the best route to Greece. She had boarded a river barge and now sat among a boatful of civilians and soldiers tending to her thoughts and her wounds. The burn was healing nicely and the ankle was getting slowly better. Her mind was full of relief-she had been clear of the terror for days- and sadness; she would most likely never see her grandparents again. Her family was gone.

The Polish army themselves were headed for Greece. It was their ordered destination as they were in retreat from not just one, but two strong armies. A couple of days before, Russia had invaded Poland from the east. It was a mystery to Janna as to why these two powerful nations- Germany and Russia- would want to destroy her homeland.

The battle for Poland was over. The Polish government went into exile. Her country was being left for the Germans and Russians to divide amongst themselves.

She overheard some people nearby saying the Russians were on their way to the Dneister but it did not bother her. Janna didn't much care. She was alone and on her way to a strange land where she would not understand the language.

The barge slowly drifted along the Dneister toward the Black Sea peacefully and without incident. There had been no sign of the Russians. Janna had been given some bread and a small piece of cheese by the couple next to her for which she'd been extremely thankful. She gained some comfort in the knowledge that there would be other Polish refugees going to Greece.

The river was calm as it carried the boat gently onward.

Finally, quite some time later, the barge had reached the Black Sea where there were British transport freighters waiting for the Polish army. There were many other British ships in the area, Janna saw. The Russians were not at war with Great Britain; the retreating Polish army was temporarily safe. She watched the Polish soldiers embarking the transports. She'd asked a soldier that had helped her climb off the barge if he could tell her the destination of the freighters and he'd told her that they were going to Greece, but that they were for the troops.

Janna hobbled after the soldier and called him as he moved along with his fellow troop to the freighter. He turned around and stopped. She had noticed that he was some sort of officer and when Janna was close enough she said, 'There are no boats for the people to Greece at the moment. Is there a way for me to be on this boat?'

'I am sorry.'

'Podobac sie.' *Please.*

The Polish officer looked at her with pity; yet, there was something about this woman, he thought. She looked so wounded and weak but at the same time he saw a kind of strength. 'Have you ever thought about espionage?'

Janna hadn't and just looked back at him blankly.

'You see, maybe I could make an exception..,' he told her.

Janna had gone out onto the deck of the freighter and was looking out at the exotic horizon that was before her. She was beginning to get enough of her strength back so as to allow her to start formulating a plan. As it was, she was travelling on this vessel under the guise of being an agent for the Polish military- albeit in a somewhat rudimentary fashion- and was feeling extremely fortunate. The officer had asked her to seriously consider contacting the Polish Embassy in Athens about joining the Polish military intelligence or maybe even the resistant movement that was already being discussed by civilians and soldiers alike.

There was so much to consider; she had to make a new life- survive and make the best of it. The warm breeze lifted her hair.

The British freighter had travelled through the Black Sea and had passed by the ancient city of Constantinople- now called Istanbul- and into the Sea of Marmara. It was a hot day and Janna felt physically well for the first time since that morning she'd left her grandparents' house. The coastline of Turkey was easily visible and she enjoyed the view, tilting her head at the sun and basking in its heat. The reflection of the sun bounced brightly off the water's surface.

A few metres away from Janna three soldiers were having a conversation and one was pointing. He remarked that somewhere not so far in the distance laid the ancient city of Troy and that the ship would later pass by near it. They all seemed to be duly impressed, she noticed, thinking: Troy must have been an important place; she'd never heard of it. Janna went back to her musing; there was much to think about.

The Greece bound transport slashed through the Strait of Dardanelles and soon would be entering the Aegean Sea. There was some anxiety aboard the ship because there was the strong possibility that German ships or U-boats were prowling the waters but it was somewhat neutralized by the calm sea, gentle breeze and strong sunbeams.

The respite allowed her thoughts to flow and she realized that some of the sadness was going away but in a strange way she didn't want it to leave because Janna felt that was akin to forgetting and she did not want to forget her family. However, the void would be replaced; first by fear and then anger: and then by hate. Janna was never the type to harbour hatred but she would soon be building her own private port; for in that moment she'd decided to go straight to the Polish Embassy in Athens and offer her services to the military. She was determined to become an agent; Janna was going to be a spy.

The ship was heading for the Greek peninsula of Khalkidhiki, near the city of Thessaloniki, and there the troops would disembark. Then, the British freighter would turn around and return through the Black Sea to the mouth of the Dneister to pick up more Polish soldiers.

Janna had found out that there was a good chance that trains would be going from Thessaloniki to Athens. Good news, except she'd realized she had only a few coins of Polish currency.

The British transport exited out of the narrow strait; it wouldn't be long now- only a matter of several hours- before the retreating Polish soldiers and Janna arrived at the port of Stavros in the Gulf of Strimon. Troy silently waved goodbye.

chapter 7

It was Massy's fifth beer. He was looking for oblivion and he'd found the directions in a bottle of cheap Scotch and a six-pack. His bespectacled room-mate, Ken, was on the couch eating corn chips. The small two-bedroom apartment living room was lit by a single bulb that hung from the middle of the room. The wallpaper was drab and peeling. The carpet was bland and stained, and the bedrooms were damp and cramped. They both thought it was great.

Ken said, 'You're drinking a lot...'

'...Yeah.'

'I'm only on my third beer. You're on, what, you're fifth? And you're drinking whisky.'

Massy went silent. He was sitting on a chair by the cheap wooden dining table. He reached over and raised his can and took a long gulp, then put the can down. 'Yeah.'

Ken stopped crunching and put the yellow bag of chips down. He asked, 'Everything okay?'

'Hmm, well...' Massy paused; then said, 'I might as well say; it's the "anniversary".'

'Anniversary?'

'You know; to the day. The car crash...'

'Oh, Jesus. Your parents...'

'Yeah.'

'Last year exactly?'

'Yeah.'

'Now I understand the whisky. Not your usual taste.'

'It's my drink for sorrow,' said Massy. He swigged from the bottle of Scotch and his face twisted momentarily. He looked at his room-mate and managed a very weak smile. 'Tastes like shit.'

Ken chuckled softly. 'You wanna play cards? Poker?'

'No. Thanks.' They both looked up when there was a knock at the door. Ken got off the couch and went over to open it. Standing in the doorway was Larry, a long-haired drop-out from Boston College who lived in one of the apartments.

'Hey, man. You guys doin' anything?'

'Nothing special. Drinking...'

'You feel like smokin'?'

Ken looked over at Massy and said, 'Uhhh...' He was really asking his saddened room-mate if he felt like having anyone around.

Massy said, 'Nah, I don't mind.' Ken moved aside and Larry walked in and sat on a chair by the table, across from Massy. Larry put down an album, face up. It was the Beatles most recent effort: Sgt. Pepper's Lonely Hearts Club Band.

'Look what I brought over,' Larry said.

Ken looked over as he slumped into the couch's soft cushions. 'Yeah, put it on.'

'Did you guys change that needle on the stereo?'

'Yeah, as a matter of fact, I did,' said Ken as he watched Larry take the record out and lean over to the stereo. 'I've only heard a few of the songs from that album...'

'Oh, man, it's fantastic. What about you, Massy, have you heard this record?'

'I'd rather hear the Supremes or the Temptations...'

'Man, you and that Motown stuff. Do you hate the Beatles?'

'I don't hate them.'

'Yeah, Larry,' Ken piped up. 'Not everybody thinks the Beatles are Olympian gods. Listen to Pet Sounds; that's pop music genius on a par to John and Paul.'

'Oh, man. The Beach Boys? West Coast warblers. You ever surf, man?'

'Yeah, funny. Okay, you win; all hail the Fab Four.'

'No, I mean it, man. This album is...it has some powerful stuff. Some really good songs. Just listen...' Larry turned up the volume and the needle found the record grooves. The song began and Larry pulled out a bag of marijuana and he started rolling a joint.

Massy drained his beer and walked over to the refrigerator and grabbed a few beers. He handed one to Ken and put another next to Larry , then opened his can and sipped it. He decided to slow his alcohol intake as he was beginning to feel slightly dizzy. And that was before the joint.

Larry spoke after he was done rolling the cigarette. 'This is some really good grass, man. Colombian. How do you guys like this song?' He struck a match and lit the reefer.

Ken listened to the lyrics and then understood the grin on Larry's face that he'd had when he'd asked the question. 'Yeah, I get it, now.

What's the name of the song?'

'"With A Little Help From My Friends".'

Smoke filled the room and they spaced out to the next tune, sitting and staring at the walls while they listened to the psychedelic words of the song. Larry rolled another joint.

They listened to the mood-inducing album mostly in silence, with Ken or Larry expressing the occasional comment. Massy continued to have thoughts about his parents' death; images of the car crash were intertwining with the lyrics that were floating through his mind.

Ken looked over at Larry's brown mane. 'Man, you're hair's getting long,' he said.

Larry turned and replied, 'No, man. You need to grow yours out, man, you look like a marine.'

Massy, who'd hardly uttered a word the whole time, said to Larry, 'Maybe you should grow yours short.' He had a sheepish grin on his face.

After a moment, Larry fell about laughing. He started coughing and leaned over, still laughing. His eyes watered and he put up his hand. Smiling through the coughs, Larry said, 'That's funny, man. The thought of your hair growing back into your head...how would it feel, man?' His laughs subsided and he stopped coughing. Then he realized, 'Shit, man. Why did I think that was so funny? Man, I told you guys, this is some good shit.'

Massy sipped his beer and went back to gazing down at the table top. After awhile Larry looked at him and said, 'So, man, how come you're not knee-deep in ancient maps? You seem kinda glum, man.' Massy didn't say anything, just stared at the table blankly. Larry continued, 'Heavy music, man...'

Ken explained. 'No, it's, uh.., his parent's accident was a year ago today.'

'Oh, shit,' Larry said, turning to Massy. 'Sorry, man.' Massy gave a slow nod in acknowledgement.

Nobody said anything for awhile. They just listened to the music and sipped at their beers in a manner that denoted a kind of respect; a minute's silence.

Massy unscrewed the lid off his whisky bottle and swigged the distilled spirit. He offered the bottle to Larry and Ken but they both declined. That's okay, thought Massy. His head was spinning. Finally,

Larry spoke. 'Well, hey, the Sox are in there this year, eh? Jesus; fucking Yaz...he's unstoppable, man. And Lonborg, George Scott...'

Ken added, 'Joe Foy; Conigliaro...'

'...Reggie Smith; Wyatt,' said Larry. He and Ken waited for Massy to join in.

Massy muttered, 'The Sox need a lefty who can keep the ball down...'

'C'mon, Mass,' said Ken. 'Me and Larry both know you want the Red Sox to win the World Series; even more than us. And you're from New York.'

'Okay.' Massy paused, resigning himself to the mild tomfoolery. With a slur he said, 'Petrocelli...'

'Rico!' said Ken.

Larry laughed. 'rrrrrrRico!'

Ken chuckled and said to Massy, 'Yeah, you know what? I'll take a swig of that after all.' Massy handed him the bottle and he raised it. 'Here's to the Sox in '67...and your parents.' He gulped, causing him to cough. Whisky dripped out of his nostril. The other two grinned.

'Was that the door?' Larry asked no one in particular.

'Yeah, I think so,' said Ken. 'It was a pretty quiet knock.'

'Yeah, man..,' Larry said while putting the bag of grass in his pocket. 'Maybe it's the fuzz.'

'You're being paranoid. It's not the cops. Don't freak out, man.' Ken moved to the door and opened it slowly. It was the two college girls who lived a few doors down the hallway in apartment 14. 'Hi Veronica. Hi Rhonda.'

They both smiled and Veronica said, 'Hi, Ken. I just wanted to return this book; thanks.'

'Oh. Yeah, thanks.'

Rhonda was peering through the doorway and waving at Larry and Massy. Massy put his hand up and drowsily smiled. Veronica said, 'It was good.' Then she looked inside the apartment. 'Hi Massy. Hi Larry.' She turned to Ken. 'Bye. And thanks again.' Rhonda, still smiling, waved slowly as the two girls left. Ken closed the door.

'You gonna ask her out?'

'No, Larry,' said Ken. 'I mean; she's just a friend...and she's two years older.'

'So? I think she likes you, man.'

'No. But I think Rhonda likes Massy.'

'Yeah, man. I wish she liked me,' said Larry, glancing at Massy. 'But I don't stand a chance against pretty boy here.' Massy stayed quiet and drank from his can. 'Massy, you should ask her to go on one of your adventure digs, I mean- expeditions. I bet she'd like Europe. Forget about Turkey, though, man.'

Massy broke his creeping melancholy. 'Maybe...'

'Maybe? That Rhonda's a good-looking chick, man.'

Larry rolled another joint and the boys listened to the songs. They smoked the Colombian and soon the album was coming to the end. Larry leapt up from his chair and moved quickly to the record player. He said, 'Oh, man, this is the last song. It's the best song they've ever done!'

Massy inhaled deeply. Larry sat down. Ken drained his can and took a hit from the joint, smoke drifting over his eyeglasses. They all listened closely as the haunting piano of the song's intro filled the atmosphere.

Then, midway through the first verses, Massy started to sob- but only for an instant. He fought it off but the action was noticed by Larry and Ken.

Larry asked, 'What's goin' on?'

'He's crying, you idiot.'

Massy wanted to say 'No, I am not crying' but he was too busy not crying.

Larry looked at Ken wearing a confused expression. Ken said, 'The lyrics, man; a car crash? Christ...'

'Look, Massy, I'm really sorry, man. I wasn't thinking.'

'It's not your fault. Forget it.'

The early morning crisp mountain air blew over the rocks that surrounded the cave's opening. Several metres inside a beam of artificial light stabbed through the darkness.

It was late summer, 1968 and Massy was on his fifth expedition. The first one had been to Ala Dag in eastern Turkey during the spring break of his freshman year. Then in the summer he'd gone to Mount Olympus. This past spring he'd seen Mount Catria in Italy and in July Mount Vallier in France.

Massy stood in a secluded cave somewhere along the French-Spanish border looking at a gold, and what Massy guessed

141

was silver, box that he'd found only a moment ago. He marvelled at the sight of it. The cave entrance was not far away so he moved toward the faint light and switched the portable battery-powered lamp off. The small box was about the size of a jewellery case, but heavy.

When Massy was in the sunlight- nobody was around for miles- he lifted the lid of the box and saw what was inside. He smiled; the box and its contents would definitely be on the return flight.

Massy was now starting his junior year and generally he felt better about life. His last expedition had been very successful and the work he'd been doing at his inherited home was starting to really show. The house was legally Massy's but he still thought of the property as his parents'. He'd done yard work, painted, changed the doors and many other improvements and soon he would put the house up for sale.

Ken was sitting on the couch. He threw an empty beer can toward the waste-paper basket; it went in. He said: 'Two points! Hey, we're outta beer, Mass.'

'Yeah, I know.'

Ken burped. 'It's your turn to go, fella.'

'Yeah, I know. And that was a free throw; only one point.'

'It's almost eight o'clock,' said Ken. 'That radio show's starting soon'. He went over to the stereo tuner and turned the dial until he found the station, which was presently playing Summer In The City by the Lovin' Spoonful. Massy grabbed his windbreaker and left for the liquor store.

Massy returned about ten minutes later. He put the brown bag on the table and took out two cans. He handed one to Ken. Two lids popped open. The Byrds were on the radio.

Ken said, 'You just missed that song you like by the Four Tops called "I Can't Help Myself".'

'Oh, yeah?'

'You should just buy the record.'

'Yeah, but I'm broke.'

'From flying all over Europe.'

'Yeah...'

The time passed and when the beer was gone Massy and Ken retired to their rooms. Ken went to sleep. Massy read through some history books hoping to find a clue about the box he'd found in the cave the month before.

His research turned up nought and he was feeling too tired to continue. The window was open and the curtains were drawn, so any cool late summer breeze was welcomed. He sipped from a glass of water. The desk lamp caused him to cast a giant shadow. It was a little after midnight when Massy dragged out the shoebox that was under his bed and took out the small gold and silver box.

He stared at it for awhile. The box was magnificent. He could not believe his luck that he'd found such an exquisite artefact. Sitting on his bed, Massy opened it and took out one of the items from the box- a beautiful ornament of some kind. He held it in his hands and looked at it carefully. A shiny silver bracelet clasp with two gold chains- one attached to an orb and one attached to a ring. He could not guess the metal of the orb, but thought the ring was possibly white gold. Another gold chain linked the orb with the ring.

Massy deduced simply that it must be jewellery and, being careful as possible, slipped the bracelet around his left wrist and closed the clasp together. Then he placed the ring on his middle finger. The orb was over his palm and when he rolled it with his fingers it moved slightly. There was a small bump, or button, on the orb. He pushed it.

A moment later Massy felt disoriented. The light was different; it was warmer. The curtains were open now, he noticed, and daylight was coming through the window. He looked at the lamp and it was off. The glass of water was gone. His eyebrows furrowed deeply as he was perplexed. Light bathed the room and the bedroom door was slightly ajar. Massy could hear the radio broadcasting a soft drink commercial. Ken must have woken up but why was it daylight? He looked at the clock; it was ten minutes before eight o'clock. Eight? Massy glanced at the daylight coming through the window and wondered if he had fallen asleep in his clothes and that it was now eight in the morning.

The radio began playing The Monkees hit song 'I'm A Believer'. Massy, still on the bed, suddenly realized the box would be in view with the door ajar. He quickly grabbed for it but it was not on the bed. The ornament was still attached to his wrist and finger; he looked around the room for the box, trying not to panic. Massy quickly found the box inside the closet in its hiding place, where it was usually kept. That's strange, he thought; I don't remember putting it back...

Massy was aware of the strong smell of hamburger that lingered through the air; last night's dinner. But why did it smell so fresh? He wondered. Oh: Ken must be making burgers for breakfast. *Massy unclasped the bracelet, unhooked the ring and put the ornament under his pillow for the time being and went into the living room.*

Ken was sitting on the couch. When he saw Massy enter the room he jumped with a start- eyes wide open- but was quickly relieved when he saw that it was his room-mate. 'You scared the shit outta me, fella. What'd you do, climb through your window?'

'What?'

'You forget your money?'

'What're you talkin' about, Ken?'

'You better hurry, fella. The show's gonna start soon. Why'd you climb through your window?'

Massy looked at the wall clock that was in the kitchen area; it was about seven fifty-one. 'Are you cooking hamburger for breakfast?'

Ken said, 'Breakfast? We just had hamburgers for dinner a few minutes ago. Hurry up and get the beer. Or did you run there already, climb through the window and stash the beer in your room? You foolin' around?'

'No; we drank it last night, remember? We listened to the show and drank beer and then went to bed...'

'No. It's almost eight, and you're gonna miss the beginning of the show. What've you been smokin', fella?'

Massy was feeling increasingly uneasy. He said, 'It's eight in the morning...right?'

Ken gave him a strange look. 'It's just before eight in the evening, the show's about to start and a few minutes ago you left to go get more beer from the store. Then you came out of your bedroom suddenly...'

'No; we listened to the show...we drank...' Massy paused. 'Remember I came back from the liquor store just before eight, the Byrds were on the radio, I handed you a beer; you said that I just missed the Four Tops- the song I like, "Can't Help Myself"...I should buy the record, blah, blah, blah...I said, "I'm broke", blah, blah...remember?'

'No. "Can't Help Myself" didn't come on and The Four Tops haven't played, so you don't know what you're talking about, fella.'

'"Summer In The City" was on the radio when I left...'

'Yeah, I remember that. *It was only five minutes ago. Then,*

144

uh...commercials; then this song by The Monkees.'

Massy felt dizzy; something very abnormal was happening. He looked at Ken.

Ken told him, 'You better hurry. It'll take you about ten minutes...'

Massy shook his head and said, 'So, you don't remember listening to the show? Drinkin' beers...any of that? You were pretty drunk.'

'The show hasn't even started yet,' Ken said. 'And I'll be able to get drunk if you'd hurry up and get more beer-'

'-Wait!'

'What?'

'Listen...the song playing...'

The song on the radio was "Can't Help Myself" by The Four Tops. Ken stared at Massy and said, 'How'd you know that song was gonna play?' Massy felt as if he'd crawled inside a television set during an episode of the Twilight Zone; or maybe dreaming. He pinched himself until it hurt: No, I'm awake. Did I go back in time? If so: how? *The ancient relic? Oh, God. What to do? Don't panic. Think. Okay, I'll go* to the liquor store and see what happens; maybe it will end. *Massy noticed that Ken had been staring at him. Ken asked again, 'How'd you know? You said it was gonna play and it did. How'd you know that?'*

Massy said, 'I was just foolin' around...'

'Huh?'

'Yeah...' Massy forced a chuckle. 'I was foolin' around. I, um...I heard the disc jockey say earlier that he was gonna play the song.'

'Oh...'

'I'll go get the beer.'

Nonplussed, Ken muttered, 'Helluva joke...'

Massy left the apartment and when he was outside it was definitely not midnight. Judging from the people and traffic about, he guessed it was more likely to be evening than morning. His mind was working overtime to find an explanation but there wasn't one that Massy could think of, bar from the ancient relic.

Just when he thought it could not get much weirder Massy saw himself up ahead rounding the corner: Himself?

Himself.

Massy thought: God, Jesus...what do I do? *He quickly moved out of view into the side area of a house he was walking past. Massy stood back against the wall, head turned toward the sidewalk, and waited.*

145

His heart pounded. What if *he* sees me? *I* see me? *Myself* sees *myself?* This is crazy. Jesus Christ, I'm hiding from myself!

He waited. Then, the Massy from earlier this evening obliviously walked on by. He was carrying a bag with a six-pack of beer in it. He did not notice the Massy from later that evening, back against the wall, breathing a sigh of relief.

Massy walked around until well after midnight, waiting for his 'past' to leave his 'present'. He went back to the apartment and he wasn't surprised to see that his bedroom light was on. He climbed through his window and saw the gold and silver box on the bed; he slid it under the mattress. The glass of water was back on the desk. Massy collapsed onto the soft bed, reaching under the pillow to feel for the ornament. It was still there.

A moment later he was asleep.

The following weeks were a cauldron of mixed emotions for Massy. He experienced a sort of joy and happy elation at times, but it was usually followed by a feeling of power- a dark power. At other times he felt incredible loneliness and solitude for a multitude of reasons, ranging from not having anyone to talk to about it all to wondering which was the real 'Massy'- him or his 'past'. The strangeness of it all made him sad sometimes, but there also were times when it made him curious and a more determined 'detective'.

It did not take Massy very long to figure out what kinds of advantages could be had in having knowledge of the future. In October, while he was doing work at the house down in New York, he bet three hundred dollars on a football game between the Boston Patriots and Buffalo Bills after having already watched the game at a bar in Manhattan. When the game had finished Massy wore the ornament and activated it before making the wager. He beat the spread and won the bet, watching the game this time at a bar in Queens. He celebrated with a Bloody Mary made with the more expensive vodka. He handed the bartender the money; who rung it up on the cash register.

Cha-ching!

Days after his third parentless Christmas, Massy sold the house.

chapter 8

The Nazi war machine had turned west and a portly English gentleman of historical extract stood on the balcony overlooking the South Downs of Kent. He was puffing on a cigar. For years he had tried to alarm European governments, including his own, of the rearming of Germany and the ruthless ambitions of its leader, Adolf Hitler.

He took another puff as he pondered the difficult tasks ahead of him: the safeguard of the British peoples, their colonies and the military forces that were preparing to fight against the well-armed followers of Nazism. His name was Winston Spencer Churchill and he had just been named Prime Minister of England.

What to do, what to do... He walked with his hands grasped behind his back as he paced back and forth. Then he stopped pacing and called out for his assistant. 'Harold!' The Prime Minister waited a few moments then the aide walked out onto the deck. It was a cloudy day and the sun did not come out to play.

Harold asked quickly, 'Yes, sir?'

The Prime Minister told him, 'Another cigar, please, Harold.' But before the aide turned around Churchill added, 'And bring me another brandy. Oh, it is late. There won't be much more done tonight- why don't you make that two brandies, Harold. That is, if you would like to have one.'

Harold complied. 'Yes sir. Thank you, sir. I would like that very much.' He disappeared into the house leaving the Prime Minister to his thoughts.

Germany had invaded France yesterday and today the King of England- King George VI- had asked Winston Churchill to form a government. Churchill had accepted. Before he could do anything at all he had to choose his cabinet Ministers.

Harold returned carrying a tray with two brandies and a cigar on it. He held the tray out and the Prime Minister picked up the cigar.

Churchill struck a match and lit the cigar, blowing out smoke. He took one of the brandies and said, 'Thank you, Harold.' He nodded once at the tray and his assistant picked up the other brandy. He raised his glass and said, 'Cheers.'

Harold held up his brandy, raising it less than the Prime Minister had, and replied. 'Cheers, sir.'

Churchill turned, heading through the balcony doors. Harold followed him and stopped just inside the door, sipping his brandy.

The Prime Minister puffed his cigar and regarded the beautiful English countryside. He told his assistant, 'Thank you, Harold.'

Harold said, 'Yes, sir.' He left.

Many thoughts ran through Churchill's mind: *How soon before the Nazis tried to goose-step over British soil? How soon would the Royal Air Force be ready? How much money would be needed? Would the United States declare war on Germany? The coastal ports? The civilians?* He was not only Prime Minister but he had also been made Minister of Defense.

The curtains swayed in the gentle breeze. The Germans were in France now and headed towards Paris. French towns burned in the wake of the Nazi invasion. This saddened the Prime Minister; he had always held a fond love for France.

Churchill finished his brandy and went to bed.

The following morning Churchill woke with the knowledge that war had once again enveloped his life and it excited him. Electricity ran through his sixty-five year old body; adrenalin of destiny. He'd always known that it would come one day.

Now it had arrived.

Breakfast was already on the table, covered and hot, when he descended the stairs. The cook had left the room and Harold sat drinking tea. 'Good morning, sir.'

The Prime Minister smiled and sat down and immediately began eating. The full impact of his new duties had not grasped him yet and he ate his meal peacefully enough.

Five days later- the fifteenth of May, 1940- Churchill lay asleep in his bed. It was five-thirty in the morning and the sun was just peeking out, spraying rays of cool sunlight over eastern England. A rooster could be heard crowing the news of daybreak. It was not the only news.

On the table that was next to the bed was a telephone. It rang. The Prime Minister woke up and answered it.

The French Premier was on the other end of the line. Churchill listened intently; it was more bad news. The Premier was telling him, 'We have been defeated! We are beaten! We have lost the battle!'

Churchill asked the French Premier, 'Surely it couldn't have happened so soon?'

But it had.

Soon, Harold was making the necessary arrangements and calls to set up an immediate flight to France.

It didn't take long. Along with his staff, Churchill boarded the government plane and was there in an hour. They met with the leaders of France and it was estimated that the Germans would be in Paris in less than three days. Outside from the meeting smoke and ash filled the air as the French burned their archives.

The meeting ended, not much having been accomplished. Great Britain would send ten fighter squadrons to France to help cover the retreat. Churchill flew back to England, looking down at the choppy waves of the English Channel.

It did not stop there. Every day, news came in of German offensive successes. The Wermacht, the name of the German army, rolled into Paris and surrounded the Allies main front. Soon, more bad news was spelled out: Dunkirk. More than a third of a million Allied troops were ferried across the Channel to England from France, fleeing from the attacking Germans. France prepared for doom. Germany set its sights on the island of Great Britain.

The Great Eagle descended and the Lion clawed mightily.

The brave remnants of the French army were cruelly run over by the coldly efficient divisions of the Wermacht and Panzergruppes. The German army stood on the north coast of France, looking toward the south coast of England. The white cliffs of Dover peered out through the horizon.

Beyond Dover, in London, Churchill readied himself as he was about to make an announcement to the nation over the radio. He spoke quietly with Harold. The room was filled with the incessant chatter of the surrounding news people.

The room became quiet and all eyes turned to the Prime Minister. Churchill shook the paper in his hand and thrust his jaw out while adjusting his blue bow tie. He cleared his throat and moved his face closer to the microphone. The nation waited.

He spoke solemnly; telling the British peoples that the fight had just begun. The Prime Minister delivered the last sentence with great deliberation: 'We shall never surrender.'

149

chapter 9

The month was January and the year 1969. The place was Las Vegas. The bar was loud, but not as noisy as the spacious sporting book that was at the other end of the well-known hotel casino. The bartender, smartly dressed in black with a long-sleeved white shirt, paused for a moment to look up at the colour television set that was situated above the spirits shelf; the Super Bowl was being broadcasted. His hand wiped at his black vest and then he tugged the matching bow-tie, perspiration trickling down his balding forehead. The bartender must have bet on Baltimore, thought the college kid who sat at the bar stirring his Bloody Mary. A few stools away some guy with massive sideburns called out for a Miller beer.

Cheers and curses burst into the air and the barman had to stop and glance at the TV screen. It was slightly comical, Massy thought, that the bartender was wearing the same look of disbelief on his face as was the television image that showed a close-up of one of the Baltimore Colts players. Massy sipped the vodka and tomato juice cocktail, savouring the taste. He was happy; the American Football League champion Jets, under the leadership of Joe Namath, were walking over the heavily favoured National Football League champion Colts.

The worst part was over, Massy thought; the game is in the bag. He'd still been worried that something would or could go wrong but it hadn't. The game had played out- and was still playing out- exactly as it had done several hours earlier when he had watched it in his hotel room across the road. Exactly the same.

Exactly the same.

It was the fourth quarter and there were just a couple of minutes left in the game. The Jets were winning 16-7 and in complete control. Broadway Joe, like any great field general, knew when to shut up and let the players around him do the talking. Snell right for a yard, Snell right for six more, Snell for four yards- First Down! Jubilant cheers!

In Massy's jacket pocket were six betting slips, each with the same wager and the same amount: New York Jets plus eighteen points; five thousand dollars. He finished his drink and held up his finger for another one. There were more cheers and curses. The bartender shook his head slowly and sadly. Massy wondered how much the man had lost on the game as the college boy's only concern now was whether or not the balding server's sweat would drip into his Bloody Mary.

The game ended and the Jets were football champions of the world. Massy drained his final cocktail, picked up the white tennis bag that was at his feet and left the bar for the sporting book's cashier window.

Later that evening he sat on a chair in his hotel room eating pepperoni pizza and drinking a coke with a big smile on his face. He was looking at all the cash that was strewn across the bed, totalling almost sixty thousand dollars. Sixty grand.

Cha-ching!

The 1970 World Cup games were held in Mexico. Massy was back in Vegas; this time he was staying in a much better hotel. He'd already bet on many of the games and had raked in a small fortune. There was one more match to be played, the final between Brazil and Italy, and that game was about to start. Massy gargled some water and spat into the sink. He walked over and picked up an empty suitcase off the bed and left the hotel room to go watch the live broadcast of the World Cup final at one of the casino bars.

He had already watched the game hours ago (that was before he'd scattered $200,000 as thinly as possible around the city's many casinos) and he knew Brazil was going to win.

Massy was no longer a college kid; he'd dropped out of Brown University a week after the '69 Super Bowl.

Brazil won 4 to 1.

Cha-ching!

Massy sat in the packed sporting book lounge drinking cola in a glass filled with ice. He didn't have to watch the screen to know who was winning the fight; he just listened to the conversations and reactions of the other people. The date was the eighth of March, 1971 and the event this time was the World Heavyweight Boxing Championship, which pitted champion Smokin' Joe Frazier against challenger Muhammed Ali. Frazier was winning; it was the fifteenth round and Ali had just been knocked to the canvas.

Ali was able to get back onto his feet but minutes later Frazier was declared the winner by decision. Massy went back to his hotel room and put on the bracelet and ring, revolved the mechanism to the usual spot and voila, back in time a few hours or so. It was never exactly the

151

same amount of time travelled back, but he tried to move and press the rotating orb part in the same spot each time because he did not want to travel back more than a few hours. Three or four hours gave him enough time to place bets at several different casinos and sport books.

Massy went out and once again wagered nearly his entire fortune, this time over five hundred thousand dollars on Frazier. When it was over this time- with the same result, of course- Massy, who had increasingly started to become a loner, jokingly thought: Y'know, history really does repeat itself. *He chuckled; it was a good inside joke. There just wasn't anybody to share it with. He had not told anyone of his excursions into the time dimension. It was a secret.*

Massy was now a millionaire.

In the spring of 1973 the college drop-out switched to horse racing and made two bets; the first a million dollars on Red Rum to win the English Grand National and then two million on Secretariat in the Kentucky Derby. Those two races made Massy over twenty million dollars. Although he was beginning to feel as if he was being watched, overall life was going well for him.

The young time traveller recalled the words his father once had told him: 'Bettin's a mug's game, son. The only thing for sure is that the bookies win in the end.' Or something like that. Massy thought it was hilarious; and he laughed.

All the way to the bank.

In the summer of 1974 Massy travelled to London and made several bets during the World Cup, which was hosted by West Germany. By the time the smoke cleared his fortune had risen to over fifty million dollars.

Massy was out of control.

The view from the balcony was spectacular. The Rhine River flowed to the left, gracefully downstream to the North Sea. Lush, dark green trees could be seen everywhere for miles and the warm sunshine accented the baby-blue sky. At this time, August in 1979, Massy had three homes spread across the globe: Nevada, England and this one in France. Each had a purpose: one for gambling, one as a central base for his expeditions and one that was close to his Swiss bank accounts. He usually lived at the house that was in Hampshire, England but he was taking a month holiday here in the Rhine Valley.

Massy had a pretty good life all in all, with plenty of money and a penchant for hard work and hard rest. He gambled for work and went on expeditions all over the world, places like Tibet and Mali, for rest. The money business in Switzerland had been taken care of and now it was time to relax. He went by many aliases, including Daniel Gerard-the named owner of the Rhine house. In a moment he would be eating a bagel with smoked salmon and garlic cream cheese and drinking Bolivian coffee. Everything was perfect except that he was all alone.

A quiet knock signalled the housemaid's entrance through the open door of the bedroom. Massy turned slightly and watched her walk through the bedroom and out onto the balcony carrying a tray of coffee and lox. She was quite attractive really, he thought. Especially for her age; she was over ten years older than him. He hadn't noticed her too much until this morning when he'd thought he'd caught her watching him, though not in a paranoid way. Massy had felt as though she was worried about him.

Then he had noticed her. Her brown eyes, her blonde hair, her large breasts, her waist, her hips, her nicely shaped...

'Thank you, Cesca,' he said, picking up the coffee cup. Massy wanted to say more; after all, she'd been working for him for over four years-although he was only in France a couple of months out of the year. He knew Cesca was from Switzerland and that her father was Spanish and her mother was German but that was about it. When he'd first met her he was twenty-seven; he'd thought of her as practically an old lady. He didn't feel that way at this moment.

She smiled at him and he smiled back. She turned and went back into the house. When she was gone Massy felt the loneliness creep in like an out of control vine.

Cesca had paused at the bedroom door and turned around. She felt so sad for the beautiful American who was so rich and yet so alone; so very alone. She continued on down the hall to the dining room where she would take her coffee break.

Out on the balcony Massy suddenly had an overwhelming desire to cry. He successfully fought it off and forced himself to enjoy the magnificent view.

Success!

A year later and a year wiser, Massy was a new man. He'd tackled the alcohol problem that had steadily worsened over the years; three Bloody Marys first thing in the morning were not enough, it'd seemed for a while. Now, it was only a drink or two in the evening. He went back into researching the ancient maps in a more studious manner. And he had finally laid his parents' memory to rest.

For a long time Massy had wondered whether it was possible to travel far enough back in time to prevent his parents' car crash. He did not experiment with the ring too much because he feared that he might go back too far. For all he knew, he could possibly end up in the First World War or even the Stone Age. He just didn't have a clue.

The complications involved were numerous, Massy knew that. When he'd thought about it he had come up with some possible ideas, but the main question was: then what? Live a normal life with the family together- his mom and dad, his past self as a teen from before 1966 and him now at aged thirty? One big happy family?

Other options Massy had mulled over included preventing the accident in an anonymous, behind-the-scenes kind of way. And then watch them from afar? Or not at all?

Maybe one day he could figure out how to go back for a day only and just look at them. See Mom and Dad one more time, walking around and talking: Just one more time.

But he knew it was likely to never happen. He put the thought out of his head; it was time to get over it.

The biggest change in Massy's life was that he was neither lonely nor alone. And Cesca was pregnant.

He would never again travel back in time. It was time to move forward.

chapter 10

Looming brilliantly against an Egyptian sunset stood two massive monuments which symbolized man's unusual ability for using a tremendous amount of energy in the pursuit of making a very bold statement.

Several miles off to the north-west more of that was occurring as German tanks from the Deutsch Afrika Korps smashed their way east towards Alexandria, the strategic Egyptian port city on the eastern end of the Mediterranean Sea. The British Eighth Army was being pushed back across the Egyptian desert by the German Commander Erwin Rommel and the Suez Canal was close to falling into German hands.

Two soldiers of the Eighth Army sat behind sandbags, smoking and talking beneath their round, peaked helmets. Their khaki uniforms were dirty but they were not worried about any inspections out here on the front. Another soldier ambled over to them, a semi-silhouette in the twilight. Stars were beginning to dot the magnificent evening desert sky.

The two soldiers were older than the ambler and when he was closer one of the soldiers said, 'Oh, 'allo, Corporal...' The other gave a ribbing salute.

The ambler didn't mind; he knew those two were grizzled veterans who were soldiers before the war had broke out. He joked back: 'That's "Corporal, *sir!*" Right; it's off to the gallows with you two...' They grinned at the young corporal and the older of the two veterans asked, 'What is it, laddy?'

'I was wondering if either of you two fine gents could spare us a cigarette,' said Corporal Thomas Smith of the British Eighth Army and formerly of the French Foreign Legion.

'Right-o, laddy me boy,' said the older soldier. He handed Tommy a pouch of loose tobacco so that he could hand-roll a cigarette. There were no explosions at the moment and the men were glad for the eerie quietude. Tommy was not able to roll the cigarette very well and by the time he was finished with it the poor thing looked like a pregnant cigar. The older soldier was not impressed. He said, 'That's it; take all me bloody tobacco, why don't you?' Then he added, *'Sir.'*

Tommy shrugged. 'Sorry,' he said unabashed, striking a match and lighting his cigarette.

'Ever heard of "Three on a match", laddy?' said the veteran because Tommy had not ducked to light his smoke.

'Flippin' 'ell,' said Tommy. 'It's not the bleedin' Somme...'

They all laughed.

After Poland had been invaded the French Foreign Legion had given legionnaires with two or more year service the option of leaving the Legion to go fight for their perspective countries. Because Tommy had not joined the Legion until the end of 1938 he'd had to wait over a year before he'd been able to enlist with the British armed services.

155

He'd been sent to Egypt and had been assigned to the British Eighth Army. Tommy's current commanding officer was General Claude Auchinleck, who was Commander-in-Chief for the Middle East.

It had been a see-saw battle in the north-eastern corner Africa for Tommy and his comrades. First, the Italians had invaded Egypt and then Tommy- fresh from the Foreign Legion- and his Eighth Army mates had chased them out and back into Libya. Newly arrived Lieutenant-General Rommel, in turn, had led his Afrika Korps (along with the Italians) into a counter-offensive that'd sent the Eighth Army reeling back to Sollum. Recently appointed Commander-in-Chief Auchinleck had responded with an offensive that'd pushed Rommel back to where he had started.

But the Deutsch Afrika Korps had only been dazed; in January 1942 Rommel had begun a startling offensive that'd drove the German forces to the heart of Egypt to a place about sixty miles from Alexandria. A place called El Alamein.

Tommy was at his post. He stood next to a lorry with four other troops. They were all young men, with Tommy the eldest at twenty-one. It was July, 1942 and the soldiers were expecting an attack at any moment. Every day there had been fighting; why would this one be any different?

He looked over at a makeshift grave, made up of two sticks tied at a ninety degree angle to form a cross. These wooden 'headstones' were scattered all over the place, a grim reminder of a daily occurrence.

The young men chatted, talking about girls and football and cars. They joked and they laughed; anything to forget for an instant of where they were. They discussed what they would do when they returned to England.

Except that it was possible that none of them would ever make it home. For some of the soldiers, like the famous King Tutenkhamen, Egypt would become their final resting place.

Tommy found a blanket lying about and picked it up, then sat with his back against a front tyre. His unit was just behind the main front. A staff car rolled up beside the lorry and he looked up to see the officers climb out and start pointing. It was a captain named Romney and Major Wellington. Tommy stumbled to his feet in quick motion and gave a rushed salute. The officers hadn't really noticed him there, nor expected a salute, but Romney acknowledged his salute with a quick nod of the head. They looked out at the horizon and spoke quietly.

Then, once again, the guns started up. The cannons to the west of Tommy roared into life. He faced the boys and told them, 'Alright, lads. Here we go...' They all started running forward when they saw the men in front of them do so.

A shell ripped into a lorry nearby, but Corporal Smith heard no screams. 'Keep going, boys!' The Germans were sending off hundreds of volleys from their field guns. One blast after another crashed into the ground around them. They neared the row of sandbags that would be their only shelter.

It wasn't long before they could peer through the haze and dust to see the Panzer tanks firing murderously. German Infantry could also be spotted scattered across the sand behind the tanks, running and firing.

'Keep firing, men!' With the constant shelling, Tommy could not hear his own commands. He looked for his sergeant down the line of sandbags. A cannon shell exploded into the sandbags near Tommy and the horrible sounds of death echoed once more in his young ears. He watched the lead Panzer exploding when an anti-tank gun found its mark. But still, more Panzers charged through; they wore the cold smile of death.

Men were dying to the left and right of Corporal Smith and he was surprised to hear they were retreating.

A few brave souls were left to cover the retreat; Tommy wasn't one of them.

Tomorrow, he thought as he jumped into a lorry. *Tomorrow* we will make a counter-offensive and regain this land.

A couple of days later Tommy and his comrades *did* regain the territory, which they in turn held for a fortnight. The major news among the troops was that of a new commanding officer. Auchinleck was out and General Harold Alexander was now the new Commander-in-Chief of the Middle East forces. And the new commander of the British Eighth Army was one Lieutenant-General Bernard Montgomery.

Rommel was denied his objective, the Egyptian oilfields, and after the Eighth Army had received a surge in reinforcements and supplies it was too late for him. He had lost his chance and the Montgomery-lead Eighth Army counter-attacked. This time the Germans were chased back into Libya and by 13 November Tobruk was bypassed and a week later Benghazi retaken.

157

The light shining outward from the windows of the public house was like a beacon. The night was quite dark and there was no moon out. It was the end of the working week and the patrons were drinking without any worry; except having a hangover at church the following day. There were several small houses and cottages between the church and the pub in this growing area at the edge of Leamington Spa, with fresh business trades at the church end.

Inside The Black Horse public house the evening was coming to an end for three drinkers who sat at one of the long tables. The atmosphere was loud and rowdy, but jovial. Late Victorian England wasn't always *a bad place to be.*

It was smoky, the air thick with tobacco and conversation. The crowd was mostly male although there were several women- a mixture of professionals and labourers alike: shop owners, builders, tailors, woodsmen, farmers and at this particular end of the table a butcher, a baker and a shoemaker. The first two were early risers because of their jobs but the third- the shoemaker- woke early because he liked to run when the sun was rising.

'Shall we have another? There is no work tomorrow,' said William the butcher.

'I must visit my mother, she needs money to borrow,' said Henry the baker.

'Tis getting late, William..,' said James Worson the shoemaker. All three took sips from their ale mugs, which were nearly empty. A man who the threesome knew to be a labourer had passed out at the table across from them, his face flat against the wood surface. The man next to him was trying to wake him.

'Yes. If you two are going then I shall, too,' said William. He lifted his mug and drained the ale down his throat. Henry and James followed suit. All three rose from the table and made their way to the large wooden door. When the door closed the noisy pub was muffled. They all lived near one another and headed toward their homes.

'Rather dark tonight, would you not say so, Henry?' They were walking away from the pub; it was the only light around.

'Yes, William. Say, Burn here says he is able to run from here to Kenilworth and then to Coventry; and then from Coventry to Kenilworth to here, all in an hour.'

William looked at James and said, 'Surely, you are not serious, Burn?' Burn was a nickname for James the shoemaker; he could run like paper on fire. That is to say: Very fast.

'No. I said; "around an hour's time or thereabouts"', James said.' I have not run the course yet, so I have not timed myself, but I am quite confident that I am able to do it. It is only about fifteen or so miles altogether, I believe.'

'Henry and I would be glad to see you do it,' said William. 'It would no doubt take place at sunrise, eh?'

'Of course. You two could follow me on horseback,' said James. 'I will attempt the feat at the end of spring when the weather is warm but not hot and when the mornings are bright and early.'

They heard the sounds from the pub increase and decrease as someone opened and closed the door several yards behind them. The person staggered drunkenly off in the opposite direction.

'What road would you run on, Burn?'

'This very road that we are walking on now, Henry,' said James. 'This road goes straight to Kenilworth, curves and leads to Coventry.'

'In an hour? Impossible..,' mused William.

'...An hour "thereabouts",' corrected James. He started to walk over to the side of the road to empty his bladder at a bush: 'Maybe two hours at most. Excuse me, fellow men, but I must have a pee...'

'We will keep walking. Will you be able to catch up with us, Burn?' William asked humourously. Henry laughed, and James chuckled.

'I will try.' James moved into the bushes and as his eyes adjusted to the darkness he watched his urine spray downward into the greenery. Then he glanced up and saw his two friends walking on. The sky was full of stars, he noticed after looking up. A beautiful night in the heavens, he thought, though it was very dark.

James looked back down as the flow lessened and the stream slowed, and something on the ground- inside the bush- caught his eye. He finished his business and crouched down to get a better look, reaching an outstretched arm into and through the crooked branches. His hand found the object and he pulled it up for closer inspection.

The shoemaker slash distance runner was taken aback by the strangeness of the object, for he had never seen anything like it. He left the bush and started walking down the road to his friends as he tried to figure out exactly what the thing was. Whatever it was, James thought,

159

it certainly was an extraordinary piece of craftsmanship.

There was a clasp-like part and he attached it to his wrist. A ring of what looked like to James to be made of gold was chained to the clasp and there was a small round ball on the chain. He bent his middle finger and slipped it through the ring. It fit loosely- his wrists, hands and fingers were all slim- but it fit.

He started fiddling with the object, turning the orb, as he began running to William and Henry. As he ran he moved his thumb over the small orb and when he neared his friends he called out to them, 'William! Henry! You should see this!' They both stopped walking and turned around to see what the shoemaker was shouting about.

James did not see the rock on the road in his haste to reach his friends in the darkness and, stepping on it, he stumbled wildly. His thumb had pressed into the orb when it was jarred and, while he flew wildly through the air towards his friends and the ground, his thumb let go and released the tiny bump that it had just pushed in.

'Where did he go, Henry?'

'I saw him stumble, William...'

'Yes; as I did. But...he disappeared before he hit the ground.'

'It is so dark. Maybe he fell to the side of the road, William.'

'That is ridiculous, Henry. He was just there...' William pointed. 'A matter of merely feet away...'

'Where is he, then?' They both looked around at the darkness around them. The light from the pub shone in the distance. There was no sign of James.

William shouted out, 'James?'

Henry yelled, 'Burn?'

William looked at Henry. 'He disappeared into thin air right before our very eyes.'

James landed with a thud, flying forward with his arms out to break his fall. His forearms were scraped and he was bleeding a little; he was sprawled on his belly and the tumble in the darkness shocked him, but he wasn't hurt badly.

The object was unscathed. He lifted himself up and unclasped the band, looking in the direction of where his friends had been. But they weren't there. In fact, they were nowhere to be seen. He called out, 'William? Henry?'

Something was very different, James noticed. It was much lighter out and some cottages were missing. He looked back at the pub and it was not there. That's strange, he thought. Then he saw that the moon was out. It was a full moon.

The shoemaker was more than a little confused; he was sure that there was no moon tonight. He looked around. There were only a couple of properties scattered around. Some houses and cottages were missing. James shouted: 'William?' A lot were missing. 'Henry?'

He stood in the middle of the road and swiveled his head and body around three hundred and sixty degrees but it did not help. His friends were nowhere to be seen and even the pub wasn't where it was supposed to be; it was not there at all. James wondered whether or not he had bumped his head in the fall.

The only thing to do was to go home.

chapter 11

A soldier pulled a dusty pack of cards from his coat pocket and started to deal them out for his Eighth Army comrades. There were three of them; they played for cigarettes to pass a few moments of the early morning after drinking cold, weak tea. They'd been up throughout the night and were quite tired and very hungry. One of them chuckled, a large red-faced man from Yorkshire. For a short moment they became engrossed in their game and forgot what they were doing.

A voice broke their fixation from the game. 'Eh, oi, what's up 'ere?' The corporal had come over.

'Oh, hello, *sir*,' said the Yorkshireman.

Tommy told them, 'We're on duty 'ere, mates. You don't want to be playin' bloody pontoon when Jerry arrives; now, do ya?' They looked at their corporal, who had a good sense of humour but when he was serious all jokes disappeared. But he did not look too serious now, though he had caught them slipping. Tommy knew they were exhausted; they'd been battling Rommel for months on end.

The red-faced man took a chance on humour. 'Oh, you are a rotter, ain't ya, Smithy? Just 'cos you don't play cards...'

'It's got nothin' to do with me liking games or not, ya bloody fool,' said the corporal.

The Yorkshireman pretended to get angry. 'Don't be callin' me a bloody fool just because you can pull rank on me. Yer only a bloomin' corporal.'

'That's "only a bloomin' corporal" *sir!'* The other soldiers laughed and Tommy and the bloody fool joined them.

One of the soldiers piped in, 'Yes, I suppose the corporal's right. We wouldn't want flippin' Rommel to sneak up and goose us!' This broke them up with laughter again. Sometimes hilarity came easy when death was lurking around each corner.

A few hours later Tommy was eating a sandwich made from his rations. Each bite was a struggle, him against the flies. They were everywhere. He looked out at the horizon to the south. The sun was out and bright as usual but it was not scorching. The Libyan landscape, at least here, reminded him of Algeria.

The town of Tripoli was quiet; Rommel had vacated only days ago and there seemed to be no immediate threat of battle. Tommy relaxed for the first time in days and found his small poetry book and began reading. It was warm and the men of the Eighth Army felt good.

He put the book down when his mind wandered back to his days in the Legion. Tommy wondered what had become of Jack. He'd heard that he'd been picked up for desertion and the word was that he was serving his time doing hard labour. Hassef had returned from the hunt and been imprisoned, but had done only a short stint considering the severity of the crime.

Tommy thought about the persistent rumour among the legionnaires that Has al Kabir and El Khajira had both been revenge attacks against Captain Versailler's men stemming from a prior incident, years before, where Versailler had ordered the slaughter of several villages when he'd been a lieutenant. At the time his sergeant, who had carried out the orders under protest, was Salvatore Bationi.

There were only few good memories from his time in the French Foreign Legion but they all faded by the time he remembered the Greek, who had supplied him with so many laughs during the tiresomely long days in the Algerian desert, because Tommy had been the one who'd found the Greek when the jovial giant hadn't come back from a reconnaissance patrol. Tommy had found the Greek's headless body under a swarm of flies.

Corporal Smith picked up the poetry book and began reading the end of a poem by Edmund Spenser titled *One Day I Wrote Her Name.*

'To die in dust, but you shall live by fame:
My verse your virtues rare shall eternize,
And in the heavens write your glorious name:
Where, whenas Death shall all the world subdue,
Our love shall live, and later life renew.'

A week later the streets of Tripoli were filled with the sound of bagpipes from the Highland Regiment. The troops marched down the dirt roads and when the parade ended the men danced wildly around the town, cheering their victory.

Three months on and the Germans and Italians had been completely run out of Africa. The Americans had been attacking the Axis forces from the west and now the two great armies were linking up in Tunis in preparation for the invasion of Sicily.

An American soldier yelled to his British allies, 'Hey, Limeys!'

Tommy grinned and shouted back, 'Bloody Yanks!'

The shoemaker had stood at the spot where his Victorian house would have normally been but it wasn't there. He'd seen that the old farm was still across the way but it had not given him much comfort. And when he had asked questions the following day everyone had thought James was strange and had given him queer looks. They hadn't seemed to be very helpful, he thought; they seemed to be much more interested in the clothes that he was wearing than in giving him an explanation.

There had been no sign of his family anywhere; neither his friends nor his business; in fact there was not one person he knew. The next day James had decided to find his brother in Northampton and set off for Daventry; he knew that Northampton was beyond Daventry.

Along the way, just before Daventry, James had received his first real useful piece of information. It had not been good news; the year was 1809. When he'd walked out of the pub with William and Henry the year had been 1873.

He was hungry and thirsty. He'd travelled beyond Daventry now and was crossing through fields toward the main road near a place called Weedon Bec. To his left and right there were wooded areas but what had caught his eye was the inn that was nestled in a clearing by the road. James was prepared to steal food if necessary. The weather was

163

very warm; there was no breeze but there were clouds on the horizon. It wouldn't be dark for a couple of hours and that would be too long to wait. He would have to try stealing in daylight.

As he neared the inn he saw that there was a well to the left of it. That was good. He thought: maybe have some water and wait for darkness to steal some food. Maybe have a nice kip afterward...

James was still heading for Northampton. He doubted that his brother was there. After all, it was 1809. It would not make sense that his brother would be there. But then again, it did not make sense that he was in 1809, he thought. So, he'd decided to press on to Northampton anyway. What else could he do?

The shoemaker still had the object; he wouldn't let go of that. James knew it had something to do with him changing years and he was convinced that he would be able to use it to get back to 1873. He prayed his older brother would be there but James knew in his heart that it was not possible. He would have to figure out this problem all by himself. Thank God that I have the object, thought James as he moved to a tree that was at the side of the road; it will get me home.

James stood by the tree and watched the inn. There was nobody outside so he decided that now was a good time to cross the road but he did not want to run in case someone was watching because it would look wrong. It was possible the innkeeper may let James have a drink from the well, anyhow. He casually walked onto the road and crossed at an angle to the well from the tree. His eyes were set on the inn.

James heard something. He looked to his left down the tree lined road: Nothing; the inn? No. The sound was getting closer. His head cocked right; it was a rider approaching at almost a gallop along the road to the right, but not visible yet. The shoemaker ran to the well and dived behind it.

He watched the lone rider, who wore a long dark cape, roar past the well. James hadn't been seen.

The well certainly had water in it: James could see that, and a bucket with a rope. It was a deep well. He wondered whether it would make too much noise but he would have to risk it. He looked at the inn's Georgian windows and could see no one about. But just as he was about to lower the bucket he heard another sound, freezing while his ears strained to locate the source.

It was more horse hooves, this time coming from the direction of the *road that the lone rider with the long cape rode into. Then it came into the clearing; a pretty carriage with two horses and a man up front. James put the bucket down, ducking behind the well. The carriage slowed and passed by the well and stopped in front of the inn.*

James listened intently and fought the urge to peek. He heard the man climb down. One of the horses sneezed. Then...voices from inside the inn. He thought about leaving and touched inside his coat pocket for the object...but it wasn't there. Panic seized him.

Frantic, he searched his pockets again- frenetically looking around the ground below him: The well? Oh. No; it couldn't have, he thought worriedly. His head moved out from the well and he could see the carriage and the man, who was looking at something at the back of the carriage: Something? Oh, no. The man in the road was holding the object; it must have fallen out of James' pocket when he'd darted out of the path of the lone rider. He was aghast; the man had put the ring on and was clasping and unclasping the wristband part. James whimpered sadly.

The man heard the sound and looked up. James ducked again, not knowing what to do. Then, a woman's voice called out from the carriage. A moment later he heard the woman shout, 'Benjamin, what are you doing?'

James was in a quagmire and he knew he had to be quick and decisive. He decided to go out and confront the man and claim his object. He had to get it back; it was his only way home.

The shoemaker stood just in time to see the man disappear. It was too late; the man and the object were gone. He crouched back down beside the well just as the innkeeper came outside and talked with the woman. James did not bother listening to what they had to say. It did not matter.

Several years earlier on that same stretch of highway rode two messengers on two beautiful, strong, fast thoroughbred horses. They were riding from London to Liverpool and carried an important message from the King. Time was essential and they rode like lightning. Lives depended on their swiftness. Eight chestnut brown legs thundered down the road in the darkness.

James had scurried off into the bushes but later returned to drink from

165

the well without realizing the irony that his precious object was only
yards away. He looked forlornly out at the road to where the man had
disappeared; he felt like crying.

No matter how far or fast he could run, James 'Burn' Worson would
never get home.

chapter 12

The bright sun bathed the Moroccan mountainside, shining over the
colourful green and brown plant life that covered the ground. Several
trails carved their way through the sloping terrain, ancient paths and
trade routes with stories and histories all of their own. Marrakech sat
below, the destination for the trade routes.

The smell of hashish lingered through the fresh hot air. Sitting on a
rock overlooking the valley was Jack, puffing away on a small wooden
pipe. He absorbed the sunlight, jutting his face out at the sky with his
eyes closed. He exhaled.

Nearby, his donkey stood staring blankly at a shrub. It was enjoying
the sunshine as well. The night had been cold, so the mid-morning
warmth was welcoming. But by the afternoon the heat would be fierce;
it was the end of spring. Jack struck another match and very slowly
inhaled the gray-brown smoke.

A wild goat stood on a trail down to the left, seemingly enjoying the
view of the ancient city. Jack laughed at the thought and smoke poured
from his mouth and nostrils. He coughed and his eyes watered. Then
he realised that it wasn't *that* funny; maybe he was just glad that the
goat was free.

Jack had been released from the Legion's prison at the beginning of
spring. The year was 1943.

He was free.

After the French police had arrested Jack that day in Marseille things
had gone downhill for the ex-legionnaire. First, he'd been kept in a
tiny, stinking jail cell- then interviewed by the police and interrogated
by the French Intelligence before being handed over to the French
Foreign Legion, who in turn had thrown him into a smaller, smellier
cell that was better suited as a hotel for flies. To say the least, the
Legion had been very angry with Jack. He hadn't just deserted; he'd

survived *and* was in France.

But there had been more to it; Jack had known that. Although nobody had given him any information he'd been able to tell that they- the police, French Intelligence and the Legion- all became a little more interested whenever Klauss's name had been mentioned. He'd understood that the Legion would really want Klauss for killing an officer- Lieutenant Bationi- but there was something else going on. He knew it and used it to his advantage.

Jack had kept to the same story: that he'd said goodbye to Hassef and gone to Marrakech where he'd picked up a scent that lead him to Casablanca; that he'd found out that Klauss had taken a boat to Spain so he'd followed on the next available boat, shedding his uniform; that he'd picked up Klauss's trail in Spain and it had lead him to Marseille: that he'd been about to contact the Legion at the time of his arrest.

After Marseille the Legion shipped Jack over to Algiers for further questioning. By then he'd also deduced that they suspected that he was a spy and that the Legion were also convinced Klauss was a spy- probably German he'd guessed, owing to the fact that several times the Legion had spoken to Jack in German in the hope, presumably, of some kind of reaction.

When the Legion were satisfied they'd sent Jack to a prison near Colomb-Bechar and he ended up serving the rest of his time in the Legion in prison, plus three months for the time that he'd spent chasing Klauss.

Jack felt sleepy. He'd been awake since daybreak, wandering the hills, and the combination of cannabis and the heat was catching up with him. The donkey snorted when a fly ventured too far up its nose. It was good to be out in the open, he thought. That was the main thing. His mind drifted momentarily to the times he had spent in solitary confinement when they'd tried to break him. His thoughts shifted quickly back to the wonderful view before him.

Jack enjoyed these hills; they were home now, at least for a few weeks. He wondered about Maria, as he had done constantly over the past few years. Jack had never mentioned seeing the Lieutenant's family to anyone as he did not want to implicate Maria nor her mother. He'd been afraid to write as all of his letters were read by the Legion.

But now he was free. He planned to move into Marrakech or Casablanca to find work and a place to live where he would have a home address. Then he would write to Maria and wait for a reply while earning enough money for passage to France.

But he had doubts; there was the very real possibility that she was married and had children or worse, what if she'd forgotten about him? And, of course, the Germans were all over France; getting there would be no easy task. At least his French had improved greatly.

Further down the hill some men with donkeys laden with carpets weaved their way through the trails to the market stalls of Marrakech. They seemed to be moving quickly so Jack guessed that they must be running late. But he was in no hurry. He and the donkey were taking their time to appreciate the splendid panorama that surrounded them.

Jack had spent the last few years of his prison term at a prison far east of Marrakech- on the Algerian border- and despite the harsh conditions of the weather and food, was not too bad a place to serve time compared to most of the other prisons. Many of the prisoners were disgraced officers who'd been caught with their hands in the cookie jar in one form or another, so the inmates were on the more civilised end of the spectrum. The prison was in the middle of nowhere so anyone who escaped would have a tough time of it. But overall the security was minimal and Jack had felt he could easily get out, though surviving the desert would be an entirely different matter. He could not risk being caught and sent to a 'proper' prison.

Jack had found work and a place to live in Casablanca and had sent many letters to Maria, but there had been no replies.

Stubbornly, after he'd made enough money, he set off for Chateaurenault.

At first it seemed as though the house was deserted. Jack knocked twice, then again. The door remained closed. He looked around but there was no sign of life. He stepped back to get a better look at the house; it was definitely the Bationi home. Late afternoon wind blew Jack's hair about.

The door opened. A tall, dark-haired man stood in the entrance straight-faced. Behind him stood a short woman; she was not Mrs. Bationi. 'Que voulez-vous?' the man asked. *What do you want?*

Jack explained that he was looking for Maria Bationi and her mother. The man told Jack that Madame Bationi and her daughter had left years ago, not long after the Germans entered Paris.

Jack felt the air go out of him. 'Ou sont-ils aller?' *Where did they go?*
'Je ne sais pas...Mais,' the man paused. *I don't know. But,*
But? But *what?* Jack's anxiety heightened, the wind flustered wildly.
Suddenly it hit him like a thunderbolt just as the man continued, '...she
has a sister that lives nearby.' Maria's aunt! D'accord! Of course! Maria
had once pointed out her aunt's house on one of their walks. His heart
jumped; there was still hope. Jack knew where it was. He told the
couple, 'Merci! Merci!' as he hurried off in the direction of Madame
Bationi's sister's house.

Wind whistled through the branches as Jack ran down the road along
the trees. The leaves were whispering, *'It's too late...'*

But he wasn't listening.

Luck had been on Jack's side as Maria's aunt had been home and she'd
told him that Maria and her mother had gone to Salvatore's family in
Italy after leaving Chateurenault over three years ago, though the aunt
hadn't heard from them since then.

All Jack had was the name of a village and a hill. He was now back
in Marseille en route to Villa Santa Lucia, Italy.

And he wondered what the hell he was doing.

Newly-promoted Sergeant Thomas Smith let the hot wind roll over
him, bringing soft kisses of water from the Mediterranean with the
breeze. The beautiful blue sea was before him and behind him was the
vast, lonely deserts of North Africa that had been his home for the past
four and a half years. He had just said goodbye to that chapter of his
life and was staring out at the shimmery sea.

Tommy hadn't seen any fighting for quite some time now and was
glad for it. He tried to keep his mind off, just yet, the inevitable battle
that awaited him and his comrades on the other side of the lovely,
shiny sea.

Upon returning to England- assuming he'd made it through the war
alive- he had made tentative plans to take up some type of gardening
work in the suburbs or maybe down in the West Country. He wanted to
plant life instead of the death that he now sowed.

The sea had had a profound effect on Tommy which had made him
feel more at peace with the world; his visions had become clearer, his
thoughts purer.

He leaned against the railing of the transport ship that was carrying scores of soldiers to their destination, which would be the heavily fortified beaches of Sicily. Tommy and his mates had had a small reprieve from battle but were about to make up for it by running off of a ship and onto sand with German bullets flying everywhere.

His thoughts drifted to a time that was long gone; his youth. Life had been so much simpler back then. Images flooded him: running around in shorts even though the weather had been freezing, picking up his small cap which seemed to be forever falling on the ground, scraping his knee- what a crisis *that* had been! Stealing apples, chasing his mates, cricket, football, his first kiss; it all seemed unreal to him, like a hazy dream.

Time arrived and time passed. He concluded that he could do nothing but keep moving forward.

'Sergeant Smith. You're wanted by the lieutenant, sir.'

'Thank you, Dobbs.'

The transport that carried Tommy and his unit neared the Sicilian coast. So far, they'd been lucky and hadn't been attacked by any German planes or submarines. Ahead and behind them the long column of ships- with a separate column two hundred metres away running parallel alongside- disappeared into the horizons. In a short while land would be visible.

It was an amazing armada heading toward Sicily. There were more than twenty-five hundred ships involved, carrying the men of the British Eighth Army and the American Seventh Army. Tommy's division would be landing just south of Syracuse. Already, the Sicilian skyline was filled with Allied paratroopers. To the west, American marines were storming the sandy beaches.

Sergeant Smith began to mentally prepare himself for the invasion. A moment later he looked at his ammo supply and filled his rifle. His weapon was the standard one used by the Eighth Army; a .303 Lee Enfield No. 4 Mk 1\2.

As Tommy put in the bullets he thought to himself: Seeds of death.

Tommy's heart raced faster when the silhouette of the Sicilian land mass came into view. *Not long now.* All around him men collected their thoughts and silently said their prayers. There would be no turning back, no strategic retreat here. The soldiers would be leaving the boat and either gain control of the beachhead or die. There was not too much in between.

He was thankful that the coastline and beaches had been 'softened' by the constant shelling provided by the armada's escorts, consisting of fifteen cruisers and six mighty battleships.

The Germans were firing back now and Tommy watched the smoke float over the Mediterranean. The men were all lined up against the railing watching and waiting, adrenalin levels jumping higher and higher.

The transport hopped through the shallow water and neared the beach. The soldiers prepared to embark and Sergeant Smith glanced around at his men. Shells were exploding in the water around them, spraying the decks. A transport not far away took a direct hit; some would not even make it as far as the beach. Machine-guns rattled bullets across the sand and shallow water. The German artillery became fierce, shells were exploding everywhere.

Tommy's boat had reached its drop off point and they all began jumping out into the small waves. Before they reached the beach they were firing. Sergeant Smith led his men onto the beach and they followed.

A shell landed near him, spraying sand. It was close but it missed him. Tommy shouted, 'Bloody hell!'

Rays of sunlight peeked through the dark grey clouds that covered central Italy and Maria was grateful for it. Rain threatened the hills and valleys surrounding her as she walked briskly along the dirt path to the doctor's house where she worked as the doctor's assistant. The house was at the far end of the only village in the remote hills and the doctor was the nearest medical help for many people in the area. Maria helped out with the ailing people, cleaned, stocked and delivered medical supplies to various places such as the large farm that was down the path from where she lived.

Bushes lined the well-worn path and the early morning mist wisped about daintily. Autumn would be ending soon and the birds prepared to fly south across the Mediterranean and over the Sahara for the winter. The clouds closed together and the temporary brightness disappeared. Maria's thoughts began to match the cool, gloomy weather which was turning colder because of the increasing wind. Her slide into melancholy usually began with thoughts about an unchangeable event: she and her mother's move to Italy. Maria planned to go back to France, maybe Paris, as soon as the war ended.

She thought: But would it ever end? The war had once again come to her; the Americans were in Naples pushing toward Rome, the British were north of Bari and the Germans were dug in the mountains and valleys. Everywhere, banditry was rampant.

Maria did not want to dwell on her woes but it seemed unavoidable; at least at times it did. Everything bad about her life would jump into view once given the opportunity and the blackened sky did not help matters. *It is too hot and then too muddy. There are too many high hills and not enough forest. I have no friends and if I stay here I will have no future. Many of the local men despise me because I am half-French and they may attack me someday: I hate it here...*

Madame Bationi had made the bold decision to leave France and though Maria had had reservations, she'd agreed to go with her mother. Complicating matters further, the day after they had crossed the French-Italian border Italy had declared war on France. The move to Italy had been very difficult on them and although they'd made it to their destination- Salvatore's sister's house in the hills east of Rome- the journey had proved too arduous for Madame Bationi; within a year, Maria's mother had died. That was well over two years ago.

Maria was alone and lonely. She did not get along with her father's relatives and now lived in a shack south-east of Villa Santa Lucia, nestled amongst the hill. She shopped in the village after work some- times or bought food from the farm that was not far from her dwelling.

The one brief respite in her depressed moods were thoughts of Jack. Though it was maddening for her not to know what had happened to him, she still held out the hope that one day she would see him again, however unrealistic that possibility seemed. But it was hope, and hope was a long stick to someone drowning.

She had guessed- correctly, though she did not know it- that Jack had been caught and sent to prison. He would not abandon me like that, she thought. *Would he?* Maria dismissed the thought because she still carried the torch for Jack and dreamed that they would be reunited after the war. *Your eyes are like diamonds.*

Over the past few years only one man, Antonio, had challenged Jack for a potential place in Maria's heart. He'd liked her and she'd known that he was nice but after the first time that he'd dared speak to her

Antonio's brother's had beat the hell out of him along with the warning to stay away from 'that French whore'.

The cloud cover thickened and grew darker by the minute. Maria quickened her pace; she was almost jogging. Walking in the hills was keeping her in great shape and the long walk to work through the hills, which she made several times a week, was easily traversed by Maria.

As Jack faded from her mind her thoughts spiraled down again; she wondered whether she would ever get away- that she was doomed to spend the rest of her life wandering through these hills. Madame Bationi had realized the mistake she'd made about relocating to Italy soon after their arrival, and had told Maria how sorry she was. Maria recalled how angry she had been with her mother that day; she then felt sad and sickened with herself and that she would give anything to have her mother around. She felt like crying.

There was a bend in the trail just ahead and Maria's commute to work was nearing an end. Light rain spat down upon her face. She didn't care.

chapter 13

The peaked mountain ridges formed a majestic, if somewhat crooked, spine that snaked along the Franco-Spanish border, linking the Gulf of Lions on the Mediterranean side and the Bay of Biscay on the Atlantic side. From quite a distance one could see the beautiful purple and yellow wildflowers that colourfully dotted the valley floors below the peaks.

Asard, a goat antelope native to the mountains of Europe, was in abundance and supplied leather goods for the people of the Pyrenees. As the Asard wandered the rocky terrain Griffon Vultures flew high above, occasionally stopping to perch sentry-like on any of the many apexes that were available to them. The vantage points afforded the carrion-eating birds of prey a panoramic view that spanned several miles.

This wondrous expanse of nature was for the most part undisturbed by the presence of concrete; there were only a few main roads. Running off one of these arteries was a private road which splintered off along a series of treacherous ridges down to a plateau that hugged the

173

mountainside. A little more than half of the flat area was roundly edged in a semi-circle by sheer cliff. On the plateau a large complex had been built over a quarter-century earlier in the early 1990's. The outlay was basically a square and most of the buildings were two or three stories high. The complex was completely surrounded by a seven metre high chain-link electric fence at the perimeter.

Where the ridge road came to the level ground there was a security gatehouse, from which it was a short drive through the recreational areas to the main building. Above the entrance stood the three-dimensional logo of the business; a blue pi symbol followed by a red 'i'- with the dot of the 'i' overlapping the 'right arm' of the pi symbol to give the initials TTi: Time Theories Institute.

Time Theories Institute as a business utilized many variable ways to generate income though it came chiefly from lectures and published works on the theory- the possibility and potential consequences- of time travel. TTi was a company more than it was an institute but there was an academic wing with students who were potential employees, and hired teachers and lecturers. There was a Research and Development department that usually kept a low profile. There was the Field Wing where some students would 'graduate' to a salaried training program for Time Travellers. In the event time travel became possible, TTi would be at the forefront of things. A very large amount was spent on security.

Between the main gate entrance and the main building's front revolving doors there was the recreational area divided in half by a road and walkway, with a football pitch on the north side and two large swimming pools on the south side- one indoors on the ground floor and the other outdoors above it. A gym and a sauna were also inside. On the other side of the pools was a mall with many assorted shops as well as several restaurants. Next to the mall- to the east by the front fence- were the casino and nightclub buildings, as well as a few more eating establishments. To the west of the pools was the housing area. The students, teachers, scientists, programmers, security personnel, maintenance, cafeteria workers and even the shop owners- excepting a handful of people- lived at TTi.

Inside, the slender old man who'd created TTi was enjoying lunch in a sunny garden area on the roof of the main cafeteria. A large umbrella kept the direct sun at bay and quiet fans circulated cool air to maximise comfort. To most of the people at TTi he was known as Professor. Some called him 'Boss'. Ishkur, his son, called him Pop. The scientific community knew him as Ernesto Fernando Garcia. Though dark in complexion, he didn't look very Spanish; he spoke with an American accent.

Accompanying the Professor at the table was his long-time friend Cyril Wilkes-Barrett and Ishkur. His personal assistant, Hadrian, was down one floor in the canteen. The Professor chewed his bacon and avocado sandwich carefully, enjoying the taste and texture. He watched his son sip from his cocktail of expensive vodka mixed with freshly squeezed oranges and was glad that Ishkur was happy- or content at any rate. The Professor knew that his sole offspring had delayed marriage and children for a complicated reason; Ishkur wanted to travel back in time one day and if that were to happen it would be best to get married then. But life was passing by quickly for his son, thought the old man; Ishkur was in his late thirties.

Cyril, from Oxford in England, was busy finishing off the last of a huge salmon quiche and already eyeing the inviting jam doughnut next to it. His portliness was more corpulent than stout, even he would admit that now. The once thick golden locks had thinned and turned almost completely grey.

A waiter came over to the table with a large mug of herbal tea with honey made from local bees and put it down in front of the Professor, who nodded at the waiter- a thank you. The server, in white shirt and black trousers, glanced at Ishkur- who shook his head- and then to Cyril who told him, 'A milky coffee, please.' The waiter's forehead crumpled. He looked at Cyril wearing a puzzled, questioning expression.

Ishkur cocked an eyebrow at his father's good friend and grinned, turning to the waiter and explaining, 'He means a latte.' Ishkur had a peculiar accent: English, American and a recognizable French lilt with traces of Spanish and German thrown into the mix. The server picked up Cyril's empty plate, nodded and left.

The Professor had been observing; Cyril must be in a silly mood. His pal, nearly fifteen years younger at fifty-six, was usually what one might describe as 'proper' but was prone to a wacky, if subtle, sense of humour. He asked Cyril: 'Springtime cheering you up, old friend?'

Cyril smiled. 'It would appear so.' He reached for the doughnut but pulled his hand back, deciding to wait for the latte. The milky coffee.

The battered old Humvee moved along the ridge road away from the front gate of Time Theory Institute. In the passenger seat sat security guard Michaelson, a veteran with fifteen years experience on TTi's payroll. Speier, the new guy, drove the vehicle. They were both Americans.

'This Hummer's one of the old bunch; it was here when I started the job. Don't want you messin' up one of the new ones,' said Michaelson as he watched the rookie drive. The cliff drop that paralleled the paved road only metres away was separated by a strong four foot high concrete wall. The veteran guard asked, 'How long you been here, a month?'

'Six weeks.' Speier was still in the awe stage. To him, the mini-world at TTi seemed like kind of a Shangri-La.

'What do you think of it?' asked Michaelson, though he already knew the answer. He could see the 'kid in a candy store' look in the rookie's eyes.

Speier almost beamed. 'It's like Disney World.'

'You'll get over it.'

'Get over what? Good pay? Easy job? Nightclubs?'

'It ain't all that.'

'...Chicks.'

Michaelson tried not to grin but couldn't help it. 'Down, boy.'

Speier, who seemed to be growing younger by the second, said: 'I can't wait to drive one of the new Humvees.' TTi had added a half-dozen brand new Hummers recently.

Michaelson nodded. 'Yeah, HumVX's. Top of the line Hummers; they're good.' The veteran had already driven one. His mind wandered for a moment and then he was looking down the cliff at the sheer drop. The heights still made him feel a little uneasy, if not nauseous. He lifted his eyes away from the view and asked the rookie: 'Does the cliff bother you?'

'No...I love it.'

Michaelson shook his head lightly and thought: *You wouldn't love it if you were falling down it.* Then he said, 'Did you hear about the snowboarder?'

Speier looked at the veteran for a moment, then straight ahead.

'Snowboarder?'

'Yeah. One of the guy's from the academy went snowboarding on his own down by the old office back in January. The old plateau is very gradual on the approach and makes for a good slope-'

'I haven't been down there yet...'

'-And so this guy goes snowboarding and...all they found was the trail of his snowboard; it lead right over the cliff.'

'Damn,' said Speier. He was now not so sure about loving the cliff.

'They never found his body. Anyway,' said Michaelson, stopping to scratch his shoulder blade, '...we'll be going past that spot when we check the faulty camera.' A security camera was not working and Michaelson and Speier had been sent to see what the problem was. The veteran continued, 'I wonder what was going through his head as he was falling...' The words drifted.

Speier's Shangri-La fantasy was slightly dampened. He stared straight ahead as he drove. His mirage began to disappear when he, too, pondered the horrible scenario. 'I wouldn't wanna know.'

The Professor was listening to Cyril and Ishkur talk about Jack the Ripper, picking up the stray poppy seeds off his plate and nibbling. There were not too many people on the roof at the moment, just a few other TTi bigwigs. The tables were far apart with lovely green potted plants everywhere.

Cyril was starting to get impatient about his latte. He wanted to get to the jam doughnut. 'I must say, the Maybrick diary was fascinating reading, though it turned out to be rubbish.'

'Total bollocks, you mean,' said Ishkur. He lightly shook the melting ice in his screwdriver. He wondered whether to order another one. He went on: 'Just like the Siskert business.'

'I don't know, my good man. Could be something there...' Cyril paused when he noticed the waiter coming over with his latte. His eyes dropped to the doughnut and then to Ishkur. 'Well, who do you think it is?'

Ishkur drank from his glass. 'Who do I think Jack the Ripper is? I don't know but one day I want to find out.'

The waiter put the latte down in front of Cyril and said, 'Your milky coffee, sir.'

Cyril chuckled, taking a quick sip. The temperature of the coffee was

177

perfect, he thought. As the server left the table with the Professor's plate, Cyril grinned around the table and then picked up his doughnut, taking a big bite. A big blob of jam oozed out the bottom of the treat and onto his white shirt; Cyril was oblivious to it but Ishkur and his father saw it.

Ishkur said: 'Cyril, old bean, it looks like you've just been stabbed through the heart.'

Cyril looked down, still chewing. 'Oh...well, thank you very kindly, Ishkur.' He grabbed a serviette and started wiping. Then he added, 'Smart aleck. Let us hope that does not turn out to be more than just an ominous statement.'

Ishkur drained his cocktail. 'No need to be like that, old codger.'

It was light tomfoolery. The Professor enjoyed it. He said, 'You both are nuts.'

The Humvee approached a sharp bend to the left. Michaelson told Speier, 'Okay, up here you wanna slow right down on the bend. After that's a straightaway.'

'Okey-dokey.'

Michaelson bit his lip; the rookie was beginning to get on his nerves. 'Just keep it nice and easy.' Still, Speier wasn't going slow enough for his liking. 'Slow down!' he said, louder than he'd wanted. The Humvee slowed to a snail's pace. Michaelson stared at the wall ahead and shook his head. 'Goddamn...'

Speier drove carefully up to the bend. 'Sorry...'

The silence did not last long. They turned to the left into a slight hairpin and as they straightened up to a more comfortable stretch of road Speier said, 'What the...' Michaelson had been watching Speier; he looked up. In front of them about twenty metres away was an armoured vehicle. A tank.

Speier said: 'What's that?'

'It looks like a miniature tank.'

'It is a miniature tank. With some friends.' Behind the tank there were several HumVX's. 'Should I back up?'

'We couldn't back outta here if we tried,' said Michaelson.

'What should we do?' Speier said, reaching for the 9mm German handgun that patrollers carried.

'Well, for starters,' the veteran warned when he noticed the rookie's

movement, 'don't bother with that thing. There could be a logical explanation. Call the gate and recheck the visitor's schedule; maybe we got another delivery of Hummers.' Michaelson opened the passenger door. 'I'm gonna go see what's going on.' He got out of the car and closed the door.

Speier asked through the open window, 'What do I say?'

'Tell them what's happening. If it's not kosher then we're at Code Yellow.' There were six Security Code Alerts at TTi: White, Yellow, Orange, Red, Violet and Black. Michaelson walked calmly away from the worried rookie, toward the tank.

Speier quickly scanned their schedule sheet and did not see anything about a small army. He called the front gate. 'Gatehouse, this is H3. We got a Code Yellow- possible Code Yellow, I mean...uh, we need to recheck the, uh...visitor's schedule. Do you read?' He waited patiently for an answer; about two seconds then tried again. 'Gatehouse? Gatehouse, do you read? This is H3...'

To buy some time for the rookie, Michaelson walked very slowly. There was no one to make eye contact with. He did not like the look of this and he was going to find out what it was all about. His adrenalin kept any fears at bay. This was his job.

Watch Commander Welch was sitting in the front gatehouse security office munching on a tuna sandwich, listening to a security guard go on about his troubled love life. Normally, Welch wouldn't give a crap but he was that bored. He could have gone out for lunch to the cafeteria or coffee shop inside the main building or any of the many places to eat at the mall but he just didn't feel like it. He was bored with the job and bored with life. Sometimes he would stay at the front gate during lunch but that'd be because there had been expected visitors. But today, he didn't have to be in the office because today there weren't any visitors on the list until later this afternoon.

Welch tried to listen, glancing out the window now and then at the activity down on the soccer field. A few of the students were out kicking a ball in the warm sunshine. Every now and then when he'd thought it was the appropriate time Welch threw out a 'yeah, I know what you mean...' But he wasn't really listening.

The guard was saying:'...And then when she saw me and Lupe going into the-'

'Shh! Hold on...' said Welch. Looking at the guard, he put one finger

179

to his lip- then held a palm up. The guard shut up and listened. Something was coming over the radio.

'-Yellow, I mean...uh, we need to recheck the, uh...visitor's schedule. Do you read?'

The guard would normally take the call but Welch rose from his chair and said, 'I'll get that.'

The radio bleated: 'Gatehouse? Gatehouse, do you read? This is H3...'

Welch was bored and grumpy. He mumbled, 'Hold your horses, for Chrissake.' He pressed a button so that the caller could hear him. 'Yeah, H3, what's goin' on? Who is this, the new guy? Speier? Where's Michaelson?'

'He's gone to the tank? Are there any visitor's on the list?'

Welch was perplexed. 'Tank? A gas tank?' At TTi they used generators and gas for power and heating.

'No; A tank tank.'

'A tank tank?' Welch was becoming impatient and angry with the obscurity. 'Speier, what the hell are you talking about? What do you mean "tank tank"?'

'You know- caterpillar tracks, heavily armoured steel, turret...big gun, go boom.'

'To the point, Speier!'

'We rounded a bend and now we're face to face with a mean-looking tiny tank, of the military kind, with about half a dozen Hummers behind it. Unknown number of personnel,' said Speier, pausing briefly. 'We looked at the visitor sheet and, uh...no one's in 'til fifteen hundred hours- food deliveries. Some VIP's at 5:30 in four vans...but this ain't them. Michaelson is nearly up to the tank now; do we have any visitors scheduled?'

'No.' Welch's anger had subsided. This sounded serious. His voice lowered. 'Tiny tank?'

'Ultra modern. Compact. Looks dangerous.' Then Speier remembered: 'Michaelson said to say if there were no visitor's then to say, to tell you, that we're at Code Yellow.'

'Not anymore,' said Watch Commander Welch. 'We're going to Code Orange: I'm calling Rentzal.' Lank Rentzal was the Chief of Security at TTi.

180

'So remember, Cyril, we're going to show the Jump Room to the Austrians at ten-thirty in the morning,' said the Professor. Seven Austrian time theorists would be given a tour and lecture the following day and Jump Room was the nickname for the Control Room. Cyril's title at Time Theories Institute was Central Operations Manager and he was in charge of the Control Room. Ishkur had gone to have a piss.

'Yes,' Cyril said, wiping the red jam stain with a wet serviette. He put the cloth in his empty coffee cup. 'I remember. They will only see what they need to see. Speaking of which...' He pulled out his eyeglasses and put them on. 'Ah, that's better. Who's doing the lecture?'

The Professor suddenly felt a chill and moved his seat into the sun, tilting his head toward the sun. 'Oh, uh...Hardine,' he said finally.

'Oh, she is good,' said Cyril.

'Coming along fine, but I wasn't sure if she had enough experience for these guys.'

'She will be fine, old fellow. The woman has a tremendous flair for presentation.'

The Professor tired easily these days. He tried not to show it because Ishkur worried about him a lot. His son wanted him to give it all up and just rest and enjoy life. But the thing was; the Professor still enjoyed seeing what was being accomplished at TTi.

Cyril regarded his old chum. 'Feeling fatigued, old friend?'

The Professor's face was tanned and leathery, absorbing the sunbeams. He smiled at Cyril. 'Don't tell Ishkur.'

Cyril smiled back. 'I won't.' They both glanced toward the restrooms and as they did the Professor and Cyril saw Hadrian, the Professor's assistant, flying out of the elevator as it opened and running toward them.

Hadrian shouted, 'Boss!' He raised the phone in his right hand as he ran.

'What the dickens?' Cyril said.

The Professor reached over and picked up his mobile phone, which was always turned off during lunch when Hadrian would take any messages.

Hadrian was at the table quickly. 'Boss, we have trouble. It's Rentzal...' He handed his phone to the Professor.

The old man spoke into the tiny microphone. 'Lank?'

The chief of security's voice came out of a tiny speaker: 'Boss, we

181

have a problem on the ridge road.' With Rentzal informing the Professor of the situation they were now at Code Orange.

Cyril watched the Professor listen intently to Rentzal's briefing of what exactly the hell was going on. His old friend did not seem to like what he was hearing.

Finally, the septuagenarian replied. 'Did you call Erlinger?' Stefan Erlinger was the Head of Internal Security and another long-time friend of the Professor's.

'I thought I'd call you first.'

'Okay. I'll call and tell him to inform the Heads of Staff. I'm on my way down.'

'Don't you think you should stay there?'

'I'll stop at the main entrance. When you get to the gatehouse give me an update. Oh, and Lank; make sure your boys don't get trigger happy.'

'Roger that. Just to confirm: you're informing the Heads of Staff and I'm putting all security forces on alert, even the off duty ones. That puts us at Code Violet, Boss.'

'I know. Talk to you in awhile, Lank.' The Professor closed the phone and passed it back to his assistant. Ishkur was standing there and when he caught his son's eye he tried not to look worried. It was probably all just a misunderstanding anyway. He usually moved around TTi riding a comfortable, slow-moving electric buggy with Hadrian walking at his side. It was down two floors by the elevators in the coffee shop on the ground floor. But he would need something quicker. 'Hadrian, get some scooters ready. Four: for me, you, Cyril and Ish. Try and get them before we get to the bottom of the elevator. Go quick.' Hadrian took off running, flicking open his mobile.

The Professor also made a call to Erlinger. 'Stefan? Listen...' He explained the situation quickly and then gave Erlinger some orders. 'Okay...you need to inform all the Heads of Staff and the other department managers. They'll need to keep everyone- students, teachers...everyone- where they are. Call Switzer first.' Jerry Switzer was Head of Staff for Research and Development. 'I'll catch up with you at the front doors. Oh, and tell Sanderson that Cyril's going to go over to the Control Room.' He stopped to catch his breath. 'Bye, Stefan.' The old man got up, struggling a little. Ishkur helped him to his feet and they started walking to the elevators, Cyril in tow. Also standing there was Antania Kurynesk, the Head of Staff for the Academics department, who had been having lunch nearby at the garden roof bar. She'd come over to see what was going on. The Professor noticed her and said: 'Erlinger's going to call you in a minute, Antania. Head down to the staff room; he'll tell you what to do.' Kurynesk nodded and left to quickly pay her lunch bill.

Ishkur ran ahead to bang on the elevator door buttons to have them ready and open. Cyril took the Professor's arm when the pace moved too fast and they slowed down. Cyril said: 'Don't overdo it, old bean. It may just turn out to be a false alarm.' The old man nodded solemnly.

A while later at the gatehouse office Rentzal was on the radio to Michaelson giving H3 the go-ahead to let one of the trespasser's vehicle's on through, a request from the intruding party. He then called the Professor. 'Boss, where are you?'

'I just got to the front doors. By the guards booth.'

'Boss, I just gave the OK for one of their Hummers to come through to the front gate. I guess the one in charge told Michaelson he wants to meet and explain.' Rentzal paused. He continued: 'He wants to talk to you, Boss... But that would have to be by phone.'

'Maybe. Have they said who they represent?'

'No. But the guy coming to the gate gave a name: Mister Black.'

'Mister Black?'

'Yes, Boss. And if this gets much worse we're going to have to go to Code Black.'

The Professor knew what that would mean: Code Black signified informing the Spanish government.

Chief of Security Rentzal stood just outside the front gate office looking through the gate bars at Rossiter and Welch as they waited for the vehicle that carried Mister Black to come around the last bend and into view. The Professor had taken Rentzal's advice and was staying put back at the main building's front entrance in the security booth, where he had access to surveillance cameras. Ishkur and Hadrian were with him. Cyril had gone to the Control Room.

Rentzal was not happy. He thought about the possibilities: they could be terrorists- Basque separatists?- or rogue bandits out for old-fashioned robbery. But this was not Basque country. Michaelson had said that he'd thought that they seemed to be Americans. Who were *they?*

He leaned into the open doorway of the office and told the trouble-some romeo who'd given Welch such an earful earlier to direct the previously off duty guards and watch commanders to certain desig-nated areas. Two other guards milled about inside the gate with Rentzal and about six more, four men and two women, were moving quickly toward him from the housing units.

There was shouting and Rentzal swiftly left the office doorway and moved right up to the gate. Rossiter, a Frenchman who was the Head of External Security, turned to him and yelled: 'Our guests have ar-rived, Chief.' Rentzal could see the Hummer-like vehicle clearly; it looked state of the art, he thought, displaying clear admiration. It moved slowly up to the front gate. Rossiter and Welch displayed a casual and calm front as they directed the unknown visitors close to the gate, although it was still closed shut.

The door of the vehicle, which Michaelson had described over the radio earlier as 'a HumVX times a thousand!', swung open and a man wearing a black suit with dark sunglasses stepped out.

Welch kept an eye on the driver, though he couldn't really see him clearly. Rossiter walked alongside the man in the black suit over to the gate, a matter of yards away. In English but with a French accent, Rossiter asked: 'Do I need to frisk you?'

The man in black just shook his head and smiled.

'We will see what the chief says,' said the Frenchman.

Rentzal was on the other side of the gate watching the two men walk closer. He was very tall and very thin and Lank was not a nickname; he was born that way and given an appropriate name. As Rossiter and the man approached, Rentzal decided to try to be subtly humourous in an attempt to see what kind of person that he was dealing with. 'Mister Black, I presume?'

The man in the dark suit spoke. 'Yes.'

Rentzal noticed Mister Black moving back a couple of feet so as not to be towered over by him. He said: 'What can I do for you?'

'I would like to see Professor Ernesto Fernando Garcia.'

Rentzal let him through the gate and held up a hand radio. 'Boss? Mister Black wants to speak with you.' He turned to the visitor and passed him the radio. The Professor was listening at the guard's booth by the main doors.

184

The accent on the other end was American. 'Hello, Professor Garcia. I am Mister Black. I would like a word. Maybe we could walk around; you could show me the place.'

The Professor spoke into the booth radio. 'Perhaps that could be arranged, Mister Black. I don't mean to be blunt, but is this a...criminal enterprise that you're undertaking here?'

'No.'

'Then why the tank?'

I will explain soon. Can I see you?'

'Let me talk with my chief of security. Thank you.' The old man looked at his son, who'd been keeping a close watch on his father. Ishkur was both worried and angry, his face contorted into a mean, questioning frown. The Professor turned back to the radio: 'Lank? You there?'

'Yes, Boss.'

'What do you think?'

'Well, he's by himself. The driver's still in the vehicle; Rossiter and Welch are out there with him. You probably saw us frisk Mister Black here. He's clean. No idea what he wants.'

'Okay. What the hell,' said the Professor. 'Escort him over here. Erlinger's on his way and you got me surrounded by about a dozen guards, Lank. I'm safe.' He made the comment more for Ishkur's sake than Rentzal's.

'Well, there should be seven with you by the main entrance doors.'

'Yeah, okay...maybe not a dozen. Any news from the bend?'

'No. Michaelson and Speier are still standing by. The convoy hasn't moved.'

'Good.' The Professor caught his breath. There was no sense in getting stressed, he reasoned. 'Okay. I'm going to show Mister Black around a bit and find out whatever it is that they're up to. I'll be with...' The Professor paused when he saw Erlinger arrive. Feeling a little winded, he took a deep breath and continued: 'I'll have Ishkur, Hadrian and Stefan close by the whole time.'

'Maybe you should take a couple of guards as well, for good measure.'

'Maybe. Notify the department heads and managers to keep everyone as they are until further notice. Remember to keep them informed.'

'Yes, Boss.'

'See you in a minute, Lank.'

'Hello, Professor Garcia. I am extremely pleased to meet you.' The two men shook hands.

'Mister Black...' The Professor regarded his visitor: solidly built but not tall, over fifty, in all black except for the slightest of white shirt showing and even though they were now indoors, Mister Black still wore his dark sunglasses.

'First: let me apologize for the theatrics,' said the man in black. 'And second: thank you for being patient.'

The Professor decided to drop a strong but kind hint. 'As you can see from my age, I cannot be too patient.' He smiled politely.

'Yes, of course,' said Mister Black. 'Shall we walk?'

'I will have to ride my electric buggy alongside you; these old bones, you see...'

'Of course.'

'We can talk alone, but we'll have some company following nearby.' The Professor turned and glanced at the three men standing and introduced them. 'This is my son, Ishkur...and this is my personal assistant, Hadrian. And Stefan Erlinger: security.'

'Gentlemen.'

'Is there anything you need? A drink?'

'No, thank you.'

First, the Professor took his visitor down the central corridor, a long hallway, riding along slowly at walking speed. Their three escorts were not far behind, maybe twenty metres, with two more guards trailing the trio another ten metres further. The group moved westerly and the old man had told Mister Black that they'd be going to the Academic Wing. 'When we get to the intersection, by the coffee bar, we turn left.'

Aside from obvious reasons, the Professor did not trust this man; there was too much mystery for this to come out right. The old guy loved a good mystery but he had a bad feeling about this. He would have to find out what this was all about, and soon, but he didn't want to push this character, who harboured an element of danger.

The walls were painted a very pale blue. As he steered with his left hand, the Professor lifted his right arm and pointed to both sides of the hall. 'These doors lead to the lecture rooms. There are "Executive"

186

lecture rooms at the far corner of the Academic Wing.'

The company logo was on each lecture room door, next to the room number. Mister Black remarked: 'I like the logo. But what does pi have to do with time?'

'I believe that time is circular,' answered the old man as he scratched at his long grey nose hairs. 'Have you read any of our books?'

The man in black did not reply right away; then after a few steps said: 'TTi's exact stand on its time travel theory seems to be somewhat elusive, Professor.' He was still looking forward; he didn't turn his head.

'We are open to several theories. There may be more than one that is right.'

'You're very fair with the existing theories that are widely accepted by the scientific community, at least on the exterior.'

The Professor's eyebrows furrowed. He did not like the end of that statement but he decided to let it go and began talking about the accepted theories, in relation to TTi's own theories. Behind them, his son was closing the gap from ten metres to about seven. Erlinger had to slow Ishkur down and with a thick Austrian accent told him: 'Your father said ten metres...'

Ishkur could hear words and parts of sentences bouncing off the hall's ceiling, floor and walls: 'string theory...worm hole...California Institute of Technology...closed loops, open loops...Stephen Hawking...time slips...Elaine de Jourdain...Institute for Advanced Study...Harvard...' There was nothing in those words to cause Ishkur any alarm but he was far from satisfied. He looked back at Erlinger, half-wondering why the Austrian was not pulling him back, and noticed that Stefan was listening to a radio earphone.

Erlinger did not appear very happy. He put his hand down from his ear and shook his head lightly at Ishkur and Hadrian, who were both waiting for an answer. His accent was thick: 'That was Rentzal. Phone mast is out; there is no outside communication. We have intercoms and shortwave but it is not a good sign.'

'I think I've heard enough,' Ishkur said. He simmered like a pot of boiling water, just below the surface.

'What can you do?' Erlinger tried not to sound unkind. Ishkur, through his nose, huffed out an audible sigh of resignation.

Up ahead, the two men moved along toward the central intersection.

Mister Black knew the old man was making a great effort to be patient and could not be kept in the dark for much longer, which the man in black appreciated; but only a little. 'You have a fine place here, Professor,' he said as though he were talking about someone's ranch in Montana. 'Tremendous. You employ some of the brilliant minds of our time; have many great admirers, respected and accepted amongst the world's scientific community...friends in the Spanish government- you certainly have a lot of pull.' He glanced over at the old man riding on the electric buggy, whose face was expressionless but whose ears were open. Mister Black continued, 'There's a lot of money in this place. Billions; right? Millions in security alone. Then you have scientists, teachers, lecturers...but you make a good profit.'

The Professor almost applied his brake but he did not want to be overly dramatic. He did want to be direct. He said: 'Is that what you're after? Money?'

Mister Black stared straight ahead as he walked. 'No,' he said.

'Then what? The suspense is killing me.'

A few steps later the man in black told the founder of TTi: 'In due time. In a way; I am explaining.'

The Professor was not amused. 'Oh, it's all clear now,' he said sarcastically. In an attempt to be amused he added facetiously: 'Thank you; can I go finish my lunch break now?'

'...Due time.'

There was nothing for the Professor to read on Mister Black's face and the dark glasses hid the eyes from revealing anything. 'Okay, well...' He fought his stress and impatience by trying to make light of the situation. '...To continue the tour: coming up on our right is the diner and on the left is the coffee bar. There are cafeterias above both of them for the staff and students. I apologize for my lack of tour guide skills; we have people trained for this. Maybe you could come back for a proper tour?' There was no reaction from the man in black, so the Professor continued. 'The hallway to the right leads to the Field Wing, where we examine the practical effects of time travel on a person: their state of mind, their physical state, psychological effects, equipment and wardrobe, type of training, historical knowledge...things like that.'

'All theoretical, of course,' said Mister Black. He turned and looked at the Professor from behind his dark glasses.

The Professor was tiring. 'Of course. It's all on the premise that time travel may one day be possible and, if it is, then at least someone had put in some forethought into what to do and how to go about it.'

'You?'

'Not me. TTi.'

'All theory?'

'It's all theoretical, Mister Black.' They were nearing the intersection.

Mister Black looked over at the old man. He said: *'So, you haven't learned to time travel yet.'*

The Professor was not sure if that was a question or a statement. He replied: *'As it stands now, we believe that the highest percentage for whether time travel is even possible lies at around three percent so there's a ninety-seven percent probability rating that time travel, to the past anyway, is impossible.'*

'A less than one in thirty-three chance...'

'It's not chance though; it's probability.'

'What about travel to the future? Does it have a separate probability rating?'

'With a self-perpetuating machine keeping a speed faster than light, tachyon photons- to tell the truth I don't know the details but the theory is if you can reach, say...Sirius in the constellation Orion, for example, at faster than light speed and be there and back to Earth and to age only thirty-three years...the sun here would revolve a couple thousand times and so the traveller would come back to an Earth that was two thousand years from the time that they'd left.' The old man was out of breath.

Mister Black was persistent. *'So you can't travel back in time?'*

That definitely sounded like a question, the Professor thought. He answered: *'No.'* Then he felt icy horror, subtle and cold, when he noticed the tiny upward curl at the far corner of Mister Black's mouth. A chill ran down his back and he shivered. Immediately, he had a yearning to be in the sun's warmth. He decided to take Mister Black to the observatory lounge that was available for staff and VIP's located two floors above the library with views of the surrounding mountain ridges, cliffs and peaks. He felt that would be a good place to talk. They reached the intersection and stopped. A moment later the escorts halted, as did the two guards who trailed behind the trio.

The Professor and Mister Black looked at one another. It was im-

189

possible to see the man in black's eyes and it disconcerted the old man. Pointing to the right, the Professor said: 'As I said- down there- that's the Field Wing.' Turning, he pointed left down the opposite hall. 'That will take us to the Academic Wing. There is a nice spot where we can talk. I'll have security make sure the place is all clear for us and we'll have food and drink, if you like.'

'Sure.' Mister Black's attention was on the hallway that continued straight to the back of the building. Five metres into that hallway there was a heavy security door. 'Where does that go?'

'That leads to the Control Room.'

'What does it control?'

The Professor sighed; half wearily, half warily. 'It's just computers mostly. Info, data...'

'And what else?'

'What else? Uh...well, beyond the Control Room at the far end of the complex is our Research and Development Wing. They deal with probabilities and other things, like reshaping molecular form type stuff that is much too complicated for me. The scientific end of things...and such.'

'And such. Of course.'

Was that mockery? The Professor felt his heart beat increase and took a deep breath to slow his pulse. 'Excuse me a moment; I need to talk to my security.' The old man turned around and waved at Erlinger, motioning Stefan to come over and as he did Ishkur caught a glimpse of his father's face. It looked tired, worn, weary and about ten years older than an hour ago. His angry son began to move closer but Hadrian touched the sleeve of Ishkur's blue silk shirt. Ishkur stopped resignedly and watched Erlinger approach the intersection and join the Professor.

'Everything alright, Boss?'

'Stefan, make sure that the observatory's clear and every adjoining room. I need a drink; have Hadrian sort us some water and I'll need a carrot juice. Have some of the guards bring up at least three or four electric scooters...'

'Boss,' said Erlinger. He threw a quick glance over to the visitor's faceless head and then looked back at the Professor. 'The phone mast is scrambled and the lines are...' He paused. 'We have no communication with the outside world.' As if to attempt balancing the news, he

190

added: 'Everything else out there is okay.' It didn't work.

The Professor was becoming angrier by the minute. He turned to Mister Black. 'Is this true?'

'It's just a precaution,' said Mister Black. He flippantly explained: 'For our protection. Nothing to worry about.' The man in black began walking, by himself, south down the hallway that would take them to the Academic Wing. The Professor zoomed up alongside him in no time. Well...in a few seconds, anyway: Zoom-zoom.

Erlinger had stayed put, waiting for Ishkur and Hadrian to reach the intersection. He was speaking to Rentzal with his tiny radio.

The old man had finally lost his patience. 'I demand an explanation.'

Mister Black nodded, but he just kept walking. Finally, drawing out the words very slowly, he said: 'Professor Ernesto Fernando Garcia...'

The Professor waited: there must be something to follow that statement. They moved along in silence for maybe half a minute. Mister Black broke the silence, but all he did was repeat himself. 'Professor Ernesto Fernando Garcia...' He could sense that the old man was about to have an outburst so he decided to fan the flame. 'You're not really a professor, are you?'

The old man gritted through his teeth to say, 'You'll enjoy the view from the observatory. Magnificent.' He could hear electric scooters from behind as the guards riding them turned at the intersection by the coffee bar. The Professor braked and Mister Black halted. 'I hope you can ride a scooter, Mister Black. They will get us there quicker.'

'I think I can manage.'

chapter 14

The streets of Cairo were busy. Busy indeed. Horns honked and the pavements were filled with men, women, goats, dogs, street merchants and almost anything you could imagine.

Just outside the city, Winston Churchill was meeting with the President of the United States, Franklin Delano Roosevelt. A phone rang.

Harold, Churchill's assistant, picked up the phone and said, 'Yes?' Moments later he said, 'Thank you,' and put the phone down. He left the room and moved across the hallway to knock on a door five times.

191

KnockKnockKnockKnockKnock.

The door opened and he was allowed in, stopping in the doorway. He said, 'Sir, the Chinese leader, General Chiang Kai-shek, and his wife have arrived.' Harold noticed that the British Prime Minister was speaking with the President.

Churchill nodded and told his aide, 'Thank you, Harold.'

Harold said, 'Yes, sir. I will be out here if you need me, sir.' He left the room and closed the door behind him.

In a few moments the leader of China and his wife were walking down the hall with their staff trailing behind. When they reached the door an American aide opened it and they entered the room where Churchill and Roosevelt already sat. Chinese staff followed them inside and then the British and American staffs joined them.

Harold sat at a desk that was set up in the hall near the conference room. In the hallway guarding the closed conference room door stood two very tough British guards. It was late November, 1943.

Inside the room Churchill, Roosevelt and the Chinese leader discussed the Far East situation, the day's main topic.

After awhile Harold gets up and walks down the hall. Soon, Churchill would join him outside with a car door opened and waiting. The next day there would another meeting.

The final Cairo meeting accomplished little. Afterward, Churchill walked with two of his generals talking quietly. In a couple of days Churchill and Roosevelt would be meeting with the Soviet leader, Josef Stalin, in Iran. The summit would take place in Tehran, filled with conflicting interests. The summit was code-named 'Eureka'.

A British guard watched Churchill pass through the doorway and straight into a car. Harold closed the door and jumped into the car that was waiting behind. The cars drove off.

Two days later in Tehran, the three leaders of the Allied nations sat down together to discuss the battle plans for 1944. Stalin expressed a great desire that a western front be set up in France so as to relieve some of the pressure off of the Russian front, thus dividing Germany's defenses.

Churchill opposed this partially. He agreed there was a need for another front that should be set up in France but not the full out front that Stalin wished, for that would mean the expenditure of all Western forces in the European theatre. Tomorrow was Winston's sixty-ninth birthday and he was not well.

Roosevelt spoke quickly as he overlaid the proposed invasion of northern France, code-named 'Overlord'. Stalin immediately jumped in to once again say that Overlord should be made the West's main operation for the following year.

The Prime Minister was feeling quite feverish. He steadied himself and spoke. 'I would like the Western forces to be split up: in France, Northern Italy and the Balkans.'

Stalin realized what Churchill was up to; the Prime Minister wanted to beat the Russian forces to Vienna, Belgrade, Prague and even Berlin. The motive was clear; the foreseen shape of post-war Europe as it was apparent now that Germany would eventually lose the war under the weight of the three superpowers all-out attack. The Russian leader silently but visibly glowered and slowly rose from his seat. Churchill shivered from the heat of his fever. Roosevelt shivered from the chill in the air.

Stalin stood at the table and said, 'It would be wasteful diversion; there must be a strong western front.' He turned and looked at Roosevelt and asked, 'Would it not?'

The President had a slight dilemma. He thought both plans were feasible but he had to think about the post-war relations with the Soviets. *Who would want to get on the wrong side of this fellow?* Roosevelt seemed to agree with the Russian.

Churchill spoke out, again raising the Mediterranean issue of a split front.

Stalin sliced in at the Prime Minister's first pause and spoke directly to him. 'Do the British really believe in Overlord?' It was sarcasm and a question all rolled into one. Churchill glowered back, smoke was swirling around him. He chomped on his cigar and said nothing.

Stalin said, 'It is the stern duty of the British to invade...'

Churchill seethed.

The Soviet leader played one of his cards. 'Do you know how many of our people have been killed?'

The Prime Minister looked over at the President and knew what was coming. The first meeting of the Tehran conference was over; the air was heavy.

At the second meeting the Prime Minister presented Stalin with a gift from the British and King George VI, a gleaming Sword of Honour for the Soviet leader's victory at Stalingrad where he'd halted the German advance the previous year. The Russian took the sword from Churchill and raised it to his lips and kissed it. President Roosevelt was visibly moved by the gestures.

Stalin immediately raised the Overlord issue. Roosevelt appeared to be in favour of it and the Russian wanted the first of May to be the target date. He also wanted the date quickly agreed on so that the Russians could co-ordinate their offensives. The votes were cast: Two to one; Roosevelt was the deciding vote. The President voted in favour of Stalin's plan; an all out attack on German-occupied France, concentrating in the north.

The main course for 1944 would be the northern coast of France.

The Tehran conference was over. In a few days Churchill would confer with Roosevelt in Cairo, just the two of them and their staffs.

Back in Cairo, the President and Prime Minister decided that the current Supreme Commander of the Mediterranean forces- the American General Dwight Eisenhower- would be succeeded so as to become Commander of Overlord; the amphibious assault that would take place on the northern beaches of France before the end of the following spring.

Also part of the plan was an operation dubbed 'Anvil', a medium to large scale operation landing many western forces into the south of France. Churchill wanted this force to be as big as possible.

When it was over the Prime Minister climbed once again into the waiting car door. 'Thank you, Harold.'

The door closed.

Part II, epilogue

The half moon allowed the messengers enough visibility to push their large horses to the limit. Speed was of the essence! The trees on each side didn't help but they could follow the road. They had both travelled this highway many times and that experience was coming in very handy at the moment for them. The horses and the riders had all had some water recently, so even though the messengers knew there was an inn just ahead with a well they wouldn't be stopping at it. Full speed ahead...

Benjamin Bathurst had time to think only a few thoughts in the millisecond after he reappeared in front of the White Swan Inn: It's dark? Noise? Horses?

TIME RING, Part III

O thou, my lovely boy, who in thy power
Dost hold Time's fickle glass, his sickle, hour;

William Shakespeare

prologue

Mist calmly swirled over the majestic but rough south-central moun-
tains of Italy. Kapitan Karl Dieter of the Wermacht stood by a parked
vehicle with a few German soldiers at his side, the winter morning dew
covering the level ground. The roadway ended and he was looking
across garden plots at a couple of buildings about fifty metres away
that were set apart from the monastery. He had escorted a high
ranking German Intelligence officer named Reichardt up the mountain
road who was to question two monks that had been detained by a short,
bald beady-eyed Nazi. The two monks were not with the monastery but
had been visiting the past several months. Eighty thousand books and
other documents from the abbey's archives had been moved to Rome
by the monks and the Germans.

Leaflets warning of an imminent bombing, dropped the previous day
from Allied bombers, still littered the ground. Dieter was baffled; there
was no military presence here. Why bomb the abbey? *He watched the*
small office that was at the side of the other building. In the office one
of the monks was being interrogated. A German guard stood outside,
keeping an eye on the other monk who was inside the very crowded
building. None of the other people were being detained against their
will. The benches were filled with civilians seeking shelter- although
the threatened abbey was only a hundred metres away- and local
volunteer doctors, nurses and helpers from the neighbouring villages
that were scattered among the hills that rolled beneath the mountain
top monastery.

The old monk could not breathe very well in the stuffy, packed room
and wondered how his companion was holding up under the fierce
questioning. Would they use knives? *The monk did not like knives. He*

was terrified. It was a cold morning but a drip of sweat slid down the monk's forehead and nose. He touched his sleeve subconsciously and when he realized what he was doing he quickly moved his hand back to his side. He glanced at the door; the guard was looking the other way. The monk felt momentary, fleeting relief. He sighed.

Inside the small office the other monk was doing what monk's did best; he kept quiet. The short, bald Nazi believed that one or both of the monks had information about an ancient scroll that the Fuhrer was after and he had brought in Reichardt to get the truth out of them. The bald Nazi, whose name was Keltner, moved his face close to the wide-eyed old monk and, speaking Italian, said: 'I have been watching you two monks for weeks. And I know you want to take that which we seek away before the bombing...' The old monk stared at the wall. 'Look at me, monk. This is your last opportunity to speak before my associate talks to you. He doesn't say much.' The old monk stayed silent; then audibly gasped when he saw the uniformed officer produce a bloodied hammer.

By the vehicle, Dieter wondered what could be so important about a couple of monks. Dieter was a German, not a Fascist. Why did the Nazi's always want to go on wild-goose chases when they should be taking care of the Fatherland? *He was annoyed by their lack of focus-which was due from too much focus, he believed. They were extremists, and Dieter liked balance. He'd heard the engines minutes earlier and now when he looked up he could see that the planes were getting close.* Were the Allies really going to bomb the monastery? *It seemed ludicrous to him because there was nothing here worth bombing. He felt tense, irritated and impatient. He and the soldier watched the Allied bombers swarm high over them, an endless trail of planes following. 'Mein Gott,' said Dieter as he stared at the bombs falling through the sky toward the mist-shrouded monastery.*

Explosions rocked the mountain, shaking the earth violently. Dieter steadied himself on the automobile, exchanging glances with the soldier. Then, to both of their horror, a bomb exploded on the small office- which disappeared along with the front end of the adjacent building. Reichardt and Keltner were no doubt dead as well as the monk that they'd been questioning. The guard who'd been at the door was in pieces. The bombs continued to rain down.

Dieter saw the other old monk emerge from the side of the burning

197

and crumbling building with one of the civilians, a girl, and run across a field away from everything. They were heading to the trees and disappeared over a crest. The explosions created a tremendous roar. He was not concerned about the monk getting away; that was Nazi business, not Germany's.

The ground shook. Dieter turned to the soldier. 'Kommen zie.' They both started running toward the burning building to help the survivors.

chapter 1

What am I doing?
Well, Jack knew what he was doing and why he was doing it, but still he pondered that question daily. Crossing into Italy from France had been difficult and travelling down the Italian peninsula was even more so. To Jack, it seemed that the desert had been an easier trek. As he'd made his way south he'd been avoiding contact, visual if possible, with anybody.

Jack was huddled under a leafy old tree watching the rain crash down all around him, creating mud and puddles that would have made him very happy if he'd been six years old. He shivered when the wind picked up, crossing his arms and rubbing them vigourously to keep warm. He was hungry and food did not come easy. He'd run out of money weeks ago. Several days before, Jack had come across a stray chicken in a wooded area somewhere west of Rimini after nightfall and, having had no food in almost two days, made good use of the four matches and dry wood that he'd had. It had been a feast fit for a king.

Jack noticed some boulders in the distance that may provide him with better shelter. When the rain ceased, he decided, he would head off toward them. His clothes were falling apart and his body did not smell that *bon*. He would have to do something about his appearance before he found Maria: *if* he found her; *if* he made it there. Jack was thoroughly fatigued and could not go much further without a proper rest period. He'd slept rough every night and had not seen a bed since he'd left France last month. He'd depleted his tobacco a week ago.

Jack hadn't found out where the Villa Santa Lucia was located, or whether it indeed existed, nor the hill called Colle Sant Angelo. But he had learnt that there was a town called Sant Angelo near the Gari

River, east of Rome. He surmised that the hill and Maria's village would be near there.

The downpour subsided and Jack quickly made his way over to the hilly rocks, sloshing through the mud. His stomach ached for sustenance; at least there was plenty of water. As he reached the rocky outcrop a rabbit appeared and then froze in its tracks. Jack stopped, eyeing the animal hungrily as he slowly moved his right hand to his coat. The rabbit's instinct told it to flee and it did, rapidly hopping back to the bushes and into safety. He searched futilely for the animal but it was gone. Jack sighed. His tummy grumbled and his bowel growled.

He moved round to the side of the hill looking for a cave and was shocked to see a small wooden building. Jack reached inside his coat to where there was a pocket; inside the pocket there was a handgun. He took the gun out and held it at his side, cautiously moving closer to the building. *Was it someone's home?* His heart thumped.

The wind picked up, making it difficult for Jack to hear. But there was no sign of life and the door swayed with the breeze. He entered the one-room shack and had the feeling that the place had been abandoned. Two wooden chairs and a table were the only furniture and there was a small stone fire pit area in the far corner next to the open air window. It had not been used for quite some time. Shelves on the wall were stocked and Jack was extremely happy to see coffee, probably stale- *so, what?*- dried noodles, sugar, salt, pepper, flour in a tin, other powders- *yeast?*- and mercifully, plenty of matches. Jack felt that his luck had changed.

Convinced that the building was indeed abandoned, Jack relaxed and put the gun back into his coat pocket. He immediately set to making some coffee. Rain pelted the roof.

As Jack drank the stale, old, wonderful coffee he contemplated his situation. Christmas was about a week away; he would rest and spend the holiday in this shack and then set off in search of Maria.

Maria.

What am I doing? Going all this way for a girl who may not want to see me; a girl that is probably married and has children. Why am I doing it? Because I...am I in love? I must be.

I must be.

I must be nuts.

Klauss was no longer in Marseille and he was no longer Claude Rozier, nor Claude Larue, nor Claude Osteine nor any of the aliases he had used during his time in France. He stood by the window of his upper floor villa watching the rain fall on Rome. He came to Italy just prior to the Italians surrender to the Allies back in September. He was now Alberto Leitter, a Swiss businessman- *uomo d'affari*- married- *sposato*- with an Italian wife- *moglie*. It was Christmas Eve, 1943 and he was by himself.

Though it had been, and still was, a major hotbed for espionage-as well as various other dark and devious enterprises- he'd done an impressive job in Marseille. So impressive, in fact, that he'd risen to second-in-command of field operations in that area. As the Schutzstaffel seized more and more power in German Intelligence over the Abwehr, so had Klauss climbed further up its ranks.

It had been dark since late afternoon and the stacked old buildings that lined the street seemed to resign themselves to the bleakness that would prevail until the loveliness of the Roman spring. Klauss soaked in the atmosphere; indeed, the worse the weather became, the better he felt. Dismal, dreary and cheerless; Klauss was in heaven.

His happiness disappeared momentarily as the war situation came into thought. He was not happy that, despite all of Germany's earlier efforts and victories, the Allies had arrived onto mainland Europe and were nibbling their way up the Italian peninsula; and that now the Fatherland was on the defensive. *Why did the Fuhrer invade Russia? Madness! The Abwehr must have given him inaccurate intelligence...*

During his time in Marseille, Klauss had learned through the grapevine- via the Vichy government- that French Intelligence had once checked up on the Swiss residence of 'Klauss Lenz'- the name he'd used while in the French Foreign Legion. It was minimally disconcerting; more of an embarrassment. He'd made a huge mistake in Algeria but had since then kept his murderous tendencies to a minimum; he had only killed when it was absolutely necessary- a liberal boundary with an individual like Klauss. But inside, he still contained the rage as a time bomb contained explosion. *Tick...Tick...Tick...*

The apartment villa of 'Alberto Leitter' was situated at the south-east end of Rome. Outside, down in the street, Klauss observed a group of young Italians laughing and cheering as they strolled along taking turns swigging from a bottle of dark red wine. They were a noisy bunch and having a joyous time; Klauss hated them. He sneered; *they were better off when Mussolini was in charge.* He heard singing from a villa nearby. *Do these people not know that there is a war on? Maybe if I killed them; that would remind them. No; must not lose what I've worked for. Must be patient. There is a proverb: all good things come to those who wait.* Then...the singing stopped. The street was quiet and empty. The rain fell mercilessly. Klauss was happy again.

The war was rapidly descending toward Rome and the Schutzstaffel figured espionage to play a key part in the battle, as it had been in Cairo a few years earlier- though it failed them there eventually. But German Intelligence was convinced that where Egypt had failed, Rome would succeed.

Klauss's superior had sent him an agent to act as his wife and she would be arriving the next day. Until now, Alberto Leitter's other half had been absent from the operation. It was not the Christmas gift he would want; he preferred to carry out his clandestine deeds alone.

Klauss did not know much about his new partner; her name was Heidi Shultz and she came highly recommended. She had recently done work in Yugoslavia and she was from Bavaria. There was a black and white photograph of Frau Shultz face down on a table.

Klauss lowered himself onto the chair next to the table and thought about his assignment. He kept his thoughts, his secret missions, to himself.

Christmas morning was dark and gloomy but Klauss knew that his joy would soon be interrupted. The agent, Heidi Shultz, would be arriving at any moment. Her name was to be Carla Leitter. During his time as Alberto, Klauss had worked with two other agents. One, a man, had acted as a business associate and the other, a woman, who had acted as 'Alberto's' mistress. Neither of them had liked Klauss and the woman had been so repulsed by him that it'd lead her into a tendency to overindulge the ever flowing *vino*. She had become a risk and had been relieved of duty; preferring to take whatever punishment that came her way as opposed to working with Klauss.

There was a single knock at the door followed by three in succession. He stood up slowly and moved to the door, which did not face the street but was at the rear of the villa where there was a flight of steps. He placed down the photograph of Heidi Shultz- now his 'wife' *Carla-*

onto the table.

Klauss opened the door cautiously and studied the woman standing before him. She was taller and slimmer than he would have hoped- she was supposed to look Italian- and she did not have brown eyes. They were blue, which confused him. He thought: Were not the eyes in the photograph dark? He still had not said a word, wearing no expression as he gazed at her. She remained motionless. *The fools have sent me a blue-eyed Roman wife!*

But she was the agent in the photograph, Klauss was quite sure of that. The woman who stood in the doorway *did* have *dark* blue eyes; maybe it was just the lighting in the camera, he rationalized. Finally, he said, 'Boungiorno.'

The woman replied in predetermined code, 'Che pensa di Roma?' *What do you think of Rome?*

Klauss answered, 'E una bella citta.' *It is a beautiful city.* He moved from the doorway. 'Avanti.' *Come in.*

The years had passed by slowly for Janna, as though they were grudgingly moving toward the future. She had completed rigourous training for Allied Intelligence and had performed several minor tasks and missions but now she had hit the big time.

A female Abwehr agent had been captured- unknowingly to the Germans- by the Allies and, as it turned out, Janna was a dead ringer for the captured spy. The plan was for Janna to assume the German spy's identity and then be placed back into the field. To quickly learn as much about the woman as possible, Janna had been present at her interrogations.

Originally, Janna was to play it safe and vacate her role the moment things heated up. But as luck would have it, a series of events put Janna in a position where she could make some major contributions.

Janna was working as a double agent, sent by the *Germans* to her new assignment.

She looked at the Nazi agent standing in front of her as she entered the room. He had just asked her to sit down. He had beady eyes and a mean mouth. They had only just met and he was already suspicious of her. The man was pointing to a thinly cushioned chair and saying, 'Si accomodi, prego, Carla.' *Make yourself comfortable.*

Janna relaxed a little as she reminded herself to remain calm. As she sat down she said, 'Grazie, Alberto.' *Thank you.*

Klauss asked, 'Would you like some coffee?'

chapter 2

Looking south-west, the Professor spread his arms out toward the large orbed panoramic windows and the steep mountainsides. 'Wonderful view, isn't it?' He and Mister Black sat in the sunshine comfortably in fat cream coloured leather chairs, their drinks on glass tables next to them. His visitor nodded. The thirsty old man drank some water, put it down, picked up his glass of carrot, celery and beet root juice and cradled it in his lap.

Ishkur sat in the darkened bar nearby out of earshot from his father, much to Ishkur's dismay, with Erlinger and Hadrian. To curb his anger and distract himself, Ishkur fiddled with a Rubik's cube that was on the bar counter. It usually took him about four minutes to solve. Hadrian had picked up a chess piece, a pawn, from one of the beautiful sets. He twiddled it in his hand while he watched the Professor, who was listening to the man in black speak.

Mister Black said, 'The early published views of TTi seem to convey that time travel were already possible- that string theories and the like were mathematical nonsense- and this is how to go at it.'

'Not true. You must have misread or misunderstood.' The Professor sipped at his juice.

'Then, over the years, your stance lightened up. Diplomacized. You gave serious nods to the great scientists and voila: Science's new cup of tea. But your acceptance by the mainstream is more art nouveau, smoke and mirrors. You don't really believe the mathematicians and physicists-'

'Not true, Mister Black.'

'...And you just swat away all the existing time theories and project your own simple conclusions.'

'I'm not a mathematician. All those numbers and letters; it's like Chinese Scrabble to me.'

'You're not a scientist.'

'I don't pretend to be a scientist.'

'But you pretend to be a professor.'

'I am a professor...I'm a scholar.'

'If you say so.'

'Am I on trial, Mister Black?'

'Professor Garcia, though you're a peasant from Sierra More-na...you don't look Spanish and your accent is American; Eastern Seaboard. Very sloppy. You must have greased a lot of palms.'

'What are you, U.S. government? C.I.A?' Mister Black remained faceless. *'Interpol? Not the Russians or Israelis. You're not Chinese, are you?'* The old man saw Mister Black's lips slightly curl as though wanting to smile at that, but held back. He thought: Mister Black was not any of those entities. No; this guy was one of the elite- the ones who more or less ruled the world. And they'd found him.

The Professor had spent many, many hours in his younger days at casinos playing two dollar poker just for fun and to pass time, learning to read people's reactions. This guy was no bluffer, the Professor concluded. He sighed heavily, even exaggerating the sigh further to make a point. The old man was tired. *'Mister Black, could we cut to the chase, please.'*

'Yes.'

'We're losing the war,' said Mister Black after a long pause.

The Professor wondered when the vagueness would end. *'What war?'*

'The war with Russia. The economic war.'

'Shouldn't you be more worried about the Chinese; or the Arabs?'

'Hush. No; this is bigger. The KGB mob had infiltrated the European states long before reunification and they have controlled the Euro from the start. The Euro is, in fact, a smart ruble. They're beating us at our own game.'

The Professor watched the man in black finally display some excitement, though it was some scary shit. He thought: where the hell is this leading?

Mister Black touched his dark glasses as though he was going to take them off. But he didn't; he just put his arm down on the cool leather armrest. *'Operation Dragoon,'* he said. *'Fifteenth of August, 1944. Ring a bell?'*

The Professor shook his head. He guessed from the date. *'World War Two?'*

'Yes. Originally called Anvil. Amphibious landings on the south

204

coast of France; the Allies follow-up to the Normandy invasion.'
Mister Black paused.

Something did ring a bell, thought the Professor. He remembered. Yes; Cyril, a World War Two buff, had mentioned it in a conversation they'd had in a New Forest pub years earlier. Mister Black was about to continue but stopped when the old man raised his hand. 'Yes, I have heard of it. Tore up the French countryside.'

'Liberated *the French countryside,'* corrected Mister Black quickly. *The Professor had hit a nerve.* 'Anyway, in the 1980's some files were found in Washington that spelled out Churchill's intentions had Dragoon been a disaster. That is, to say, he would have swung his forces south and east to the Adriatic and the Danube, which was long rumoured. Our computer analysis for this scenario shows a favourable outcome for postwar Europe.'

'And what does this have to do with the tea in China?'

'What?'

'In English...'

'Yes. So, if we go back to the Second World War and somehow leak information to the Germans about the Dragoon landing then we will end up beating the Soviets to not just Berlin but also Yugoslavia, Hungary, Austria, Czechoslovakia, Albania and western Poland.'

'All very interesting, but it has nothing to do with me or TTi.'

'It has everything to do with you and TTi,' said Mister Black ominously. *The Professor did not like the sound of that. The old man braced himself for what might come next.* 'We need you to send one of our people back in time. It's my job to make sure it happens.'

'You're nuts. We can't travel back in time. It's theoretically impossible.'

'Cut the crap, Professor. We've been watching you a long time.' Mister Black let the words sink in. *The old man felt very numb and light headed; as he reached for his juice his arm visibly shook. The man in black continued.* 'We had someone pose as a student in your Field training. He finally left last January but not before befriending one of your Field agents- Melena Wohler. We found out a lot of great stuff from her; especially after she'd left TTi.'

The Professor's dizziness cleared, thanks to adrenalin. Thoughts ran through his head: Last January? Melena Wohler? After she'd left? *He processed the logic.* Last January a snowboarder went over a... *He then realized; the snowboarder was their spy. Melena Wohler had been one of TTi's top Field agents: hardworking, enthusiastic and intelligent. But then she'd become depressed, sullen- even angry. She'd left TTi at the end of the previous year. The old man wondered what his visitor had meant by 'after she'd left'. Had they blackmailed her? Tortured her? He looked at Mister Black, who was giving the Professor time to think about the situation, and thought: you bastards.*

'Any resistance would be futile, Professor. We even have rocket launchers in position to take out your helicopters. There is no escape. We know you can help us and you will.'

'What if I don't help?'

'Where do I start? Identity theft is the least of your troubles. Our people sniffed out a trail: your deceased wife's ex-husband Daniel Gerard, a very rich man of whereabouts unknown, had left his fingerprints all over his former residences and we found matching prints in a Boston Police file from the late 1960's; a Brown University student was arrested at an anti-war protest rally.'

The Professor gulped. Uh, oh... He now knew what it felt like to be a deer caught in the headlights. The headlights in this case being the flash of a school photographer's camera. 'Smile!'

Mister Black reached inside his suit pocket and pulled out a small black and white photograph, cut from a school yearbook. He placed it on the glass table beside the Professor's juice drink. He smiled at the Professor and said, 'You haven't changed a bit.' The old man's heart sank; he'd been found out completely. The man in black then threw in: 'Except, of course, for the wrinkles...huh, Professor? Or should I just call you Massy?'

'No. What makes you think I would help you even if I could?'

'We know you can do it. Don't make me say the obvious. You will help us.'

'And what if I don't?'

'Your son...'

'My son?' The old man glanced around quickly at the bar area. The three musketeers were sitting on bar stools. Ishkur was alright. 'What about my son?'

'We know you can travel back in time, Professor.'

'What about my son?'

Mister Black ignored him. 'Dernier told Wohler all about his "jump"...'

'What? Dernier?' The Professor straightened when it hit him: damn; they knew. *Alain Dernier had been a Field agent a few years earlier. There had only been three missions where agents were sent back in time and Dernier had been one of them. He'd also been a close friend of Wohler; she'd only know about anything if Dernier had waited years to talk to her. But where was he now?*

Mister Black seemed to know what the old man was thinking. 'Dernier blew his brains out just before we got to him...'

'What do you want me to do, Mister Black? If that's your real name...'

'It is.' It was; his name was, in fact, Foster Worthington Black. 'The plan is simple: our man is at the front gate. He drove me up and his name is Clayton. Bring him in here. Then you send him back to circa 1942 and that's it; done.'

'That's all?'

'That's all...'

Massy's creaking bones rose from the chair. 'Excuse me, I must talk with my people and arrange for your man to be escorted over here.' He walked steadily enough but he could sure do with a drink. A real *drink. And he was entering a bar. He made eye contact with the trio. He told his son, 'Ishkur, make me a Bloody Mary, please.'*

Hadrian cut in. 'No. I mean...sir, you shouldn't.'

The old man looked at his son, who hadn't moved and sat stirring ice in a glass. He took a deep breath. 'Okay. A Bloody Mary without the vodka.' Ishkur went behind the bar. Turning to Erlinger, he said, 'Stefan, the driver by the gate needs to be escorted over here but wait a minute and take your time. Hadrian, get Cyril over to me on the double.' He sat down on a bar stool and a moment later his son placed the Virgin Mary down onto the counter.

Massy had now briefed Cyril of the situation. They were in the bar, strategically behind a large potted palm. Ishkur had gone to the toilet again and Hadrian stood away by the windows. Erlinger sat silently with Mister Black in the lounge. Cyril asked his old friend: 'But what about TTi's "Rule Number One: Do not interfere"?'

'They have me by the balls, Cyril,'

'Operation bloody Dragoon...who would have thought?' Cyril

207

paused, thinking deeply. 'I suppose it does make sense logically if it was, indeed, successfully carried out.'

'Cyril, we can't let this Clayton go back with the bracelet.' Only a select group of people knew about Massy's bracelet: Cesca- his beloved and departed wife, his son, Cyril, Bill Sanderson- the Control Room manager, Stefan, and the three Field agents who had time travelled. A handful of Control Room personnel knew about the time travelling but did not know exactly how it was done.

Cyril contemplated a moment, then said, 'What if we send someone first and they wait for this Clayton fellow and just take it from him, at gunpoint if necessary.'

'Maybe. Which Field agent could we send?'

There was a long pause. The two men thought of the options. Then Cyril said, 'Me.'

'Cyril, be serious. At your age?'

'I get the bracelet back, put it down the cave chute for retrieval and live happily ever after.'

'I know you're a big fan of World War Two but this is ridiculous.'

'In fact, as war espionage is a forte of mine, I could set up the meeting for the leak before Clayton gets there. Their man could not possibly know what to do. I would leak Anzio at the last moment to attain credibility; then have Clayton...meet in Rome shortly thereafter. That would give the Germans enough time to act on it.'

'You want them to succeed?'

'Of course: If we do not, my guess is that they will kill you- and probably Ishkur- and take over TTi anyway.'

'I'd never see you again. Who would I talk to?'

'I divorced at twenty-four, old bean,' said Cyril. I thought I would get married again one day but...well, this allows me a fresh start.'

'Goodbye, Cyril.' The old man looked strongly at the closest friend that he'd ever had.

'Goodbye, Massy.'

Cyril was soon on an electric scooter roaring down the hallway north to the Field Wing. He knew exactly what clothes he wanted from wardrobe. He would also grab a pair of old German field-glasses and an operable Webley Colt .38 revolver. Cyril chose to not take this all too seriously. It was a game: The ultimate three-dimensional war game. Better than Nintendo. He was almost grinning; he felt like a kid again.

Meanwhile, Mister Black and Massy waited in the observatory lounge with Erlinger and Ishkur nearby. Hadrian had gone to get several sandwiches and French fries from the roof garden cafe, anything to give Cyril a little time. Rentzal was stalling at the front gate office and Clayton was still outside the gate.

Mister Black put a finger over the tiny round radio plug that was in his ear. He turned to Massy and said: 'My guy's not in yet. What's the delay?'

The old man called out to Erlinger. 'Stefan, see what's going on. Lank's probably double-checking everything.'

'Yes sir.'

Cyril sped up to the Control Room already wearing his war-era clothing that he'd got from the wardrobe in Field Wing. Sanderson, a tall and thin dark-bearded Canadian, was waiting for him with the door open.

The room had computers near the walls, chairs facing inwards, and in the centre of the room there was a raised area with a dark tinted booth. Cyril asked, 'Do you know what's going on, Bill?'

Sanderson glanced up and down at Cyril. 'It's Halloween? Just kiddin', man. The Boss spoke to me briefly over the intercom. It was coded but I got the gist of it. Ready to go?'

'As I will ever be. Nobody can set the "time" better than you, Bill. Send me to 1942, please. April, if possible.'

'I don't think I'm that good. But I'll try.' Sanderson handed Cyril the bracelet. 'Cyril...good luck, man.'

'I will need it.' Moments later, Cyril was gone.

Chadwick Theodore Clayton stepped from the elevator accompanied by Lank Rentzal and two guards. He walked casually over to Mister Black and TTi's founder, who had both just started eating and had mouths full of roast beef sandwich. Clayton said: 'Looks like a picnic.'

Mister Black told him, 'If I were you I'd dig in and eat up. You don't know where your next meal will come from.' Then to the old man: 'Professor, this is Clayton.'

'That would have been my guess,' said Massy.

Well over an hour after Cyril had 'jumped' back in time over seventy-five years to 'land' on the plateau, Sanderson climbed into the

209

Control Room elevator and descended, heading to a cave chute underground to see if the bracelet had returned now that 'time' had caught up. He'd picked out a select group of computer specialists to monitor any alterations in history. There hadn't been any. Only people who Cyril had interacted with would have had a tiny change but there'd been no significant changes in history, the computer group had concluded.

All doors leading to the Control Room were guarded by Erlinger's men. Inside, the four people- three men and a woman- were sitting in front of computers, relaxing and drinking fancy coffees while they waited for the Professor and his guests to arrive, who were on their way over from wardrobe.

Except security and a few chosen individuals everyone at TTi had been informed that the crisis had been a false alarm and everything was carrying on as usual, though the heads of staff could tell that there was something odd going on. Communication with the outside world was back. The convoy on the road had not moved and Rentzal had sent five guards to join Michaelson and Speier at the bend.

The elevator door slid open and Sanderson calmly entered the Control Room, four pairs of eyes watching him. 'So, I see our guests haven't arrived yet.' He had some good news but it was for the Boss's ears only. The bracelet had come back via a cave chute where Cyril had dropped it when he'd 'landed'. The chute- drilled from under by TTi to reach the deep, narrow natural hole in the cave- sent the bracelet into the chute basin for retrieval. Over the years Cyril had also left several notes, the first dated October 1941 and the last one June 1957. It was how all TTi's time travellers had sent notes and, more importantly, the bracelet back.

The Control Room's east door opened and in walked Massy; followed by Mister Black, Clayton, Erlinger and Ishkur. The old man looked at the anxious faces worn by his employees, sitting at their computers: Stenvaag- white beard and bespectacled with a heavy Norwegian accent; Winthorpe- Englishman with ginger hair and rosy cheeks; Mitsusaka- pretty and demure with porcelain skin; and McPherson- Canadian giant teddy bear. His eyes met Sanderson's, who with a tiny single nod let Massy know that everything was under control.

Clayton was dressed as an American businessman from the era.

Against Massy's will he was also armed with a P45 handgun. He also carried old dollars, some of it counterfeit. He stood listening to Mister Black.

While his two visitors were busy, Massy moved over to Sanderson. He said very quietly: 'Bill?'

Sanderson spoke quickly, just above a whisper. 'Bracelet came back in eighty minutes. First note- 1941; last, 1957. In January 1944 Cyril leaked Anzio in Lisbon and set up the Dragoon leak for Feb 1944 in Rome via Sardinia but when Clayton didn't arrive he went to Sardinia and missed the rendezvous by four days. Went back to Lisbon but never saw his contact again and gave up after the landings. Shacked up with a woman named Rosabella in the hills around here and lived happily ever after.'

The old man ingested the information. He smiled. 'He's probably buried nearby.' Then he calculated. 'He lived to about what, seventy-three?' Massy stared blankly for a moment then he said: 'What about the gun Clayton took with him?'

'Don't worry, Boss. You ever play chess with Cyril?'

Massy knew what Sanderson meant. 'Oh, yeah. Many times.'

Twenty minutes later Clayton stepped into the booth at the centre of the room where the bracelet was attached to his right wrist by Sanderson; then the ring was put on. Clayton's arrogance disappeared; he started to sweat and hoped that it wouldn't be akin to a roller-coaster ride through space. He hated roller-coasters. He felt thirsty.

Sanderson told Clayton: 'Push down here...and here...' They all watched with great interest. Massy hated this part; when someone else 'jumped' with 'his' bracelet. The possessiveness- it made him feel like Gollum. Sanderson continued instruction. 'Now keep it pushed down and don't move...' He set the 'time' on the orb; his instructions were to set Clayton's 'arrival' for approximately late 1942. 'Okay. Ready? Now...let go!'

Clayton was gone. He'd disappeared. The time was 4:58 pm.

'I'll be damned..,' said Mister Black.

The next couple of minutes passed in silence.

'Now what happens?' asked the man in black impatiently.

'Still waiting to monitor history,' said Massy turning around. 'Okay, computers; it's nearly been three minutes. Anything up, yet?'

Stenvaag said: 'Present time is...hmm; there's no old data on my computer.' Winthorpe's computer was having the same problem.

McPherson looked up from his screen at Massy and shook his head. Massy asked Mitsusaka, 'Mitsy?'

Mitsusaka was the smartest of the four. Her voice was so soft that it could hardly be heard. 'Boss, my guess is that something has changed so drastically that computers did not...had not...' She paused long enough for Massy to realize that history had probably changed.

'What's going on?' demanded Mister Black.

The old man ignored him and paced in a circle. 'Let me think...Winthorpe, check the microfilm connection. McPherson, try old computer lines. Sten, just keep on the present; it may be that no history changed at all.'

Stenvaag said: 'History seems normal, Boss. Maybe we need to wait.'

'We should have seen something old by now...'

'Boss...' It was Mitsusaka, speaking gently. 'I think it's time to try out Dzyan.'

Dzyan was a system idea by Massy, based on the Book of Dzyan legend, and programmed by the four computer geeks- lead by Mitsusaka. The concept was to have present day computers 'read' old books and newspaper and display the data onto the screen, thereby allowing events to be followed as they 'change'. It wasn't completely finished but Massy decided it would be worth a try. 'Yes. Let's do it. Bring it up, Mitsy.' Mitsusaka tapped away furiously at her computer.

Mister Black was not happy. He asked: 'Well?'

'We should have seen something by now. We weren't getting any old computer data on the-'

'Boss!' It was Mitsusaka. Massy had never heard her speak so loud. She was pointing at her screen.

The old man stood in front of the screen, behind the seated Mitsusaka. 'What is it?'

'It's from the War Library series; an old book from the '40's. There was a map, here...' Tap, tap. 'Back on page...' Tap, tap, tap. 'Here; see?'

'Bill, look...' Sanderson peered closer, Mister Black and Ishkur right behind him. The old man's shaky hand pointed toward the screen as he said: 'That's not the way the borders were, was it?' If he'd turned around he would have seen the man in black grinning from ear to ear,

which would have given him the answer.

'No,' said Sanderson. 'They weren't.'

Dzyan was only set up on Mitsusaka's system and the other three were not getting anything on theirs, so everybody crowded around the petite Japanese woman's computer to watch history unfold before their eyes. She said, 'On pause, Boss. That's it: postwar borders, October 1945.' Mister Black's eyes feasted at the result: the Soviets had been kept east from the Vistula to Belgrade. Just what the doctor ordered.

'Okay, Mitsy. Good,' said the old man. 'Now, keep an eye on developments. In fact, check old newspapers: London Times, New York Times...'

Mister Black moved close to Massy's side and said: 'Looks like mission accomplished.'

'I'm glad you're happy.'

Winthorpe read out something Mitsusaka had found. 'London Times, April, 1946: "Soviets demand parts of Poland and Yugoslavia"...'

Mitsusaka continued to tap at the keyboard, click her mouse and touch the screen. She stopped when Stenvaag cried out, 'Hold it! Back up a bit...' She tapped and clicked. 'There!'

Everyone turned as Sanderson read the huge front page headline aloud. 'New York Times, June 7: "STALIN SAYS CHURCHILL LEAKED DRAGOON".' Then he muttered, 'That sounds ominous.'

Mister Black and Massy exchanged glances. The tired old man thought: that's Not Good.

chapter 3

Jack was lying prone under a large leafless tree, his palms planted against the dirt. He pushed down on them in order to raise himself a few inches up. He vomited; again. *Was it ever going to stop?* He watched the projected sick mingle horribly with the previous offerings and prayed for the strength needed to move away from this foul image. *What did I eat?*

The mid-January weather only added to his misery. He had made rapid progress since his Christmas holiday at the abandoned shack; travelling from Pescara on the Adriatic coast through a valley below Mount Amara and past Isernia.

Jack's clothes smelled and were torn and shabby. He smelled, was fatigued and had lost a lot of weight. His beard was scraggly and contained pieces of vomit. He wondered if he was dying.

It would be dark soon. Jack did not like the idea of dying with some wild animal feeding on him. Raindrops started to slowly fall from the dull, grey sky. He managed to roll over once, to his left away from the sick. It made him dizzy.

Sant Angelo was not far but for now Jack could go no further. He pushed up on his palms and opened his mouth; he knew it was coming. He moaned. 'Uhhh, ckkuh...nn-ohh, not again- *bleagh!*...uhh, *bleagh! Bleagh!* Bleaghhh!' He stopped to get some air but the fumes made him gag and vomit more. *'Bleaghh!'* The muscles in his stomach tightened as it emptied; Jack was retching and could not breathe for a moment. He was exhausted and sweating.

Jack moaned quietly, his chin on the ground. The rain began to fall in large drops and Jack watched them splash into his vile yellowish personal pond, just inches from his face. One of the splashes spat vomit into his right eye.

Jack was too tired to curse his bad luck and was soon asleep, his cheek pressed against the earth.

chapter 4

Stenvaag asked no one in particular: 'Why would Stalin accuse Churchill of leaking secrets? It does not make sense; they both won the war together...'

'Read on,' said McPherson. 'It's about the Allies swinging east through Austria.' The computer crew did not know the exact details of what was going on. They knew this mysterious VIP had coerced their boss into sending one of his own men back to the Second World War and that they were to monitor changes but that was all.

Sanderson had been briefed by Cyril and Massy so he knew more or less what was going on. He stayed silent, keeping an eye on Mister Black.

Massy called out:'Time?'

Winthorpe answered. '5:05 and thirty-sev...forty seconds.'

Stenvaag read out a headline. '..."SOVIETS EXECUTE AMERICAN

SPY".'

Mister Black leaned in closer to read the story before Mitsusaka changed to a new screen. There was a picture of the murdered spy. Massy turned to him and said, 'It's not your guy...'

'No.' The screen changed.

Massy asked: 'Where are we?'

A soft voice: 'End of '46.' It was Mitsusaka. Ishkur moved to the door that lead to the Field Wing and put his ID card in the slot. The door slid open and he glanced at his father, who had turned at the sound. Ishkur went into a hallway and the door slid shut behind him.

Winthorpe: '5:06!'

The screen paused. McPherson pointed. 'That one. The U.S. is building nuclear sites in England, France, and Norway...'

Mitsusaka typed rapidly, her fingers a blur as they moved over the keyboard, touched the screen or clicked the mouse. Mister Black strained to see over the heads. Winthorpe called out the time, '5:06 and twent-'

McPherson: 'Oh, no!' Everyone's attention was on the screen where Mitsy had paused, which displayed a massive headline from the New York Times dated April 27, 1947: SOVIETS HAVE BOMB.

They were all silent. Nobody exchanged looks; they all just stared at the screen, waiting. Mitsusaka typed away and the screen changed. Stenvaag said, 'The Russians have blockaded the Norwegian Sea...'

Two clicks on the mouse. McPherson pointed. '...They've backed off.' Another double click. '...U.S. military presence in Norway, air bases, army...Trondheimsfjorden...'

Winthorpe: '5:07!'

Mitsusaka typed away, the screen changing several times. Stenvaag said: 'Wait; go back!' Mitsy clicked. 'There,' said Stenvaag. 'London Times..."US PLANES SINK SOVIET SUB"...on training mission. Off the coast of Norway.'

McPherson: 'It was a mistake; "US APOLOGIZES".'

'That was close,' said Massy. Sanderson had been sneaking a look at one of Cyril's notes to see if perhaps the reports had changed. When the date on the note matched the 'time' they were 'at' on the computer the note vanished in his hand.

Stenvaag didn't like what he was seeing on the screen. It was changing rapidly but he could see that much of the news centered

215

round his homeland. He saw the headline before McPherson said loudly, "'SOVIETS INVADE NORWAY"!'

Single click. Stenvaag summarised. '...Just the northern tip. No battles; but NATO mobilizes.'

'5:08!'

Click, touch, click. McPherson: 'London Times! "NATO-SOVIET SKIRMISH".'

'Not good.' Massy took a deep breath and huffed. He glanced at the sign that proclaimed TTi's now shattered motto: 'Rule Number 1: DO NOT INTERFERE.' He sighed.

'Mitsy, slower...look.' McPherson pointed. 'Soviets attack NATO forces...' A pause. '...The Soviets are retreating.'

Stenvaag: 'Yes, but they are reinforcing.' Massy wondered. Where the hell did Ishkur go? *Mitsy paused the screen.*

McPherson: 'New York Times..."SOVIET JETS ATTACK US SHIPS"...'

'Shit, where?'

'Baltics and Norwegian Sea.' Mitsusaka touched the screen and it changed.

Sanderson sidled over to Massy's side. 'Boss, come here a second.' They moved out of earshot from everyone. 'I took a look at Cyril's notes to see if they'd changed...'

'They shouldn't; or should they?'

'Well, as time catches "up" they disappear.'

'What?'

'Watch.' Sanderson held out a note of Cyril's dating 24 December, 1949. Massy took the paper and started to read Cyril's old message but after a few seconds the note vanished into thin air. The two men exchanged semi-amused looks.

Winthorpe: '5:09!'

McPherson: '1950!'

Sanderson spoke quietly to his boss. 'It's gotta have something to do with why there's no old data from the current systems; whereas Dzyan is running straight off images of old newspapers and books.'

'True. But, that means...'

'That means something bad happens, Boss. Something bad happened; and something bad's gonna happen. Right?'

'Doesn't sound good.' The old man had to think hard and fast.

Mitsy turned toward Massy and Sanderson. 'Boss...'

As Massy moved back to the computer, McPherson read off the screen. 'NATO bombs Soviet missile sites!' He continued. 'Conventional bombing; not nuclear...uh, oh; here we go...'

Mister Black seemed excited, getting in on the reading: 'NATO bombs Minsk and Kiev...Novgorod...' He was thinking: Yes! Kickin' their ass!

McPherson said: 'Soviets mobilizing...' Click, touch, double click. 'Soviet tanks engage NATO...middle of Europe...'

Little Mitsusaka stopped and leaned away from the computer. She looked up at Massy with doe eyes and said softly, 'What is going on, Boss?'

chapter 5

22 January, 1944.

Klauss and Janna sat in silence on soft chairs in the lounge area of the villa across from each other listening to the Italian radio news reports about the large Allied landing assault that was taking place on the beaches of Anzio, some sixty kilometres south of Rome. Even when the radio wasn't on they rarely spoke and the quiet was never comfortable for Janna. But, ultimately she was glad for the silence; every time Klauss had spoken to her she'd felt as though she were being interrogated. Usually, Klauss paced around- sometimes quickly, sometimes slowly- keeping his thoughts to himself. In her mind, because of her grief and hate, she had mistakenly identified him as the typical German: What he *was,* was the typical madman.

The lounge was dark because Klauss preferred the curtains drawn together, even during the day. A small amount of grey light seeped into the room from the kitchen's lace curtain windows through a doorway. The decor was extremely drab but not cheap and the room was practically bare of items other than books. There was one painting- an oil of Mount Vesuvius erupting, with the citizens of Pompeii looking on. It was badly painted with bright, showy colours. Very gaudy; Janna hated it. Though sometimes, strangely, she'd felt as if the painting was her only friend during this cold, bland, perilous winter. It hung on the wall across from 'her' chair and Janna had spent many minutes looking

217

at it, pretending that she was intrigued by the image; a good excuse to avoid making eye contact with the dangerous Nazi, who would sometimes just sit and quietly stare at her.

Janna sipped at her cup of tea, while Klauss drank coffee. She had not eaten since lunch and longed for some of the fine cheese that was only feet away in the kitchen. But Janna was waiting for Klauss to get hungry; she didn't want to annoy him by eating. Her stomach rumbled; she took a chance and asked: 'Le piaciereb-be pane? Formaggio?' *Would you like some bread? Cheese?'*

Klauss waited several seconds before answering. 'Si.'

'Ancora caffe, Alberto?' *More coffee?*

'Si.'

Janna wanted to jump out of her chair but instead paused a moment before casually rising and moving to the kitchen. Klauss watched her as she walked away, not for sexual reasons- she was an attractive woman, especially for her age- but to study her body language.

Klauss had had his suspicions about Janna from the beginning, when they'd met at the door some weeks earlier. He'd tested her several times, making odd remarks out of the blue to see what kind of reactions he could get out of her.

Janna stood in front of an open kitchen window slicing bread. She thought of her dead son and daughter, reminded by the sounds of Roman children chattering loudly as they played in the street below. The thoughts were quickly hidden away; it was too dangerous to allow them into her head.

Life outside seemed normal to a degree but the people could not be oblivious to the fact that the Allied forces were not far away and zeroing in on Rome. Janna glanced out the window; the late afternoon's dull daylight was fading. She grimaced when the knife cut into her finger, breaking the skin. She looked down and saw that she'd nicked herself but it was not bleeding. *Wouldn't want him to see blood on his plate!*

A child outside shrieked and Janna jumped nervously and sighed stressfully through her mouth. She composed herself and continued slicing, making sure not to make any more mistakes.

chapter 6

The Professor explained mega briefly to the computer crew what was happening. Mitsusaka looked sad, Winthorpe was worried and Stenvaag became sombre. McPherson, angry, threw an accusing eye in Mister Black's direction. Erlinger and Sanderson already knew. His son was still out of the room and he'd guessed that Ishkur must have gone to the toilet but that was a few minutes ago. The tired old man told everyone, 'I must have a drink; keep watching the screens.' He turned and moved to the intercom buttons that were by the east door.

Winthorpe announced dully, 'NATO, Soviets...tank battles, Czechoslavakia...'

Massy pressed the intercom and said, 'Pete?' Peter Drago headed the Field department. He waited a moment and then someone answered.

'Hello, Boss. Pete went to the coffee bar by the main crossroad. Things are back to normal, right?' It was Raj Suryet, Drago's main assistant.

'Uh, well...listen, Raj. Go to wardrobe and get me one set of clothes, early 40's, cash in pounds, dollars, francs, marks...' The old man stopped to catch his breath. '...Uh, Colt .45 with bullets, French and English passports of a male aged about...around seventy; and...what else? European style hat. Got all that?'

'Yes, Boss. Clothes, money, gun and passport.'

'Good. On the database in wardrobe you will find my measurements. Use those sizes.'

'Your sizes, Boss?'

'Yes, Raj. I'll have Bill zoom down the hall to pick them up from you. Hurry.'

'Okay. But why didn't Ishkur pick them up when he was here a minute ago?'

'What? Ishkur was there?'

'He picked up some books, Encyclopedia Americanas...'

The old man had to think: Of course; Cyril must have left a scooter in the hall between the Field Wing and the Control Room. Then he thought, but what was Ishkur doing? Never mind. 'Okay, Raj. Get those things ready and out the door. You don't have a scooter there, do you?'

'No, I don't think so.'

Massy heard McPherson in the background saying something about Korea and China. 'Gotta go, Raj.' He left the intercom and headed toward Sanderson, who was standing on the outskirts of the crowd. Just then, the Field Wing door slid open and Ishkur walked through carrying several encyclopedias. He changed direction and moved quickly over to his son.

'I got these books, Pop. To check the...look, history's chang-'

Massy interrupted. 'But Dyzan is doing that.' Dyzan was hooked to a computer that read hundreds of old books and newspapers simultaneously, inside a vault nearby.

Earlier when Ishkur had gone to powder his nose he'd seen the scooter that Cyril had used and decided to ride to the Field Wing. 'I thought perhaps these normal books might be a few seconds, maybe even minutes, faster.'

'I doubt it. I mean, how? Look, forget that. Listen.' The old man dropped to a whisper. 'You gotta get over to the house and bring me back something.' The house was Massy's residence on the premises, situated between the Research and Development Wing and the Academic Wing. His home, where Ishkur also lived, was a huge ranch only a few miles from TTi.

Ishkur put the books down. 'Something?'

The old man paused, enough for them to hear McPherson announce: 'Soviet-NATO cease-fire...Soviets in the Balkans...'

Massy looked at his son. 'Yes. Something. The...' He stopped, then said, 'You know Mother's jewellery-'

McPherson was louder this time. 'NATO resumes bombing!'

'-You know your mother's jewellery box, right? On her old dresser...'

'Yeah, the box you-' His father held up a palm.

'Ish, listen. The painting above it, the swans, look behind it- on the wall. In the middle there's a tiny off-coloured speck. Find it but don't touch it. Unhook the painting, put it aside and move the dresser aside. On the floor...' He had to catch his breath. 'On the floor under the carpet is a square cut in the wood. From where the wall meets the carpet you'll see two slice cuts parallel about a foot apart. Pull back the flaps. Underneath, the wooden square pulls out easy. Under it is a floor safe. The safe has a handle and a spot in the middle where a finger is placed but don't touch it. It's easy to see.' He paused. In the background McPherson was saying something about an air raid in

220

Norway. *'Got it, Ish?'*

'So far...'

'Okay. Find the speck on the wall. Press it, then quickly- within ten seconds, anyhow- press the spot on the safe. Use your right index finger. It only works for your or my fingerprints. Then pull up the handle on the safe.' The old man was stressed and tired. *'There is only one thing in the safe. Bring it to me: On the double. There are those scooters outside the Academic Wing door. Come back to that door. I'll be waiting.'*

'But, Pop. What is it?' Ishkur's strange, mixed accent made the word *'what'* sound like *'wert'*.

His father ignored him. *'If the safe doesn't open at first, try again. Ten seconds, remember?'*

'But, wert am I getting?'

The old man took his son by the elbow and guided him to the door that lead to the Academic Wing, glancing subtly at Mister Black whose attention was consumed by the computer screen. He leaned his face close to his son's. *'Ish, when I found the box in the cave that day there wasn't just one bracelet.'* He paused and let out a breath. *'There were two.'*

Ishkur didn't know what to say. Then, a flash bulb lit up in his mind: his dream of going back to the late Victorian era. He started to grin but his father stopped him with the slightest of head shakes, accompanied by a look of disapproval.

Massy said, *'Okay, Ish. Don't let on. Now hurry on and meet me back outside this door quick as possible.'*

Ishkur nodded; then realized something. *'Wait a minute, wert are you going to do with it, Dad?'*

'I'm going back in time to stop this mess once and for all.'

McPherson shouted: *'NATO bombers level Minsk!'*

'Wert?' Ishkur was confused. His light bulb puffed into thin air. He also thought: Pop can't go back. He stammered, *'But, but-'*

'No buts. Now get going. Quick.' His son stalled, staring at him. Louder than a whisper, he told Ishkur: *'Now!'* Ishkur turned and put an ID card in the slot and the door slid open. On his way over to Mister Black, Massy passed by Sanderson and said, *'Bill, you need to take the scooter that's outside the Field door there and ride down to the Field Wing where Raj will have some stuff for you to bring back to me. But*

bring it back over there; via the M25.'   Massy nodded toward the door which led to the Academic Wing corridor. The M25 was the nickname for staff at TTi for the hallway that circled the Control Room about halfway between each wing. 'It's longer, I know, but I'm meeting Ishkur there in a couple of minutes. I'll explain when you get back. Go.' Sanderson turned and left for the door. Massy went and stood next to Mister Black.

McPherson: 'Soviets bomb NATO and American air bases...Norway, Germany...but, little damage. Kiev levelled!'

Massy said to Mister Black, 'There's some whisky in the cabinet over there if you'd like a drink...'

The man in black smiled enthusiastically: 'To celebrate?'

'Celebrate? Are you nuts?' Massy was incredulous.

'Well, we're winning, aren't we?'

'We're headin' for Armageddon, you fool.'

'Nah. I think our forces will come out on top.'

Massy shook his head in disbelief. At least someone's enjoying this, he thought bleakly. McPherson's commentary was becoming increasingly scarier. 'Major Baltic naval battle...Prague entered...Soviets destroy American fleet in Black Sea...' A pause: Then, 'Leningrad bombed! Moscow! It's getting crazy!' Massy's tired old eyes met Mitsusaka's and he felt shame for letting this happen. McPherson jerked his head from the screen and told Mister Black, 'I oughta rip your head off!' The man in black recoiled.

Massy said, 'Never mind him, Mac. He's just the messenger boy for some very dangerous people. Calm down.' The uneasy silence was broken by a loud gasp.

It was Stenvaag. 'God in heaven, no!'

Mitsy cried out, 'Boss!' They all squeezed closer to the computer screen.

McPherson said loudly, 'Norway! Atomic bomb on Trondheim!' The Soviets had used the bomb. Then, 'What's that smell?' He sniffed: 'Bacon?' They all sniffed into the air, looking around, except Winthorpe; whose mouth was agape; pointing at the empty space beside him.

Mister Black: 'He just...disappeared.'

Massy: 'Who?'

Winthorpe: 'Sten...' He was still pointing to where Stenvaag had been sitting. The chair and Stenvaag were both gone.

McPherson: 'What's that?' He was looking at the spot where Winthorpe was pointing. 'The bottom part of the chair?' It was smouldering. They all bent closer to see.

Mister Black: 'It's a foot!'

McPherson: 'Holy shit, it's Sten's foot! That's his shoe...'

Massy: 'What the-'

Mitsusaka: 'Spontaneous Human Combustion.'

McPherson: 'Why? How?'

Massy: 'Because...Nils Stenvaag was born in Trondheim. In February, 1952. What's the date, Mitsy?'

Mitsusaka looked at the screen. 'It's April, 1952.'

McPherson: 'Great. We're toast. How long do we have, Boss?'

'An hour...at most. But really, could be any time.'

Winthorpe had seen Stenvaag vanish before his very eyes. He broke from the shock to say, 'Unless there's a permanent cease-fire...' Nobody else in the room felt that optimistic. The war had escalated and was now spiralling.

Raj Suryet stood in the white-walled corridor holding two knapsacks, watching Sanderson ride toward him. One knapsack contained clothes and shoes. Inside the other was money, passports, a pistol and a hat.

Down the long halls, on the other side of the Research and Development Wing, Ishkur had entered the house. He'd also decided that he was not going to let his father go back in time; he himself would go.

Back in the Control Room things had looked extremely grim after the United States retaliated with a nuclear strike on Smolensk. But everyone in the room was relieved, at least for the moment, when a cease-fire had been announced. There was still intense fighting around the globe. There were civil wars in Greece, Yugoslavia, Italy, Algeria, the Middle East and South America. The Soviets claimed Albania. In Turkey there was a blood-filled Communist revolution.

Massy was standing next to Mister Black wondering how he was going to get his visitor out of the room. He wanted to make his 'jump' without the Man in Black's knowledge. Time was running out. McPherson was saying the US and NATO had sent forces to the Balkans. The man in black turned his head and Massy asked him, 'Still wanna celebrate?'

223

'No,' said Mister Black. 'But I think I'll have that whisky. Bourbon, if you have any. I still think the Soviets will be subdued.' Massy went over to the cabinet. Mister Black followed him. 'Will that...what, uh, happened to Stenvaag- will that happen to all of us?'

'Quite possibly. I don't know.' Massy poured and then slid the glass over.

Mister Black picked it up and drank. 'Delicious. Well, Professor, it has been very quiet between the two superpowers since the cease-fire...' He noticed that Massy was not drinking; then continued: 'Not much is happening.'

'Oh, yeah it is. They're both bulking up their nuclear arsenals.' Massy paused, hoping that Mister Black would finally get the message. He spelled it out: 'They're going to blow each other up.' He poured whisky into another glass.

McPherson: 'NATO-Soviet skirmish in Hungary!'

Massy picked up the glass of spirit and told Mister Black, 'I'm taking this to Erlinger and then going to the toilet. Help yourself to more of that whisky, if you like.' He turned and went over to Erlinger. Mister Black poured another drink.

Massy said a few words to Stefan, looked sadly at the remaining computer crew- especially Mitsy- and then left the room. The door slid shut behind him.

Sanderson had passed the Research and Development and was on his way to meeting Massy in the Academic Wing corridor via the 'M25' when he saw Ishkur entering the corridor from a hallway on the right and, on a scooter with his back to Sanderson, was riding off. They were both headed to the Academic Wing hallway. Then Ishkur stopped and sat upright on the scooter, reaching into his pocket and fiddling with something. He did not hear the electric scooter glide up beside him.

Sanderson stopped and started to speak but his eyes fell onto the small vial that Ishkur held near his nose.

Ishkur was startled. 'Bill...' He closed the vial and put it away. 'I gotta go!' He roared off and Sanderson followed. Not far ahead was the intersection where the 'M25' met the Academic Wing corridor. Ishkur's father suddenly appeared from the intersection, heading in their direction. In moments, they all met up and stopped in the corridor.

Massy spoke first. He asked Ishkur, 'Did you get the bracelet?'

'Yes, Pop.'

'Bill, might as well dump out the clothes so that I can change into them.'

Sanderson guessed. 'You're going back, Boss?'

'Yes.'

Ishkur shook his head. 'No.'

'No?'

'No, Father. I'm going.'

'Don't be ridiculous Ish.'

'Whatever it is you have to do...I'll do it.'

'Clayton has to be stopped; probably killed.'

'I can do it. For once, I want to be able to do something important. Besides, I don't want to live in these times. I want to live in the past. I've started doing coke again...I need to get away from all...there's nothing for me here. Please, Father. Let me go.'

The old man was tired. His son wanted to make a fresh start. He looked at Ishkur and nodded approval. 'This is goodbye, you know...'

'I know.'

Massy looked at Sanderson. 'Bill, I was hoping to do the jump from the Control Room but we'll have to do it here.' Ishkur pulled out the bracelet. He knew how to put it on. 'Well, Ish...the floor's yours.'

Sanderson said, 'I hope you two have the same measurements.' Clothes were strewn on the ground.

'Not really,' said Massy. 'Anyway, we're running out of time. Just buy some clothes. Catch up with Cyril. He'll be there from- what was it- late '41? Bill, set the time for about...1942.'

Sanderson handed Ishkur the remaining knapsack. 'This is cash, passports and a gun.' He strapped it to Ishkur's waist.

The old man and his son faced each other. Old memories flooded in. Massy used to take his little boy on exotic archaeological digs all over the world. 'Say hello to Cyril for me, Son.' They hugged.

Sanderson set the time. 'Okay, be still, Ish. Want to say anything else?'

'I love you, Father.'

Massy told him, 'Good luck, Son.'

Sanderson said, 'Okay, ready?'

And then Ishkur was gone.

Ishkur suddenly found himself in mid-air, falling. He was terrified for a moment, like when one falls in a dream. Then he hit the ground awkwardly. He yelled out in pain. His right wrist and hand throbbed before the agony set in. There was little light but he could see that he was on the plateau where TTi would one day be built. At first he'd thought that he'd hit the ground leaning on his right but realized he'd hit the side of a large boulder just before hitting the hard dirt. The pain was excruciating and once again he screamed out.

Ishkur was disoriented and looked around to center himself. His left hand held his right wrist and he was still lying on the ground. The right side of his body ached tremendously and both his ankles, he guessed, were sprained. He hoped they weren't broken. The air was crisp and he started to feel the cold. Since he could see the light was coming from the east he determined it to be morning. Ishkur was becoming more aware of things but he felt dazed and the pain would not go away. He shouted and cursed a few times.

Then, the now official time traveller noticed the bracelet. The chain between the orb and the ring had broken. The orb was scuffed and the bracelet part dented slightly. Ishkur took it off carefully with his left hand and put it aside. Doing his best to ignore the pain, though still allowing the occasional outburst, he pondered his predicament. He would need water at the very least. He did have something that would boost his spirits, he reckoned, reaching for his coat pocket. But he froze when he saw a figure cautiously approaching him, about thirty metres away.

Ishkur reached for his knapsack, still tied around his waist. He knew there was a gun in there. He fumbled about but managed to get it open, then looked up briefly. The figure was closer, a man, holding what looked like a gun at his side. Ishkur's heartbeat jumped but then he realized the man looked familiar.

The figure shouted. 'Ishkur?'

Ishkur sighed, a massive breath of relief; it was Cyril. The body pains returned when the adrenalin subsided. He waved at Cyril, who started jogging over.

Cyril came to Ishkur and stopped, dropping to his knees next to him. 'Good God, Ish. Are you hurt?'

Ishkur huffed at his bad luck. 'Yeah...goddamn. Hit this boulder hard.'

'Ouch. Your wrist?'

'Yeah. Mm, ankles too. But I don't think they're broken, after all. Uh, right ribs...knees, a bit. I think the wrist is broken.'

'Can you stand?'

'Don't think so.'

Cyril pointed to the north-east. 'I landed over there; after my jump. That's where the Control Room was- *is*- I mean, *will* be...' He pointed to a crest nearby. 'And see that wooden shack, past that little crest, I built that to wait for Clayton. I went to sleep at dusk last night so I was awake; I heard you yelling.' Ishkur was listening, occasionally groaning. Cyril went on. 'Why did you land over here? Did you jump from the Control Room?'

Ishkur shook his head, grimacing from the pain. 'No. We were in a hurry? What about Clayton?'

Cyril had so many questions. 'Wait a minute, old bean. How did you get here? Your father told me not to send back the bracelet that Clayton wears...I've put it down the other chute; the one that leads deep into the mountain crevices.' Then Cyril said to himself: 'I suppose they could-'

Ishkur cut him off. 'Cyril, where's Clayton?'

'And why are you here? That's the big question?'

Ishkur grunted, trying to shun the pain. 'No,' he said. 'The big question is: where's Clayton?'

'He was here. Over a week ago. I arranged a boat for him to Sardinia where he has a rendezvous that will take him to a river house on the Tiber. The rendezvous in Sardinia is to ensure Clayton's passage to Italy, but I know where the river house is. As to where he is at this moment, I-'

'So, he's left! Damn...'

'Ishkur, my dear boy. What is going on? And we must get you some help. I have food and water in the shack. And a donkey. As soon as possible, we'll get you over to where my home is. But first, what on earth is happening?'

'I was sent back to stop Clayton, even kill him. But why is he here already? Wouldn't he meet you in 1944?'

'This *is* 1944. January.'

'But Sanderson sent me back to 1942. This isn't...?'

Cyril shook his head. 'No. Bill must have got it a little wrong.'

Ishkur felt crushed. 'Oh, man. I have to stop him. I have to.'

227

'What is going on back at TTi?'

'You wouldn't believe it, Cyril. History was normal after you went back but when that Clayton git went back all hell broke loose. It's the late 1950's and America and Russia are about to blow each other up. Pops was going to go back in time but I told him I would do it. You know; do something right for once. Something important.' Ishkur sighed heavily. 'And now I can't even fucking walk.'

Cyril had a thought. He looked at the bracelet. 'Well, we could just-' He stopped, looking closer at the bracelet because something was odd. 'Oh, no...' Cyril could see that the bracelet was broken. Ishkur understood what Cyril was thinking. That they could've used the bracelet to go back a couple of weeks and wait for Clayton.

'Oh, yes. It's snapped.'

'We could maybe try it...' They both paused to look at the broken bracelet.

Ishkur said, 'I don't wanna try it...'

Cyril agreed. 'Me, neither.' He paused to assess the situation. 'The bracelet I used has been put down the vault chute and Clayton was sent back wearing that same bracelet. I took that bracelet from Clayton-'

'Really?'

'-Yes, really. At gunpoint. Made him strip. Clayton had only one gun, massive, but lots of ammo. Gave him his clothes back, gave him directions and sent him on his merry way. Seemed like a right bastard.' He reflected. 'But I guess he got the job done. Or should I say; *gets* the job done.'

'We have to stop him...'

Cyril glanced back at the crest. 'I should run over and get you some food and water, and bring the donkey. The donkey can carry you out of here.' The morning light grew brighter but it was still quite cold.

Ishkur: 'Maybe some blankets?'

'Of course. So, anyway, I took the bracelet from Clayton and only yesterday I put it down the graveyard chute; the one that goes nowhere. But we can't retrieve either of them, they are too far down. Impossible. The broken bracelet would be dodgy...'

Ishkur was still in agony but the sight of the plateau as it was before TTi had been built was wonderful and nostalgic, for he had seen it like this as a boy. He sat with his butt on the ground, legs straight out. He bled only a little, on his right side and right arm.

Cyril said, 'Of course, we could find the cave where your father found the gold box and get the original bracelet out of it. By the way, how *did* you get here?'

'That's the thing. The gold box; it had two bracelets all along. Pops only just told me...'

Cyril grinned. 'The sly old fox. That explains it.' He looked to the west and raised an arm toward the beautiful ridges- lit up from the morning's rays- across the deep ravine. 'The trail is over there somewhere, I know. But I have never been to the cave.'

'I've been there.'

'You've been there?'

Ishkur rubbed his neck. 'But it was about...over twenty years ago.'

'Think you could find it?'

Ishkur thought for a moment. 'Maybe. I mean, it would take awhile. Some of the terrain is treacherous. Maybe not with the ankle messed up but still, could be days or weeks. Or I may never find it. I can't remember where, exactly. It's over that way, I know, but where it starts...' His words trailed.

'I do not think we have time to find the cave, dear boy.'

'If we did find the cave, I will easily be able to find the box. Father showed me the spot. You know; in the cave.'

'We do not have time, old bean. I am going to have to go after Clayton.'

Ishkur felt pathetic. Cyril would have to do the job for him. But somebody had to stop Clayton from relaying the information to the Germans. 'I'm sorry, Cyril.'

'For what? Oh, I see. Look, you could not help your unfortunate crash landing. You should have jumped from the Control Room. What was your father thinking? The jump booth is situated purposely over ground that would not change, but for the couple of inches of concrete in that spot. So anyone jumping pre-TTi would fall only a couple of inches, as I did. And I got a jolt from that. You must have fallen several feet; you are lucky that you did not shatter your legs. Did you brace yourself?'

'Hitting the boulder brought me to life quickly...'

Cyril was standing now. 'I better get cracking.' He began walking toward the shack.

Cyril had brought back food, water, blankets and the donkey. He'd watched Ishkur eat and drink, and then they'd carefully put him up on the strong donkey. Ishkur did not weigh very much. They'd left the plateau and were moving along the ridge trail to the home Cyril shared with the love of his life, Rosabella.

Cyril patted the donkey as he walked alongside the beast and its human cargo. 'If it were not for Neddy here I would go loony,' he said, referring to the donkey. 'I waited over two years for Clayton to show up: Nobody to talk to except Ned.' He turned his head toward the donkey's ears: 'Eh, my good friend.' The sun was showing now and was in their eyes. 'Neddy kept me company all that time; down here, anyway. I would go up to the house every now and then. Luckily, I was down here when Clayton arrived.'

Ishkur was still in pain but knowing there would be a home to convalesce at was extremely uplifting. The trail was getting rougher as it angled toward the apex.

Cyril continued. 'Rosabella's a fabulous woman. She will take care of you but if it gets worse you would have to take the automobile to a doctor. I will take the scooter, drive to the Gulfo de Rosas where I know some people and buy a boat and a captain.'

They eventually reached the top of the trail and moved along level ground, striking views of deep ravines to their left and right. Cyril did most of the talking. After awhile they stopped at a nice spot and Cyril helped Ishkur off Neddy. A large bird of prey flew nearby; then disappeared behind a ridge.

Ishkur asked, 'So, then...you kill him. Then...?'

'Guess I will have to kill him before he talks. He is the only one that knows. And then...I come back here.' Cyril raised his eyebrows and smiled. 'And then I get ready for Normandy.'

Ishkur wanted to laugh. 'Wert? Normandy? Cyril, you aren't...'

'Yes, of course I will go there. Would not miss that opportunity for the world, old bean. The landings...the beaches. Watching major history unveil before my very eyes...' Cyril looked at the expansive view, a dreamy glaze over his face.

'Cyril, you'll get killed...'

'Ishkur, I will watch from afar, naturally. 'Tis a dream come true.'

'You're nuts. You'll get killed, Cyril.' Ishkur didn't think it was so funny anymore.

'Do not worry. I have these authentic World War Two field-glasses...'

'They'll think you're a spy-'

'They are German field-glasses...'

'Great,' Ishkur said sarcastically. 'An Englishman with German binoculars in France. Nothing suspicious there. Whoever finds you will think you're an enemy spy and torture you or worse. They *kill* spies.'

'I think not, dear boy. Do I look like a spy?'

'Yes.' Ishkur paused; then said: 'What am I saying? You *are* a spy.'

'Ishkur, my good man, you are a funny chap.'

'Cyril, I've known you since...well, almost my whole life. You're my Dutch uncle...'

'Do not worry about me, Ishkur. You take care of yourself. If I die, I will die a happy man.' They sat in silence for a few moments.

Ishkur said, 'I was going to use that bracelet to jump back to the Victorian age; after I'd dealt with Clayton.'

Cyril smiled. 'Because you want to see who Jack the Ripper is; right?'

'Well, yeah. You know that.'

It was Cyril's turn to be sarcastic. He said in fun, 'Yes. Nothing dangerous about *that*, old bean...'

Ishkur tried to suppress his growing grin. 'Touche, old bean.'

'Touche.' Cyril stood up and reached an arm out to Ishkur. 'Guess we should get going again.'

In the Control Room McPherson continued to announce the developments displayed on the screen as Mitsusaka typed, touched and clicked away. Winthorpe had shifted closer to the computer, moving his chair into the space where Stenvaag had been. Strangely, Stenvaag's chair had vanished along with him but his left foot and shoe had fused with the bottom of that chair. After it had cooled McPherson'd put it in a bag, placing it aside. Still, Winthorpe felt a little uneasy sitting there.

NATO had sent forces to the Balkans and the fighting had escalated quickly, leading to another cease-fire. It lasted only two months, which was about ten seconds to the five people in the room: A small reprieve. McPherson read off the glaring Los Angeles Times headline: '"SOVIETS INVADE CZECHOSLOVAKIA"!'

Mister Black looked up; he'd pick up an encyclopedia and had been astonished and fascinated to see the history pages change before his very eyes. He could tell what the date was on the computer by seeing when the history changed. 'It's the fall of '57,' he said. 'Right?'

Winthorpe answered. 'Yes. Autumn...'

McPherson: 'They're attacking over the German border! ...Northern Italy! NATO on the run...Americans send massive army to Europe...' Then, to no one in particular, 'Think I'll pour me a Scotch.' Erlinger, who'd been standing behind them alone with his thoughts, joined him.

Earlier, Massy had told Erlinger that he was 'not really going to the toilet and that Bill would explain later.' Erlinger wondered what his boss, Ishkur and Sanderson were up to.

Winthorpe took over the commentary. 'NATO warns Soviets to stop...'

McPherson poured two glasses and handed one to Erlinger. 'Anyone else?'

Winthorpe joked blackly, 'A pint would do nicely...with a strychnine chaser.'

'No such luck,' said McPherson before draining his glass.

Mitsusaka paused the screen for a moment. Winthorpe pointed: 'Russians capture Prague!' Mitsy typed with her left hand and used the mouse with her right. McPherson returned to the computer. Winthorpe said, 'Russians fighting toward Berlin...'

Mister Black looked up from the encyclopedia and exclaimed, 'I just read that! Just that moment!' He was excited when he should be worried. Erlinger looked at the man in black and shook his head incredulously.

McPherson told Mitsusaka, 'Wait!' She knew what he meant and side clicked, which brought back the previous frame. The big Canadian read aloud the Los Angeles Times headline, bellowing: "'SOVIETS BOMB BERLIN"!' Everyone was silent for a moment. Mister Black closed the book and put it down. McPherson, almost reluctantly, continued, 'NATO responds, bombs Minsk...Lvov, Kiev...' The door to the Academic Wing slid up and Massy and Sanderson walked into the Control Room. McPherson looked over and said, 'Just in time for the end of the world, Boss.'

Massy didn't like the sound of that. He knew it would be a couple more minutes before there'd be any change from Ishkur's going back.

The old man asked, 'What time is it?'
Winthorpe: 'Coming up to 5:17...'
'No; I mean, the year?'
'1958...January.'
McPherson: 'Soviets bomb Bonn, Brussels...' He stopped abruptly,
staring at the paused screen. 'Jesus...'
Massy didn't like the sound of that either. 'What?'
A photograph of the Parisian outline, minus one very famous
landmark, accompanied the New York Times headline that said it all in
two words: EIFFEL TOWER!

chapter 7

Klauss had been awake since before dawn. He was fully dressed and
had made himself a breakfast of eggs, fried potatoes, ham and toast
with coffee. The cold, mid-February morning covered Rome with low
clouds. Although the weather was gloomy Klauss was ecstatic. It was a
big day for him.

He was making more coffee when Janna came into the kitchen.
Puzzled, she asked in Italian, 'A special occasion, Alberto?'

'Good morning, my beautiful,' chirped Klauss, ignoring the question.

My God, Janna thought. *Was that a real smile? Why was he so
happy?* Klauss gestured toward the coffee. She said, 'Yes, please. It
smells very nice. You have already eaten...'

'Yes.' He poured coffee and handed her a cup on a plate.

She took it. 'Grazie.'

Klauss then spoke quieter, in German- which he rarely did and only
outside far away from anybody- with a gentle tone. 'I never ask about
your old life, Heidi. What region of Germany are you from?' He sipped
at his coffee, picked up a plate of sweet pastries and moved into the
other room. He looked back at her and smiled. 'Come.' He sat down in
his chair and Janna followed suit.

She thought that it was very unprofessional of Klauss to speak
German at the villa and to call her by her real name, although Heidi
wasn't her real name. It was somewhat disturbing. *What was he playing
at?* Janna wasn't sure whether to answer in German or in Italian. She
said the name of the town that Heidi Shultz was from. 'Finsterwalde.'

Klauss could see that she was uneasy. He held the plate of pastries out to her and said in Italian, 'Here, have one of these...' He smiled warmly at her.

Janna was still sleepy. She did not know what he was up to but at least he was being kind. 'Grazie.'

Again he spoke in German. 'It is alright to speak our language. Nobody will hear us. Go ahead. Please, you will feel better.' He smiled again.

Janna decided to indulge him, not wanting to anger him. She spoke in German, almost whispering. 'I was born in the hills outside of the town, in a church.' She was reciting from data stored in her memory.

'Jawohl...ah, yes. I have been there.' He sipped. 'The hills are very lovely, like you are.' He smiled brightly.

It all seemed absurd to her but Janna had to go along. She was about to say thank you in Italian but changed to German. 'Dzie-': She froze, just for the tiniest of instants. Then quickly: 'Danke, Alberto.' She dropped her head to her cup of coffee, avoiding eye contact. Janna felt sick. *Had he noticed?* She did not want to look up to see if he had. Janna forced herself to peer up and look into Klauss's eyes, asking for another sweet pastry.

He handed her the plate and she took an apricot-filled one. Janna searched his eyes for any sign; any signal that would tell her whether or not he had noticed her slip up a moment earlier. Her heart hammered against her chest. There was no recognition in his eyes. She felt a little better. Maybe he hadn't noticed. After all, she rationalized; it had only been an instant.

Klauss leaned back in the chair and said in Italian: 'Ah, yes. As for today, I have a special assignment. You have nothing to worry about. You stay here at the villa until I return. I will not be too long.' He smiled once more at her.

Funny, she thought. His smile wasn't quite as warm as it had been thirty seconds ago. It was more...satisfied.

Klauss went over to the door and put on his long, dark grey coat. 'It is very chilly,' he said, closing the door behind him.

Janna thought: As it always was.

Klauss drove his automobile out of the eastern end of Rome south-west toward the Tiber River. His direct superior had been told by the Fuhrer himself to go to the front on some very important assignment and so Klauss was given the responsibility to show up at a separate urgent meeting; one his superior could not attend. Klauss was thrilled.

Cyril had found a boat and captain in the Golfo de Rosas that would take him to Italy, though it had been very expensive. There'd been no reason for him to try and make the rendezvous in Sardinia because it'd been too late for that, though he would rather have had to deal with Clayton before the rendezvous. Clayton would have had safe passage from Sardinia to the meeting point, which was a river house on the south bank of the Tiber just outside of Rome. Clayton had already been there for days. The actual meeting was to take place in less than fifteen minutes.

Cyril was riding his scooter- he'd brought it on the boat with him-under a dark grey, low clouded sky. He wore a heavy, brown coat and was thankful for the warmth it gave on this chilly morning. He'd not been able to persuade the captain to take the boat up the river so he'd disembarked near the mouth of the Tiber; but it hadn't mattered as Cyril was late and he was making faster time riding on the road that ran alongside the south side of the river.

The river house was not far, he was sure of that. The main landmark he was looking for was a prominent bridge that was just north-east of the meeting place. There was little other traffic on the road but in some parts of the riverside it was quite busy, he noticed as he sped along. Even an hour earlier would have made a world of difference, thought Cyril. But now he was cutting it too close. He had to get to Clayton and kill him as Cyril did not think Clayton would comply. And he had to do it before Clayton passed on the information to the Germans or it would be nearly impossible for him to achieve his task.

There was still no sign of the bridge. As Cyril rode north-east he could see the south side of the river was lined by trees and bushes. There were few riverside dwellings along here and he was feeling anxious. He saw a couple of houseboats and wondered if his German contact in Lisbon had made a mistake in the translation, for the contact spoke to Cyril in English. Up ahead on his left he noticed a long rectangular building but it did not look like a home, he thought as he gave it a long look. Cyril swerved quickly when he realized he was about to run over a cyclist, who he could hear cursing behind him. As the road curved closer to the river it rose a few feet and then Cyril saw the bridge. He quickly looked for any sign that confirmed the bridge's name and also kept looking for any river house just south of the bridge. The bridge was not far and he could see there were no buildings between him and the bridge, unless they were obscured by the heavy foliage that ran along the south side of the river. He was sure that this was the right bridge and his instinct was right. A sign read: Verdezza Bridge.

That's it, Cyril thought. He slowed to a stop, on the side of the road. A large lorry roared past him, heading south-west. He looked to his left toward the river. There was nothing he could see that looked like a river house. He deduced it may've been the rectangular building that he'd passed a moment earlier. He spun his head back to the road and started turning the scooter around in one motion. Cyril looked up and stopped abruptly when an automobile travelling from the direction of Rome approached and sped by.

Klauss was annoyed that the man had tried to turn his motor bike around in the middle of the road like that. It could have caused an accident. Klauss quickly forgot about it and scanned the riverside for the site of his important assignment, a meeting with an Allied double agent. He knew the place was just up the road on the right.

It was the first building Klauss had seen since he'd passed the bridge and he drove down a dirt path to it and stopped.

Cyril had turned around and soon saw the rectangular building, now up ahead on his right. He also noticed with some dread that the black car that had sped past him a moment ago had turned down a dirt path and was stopped in front of the building. The lone driver was getting out of the vehicle. Cyril slowed and veered off the road to the right towards the riverside. The building was still some distance away but he could see the driver getting out. The ground beneath Cyril was uneven and the scooter bounced around. He saw a uniformed German officer emerge from the door at the front of the rectangular building and the two men were speaking. Cyril nearly lost his balance so finally he slowed the scooter to a stop and hid it behind a bush.

Cyril quickly reached under the seat to a specially built compartment and pulled out his Webley .38 handgun and his field-glasses. He started moving toward the building but stopped when two German

236

soldiers also emerged from the front entrance. They'd joined the uniformed officer outside but Cyril noticed that the driver of the automobile wasn't there. He must have gone inside. Cyril quickly lowered his body and in a crouch moved to his right where there were trees. As much as he could, he angled closer to the building. If the Germans out front looked over they would probably see Cyril.

He moved into some thick bushes and rested a moment. Cyril could see three windows at the side of the building so he got up and ran a little closer to some other thick bushes. He glanced back at the front; they hadn't seen him. His heart pounded. Cyril had a clear view of the windows and through the middle one he saw Clayton's left profile. Cyril's heart jumped. Clayton was sitting, arms resting on a table.

Cyril held up the field-glasses, thinking he would have to get much closer to get within accurate shooting range. Also, he had the problem of the soldiers out front. How could he get away? Clayton suddenly sat straight up and a second later Cyril clearly saw the driver of the automobile sit down at the table, across from Clayton. Cyril had to think carefully; he couldn't just run over there, guns blazing.

Klauss sat with his hands at his side. He spoke German. 'Guten Tag, Herr...?' He did not offer a hand.

The man sitting across from Klauss could understand the greeting, but replied in English. 'Clayton is my name. *Mister* Clayton. Not *Herr* Clayton. And I don't speak Kraut. You speak English, I hope, Herr...?

Klauss told him in English, 'Never mind my name. I am the one for who you need to give the information to, *Herr* Clayton.'

Clayton sneered, thinking: Great, I get an asshole to deal with. The two men stared at each other for a few tense seconds, neither of them blinking.

Klauss had had enough. 'Well?'

Clayton did not like being ordered around by this guy. 'I'm trying to help you fucks.'

'Tell me. Why do you want to help Germany?'

'None of your business, pal. Just know that the information is completely accurate.' Clayton had already decided how he would present the facts and wanted to pace himself so that he could go through it all in the correct order. 'This is extremely important,' he said.

'I am waiting, Herr Clayton.'

'Hold your horses, Fritz. Jesus...' The room had no heating and though it was cold Clayton was beginning to feel very warm. 'There will be a major Allied amphibious assault on France by the-'

'When?'

Clayton ignored him and continued. '...By the Allied-'

Klauss persisted. 'When?'

'Listen, goddamit, and I'll tell you. But first-'

'When? Answer, Herr Clayton!'

'Jesus. August, but-'

'Not until August?'

'Yes, but it was originally planned to take place in May-'

'May? Or August? Tell me, Clayton!'

'I'm trying to tell you, if you'd only let-'

'Stop your stalling!'

'I'm going to pop you in the mouth if you don't shut up! Let me explain it through.'

'I am listening.'

'The operation is code-named "Anvil" but will later be renamed Operation Dragoon. Fifteenth of August: amphibious assault. About a thousand ships, including ten carriers and five battleships with the initial wave bringing in a hundred and fifty thousand troops. Over the next-'

'Where?'

'I'll get to that.' He glared at Klauss; then continued. 'Next couple of days that number will double and in the following few weeks over a million Allied troops will come ashore on these beaches. The night before there will be seaborne and aerial commando raids, and in the early morning parachute drops behind lines.' When Clayton paused, Klauss raised a fist and slammed it down on the table.

'Where?'

'South coast. East of Marseille, between Toulon and Nice. Objectives are Lyons, Paris and the Rhine. The planned liberation of France. Here is a list of the commanders, divisions, army groups, objectives, commando operations...everything.' Clayton put a small folder onto the table and pushed it over to Klauss. 'It is imperative that this information goes straight to the Fuhrer. That was part of the deal.'

Klauss was to take this information straight to his superior, who had gone to the front line, and his superior had a direct line to the Fuhrer. It was only a small lie. 'Jawohl. Yes. From me straight to the Fuhrer.' Klauss stared at Clayton with little expression. Then added: 'You small pig. Is that all?'

'Listen, buddy, this...,' Clayton said, pointing at the folder, '...is going to keep the Allies from overrunning France.' He was about to add the word *temporarily*, but thought better of it. Wouldn't want to ruin the Kraut's hopes, he thought spitefully.

Cyril knew without a doubt that Clayton was relaying and giving the information about Anvil to the man at the table. He also knew that he would have to kill both of them and then escape before the other soldiers caught him. He'd moved down into the foliage near the river where he was well concealed. Cyril could hear the river water slap up against, he guessed, small wooden docks. He was moving closer to the building's back end where he hoped to make it unannounced up the side to the middle window.

A moment ago Cyril had seen one of the soldiers look in his direction but he'd been relieved when the soldier had looked away uninterested. Cyril stopped when he noticed he had a good, concealed view through the window and lifted the field-glasses to his eyes for a close-up. He could see the folder on the table; he knew what it was. He had seen it when he'd strip-searched Clayton back at the plateau in Spain.

The man who'd driven to the river house was talking to Clayton. Cyril moved the field-glasses to the right a smidgen and saw the side of the American's face; enough to see the anger on it. He moved the view back to the other man. Incredibly, Cyril saw the man lift a gun- he could see it was a Luger- and, still sitting, calmly fire across the table. Cyril quickly looked to the right and could see Clayton grab his own chest. He put the field-glasses down so he could see both of them at the table, even though they were now smaller to see. The man fired again, this time into Clayton's face, and Cyril saw the American's head fall down onto the table. The other man calmly picked up the small folder and turned around and left out of view.

Cyril looked at the front of the building and could see one of the soldiers standing at the corner looking toward the front doorway. He couldn't see the other soldier or the officer. They probably would have gone to investigate the gunshots. He thought: What if the man tells them about Anvil, too? Cyril would have to kill all of them. He wished the scooter was closer. He couldn't possibly get out of there alive by running up now and shooting. He quickly decided to run to his scooter and ride over there, pretending to be lost. He would ask directions and then shoot them as they would not be expecting that. Cyril shook his head at the ridiculous idea: Ludicrous. But he had no other plan and so he kept moving along the foliage toward the scooter.

Please think of a better idea, he told himself. He glanced back. The man who shot Clayton emerged from the building quickly and headed straight for his car, ignoring the officer who was following him. There was one soldier outside. Cyril guessed the other one must be inside, checking the body. He tripped and stumbled but kept moving. Looking back again, he saw that the driver was reversing back down the dirt path. The uniformed officer's hands were fanned out, still walking after the departing automobile. Cyril deduced that the killer had not said anything to the officer. Cyril was running hard and could see the bush that concealed his scooter.

Past the scooter, to the right, the man who killed Clayton sped along the road that led to Rome. Cyril jumped on his scooter and followed him.

chapter 8

Jack had been found sleeping in his vomit by the son of an Italian baker, who told his mother and father about the man who looked dead. The parents had the boy show them where the body was and they'd been surprised to see that the man was still alive. They'd helped Jack back to their home and took care of him for a few weeks. After he had restored his health he'd said goodbye to the family and continued on his way to Sant Angelo in search of Maria, although he'd practically given up hope that he would actually find her.

He had found Sant Angelo only to discover that Colle Sant Angelo, the hill near Maria, was still a few miles away to the north. That wasn't bad news but the problem was that he was at the front line of battle, at the heart of the Gustav Line. He travelled at night, walking through the trees under the cover of darkness. Crossing any roads left him extremely vulnerable. He'd seen Americans the last few days and now he was seeing the occasional Germans. He'd crossed over the front line.

Jack rested among the trees in the misty morning dew. He shivered, looking up the green incline to the steep hills that led to where Maria lived. *Up there; somewhere.* He knew it would be a fair hike and Jack was glad to be back in good health. Doubtful thoughts constantly played on his mind. *What if she doesn't even acknowledge me? Or won't speak?* He pushed the thoughts out as quickly as they came in.

He still had some bread and cheese but he would need to have a proper meal again soon. Back at the baker's house Jack had realized how important a simple home cooked meal was. Over the last few days he'd heard explosions and periodic gunfire. Since he'd been travelling at night, that meant he'd sleep during the day. Jack was often jolted awake by the sound of artillery shells exploding in the distance. It made for disturbing dreams.

But this morning he would only be resting awhile. He was not going to sleep, yet. Crossing over the front line and making his way into these mountainside woods had given Jack a lift in spirits. He was closing in on Villa Santa Lucia and he needed to find out about Maria, whether it would be good news or bad news. The village was probably only a mile or two up this rugged terrain, thought Jack. He looked at the dense, wet greenery around him. It would not be easygoing but with a little rest he should be able to make it to the top of this first incline with little difficulty. It was daylight now and he would have to be very vigilant. Jack would have to traverse very slowly up the mountainside.

Reaching into his coat's outer pocket, Jack produced some cheese and stuffed a chunk into his mouth. He chewed slowly and let it melt in his mouth. It tasted wonderful. Jack did his best to appreciate the cheese, savouring the taste.

He just wanted to find Maria safe and sound.

chapter 9

Cyril had followed the black automobile into Rome, putting off making his move until the car stopped. After heading north-east from the river house the murderous German contact drove to the city's eastern side. Cyril still hadn't been noticed tailing the vehicle, keeping some distance behind. The early morning sky was still dark grey.

The man who'd killed Clayton had not had yet spoken to anyone about Operation Anvil and Clayton was dead, Cyril was sure, so he still had hope. He would just have to kill this German agent before he had a chance to speak.

Up ahead he saw the black car turn right, heading east. Cyril was feeling very nervous and wished he was somewhere else. He slowed the scooter and made the right turn onto a residential street. He panicked when he did not see the car down the road- thinking for an instant that it must have turned onto another street- and started to accelerate. But he quickly saw the black automobile parked just ahead on the right side in front of a row of villas. Cyril caught sight of the man walking away and disappearing around a side entrance to the villas. He slowed rapidly and veered to the left to the opposite side of the road and stopped. He was too chicken to park next to the black car.

Heart pounding, Cyril reached under the seat for his gun. He looked up and saw a second floor light go on in one of the villas. He waited a moment, looking through the lighted window, and then clearly saw the agent who'd been driving the black car. Cyril watched the man, now seeing his left profile. He'd seen the man's right profile at the river house. Cyril did not like either side.

The man was talking to someone but Cyril could not see who, although there was another window. But it had lace curtains and he could not see the other person. Cyril sighed sadly, thinking, that means someone else has to be killed. He could take a shot from here at Klauss but that would alert the other person and they'd still have the folder. He knew he would have to cross the road and possibly be seen but he had to get closer. There was very little traffic about. A few cyclists were coming down the street and further down there were pedestrians but for the most part it was deserted here. He decided to head for the side entrance where there must be a flight of stairs. He waited for the cyclists but really he was just stalling. He was scared. In fact, he'd never been so frightened in all his life. Cyril watched the man through the window, knowing he could not stall forever.

Inside the villa Janna stood listening to Klauss, who seemed to be excited but also looked very manic. She glanced through the lace curtain and front window and espied a man standing next to a motor scooter. He seemed to be looking through the other window, where Klauss stood, watching intently. The other window did not have a lace curtain. The man held something in his hand that looked suspiciously like a gun. She looked back at Klauss who was speaking non-stop.

Klauss spoke German. 'So you see, Frau Shultz, I am at this very moment not only the most important German spy in Rome...but the most important *anywhere*.'

Janna glanced out the window. The man across the street still watched Klauss, hands now in his pockets. Three cyclists rode by in front of him. She returned her attention to Klauss. He told her, 'And now I have information that will turn the war back in Germany's favour...' He waited for a response. She shuddered at the news but did not display any emotion. 'You seem quiet for one who has just received such joyous news.' He looked hard at her.

Janna said, 'That's wonderful...' She was also speaking German, confused whether to call him Alberto or not. She scratched her face so that she could peek out the window. The man still watched Klauss through the other unobscured window and had not moved away from the motor scooter. He stuck out like a sore thumb, she thought, thinking of the phrase from her British training period with the Special Operations Executive. She wondered: What was he up to?

Klauss smugly told her, 'However, your lack of enthusiasm does not surprise me.' He now had her full attention. 'You do not know it but last week the Schutzstaffel took over all German Intelligence duties. The Abwehr is, well, no longer. It will soon be official. We have taken your hero Canaris as he is, like all Abwehr, a traitor at best and a double agent at worst.' He smiled at her; it was a horrible smile. Janna's forehead started to tingle and her mind crushed as the brain screamed alarm.

Janna wanted to learn what the valuable information was but something else was going on here. She was on high alert, staring intently at his cold eyes. She needed to bring the conversation back to what Klauss had found out earlier this morning. But before Janna could speak Klauss continued his monologue.

'I know you are not SS, Frau Shultz, so this would normally be bad news for you and I could understand your dismay, but,' he said, pausing to smirk. Her ears were ringing; something in his voice. She then understood why he was speaking German so openly and carelessly. He wasn't coming back. Klauss continued: 'You are not even Abwehr.' Janna's eyes widened slowly and she found it hard to suppress the expression. She wondered whether her cover was blown or was he just trying to trick her. Then Janna realized. He was toying with her like a cat with a small mouse.

Klauss told her, 'I am a language specialist and a few times, like at dawn when I told you that you were lovely like the hills of Finster-walde, you made a mistake.' *Oh, no!* He *had* noticed, Janna thought as she felt the double slam of realization and fear crash into her mind. She was frozen in terror. Janna hadn't expected to freeze but she wasn't sure what his intention was.

Klauss said: 'Let me guess; Polish?' Her heart sank; he knew that she was a double agent and he was going to kill her. Janna glanced quickly through the window pleadingly, as if there may be hope out there. The man had left the scooter and was running across the road with a gun in his hand, looking up into the window Klauss stood by and then stopping at the black car.

Klauss peered outside to see what had caught her attention and immediately saw who she was looking at. Then he noticed the scooter across the road, recognized the man as the rider who was on the road just before the river house and put three and three together; he had good instinct. The man was climbing onto the bonnet of the car. Then Klauss saw the rider's gun. In a flash, Klauss pulled out his Luger and took aim at the man, who was now clambering onto the roof of the car. Only a few metres separated them and Klauss was about to take an easy shot at the intruder.

Janna's hand came down on the gun as Klauss fired a shot. It missed, hitting the car and sending the startled man sliding to the side for cover. Klauss waved the Luger away from Janna's hand to take another quick shot at the man in the street, now shielded by the automobile. It missed and Klauss turned quickly to Janna, who was running for the kitchen. He fired quickly, hitting her in the leg. She screamed but managed to make it through the kitchen entrance.

Klauss glanced back outside. The man was gone. With gun pointing Klauss ran to the kitchen where Janna was picking up a knife. He slowed and fired twice, the bullets ripping into her chest. She fell to the floor but still held the knife and looked hatefully at him. Then, Janna let go of the hate because she wanted her last thoughts to be of her children. Klauss walked closer and aimed, firing three shots into her crumpling body. He felt for the small folder in his pocket and found it, quickly moving back to the windows in the other room.

Cyril was daunted as he cautiously, but not slowly, climbed the stone steps leading up from the ground to the entrances of the villas in the rear above, the Webley raised in his hand just inches from the wall. He was very tired and his coat felt heavy. Over two years in the rugged Pyrenees had toned his body and he was much leaner. But he was pushing sixty and though he was in good shape, Cyril was not cut out for this.

He thought: Should I just run in and start shooting everyone? What if I guess the wrong villa and I kill a family of Romans? If I make sure it is the right villa and I hesitate, the Germans would kill me. I don't want to be here...

Cyril decided it was not like Nintendo anymore.

He'd heard three shots but they hadn't been aimed at him. Even so, he crouched as he moved along. He was nearly at the top and could see a walkway with several doors on the right, leading to the villas. It had to be one of the first two doors. He looked at the distances and made an educated guess; the first door. Reaching the top of the steps, Cyril realized he was shaking. At any moment the Germans could come out of any of those doors and start firing. The tension and nerves got to him; he ran for the door.

The wooden door did not seem formidable but he doubted that he could kick it in. It was locked. Cyril's blood pumped hard through his heart. He knew the world was at stake. Failure meant the end of the world. But he could just walk away. He thought about it.

He thought about it because going through that door meant certain death.

Cyril had a brainstorm: Get back to the scooter and wait. He started to run for the steps leading down but abruptly halted and, with crazed eyes, turned around; then with all of his force kicked at the door. It flew open easily, the lock broken.

Cyril pointed his gun and ran into the villa; in his mind the deranged, insane, scream of a lunatic filled his soul. He would rather die here and now than deal with *that* kind of guilt the rest of his life.

Cyril aimed the Webley left, middle, right: Nothing, nobody. He heard an engine as he ran into the kitchen, gun pointing. Seeing a dead woman, who seemed to have a peaceful look on her face, he turned and ran to the open window in time to see the black car pull onto the street and drive away to the right. Cyril cursed, noticing that the roof of the automobile was dented; the German agent must have gone out the window. A quick look into the bedroom: no one there. Cyril thought: Just me and that psychopath.

He went running for his scooter. The black car was headed east.

Klauss drove through the streets, lined with buildings and dwellings. There was more traffic about but he never had to go slow. His superior was at Aquino and Klauss was making a - albeit haphazard- beeline for him. This information will go straight to the Fuhrer. For once, Klauss felt very happy about life. He was in a good mood.

When he'd left the villa, Klauss had turned on the first right, then the next left, then right several streets before making another left. He was looking behind on turns to see if he was being followed but there was nobody. Klauss especially kept an eye out for any scooters. He wished he'd killed the man but when the opportunity had presented its self to escape, his instinct told him to flee. Staying at the villa allowed a certain degree of risk; the most important thing was to get this folder to his superior at Aquino.

The weather was gloomy but that didn't bother Klauss. He liked it.

Cyril had initially ridden east but when there was no sign of the black car he'd tried south for a few streets, then east again. Nothing. The car could have turned left at the beginning and was headed north or north-east, he deduced, and the more he continued this way- if it was the wrong direction- the less chance he'd have of ever catching up with the homicidal German agent. Cyril was indecisive, rationalizing that he could go a few more streets east before deciding what to do. Then his option will be left to the north or right to the south. His logical conclusion came to two possible destinations, north-east or south-east. He sped on.

At least the narrow back streets were almost empty, he thought as he wove his way through the neighbourhoods. Cyril couldn't procrastinate any longer. He was coming to the far end of the city. There was an intersection coming up. *Left or right? North-east or south-east?*

Cyril turned right and was now going south. If the black car was heading north-east or north anywhere, he would never catch up. But he'd gotten a good jump on the two directions left open for him; south or south-east. There was the possibility that the black car had already reached its destination and the agent had relayed the information. The German agent could be anywhere.

The tired Englishman was about to give up hope when he saw a black automobile cross the next intersection, moving east. Cyril could not tell if the roof was dented. It did look like the car but it had gone by so fast that he was not sure.

Cyril turned left and followed. The car ahead had picked up speed and was gaining distance from the scooter. There were fewer and fewer buildings and the road was turning into- albeit an empty one- a thoroughfare. He hadn't been seen yet. Cyril decided to back off a little and just keep the car in sight because the landscape was opening up and he had a good view in front of him. He was sure that he was following the correct car: Almost sure.

Sure enough to bet the world on it.

'The Eiffel Tower?' Massy looked gravely at Sanderson. They'd figured that in a couple of minutes it should be known whether Ishkur's 'jump' had changed anything and they were hoping that the superpowers did not blow up the world first.

McPherson: 'US jets and subs, Baltic Sea, Black Sea...' The screen changed rapidly from one headline to another. 'Tank battles all over central Europe...civil wars in southern Europe...'

Winthorpe added, 'Spain and Norway drop out of NATO...'

Massy craved a cold drink of carrot, celery and beet root juice. All we need is a little bit of time, he thought.

McPherson held a Scotch in his hand. 'Soviets after the Suez Canal...aerial and artillery bombardment of Berlin. Tank battles in the south of France...and Italy in the north...'

Mister Black stood next to Massy, swirling a drink. On the other side of the computer crowd Sanderson subtly updated Erlinger on the situation. Winthorpe sat up and went to get two coffees for him and Mitsy. McPherson said, 'NATO taking a beating in the Balkans and Italy...US force in southern France...Offensive on Berlin...'

Mister Black and Massy were a few feet behind the others. The man in black was feeling a little less confident about the chances of any favourable outcome from this experiment. He turned and looked at Massy. 'Professor, you rolled over pretty easy, I mean it was a good thing for you that you did, but I got to ask; how come you didn't play harder to get? How did you know I wasn't just bluffing?'

Massy told him. 'I didn't play poker for money. At the casinos while waiting for my large bets to win, I used to play the two dollar tables for hours. Just for fun.' He paused when McPherson called out.

'NATO nations call for peace! Civil rioting all over southern and Central Europe!'

Massy watched Winthorpe bring a coffee over to Mitsusaka. He saw her smile and thank Winthorpe, stopping her typing to accept the coffee. Massy was always intrigued by how elegant Mitsy was. She sipped and placed the cup in front of the computer but before she began typing again, McPherson joked, 'Maybe you should just leave it on that headline.' Most of them could see the screen but Sanderson and Erlinger couldn't, so McPherson filled them in when they looked over. 'London Times: "ARMAGEDDON"!'

Winthorpe remarked, 'Technically, I don't think Armageddon could have a headline. Everything is destroyed. So that means-'

McPherson cut in. 'No. The Day of Judgement is the day after *Armageddon. It would be the headline on Judgement Day, morning edition.' A couple of them cracked up with chuckles, a forced attempt to lighten a tense situation. Massy watched Mitsy smile again and he was glad that they were all happy and grinning, even if it was just for a moment.*

Mister Black had not smiled at McPherson's joke; he suddenly didn't like the idea of a Judgement Day. He said to Massy, 'You were saying, Professor? About the poker and two dollar tables...'

Massy looked at him. 'Yes, Mister Black...poker for fun; just reading people's reactions.'

McPherson: 'Berlin's a mess...Soviets have pushed to the Rhine with a conventional army...Berlin has fallen!'

Massy continued, making eye contact with Mister Black. 'Some people say they read the eyes of the other players and some say they read the faces; I read the body. I spent a lot of nickels learning about bluffers and I'll tell you one thing, pardner...' Massy changed his accent to a Southern drawl. 'You ain't one.'

chapter 10

Klauss was speeding east out of the city and was confident he wasn't being followed. But he was having a personal crisis; one major problem that he had to solve. Once he relayed the basic information, Klauss finally realized, he was useless. The small folder harboured all the facts. His superior would likely get the credit and Klauss Gelfroher could fade into the background: *A nobody*. His mind delved deeply for a plan.

Klauss quickly decided that he would become the folder. His memory was photographic and precise, helpful in his ability to speak several languages, and the facts would be kept in his mind like a vault. He would need a driver and then sit in the backseat reading the entire folder. Sometime before Aquino he would destroy the folder. That would give him around an hour, more or less, to study and memorize the entire contents. Klauss was sure he could do it. An old, rusty automobile pulled out in front of the black car and Klauss reacted slowly, skidding for a moment when he veered and touched the brakes, and then continued on. He hadn't been paying attention; he still had to smooth out the edges of his plan and he needed to think it carefully through.

After destroying the folder- Klauss decided on burning it- he would tell his superior very little; only that he has all the facts in his head as he was given them orally and...and...*think!* And...that part of the deal was that this information must be given to the Fuhrer in person. *Brilliant!* He was happy with that plan. Klauss would be famous for sure. The role of heading German Intelligence flashed dreamily in his mind. Coming back to earth, he knew his superior would not be happy about it. He sped along, the road veering to the right. Klauss was now heading south-east.

Several streets behind Klauss, Cyril was reluctant to try and close in on the black car just yet. The road was dipping slightly and he could see mountains in the far distance; to the north-east. And he'd clearly seen the roof of the car that he was following; it was dented. The road was changing course and Cyril guessed correctly: south-east.

There were surprisingly few buildings out this way, he noted. He had plenty of petrol. There were many low clouds but the road was dry. Cyril was starving and he'd seen only two shops open for business other than tobacconists. They'd both been bakeries and he'd smelled them as well, but stopping was not an option. Several small groups of men and women walked along the road. Probably factory workers, thought Cyril. The buildings seemed to be bigger along here.

He watched the black car as it alternately moved past large buildings and open spaces. It might be a good time as any to attack the German agent in the open before he reached any friends, though his approach would be visible. *What are my options?* Cyril had a good view of the road and now noticed a group of cars stopped in a line about a half kilometre ahead of the black car: A checkpoint.

Thinking quickly, he scanned the area and saw an offshoot that lead to a hilly spot overlooking the checkpoint. There was a booth to the side of the road, in the middle of the stopped vehicles, and German soldiers were in the road talking to drivers and pedestrians. He saw an automobile waved through at the checkpoint but Cyril doubted it would be easy because he did not speak Italian, making it difficult to pass for a citizen. The turning came up and he slanted right to another road, moving up a small hill.

He came to the crest of the hilly street and stopped. It was a perfect vantage point and he saw the black car pass the vehicles in line and drive straight up to the checkpoint. He pulled out the field-glasses.

Cyril could see the agent get out of the car and talk to a tall German soldier, pointing at the steering wheel and then getting into the backseat. The soldier, with rifle slung behind his back, held his palms out, turned and called toward the booth. An officer appeared and walked over, saying something to the soldier. The agent was out of the car again and held out some papers that the officer took and studied. The agent spoke to the officer as he read.

Cyril was by a bush but he was still conspicuous and knew he must look suspicious. But he dared not look away. The officer handed the papers back and nodded. Cyril could tell that it was not the small folder, probably just identification. The agent once again was in the backseat, door closed. Cyril moved the binoculars up a bit and watched the officer talk to the soldier, who did not look very pleased. He also looked very young and when the officer pointed at the black car's open door he seemed reluctant to move but finally the teenage soldier went and sat down behind the wheel.

The agent was opening the small folder and saying something to the driver. The black car started moving, continuing south-east. Cyril had seen that most of the people had been let through. It wasn't like it was a roadblock but he made up his mind to avoid it. Looking to where the main road lead he saw plenty of crossing points but no clear street to the thoroughfare. He was sure the agent wouldn't be stopping soon, Cyril deduced. *Why else would he ask for a driver?*

He jumped on the scooter and roared off.

Klauss sat in the backseat silently reading every detail of Operation Anvil in the documents. There was a lot to memorize. He'd given the young German soldier instructions to drive straight to Aquino, over eighty kilometres away, but to stop a few kilometres short of it. That was when Klauss would burn the small folder. He also told the driver to keep his mouth shut.

The black car glided swiftly along the straight road. Soon, everything was rural. Hills could be seen up to the right; to the left far in the distance the Abruzzi Mountains loomed through the greyness. The driver could not appreciate the view knowing they were headed for the front; he'd already been wounded in battle once. He was happy with his checkpoint duties.

Sometime later, maybe fifteen minutes, Klauss stopped from his study to roll his neck muscles. He noticed the dent in the roof over the passenger seat and thought of the man back at the villa. He leaned forward and told the driver, 'Make sure we are not being followed. Automobile or motor bike...whatever. If you see something, tell me immediately.'

'Jawohl.'

Klauss relaxed and began reading again. The black car whizzed past an old wooden sign that read: Valmontone 1km.

Cyril had found his way back onto the main road having avoided the checkpoint. It'd been easier than expected but no less terrifying. He'd lost the black car temporarily but after an extremely quick stop up an incline by the road he had seen it through the binoculars racing several kilometres ahead, still on the main road which he now knew was called Route 6.

The road was straight but that wasn't advantageous to him. The scooter could not go as fast as the car so Cyril was sure he'd fallen even further behind. He needed curves or a miracle to close the gap between the two vehicles.

The soldier driving the black car checked the gauges on the dashboard. 'We are very low on petrol-'

'Quiet! There is a jerrycan in the boot. No more talking.' Klauss looked down and continued studying. A rail track had ran alongside Route 6 since San Cesareo but now it was splitting away from the road, to the south. The black car was making good time as it sped through the sleepy village of Torre Santi.

Cyril entered the town of Valmontone, slowing a little as a few people were starting their day. The gloomy weather canvassed a surreal postcard. The coat he wore was not warm enough for the ride and he shivered constantly. He looked out for a bakery, his hunger becoming a distraction, but the tired Englishman decided there would be no time for that. He was too far behind.

Klauss paused from reading and looked out the window at the low hills around them. 'Where are we?' he demanded.

'Ferentino. About halfway to-'

Klauss interrupted the driver: 'How far until Frosinone?'

'I do not...maybe ten kilometres.'

'Drive.' Klauss returned his attention to the documents and they rode in silence. It wasn't long before the black car went through Frosinone.

A fair distance past Valmontone Cyril had found a rise just off the road with a good view of the valley and he'd quickly made out the black car more than a few miles ahead on Route 6. He'd seen that the elevation was rising slowly but steadily and had noticed when the rail track split away from the road. There had been a wooden sign on a tall post: Torre Santi.

At the moment, Cyril rode up the small hilly village of Ferentino which nestled to the south side of steep, green hills that were covered with a delicate, grey mist. Very beautiful, he thought while he tried to control his shivering. The road was curvy through here and Cyril hoped that the bends had slowed the black car, wherever it may be. When he reached the crest of these hills he would find a place to use the binoculars.

Massy went over to join Sanderson and Erlinger on the other side of the computers. Mister Black moved closer to the screen. Mitsusaka typed and clicked, occasionally stopping to sip her coffee. McPherson read the screen. 'Phillippine civil war with Chinese-backed communists...'

Winthorpe: '5:18...'

'Revolts in Africa...Ethiopia, Egypt, Sudan...Chad.'

'January, 1959!'

'Wars in Central and South America. Bolivia, Colombia...NATO calls for cease-fire. Balkans a mess.' McPherson drained his glass and turned around, looking at Mister Black. The big Canadian gestured with the empty glass, handing it toward the man in black. 'Get me another one of those, will ya, pal?'

Mister Black was only too glad to oblige. He took the glass and went to refill it immediately. If he started being a kinder person, he figured, then maybe he would get a better deal on Judgement Day.

'Riots in England! London. Riots in Malaysia.'

Massy said to Sanderson and Erlinger, 'Doesn't look good, boys.'

Erlinger's Austrian accent was thicker than usual. 'No, Boss. All we can do is wait?'

'Yes.' He turned to Sanderson. 'Bill, it couldn't be too long, now. What do you think?'

Sanderson took a logical guess. 'It's got to be in the next two, three minutes. No, wait a minute. Less; I think.'

Massy rubbed his chin. 'Yeah, less than that. Two minutes at the very most.'

McPherson: 'Soviets attack US fleet in Pacific! Sink two carriers! Mediterranean...United States and NATO bomb Russian cities...massive raids.' He looked up and over at the trio. 'They've hit Stalingrad and Moscow!' A small pause, then: 'Boss, are we all going to combust like Stenvaag?'

All eyes in the room fell on Massy. 'I hope not.' It was all he could say.

'The Russians have crossed the Rhine! NATO air raids on the army invading France!' McPherson stopped to have a swig of whisky. He joked, 'I bet they sell a lot of papers with these headlines.'

This time nobody laughed; they were all too busy dreading the worst. Massy felt remorse and was very sad: He was much sadder than he was scared.

'USA calls for peace plan and summit! That's good!' But then

McPherson stopped and said, 'Oh.' His expression dropped to a frown.
'What is it, Mac?' asked Sanderson.
'Soviets claim they have enough nuclear power to blow the United States into dust a hundred times over...'
Sanderson muttered to himself, 'That's one hell of an RSVP.'

chapter 11

Klauss sat eating a cold sausage, chewing very, very slowly as he went over the details of Operation Anvil for a third time. It had been the better part of an hour since they'd left the checkpoint. The road had been mostly curvy since Frosinone. The black car slithered through the village of Ceprano. There were more civilians about but they seemed to be staying near the shadows and looking vigilant; the war was coming to town.

The driver said, 'We are heading straight for the front lines.'

Klauss: 'Do you think I do not know that? Drive.' An old woman carrying a sack was being followed by a young boy and a pig, crossing the road ahead. The driver slowed down. Klauss exploded. 'What are you doing? Forget about them! They will move. Now, drive!' The black car hurried the group out of the way and accelerated but soon was in a series of tight bends. The car screeched when they slowed abruptly for a sharp curve then went on. At the next bend the driver nearly lost control and slammed on the brakes, jerking Klauss forward and disrupting his concentration. He nearly lost his sausage.

'Dumpkof! Slow down!'

The black car departed Ceprano and slithered through the winding curves.

When Cyril had reached the crest at Ferentino he'd had another magnificent view of the landscape and, sure enough, with his field-glasses he'd seen the black car in the distance. He hadn't gained any ground. The agent was heading straight for the front line and Cyril knew he was running out of time.

Frosinone had a couple of rivers running through and Route 6 had become very twisty. He rode as quickly as he could, especially on the curves. The scooter manoeuvred wonderfully and Cyril flew along the road unobstructed until several military vehicles appeared up ahead.

He steered down the street on the right and sped on a couple of streets and turned left. The small neighbourhoods were sprawled out but the roads were straight. The scooter went over a small bridge, veered onto another road and suddenly he found himself back on Route 6. A bit of luck, he thought, realizing he'd found a short cut.

Klauss kept reading the documents over and over, drumming each detail into his brain. But the constant curves were getting on his nerves and he was becoming anxious. Aquino was only about ten minutes away and he would soon have to burn the small folder. He would soon be lying to his superior. Paranoia was setting in. If there was an investigation into this perhaps the driver would be interviewed and mention the folder. That was an easy problem for Klauss to solve. He just needed five more minutes with the precious documents.

The car started to jerk a little, then slow. They were out of petrol. Klauss shouted. 'You idiot!'

The driver got out of the car saying, 'You said there was a jerrycan in the-'

'Yes, get it. Fast!' Then Klauss jumped out of the backseat, the folder in his hand. 'Do not use all of the petrol. Save some.' He took a box of matches out from his coat pocket. 'Schnell! Hurry!'

The German soldier was experienced but not hardened. He tried to rush, spilling some petrol from the jerrycan. 'Don't lose any! Dumpkof!' The tall soldier could not believe he was shaking because he knew he could crush this man with his bare hands. Just obey the orders, he reminded himself. Klauss was like a rabid dog. 'Hurry! Schnell! Schnell! Don't use it all!' The soldier spilled a little more. 'Dumpkof! You idiot!'

The soldier muttered, 'Shut up...'

Klauss's eyes narrowed. 'What?' The soldier poured more of the liquid into the petrol tank and then stopped, looking at the crazy passenger. Klauss looked at the jerrycan and told him, 'Pour the rest on these documents.' He scattered the contents of the folder onto the ground and gestured. The soldier poured, soaking the papers. Klauss lit a match and burned the documents. They both watched, sometimes separating the sheets, until the fire was just a pile of ash.

Then Klauss calmly fired five shots into the soldier's face and body.

Cyril breezed in and out of the curves, the elevation rising. He was

255

quite sure the black car had not reached its destination and that he was gaining ground. There was still little traffic, though his heart hammered whenever he came across military vehicles going about their business. He came to the town of Ceprano and his eyes strained for any sign of the black car. There were a few crossroads but he decided to press on. It seemed very quiet in Ceprano. Too quiet for a character like that madman in the black car, Cyril thought.

He left Ceprano and Route 6 curved north-east and Cyril began to worry. To the east, steep hillsides and mountains became more and more prominent. The road was going straight north and he was beginning to lose hope. To his right he saw across the small valley and could see a road. He stopped. Through the field-glasses he could see that Route 6 appeared to curve back around in an arc to the other road, continuing on a south-east course. Moving the binoculars back to his right Cyril scanned the road across the valley. It was only a couple of miles and the view was unobstructed. He saw the black car speeding along. He jumped on his scooter. Zoom-zoom.

Klauss entered Aquino. He was questioned by an officer upon arrival and quickly learned that his superior, whose name was Reichardt, had gone to Monastery Hill on urgent business- orders straight from the Fuhrer. Klauss was furious, glancing around at the soldiers that surrounded the headquarters. There were half-tracks and other trucks but Klauss saw no tanks. He asked the officer how he could reach the monastery and was told it was just beyond Coppola, to the left after the military checkpoint. The officer informed Klauss that the area behind and to the side of Monte Cassino was crawling with the enemy. They both saluted and Klauss left for the monastery.

Luckily for Cyril, Route 6 did curve back around and was the same road that the black car was on. He rode past a large family walking west. The man was pulling a large cart and all of them carried luggage. The road straightened out and Cyril could see something lying on the ground ahead. It was a German soldier, dead. Tall, young; Cyril identified him as the guard at the checkpoint back on the outskirts of Rome who drove the black car for the German agent. He sped on.

Cyril soon came near a town that was on the south side of Route 6. There was a strong military presence and he was sure that here was the agent's destination. Anything beyond here, if Cyril remembered correctly, was Allied territory. He saw a signpost pointing to the right: Aquino. The road here was clear but if he moved toward Aquino he would be questioned for sure. Cyril rolled on past the signpost and kept going but not at full speed. He was stalling but turning right would be the only logical thing to do. Another turning on the right presented itself and he was hoping shame would force him into making the turn. No. He couldn't do it; maybe the next one. He rode straight and nearly jumped when he saw the black car turn onto Route 6 at the next intersection.

Cyril accelerated but the car was racing away at full speed. This was his last chance. The rail tracks had rejoined Route 6 some time ago and were just down on his right. He was seeing more and more German troops and he wasn't seeing any civilians on the road. In two minutes the car- *and then the scooter a few moments later*- passed an old beat up signpost: San Germano. A large lorry passed by the black car and Cyril gulped. A moment later it went by and he sighed.

Two more minutes on and the scooter had not closed any distance on the black car. Then he saw the military checkpoint with many soldiers and German half-tracks. The black car was slowing down and easing into a short line of vehicles. Cyril noticed that the agent did not roar to the front of this checkpoint. Thinking quickly, he veered to the left onto a side road to find a spot where he could look through his field-glasses. By the time he did, the black car was leaving through the checkpoint. Cyril watched it continue east until it disappeared behind trees. He kept looking though and then saw Klauss heading north into the steep mountainside. In seconds, the scooter was whizzing away. Cyril saw a signpost: Via Santa Scholastica. But soon that road curved west and Cyril panicked, wondering how on earth he would get over to the other side of the checkpoint. He turned around and moments later stopped at a crest looking across the deep ravine. Once again, there it was; the black car, only a half-mile away carving its way up near the top of the very steep mountain. Lower to the right he espied a roadway that splintered off the mountain road but seemed to be a dead end. The scooter descended a little and Cyril noticed a dirt path to the left and went down it. It was the right direction but soon the ground became uneven and he was riding through trees, bumping over roots and nearly losing his balance. It took him a few minutes but he made it to the dead end street that lead to the mountain road. Though he doubted his chances of ever catching the agent, he took a few deep breaths and carried on.

chapter 12

Tommy had survived the beaches of Sicily, just as he'd survived the French Foreign Legion, El Alamein and Libya. He'd fought up the Italian peninsula on the Adriatic side and was now in the Cassino area at the middle of the Gustav Line. Lower level commissioned officers had been dropping like flies and Tommy expected that he would soon rise to the rank of lieutenant.

It was early morning for some but Tommy had been up for hours leading a scouting patrol to the south-west end of the Montecassino massif. There'd been communication problems among the several army divisions in the immediate vicinity, mostly between the upper and lower echelons, and a few units took it into their head to gain information by sending out reconnaissance squads. Many hours earlier, before dawn, Sergeant Thomas Smith and a group made up from soldiers of the 4th and 7th Indian Divisions had slunk down from an area called Point 593, crossed the Albaneta Farm Road and descended into the heavy woods below: Enemy territory.

He had two Gurkhas with him, a corporal from the 7/1 Royal Sussex Regiment and a marksman from the 4/6 Rajputana Rifles. They were all part of the 2 New Zealand Corps and there was little comfort knowing that most of that army was only a couple of miles away, just south of the town of Cassino. To the north of Cassino, across the Rapido River, the massive 2nd US Corps stood poised.

The patrol had been out too long, thought Tommy, and they were headed back. They had no radio and he was keen to tell his lieutenant about the strange leaflets the patrol had come across warning the inhabitants of Monastery Hill of an impending bombing, by the Allies, that was to take place this morning. It was news to him. He looked east at the high hill plateau that housed the monastery; then at the sky. No bombers. The clouds were thinning and there was even sunshine but early morning mist still swirled at his ankles.

It was dull and grey but there was enough light to keep the patrol extremely vigilant and they moved slowly through the small, dense forest toward the steep mountainside that would lead them back to their units. No one spoke and they communicated with gestures.

Sometimes Tommy liked to dream about the garden he would eventually have, once the blasted war was over: lovely and green with plenty of roses and other flowers. A long, Alice in Wonderland-type lawn stretching to tall, leafy trees, flanked on both sides by thick, dark green hedges. He was not thinking of the garden now.

The silent patrol continued stealthily through the misty woods.

chapter 13

Klauss had made his way swiftly up the mountain road, throwing caution to the wind. He'd turned right at Albaneta Farm Road and in no time was roaring onto the plateau, the huge monastery of Montecassino dominating his view. He veered right toward the German military vehicles, including a staff car, and skidded to a stop. Two soldiers ran up, one pointing a Schmeisser machine-gun at him, as he got out of the black car with both arms held high holding identification papers in his right hand. As the soldiers approached he asked, 'Who is in charge? I need to see an officer named Reichardt.' Klauss handed them the papers and as they went over them carefully he saw an officer nearby, looking at the sky. He could see that it was not Reichardt. Klauss: 'Who is that?'

The soldier with the Schmeisser told him, 'That is Kapitan Dieter.' The other soldier handed the papers back to Klauss, nodding approval. Klauss ran over to the Kapitan who stopped looking at the sky when he saw him running.

'Kapitan Dieter? I am Klauss Gelfroher and I need to see Reichardt. I know he's here. Urgent. Where is he?'

Dieter knew that Reichardt would not want to be disturbed while in the middle of an interrogation and so he stalled; he didn't want to get caught in the middle of whatever business these Nazis were up to.

'Now! Dieter, tell me, now! Orders from the Fuhrer!'

In *that* case, thought Dieter as he pointed to an office across the way that was next to a long, narrow building. 'He's in that office interrogating a...someone. He's with another officer, named Keltner.'

'Danke,' said Klauss, who rarely thanked anyone for anything. He took two running steps toward the office when suddenly it exploded, taking out the front of the building next to it. Someone behind him was yelling and then he saw them all looking up at the sky, running or ducking in various directions. Then Klauss knew; bomber planes were dropping their loads. Looking back at the office, he also knew that no one had survived the office blast because the office had disappeared. He shouted back to Dieter, 'Who was he interrogating?'

The Kapitan felt it did not matter to tell the agent because the monk was no doubt killed in the explosion. He wouldn't mention the second monk, though. 'They were interrogating a monk.'

Klauss said, 'Well, they are all dead now.'

A soldier standing by remarked, 'Yes, but there was another monk who was in the long building waiting to be interrogated next. Look, there he goes now, running across the field away from everything.'

The murderous German agent asked, 'Why were they interrogating the monks?'

The soldier had been by the office earlier and had overheard Reichardt and Keltner. He told Klauss, 'They have something the Fuhrer wants...' Dieter shook his head disapprovingly at the blabbermouth.

Klauss was intrigued. 'What is it they have?'

The soldier didn't know. He shrugged. 'Weiss nicht.' *I don't know.*

When Klauss tried to get the soldier to chase after the monk, who was running with a young woman, Dieter told him: 'Absolutely not. My soldiers are coming with me to help the civilians.' The Kapitan gave Klauss a cold, hard look as if to say: *Do you want to tangle with me and my boys?*

Klauss got the message. He sneered at Dieter and began running after the monk, who was quite a distance away now. There were explosions everywhere and after several steps Klauss stopped when one exploded halfway between him and the monk. He turned around, shouting above the explosions at a running soldier. 'Where does that go?' He was pointing at a small hill crest where the monk and the girl had just disappeared over.

'The side of the mountain, back down to the road.' The soldier ran on toward the burning building.

Klauss ran quickly to his car. Reichardt was dead; that was probably good for him: No one to have to share any credit. And Reichardt was obviously doing something very important up at the monastery or else why would he have passed up the extremely important meeting at the river house. *Something more important?* If Klauss found the monk he would make him talk and then Klauss would have *two* major pieces of information to present to the Fuhrer: Dreams of glory. He started the engine amid bombs falling and the black car screeched away from the mountain top monastery. Then bombs landed not far in front of him, creating craters in the road. He gingerly manoeuvred around the gargantuan potholes, snaking his way to the Albaneta Farm Road which lead back to the mountainside road- hoping it would take him straight to the spot the monk was running. Beyond the initial craters, though, he could see the road was clear.

The old monk's heart beat like a hummingbird's and his legs were tiring. He'd grabbed the young woman's arm inside the building after the first explosion and asked her to come with him, which she had. He now had a bigger favour to ask from her.

They'd run across the field, bombs exploding endlessly, and she had ran with him without questioning why. She seemed wise, thought the monk, and knew that he needed her help. They'd run over the crest of a hillock, then down through the trees. The road was in view. Suddenly, he dropped to his knees next to a large, very old tree. He was gasping.

Speaking Italian, the young woman asked, 'Lei e bene?' *Are you alright?* She looked at him, full of concern.

The monk looked at the woman's deep brown eyes and nodded, catching his breath. He felt she was trustworthy and that was the most vital thing at the moment. He held out an arm and from his sleeve produced a very old, rolled up scroll. He looked at her; she looked at him.

The pretty young lady asked, 'Che cos'e questo?' *What is it?*

The monk put it carefully down a hollow in the tree. It was a perfect fitting and she wondered if he had been to this tree before. He was finally getting his breath back. He looked around and saw no one, but he thought he'd seen someone chasing after him just after the explosion. There was no time to take a chance. The monk quickly explained. 'It is an ancient scroll, with maps and...' He looked back up at the crest, looking worried. 'If they capture me you must remember this tree. When it is safe, take it to-' several bombs crashed into the crest, a deafening roar. Taking her arm again, he said, 'We must go.' He looked

at her, almost sympathetically. The monk asked, 'Che e suo nome?'
What is your name?

'Maria. Maria Bationi.' They both began running down the mountain toward the road below, the explosions behind them unremitting.

The grey-black sky was filled with smoke and the mountain shook from the constant pounding. The monk did not know where to go from here so he was giving the young woman the lead. Maria's home was on the other side of Albaneta Farm, which was to the right when they got to the mountainside road and then left at the T-junction of Albaneta Farm Road. The farm was about a mile away. There was a footpath that ran just below the mountainside road which curved left at the T-junction toward the farm that locals had used for centuries and Maria decided it would be safer than travelling on the road.

The monk and Maria crossed over the mountainside road and were running up the footpath, large enough for a few mules. The path was obscured from the road above by the thick trees and bushes that created an almost continual hedge. They ran hard, the incline steadily increasing.

Klauss had weaved slowly through the craters but was now roaring down the Albaneta Farm Road away from the bombs, which continued to pour down incessantly, to find the monk. But he'd lost time and thought that if he didn't capture the monk then it was no skin off his nose. The mountainside road was on his route back to Rome so, he thought, if he saw the monk on the road then he would capture him. Otherwise, he wasn't that bothered. A bird in the hand was better than two in the bush, he reminded himself: Must not be greedy.

Cyril had rode the scooter up from the closed part of the dead end road and had joined onto the very steep mountain road and was moving upward, sheer mountainside on his right and sheer drop on his left. As the road curved around he noticed the slope on the right was gradually becoming less steep and on the left side also, trees and bushes appearing by the roadside. Explosions thundered and Cyril remembered enough about the war to know where he was and he had an inkling which way Klauss was headed. To the Abbey of Montecassino: atop Monastery Hill.

Cyril didn't know what he would do or how he would do it but he had to do something, even if that meant riding a scooter through hell. Cyril had a strange thought which exposed his dry humour: An opera in Hades would be *fortissimo*.

He knew that he would need to go to the right to get to the mountain top. Wisps of smoke swirled about the air above and around him. The road was not so steep anymore. The slope to his right was becoming fairly level; Cyril was nearing the top. He came to a straightaway and accelerated. There was a T-junction not far up ahead and a right turn would lead to the abbey, Cyril surmised.

The monk and Maria were running along the dirt path that was parallel to the mountainside road, completely obscured from the roadway by the almost solid row of trees and bushes. The explosions still rocked the mountain top to their right. Maria would soon lead them west away from the abbey and into, with any luck, safety once they'd gotten far as the farm. Then she would only be a mile from home. The Germans were at the farm but she knew the area well and could get past it. As they ran Maria called out, 'Do you want to stop?'

The old monk was breathing hard but he kept running, shaking his head. A few moments later she heard him say, 'Soon...' The path was straight and shortly they would be coming to the turning, which went to the left and continued along just below the Albaneta Farm Road. Below them, to their left, it sloped down rather sharply into a forest of deep, green woods and thickets.

The noise from the bombs still booming, neither of them heard the scooter whizzing by them on the other side of the trees and hedgerow, approaching the T-junction.

Klauss was about to leave the Albaneta Farm Road and turn left down the mountainside road toward sanity. The explosions were creating havoc with his nerves and his anger rose with every boom. He couldn't wait to get off of this crazy mountain. Klauss pushed down on his accelerator and sped into the left turn.

Cyril was scared again as the T-junction rapidly got closer and closer. He was shaking. He thought of turning around. 'Not cut out to be a hero anyway,' he muttered to himself. Cyril slowed the scooter at the last moment, the T-junction upon him. Then: *No. Do the right thing.* He increased his speed and moved into the intersection to turn right toward the abbey. *Do or die!*

To his horror a car was running into him and all Cyril could do was slide to his left, the left leg catching the ground and sending waves of pain crashing into him. The car did not have time to steer away and clipped the scooter, sending Cyril spinning and off- landing several feet away and clutching himself in many places. He was bleeding and mangled but could see that it was the black car, now skidded to a halt, which had collided with him. Cyril was dazed and blearily saw the German agent out of the car, moving toward him.

Klauss was seething. His right shoulder hurt badly and his leg felt a bit funny but that didn't stop him from jogging to the man in agony- the man who had followed him from the river house. He recognized the brown coat. The man was struggling to get up and was up on one knee.

Slowing to a stop, Klauss reached inside his own coat- long and dark grey- and produced a sharp knife. He kicked Cyril back down, quickly glancing back at the scooter where Cyril's British revolver laid on the ground. Klauss leaned lower and asked in English, 'Who are you? Who sent you?'

Cyril didn't know what to say, he tried to get up but Klauss used his boot to push him back to the ground. He sneered at Cyril and said, 'Fool.'

Then Klauss stabbed Cyril in the middle of the chest several times until the body was lifeless.

The monk was gasping for air and came to a stop on a small rise where the dirt path would continue left. Maria wanted him to wait until past the bend because below the T-junction there was a bare spot on the path with no concealment from the trees. But he was gasping for air; she couldn't force him to run. Several bombs exploded not far away. Maria saw him grab his chest, his eyes were wide. Running back to him quickly, she guessed he was having a heart attack.

His eyes changed to a different kind of fear and it puzzled her for an instant until she saw that to his right, with a plain view of the T-junction, he was looking at a crash scene and a man carrying a knife was moving menacingly straight toward them. Now the man was running.

Maria went to flee but the monk did not move. 'Run,' he told her.

'No,' She reached her arm out and said, 'Come. Quick.' The monk turned around; Klauss was upon him, brandishing the knife.

Klauss grabbed the monk roughly by the neck and put his face close to the monk's ear. 'Dove va?' *Where is it?*

The monk said nothing, and neither did his eyes. He just stared.

Klauss rubbed his painful shoulder and put the knife away and replaced it with his Luger. His eyes narrowed. 'Why were you being interrogated?' Klauss raised the gun and pointed at the monk's face. 'You have something! What is it?' He moved the pistol closer; it was almost touching the monk's nose. 'Che e la cosa? Dove e? Mi dice!' *What is it? Where is it? Tell me!*

The monk wished Maria had run when she'd had the chance. This kind of man did not leave witnesses. The monk had spent most of his life staying silent; this was a cakewalk. The monk would never talk. And Klauss knew it: Instinct.

With bombs falling through the black-grey smoke-filled sky and never-ending explosions crashing, Maria felt like she was visiting hell as the bullet ripped into the old monk's face, sending him straight to the ground. She stared at the monk's lifeless body and then screamed at Klauss in French, 'Vous etes un cochon!' *You are a pig!*

Klauss's eyes narrowed to slits. He thought: Oh. A French bitch. He looked closer at her face, especially the eyes; something vaguely familiar...but something else. Explosions crashed in the distance. She was backing away slowly from him, staring coldly. He moved closer and said in French, 'Vous savez quelque chose.' *You know something.* He waited. When she started backing away further he held up the pistol and she stopped. Klauss demanded, 'Que savez-vous?' *What do you know?*

Maria believed in direct communication. 'Que pensez-vous?' *What do you think?* She glared at him.

Then turned and ran like the wind, west down the dirt path toward Albaneta Farm. Klauss fired a shot and it slammed into a tree next to the fleeing Maria. He grimaced from the pain in his shoulder and started to run after her. He wondered whether it was worth leaving the car but he was sure she knew something: Instinct. *What do you think?* She would only say that if-

Maria was running so hard her feet hardly touched the ground but Klauss was still behind her. She didn't dare turn around. Maria decided her best bet would be to veer left, down the steep ravine into the woods below. She was fairly familiar with this area and she knew ways to get

265

back up to her home from here.

Klauss couldn't gain any ground on her so he stopped and aimed carefully, leading her steps. He fired and Maria stumbled on a rock, the bullet whizzing by just above her. She didn't fall and kept running. The shot would have hit her and Klauss cursed, rubbing his shoulder. He ran again, tentatively at first because he wasn't sure if it was worth continuing the chase, then into a full charge when he decided that it was. Klauss knew he could catch her, eventually.

Jack moved stealthily up through the thick wooded incline. The explosions were tremendous but he was glad the bombs seemed to be concentrating on the high mountain to his right, almost behind him. He'd had a rest and normally would have slept, having crept through every moment of darkness the night before, but wouldn't have been able to sleep anyway in this madness.

Jack was still very tired but he knew he was getting close to Colle Sant Angelo, just up over and past these high hills. He was looking up the steep wooded area ahead of him so he did not see the tree root and he stumbled and fell to his knees, his palms to the ground. Jack noticed the pretty swirls of mist inches above the ground; it stopped him from cursing.

Jack had not seen anyone, thinking it strange considering the amount of activity. Looking around briefly, he stood and continued his hike up through the trees and bushes.

Tommy and his patrol had stopped when the bombing started and found shelter among some boulders in the woods but when it was obvious the mountain top was the bombers objective they proceeded to scale the bushy hill north back toward Albaneta Farm Road where they would have to cross the road in daylight to make it back to their units near Point 593 which was just below dangerous Snakeshead Ridge, a high strategic mountainous spine that ran south to north through the range and towered menacingly just north-west of Monastery Hill.

The corporal from the Royal Sussex Regiment carried a Thompson machine-gun but the two Gurkhas and the marksman from the Rajputana Rifles, who had a scope, carried rifles that were slung over their shoulders. Tommy preferred his Enfield rifle. They trudged through the leafy mist, moving silently up the noisy mountain.

Maria was running down the dirt path at breakneck speed but when she had dared a glance back she'd seen that the murderous German was still the same distance behind her. He had not gained on her but she had not pulled ahead either. Maria was tired but knew she could run quite a ways, even at this speed. She was more worried about the straightness of the path and sure enough, a bullet crashed into the ground by her feet.

Klauss was running and taking pot-shots at her. He wanted to get at least close enough to stop and get off an accurate shot but couldn't close the gap on her. Klauss most certainly didn't want to run all day and she did not seem to be tiring so he wanted to bring her down with a bullet. He did not want her dead; she had information. He fired at her legs again but missed. The sounds of the explosions were getting further and further away but it was still loud. The path was straight, running parallel below the Albaneta Farm Road, and Klauss knew that if he could just get a little closer...

Maria suddenly veered left down the steep hillside into thick woods below. Klauss saw her run down the narrow pathway and he followed. They were both a blur as they sped through the trees and bushes. Klauss thought he'd stumble and go crashing at any moment; he was going so fast.

But he was finally gaining on her.

Jack was keeping to the left of the main mountain massive just as he was told back in Sant Angelo, days ago. Once he was in the hills he should easily find Villa Santa Lucia; and hopefully Maria. But now he was coming to a very steep incline and feeling very tired. He noticed boulders everywhere and up on his right there was a large group of them. If it weren't for the continuous explosions he would have stopped to rest or even sleep there. But he had to keep going; under the trees, through the bushes and up the hill.

Tommy stopped his patrol to rest a minute when they came to a set of boulder settlements; one on the left and one on the right, creating a miniature valley. They moved in between and Tommy sent the two Gurkhas up to the left.

They'd easily identified the aircraft through the drifting high cloud as

Allied bombers but he wondered what the purpose was; the Germans were centered further up the mountain at Snakeshead Ridge. Tommy adjusted his helmet a little. Only a few bombs had strayed down into the forest but Sergeant Smith and the men were still wary.

As Tommy silently ordered the soldier from the Rajputana Rifles to stay put now and watch their rear, the corporal tapped him. When he turned, the corporal, who was older than him, gestured at the Gurkhas. They'd seen something.

Tommy and the corporal jogged up to the Gurkhas, peering through a gap in the group of boulders. The corporal held his machine-gun up as he moved, just behind Sergeant Smith.

One of the Gurkhas pointed and Tommy looked through the gap, immediately making a double take. He said, 'Crikey. I know him. That's Jack. We were in Foreign Legion together.' Then he thought: What in bloomin' blazes is he doing here?

The corporal, gun held down now, said: 'Foreign Legion? Maybe he's with the CEF.' The CEF was the French Expeditionary Corps, which had units a few miles north.

Tommy shook his head. 'No, he's not wearing a uniform. Stay 'ere.' Tommy jogged to the end of the boulders and stopped, looking left. When he saw his old comrade he waved and called out, but not loudly, 'Jack!'

Jack was just noticing Tommy when he heard him call out his name. The weary travel-torn American wasn't sure whether he was seeing things or not. *Tommy? Here? Appearing from out of nowhere, these boulders, this mountain...* It was a lot to take in but as Jack saw it to be true he was glad it was Tommy. He'd thought about him over the years. Finally, he moved closer to greet his old friend. 'Tommy, I can't believe it's you. What're you doing up here?'

Tommy smiled. 'There's a war on, mate. What're *you* doing up 'ere?'

'I'm on my way to Maria-' he stopped, realizing Tommy wouldn't know who she was. He looked at Tommy close and noticed the chevrons on the uniform sleeve. The years had chiseled into both their faces. 'Lieutenant Bationi's daughter; I delivered the message to his family and...well, fell in love with his daughter.'

'But the lieutenant's home was in France...'

'Long story.' Explosions still screamed from the mountain top. 'I'm going to Colle Sant Angelo, near Villa Santa Lucia.'

'You're kiddin', mate.' Sergeant Smith glanced back down the boulders. Everything was okay. The Gurkhas were behind and down a bit with the corporal from the Royal Sussex. Further behind them the marksman kept watch on the rear, looking to the south-east.

'Why's that? You-' Jack bolted upright, looking to the left of Tommy and just beyond him. Out of the thick foliage someone suddenly appeared. Tommy turned around and saw a young woman running at full tilt down the steep hillside. Jack recognized her instantly. He shouted, 'Maria!' But she kept running and barely turned her eyes in the direction of Jack. Only a few metres separated them. He was sure it was Maria and immediately began running after her. He was too busy starting after Maria to notice a second figure emerge running from the bushes. But Tommy did.

Klauss almost ran into Jack- oblivious to the sprinting German- and rapidly slowed to a full stop, gun still in his hand. He raised the Luger and aimed it at Jack, only feet away, who was interfering with the madman's pursuit: an easy shot.

Tommy shouted- screamed- above the sound of the explosions: 'JACK!'

Jack stopped and turned around. Klauss had changed his aim when he'd heard the shout and seeing Tommy whipping up his rifle Klauss fired quickly. Tommy dropped his rifle and put his hands to his chest, falling to his knees, shocked.

Jack was firing at Klauss. *Bang! Bang-Bang!* Three shots, tightly grouped. The first two hit Klauss in the heart and the third caught him in the neck. Klauss fell into a heap. Jack ran a couple of steps toward him and could tell that the man was dead, though he didn't see the face.

Klauss was dead.

The stunned American ran quickly to Tommy who lay flat on his back now, staring upwards at the dull sky catching glimpses of bombers through the trees, flying high among the clouds. The Gurkhas got to Tommy before Jack and immediately started to attend to his wound. As Jack neared he could see the gaping wound that bubbled hideously in the middle of Tommy's chest.

'Oh, god, Tommy, no...'

Tommy's mind wandered from the clouds to gentle streams and brooks and birds. He made eye contact with Jack and started to speak. 'Jack...'

Jack leaned closer to Tommy's face. 'Save your strength.'

'I...was gonna...'

'Tommy, you need to-'

'House with...with a garden...'

'Hang in there, buddy.'

'Find me a...lovely wife...some...children...'

'Tommy, no...' The Gurkhas worked furiously on Sergeant Smith but there was little they could do. The corporal and the marksman stood by, scanning the area all around them intently and guns at the ready. More explosions shook the landscape.

Tommy looked upward. He remembered verses from a poem called The West Wind and began reciting them, though Jack couldn't hear the words. Tommy's lips were moving...then his eyes stared blankly at the sky. He was dead.

A lone tear rolled off Jack's cheek onto Tommy's. Jack looked at the Gurkhas sorrowfully and noticed that the corporal was pointing the machine-gun at him, looking angry and suspicious but not completely alarmed. He heard a feminine voice call out from behind him, where the corporal was looking. 'Jack?'

Jack knew right away who the voice belonged to. He turned and ran to Maria, who was walking very tentatively toward the group. When she saw Jack's face she ran to him and they embraced, explosions still pounding the mountain.

Maria said, 'I knew you would come back.'

Jack promised her, '*Mon petite chou*, I will never leave you again.'

Part III, epilogue

Winthorpe: '5:19!'

'1960! Soviets cross the Rhine!' McPherson turned around and smiled at Massy. 'Boss, I hope spontaneous combustion isn't painful...'

The old man replied wryly, 'Probably not...'

Erlinger went to pour a Scotch. Everyone else was watching the screen. Sanderson asked Massy, 'Boss, why didn't you just jump to yesterday and nip this all in the bud?'

McPherson shouted, 'Heavy in the Balkans! North Italy...Marines in the Baltics...'

270

Massy answered Sanderson, 'We needed to jump back before the point of change- August '44. I'm pretty sure, anyway.'

Winthorpe: 'Riots all over South America, civil wars in...'

McPherson: 'Street fighting in Berlin...Soviets sink carriers in Atlantic...China at war with Japan!'

Sanderson said, 'We're running out of time.'

'Yeah,' said Massy. Then he called out to the computer crew, 'What month?'

'Early May,' said Winthorpe.

McPherson: 'Russians major offensive in France!'

Winthorpe: 'Air raid on Leningrad...'

Erlinger rejoined Massy and Sanderson. His Austrian accent grew thicker after every drink. 'Doesn't look good, Boss.'

Massy's eyes displayed sombre agreement. He was thinking: No, it's Not Good.

Winthorpe shouted: 'Late June!'

McPherson: '"US BOMBERS LEVEL LENINGRAD"! Jesus...'

Sanderson: 'Oh, no. Here it goes-'

McPherson: 'Soviets retaliate...Oslo, Paris...East Anglia, Dover, Bordeaux...'

Winthorpe: 'London! Manchester...'

Massy shook his head slowly and sadly; they were out of time.

McPherson: 'Shit, that's it! "SOVIET NUCLEAR SUBS STRIKE LOS ANGELES"!

Winthorpe: 'And San Diego!'

Mitsusaka: 'No more Los Angeles Times feed...' She put up the New York Times.

Winthorpe: 'San Francisco! Seattle!' Then the screen went blank.

McPherson called to Massy. 'Boss, the screen's gone blank. I think they've done it.' Massy moved to face the computer.

Winthorpe looked gravely at the empty blue screen. 'They've blown each other up, right?' They waited silently for several seconds with great apprehension.

Mitsusaka was startled. 'Oh...' The screen came back on.

Winthorpe: 'Back on! New York Times...October, '60. World Series headlines...'

McPherson: 'How come there is no war news..?'

Massy smiled. 'But there is good news. Mitsy, go back a couple clicks, please.' Clickclick. 'There; Mazeroski! Don't you see?' They all looked at him puzzled. He explained. 'That's what had happened originally...the homer in the World Series.' More looks of perplexity. 'What I mean is Mazeroski...never mind that. Mitsy; try War Library...say, late '45.' Mitsy typed and the screen showed a table of contents. She went to the spot before Massy could tell her. He said, 'Yes, that's it. Postwar borders, for May 1945.' They all moved in to look at the screen.

Mister Black broke the silence. 'The borders are back to normal! Like they were to begin with!' They all exhaled a huge sigh of relief: Stunned grins all around. Then cheers.

Massy exchanged a quick glance with Sanderson, both smiling. Massy thought proudly, though mistakenly, that Ishkur must've stopped Clayton.

Mister Black stood next to Massy. Massy said to him, 'Sorry your plan didn't work out.'

The man in black was reeling from being spared from damnation and felt over the moon. He answered, 'That's quite alright.'

Ishkur recovered from his injuries and waited with Rosabella for Cyril's return, which never came. He'd waited until June of 1945 to see if anything changed and it had; the borders were back to normal. He'd followed the war and it'd seemed okay but now he was sure. Ishkur surmised that Cyril had stopped Clayton but had died along the way. He'd said goodbye and thank you to Rosabella. Then he'd gone to the cave, which he'd eventually found during his wait for Cyril, and had taken both of the bracelets. Ishkur had put one down the old chute that lead deep into a crevice, never to be found, thinking: Father wanted a normal life; if he never finds the bracelets he'll have one. Ishkur'd kept the other bracelet to transport himself back to the late 1880's and reasoned that he could always put that bracelet back later if he changed his mind.

Ishkur had then left the Pyrenees and made his way to Lyon, where he'd put on the bracelet and set the time as best he could. To be safe he'd aimed for 1905 because he did not want to go too far. But Ishkur had "landed" in 1879. He'd then left Lyon for London and headed up the Rhine valley, where he had lived much of his youth, and detoured to the Black Forest in Germany. He'd been there many times, a favourite haunt. He spoke German and felt safe.

Seeking for a place to sleep in the darkening forest Ishkur had found a fire pit in a clearing off a faint trail and made a fire. An owl hooted.

Ishkur enjoyed the warmth and drank wine from a flagon, thinking about the bracelet and what to do with it and getting a little drunk. He pulled the bracelet from his coat pocket and snapped it on his wrist, mucking about. He decided to put it back in the cave some day; but not until after 1888. Then Ishkur heard the distinct sound of a stick snapping. He called out in German, 'Wer gibt es?' Who's there? *He quickly put the bracelet away and scanned around the dark fringe of the clearing, squinting his eyes until he saw a shape. Ishkur moved forward slowly, right hand over the gun in his pocket. A bit wobbly, he stopped and stared until his eyes adjusted. He said, 'Seien Sie erschrocken nicht.'* Do not be frightened.

Ishkur nearly jumped when a small figure emerged from the shadows. 'Bloody hell, it's just a kid..,' he said in English, looking at the young boy who seemed equally scared. Then switched to German, 'Was ist Ihr Name?' What is your name?

The boy smiled warmly. 'Mein Name ist Kaspar.'

As Ishkur was travelling through Germany, he'd decided to use a German name. Ishkur said, 'Ich bin Hansel.' I am Hansel. *He then invited the boy to share the campfire. They exchanged stories and both fell asleep by the fire.*

In the morning, with a fuzzy head, it did not take long for Ishkur to realize the boy must've stolen the bracelet. He ran looking for the boy named Kaspar but he would never find him. He continued on to London.

The boy, Kaspar, accidentally used the bracelet and 'jumped' from 1879 back to 1828 and in 1833 he was robbed of it and murdered by Rolf's gang who pawned it in Berlin where it was sold in 1863 to a wealthy Englishman from Coventry whose mansion was burgled ten years later, the thieves dropping the bracelet near Leamington Spa. It was then found by James Worson who tripped and ended up 'jumping' back to 1809. The bracelet fell out of his pocket as he was crossing the road by the White Swan Inn and he watched Benjamin Bathurst pick it up and vanish.

Benjamin Bathurst had time to think only a few thoughts in the milli-

second he reappeared in front of the White Swan Inn: It's dark? Noise? Horses?

The two large horses that carried the riders who were delivering the King's message stormed into the clearing; the inn was on their right. The clearing gave the messengers some visibility. Then-

Wham! *CRUNCH!*

'AAAAAGH!' Benjamin's scream quickly faded.

The horse went into a dive and fell, throwing its rider. The horse landed on Bathurst, killing the hapless businessman instantly. The rider was injured, but alive. The other messenger had stopped his horse quickly after avoiding the collision. Both riders had had fair vision of the road and both had seen Bathurst suddenly appear from out of nowhere.

Both riders failed to notice the object that had flown off the wrist of the dead man: The object that had landed several feet away.

The object that had gone straight into and down the well that was next to the White Swan Inn. Years later, the well was abandoned and filled with stones and so to this very day the bracelet rests down there. Therefore, Massy found an empty gold box in the cave and lived a normal life.

And one happy gardener got his life back...

The bright morning sun splashed warm rays generously from the east over England's West Country, brightening the thatched cottage and the long, narrow lawn gorgeously. Colourful flowers bordered the green and two little girls ran happily on the grass, shepherded ever so lovingly by a beautiful Border collie.

Their father was nearby on his knees working a trowel into the soft, brown earth. Their mother appeared from the cottage holding a small book of poetry. She called out to her husband, 'Here's one, luv: The West Wind by John Masefield. It's the one with the violets and brooks and birds singing...' She smiled. 'It's a lovely poem, Tommy.'

'Yes. It's always been one of me favourites.